MW01139957

HYDE
and
Seek
Sweet
LAYLA FROST

Dedication

A giant freakin' special thanks to:

Everyone on GR that gave me advice, feedback, and encouragement. You all seemed to know when I needed an extra push. Thank you.

My girls, Tina, Jessie, and Lindsay. If you were any more supportive, you'd be my Wonderbra. Thank you for always having my back.

Renee, you helped me take an awesome story and make it a *book*. Your advice, criticism, and encouragement always meant so much to me because it came from the heart. Thank you for your time, honesty, and perspective. And most of all, thank you for the laughs!

Jess, lovely sister of mine. As a kid, I used to see you up on the porch roof, your blond hair blowing around in the breeze. You'd sit out there and read, like it was no biggie that you were so high up on a slanted rooftop. You were the epitome of teenage awesomeness and I wanted to be just like you. In those early days, you made reading *cool*. Years later, you handed me a romance novel and I didn't put it down until I finished it in the wee hours of the following morning. Thank you for influencing and expanding my love of books. Thank you for being my best friend. Thank you for being *you*.

To M—

Without you, I'd have never had the guts to go for this. Thank you for encouraging me, listening to me talk about the characters in my head, and for picking up the slack when I was in this other world. I love you whole bunches.

Happy endings don't always happen.

In fairy tales, the hero and heroine go through obstacles and trials, but their happily ever after always comes. It's kinda the whole point of the story.

Real life doesn't offer that same guarantee.

Time passes and the pages turn, but there's only obstacles and trials, followed by more obstacles and trials with no happily ever after in sight.

Sometimes people never find their grand romance. Sometimes people lose their grand romance before their life is over, leaving them with regrets and heartache.

And sometimes, people lose their lives.

Scorching

"Babe, that van you?"

It had only been me and two guys, who based on their leathers, were most likely guys of the biker variety, in the waiting room. And neither of those dudes struck me as the type to be called 'babe' by another dude.

Not that I judge, of course. It just seemed unlikely.

Seeing as I was reading, and lost in my thoughts, I hadn't even noticed anyone else entering the room until the deep voice called out.

Another quick room sweep out of the corner of my eye confirmed I was the most likely candidate to be called 'babe'. Probably the only one there with a van, too.

"Babe, van?" he asked again as he turned around and began rifling through papers.

"Um, yeah," I answered to his back.

It was a back. I'd seen lots of them. Backs were backs, right?

Yeah, no.

This was a *back*. Broad shoulders, and what I was sure were a lot of muscles somehow visible through his dark gray t-shirt. I'd never thought of backs as anything, but this was a *good* one.

"They do the paperwork with you?" he asked, turning back

around with a stack of papers.

"Uhh," I mumbled. They hadn't. I knew they hadn't. My brain fully acknowledged no paperwork had been done with me. Getting my mouth to communicate that, however, was not happening. Not once my eyes saw his front. I liked his back, but I liked his front a whole hell of a lot more. So much more, in fact, I couldn't say the word 'no' about some simple paperwork.

There's a whole lotta other things I wouldn't say no to either.

Facing away and bent over, I'd noticed he was tall. Straightened up, though, I saw he wasn't just tall. He was *tall.*

As in *very*.

At five foot four, I was used to looking up at people. Since he was at least a foot taller than me, I could develop a serious crick in my neck from craning my head to look up at him.

It was a sacrifice I was more than willing to make.

Because, along with being tall and built, he was hot. Beyond hot. I don't think there's a word to describe what he was. Scorching, maybe, if the heat I was feeling was any indication. His damp, dark blond hair was pulled into a messy knot at the back of his head. It wasn't very long, probably only around shoulder length.

Since he looked to be in his early thirties, his face had long ago lost any boyishness. Amazing bone structure and hard angles came together in an almost beautiful way if he weren't so overwhelmingly masculine.

His strong jaw was covered in at least a few days' worth of stubble. Scruffy stubble that should have screamed "I need a shave!" Instead it beckoned "Run your fingers over me!"

I clenched my fists, fighting the urge to do just that.

The thing that seemed to cut off communication between my brain and my mouth, though, were his eyes. Vibrant green eyes, lined with thick, long lashes. Sexy as hell, they left me mumbling like I didn't have a brain.

Get it together! So, he's tall. And hot. With those green eyes. And those muscles. And... Where was I going with this?

Oh yeah. Get it together!

He shook his head, his eyes shining with amused frustration. "Nope, no paperwork. Not a surprise, they never do anything that even slightly feels like work. Come on up, babe. Let's take care of this."

The sound of my heels clicking on the linoleum echoed in the room. I cursed my decision to wear them. High heels, in general, weren't known for being easy to walk in. Four-inch ones, especially. Heels with jello knees forced me to focus extra hard on the simple task of putting one foot in front of the other.

I'd already mumbled like an idiot. I didn't need to fall on my face like one.

I reached the counter, staying upright the whole time, and silently congratulated myself. When I looked up at him, his gaze was intense as he looked through me. And I mean *through*. Into my mind, my soul. I was sure he was sifting through my deepest and darkest secrets.

What he found must have bored him because his eyes quickly lost their intensity. Using a pen, he tapped a beat on the counter. "Name?"

"Piper," I breathed. Yup, I breathed it. My voice came out soft, airy, and slightly raspy. I internally shook my head, attempting to lift the fog.

Way to go, Piper. You remembered your name, and were even able to talk this time. Now let's see if we can't start sounding less like a wannabe phone sex operator, hmm?

"Yeah, definitely no paperwork with that name. Last name?"

"Skye." I spelled it out while he wrote.

"Piper Skye." My name rolled off his tongue like it was one he'd said often. His lip quirked up. "I like it."

I liked my name. I always had. Hearing his deep, gravelly voice rumble my name, though, made me *love* it. I found myself wondering how it would sound if we were doing other things, none of which were appropriate to be thinking about.

My cheeks flushed and I tried again to clear the mental fog. "Thanks."

"What's going on with the van, babe?"

I liked the way he said my name, but I really liked it when he called me babe. I knew he probably called every chick that, but that didn't mean it wasn't hot.

"It needs to be colder in the back."

"Air not workin'?" He raised his eyebrow. "Why'd you come here for a repair?"

Hyde was a body and custom job shop, not a regular garage. I, along with most everyone, knew that. It wasn't where you came for an oil change and a tire rotation. Hyde was where you brought a sweet ride you wanted made sweeter.

"Um, no, it works. It works great but it needs to be colder. I use the van for work and my stuff keeps melting in the back."

"What type of stuff—" he started before being interrupted by a golden god entering the room.

"Jake, dude, you will not believe the sweet piece I had last night..." His words trailed off when he saw me. "Sorry, didn't know you were busy," he said to Jake, though he was definitely still looking at me. "Hey. Kase." He extended his hand.

Since he was only an inch or two shorter than Jake, I still had to crane my neck to look up at him. It was not a hardship. His dark hair hung in dreads past his shoulders, and his groomed facial hair was slightly longer than Jake's scruff.

I was sure he had to be wearing color contacts because no one had eyes like his. They were the most startling crystal blue I'd ever seen. Rimmed with black lashes and his golden skin, they stood out in sharp contrast.

Starting from his fingers up, intricate ink covered his arms, small patches of tanned skin peeking through here and there.

His skin tone and dark hair hinted at some exotic heritage, but I couldn't put my finger on it.

But I'd totally be willing to try. Finger, hand, tongue, whatever.

"Piper." I reached my hand to meet his. I smiled, unsurprised by his sudden personality change. I knew I came across to most as more conservative, shy, and quiet. My real friends knew that couldn't be further from the truth, but I was only that close with a handful of people.

My general vibe screamed 'introvert!'

Actually, I don't think you can scream introvert, but it definitely mumbled it.

I understood his thinking. I was in a body shop waiting room in four-inch heels, stockings with the seam up the back, and a white fitted blouse tucked into a pale pink pencil skirt. My black hair was pulled back in a neat twist. I knew I looked conservative, uptight, and very out of place.

However, I'd come straight from a meeting at the bank that had been unexpectedly moved up. And, unfortunately, meetings at the bank require you to look conservative, uptight, and very *in* place there.

It'd been a minor miracle I was able to get my van into Hyde. I wasn't about to cancel just because I was in a skirt.

Kase lifted his chin. "Nice to meet you. Sorry about that. I, uh, I didn't know there were customers here."

I fought the urge to laugh. He came through the garage, which meant he saw vehicles there. He had to have guessed there were people waiting, and he was talking loud enough that I had no doubt the bikers against the far wall heard.

"Seriously, not an issue," I said. "Congrats on the sweet piece."

Kase's smile turned sheepish before I was distracted by a throat being cleared. The throat of a very tall, very hot, impatient man.

"Kase, if you're done, you got work to do," Jake said, glaring at Kase.

Kase grinned at me, unfazed by Jake's look. "Nice to meet you, Piper. Let me know if you need anything."

I returned his smile. "Thanks."

As Kase left, Jake turned back to me and began tapping his pen to a fast beat. "So, coolin' in the back, got it. Anythin' else?"

"Yeah, uh, Z is installing some new speakers." I congratulated myself again on being able to actually form words while looking him in the eyes.

In an attempt to not blurt out something embarrassing or start drooling at his hotness, I distracted myself by thinking about Z. Since I doubted his real name was Z, I started forming ideas about what it stood for.

Jake finished writing something and looked amused. "Your work need louder speakers?"

"Well, yeah, kinda." Maybe not my work, but I definitely did.

Leaning down, he placed his forearms to the counter. His head tilted to the side as he looked at me. "How so?"

"I drive a lot, for deliveries."

"What stuff you deliverin', since I'm doubtin' it's pizza?"

"Desserts. Mostly cakes and cupcakes."

"Really? Awesome. What bakery you work at?" Kase startled me by asking.

I belatedly noticed him and three other hot guys standing in the doorway.

Apparently name guessing is a good distraction technique.

"No bakery. Not yet, anyway."

"Hey. Eli," one of the other hotties said as he stuck his hand out. He was shorter than the rest, around five foot ten or so. With his short brown hair and warm, brown eyes, he looked wholesome, boy next door. He almost seemed out of place at the shop, until you took in his ink. It was good ink. He must have agreed as there was a lot of it.

I took his hand. "Piper."

"Xavier," another introduced himself with a nod. This yummilicious man was all dark eyes and overgrown dark hair. It was hot, and worked for him. "Your desserts any good?"

"Well, people order. A lot, actually. So… yeah." I knew my desserts were good. Based on the swell of my chest, hips, and ass, I knew this fact well. I had to sample stuff though. Quality control and whatnot.

You're so good at lying to yourself.

The popularity of my desserts was what had brought me to the bank that morning. When I'd started making cakes for friends, I did one or two a month. Those one or two turned into three or four referrals, which then turned into three or four more referrals.

Before I knew it, my side hobby became a business, a Piper's Cakes was born.

Up until last semester, I attended college but hadn't picked a major. Since Piper's Cakes was quickly growing, thereby solving the dilemma of what I wanted to do with my life, I cut back my classes and switched to a business major.

It was a scary decision, but in a good way.

In order to do all I wanted to do, I needed money for better equipment, more space, and maybe even some help. I was turning away a lot of orders because I didn't have time. I couldn't make money turning away orders. It was a cycle I was trying to break.

"Key," a quieter voice said with a nod, the last of the hotties. He was a leaner and lankier hot, more Steven Tyler or Mick Jagger rock 'n' roll. He had slightly shaggy, light brown hair with moody looking brown eyes. "You got any dessert on you?"

I shook my head. "Nope, sorry. Maybe if I come back."

I was rewarded with a half-smile from Mr. Brooding. As I was pretty sure that was as close to happy as he got, I was cool with it.

My answer was welcomed by a bunch of smiling, eager faces and murmurings of desserts to come. Most guys were predictable when it came to food. I'd delivered cakes for children's birthdays, and it was the men that were hanging around, looking for a chance to swipe some.

"Guys, seriously, work," a rough, annoyed, and very in control voice bit out. I almost jumped up and started working at his order, it was that firm. I, apparently, was the only one since the guys still stood around talking about desserts they liked. Jake looked up and inhaled deeply before going back to his paper. "Moving on. Why do baked goods need better speakers?"

"No, the baked goods don't. I do."

"Yours broke?"

"No."

"Then why the speakers?"

"I spend a big chunk of time making deliveries. Have you ever tried driving without being able to really crank up your music?"

"What do you listen to?" Kase questioned.

If my vibe mumbled introvert, Kase's seemed to shout extrovert, complete with neon sign, marching band, and flares. His friendly bordered on flirtatious, but there didn't seem to be any actual interest.

In fact, all of the men appeared to be paying more attention to Jake's reaction, not having any of their own.

Too bad for them since Jake was sticking to the mostly silent glowering.

"Almost anything," I answered Kase. "But mostly rock. Can't listen to rock at a ten when you can have an eleven."

"Fuck," I heard Jake mutter softly to himself.

"Did you just make a Spinal Tap joke?" Xavier asked.

Before I could answer, Kase laughed. "Damn, you're full of surprises. Hiding a body of tats under that sexy librarian outfit you're workin'?" he said jokingly. Which, of course, resulted in an immediate blush from me. "Oh, damn, I'm sorry, Piper, I didn't mean to offend you, or make you feel uncomfortable. I don't have a filter, so I—"

"Fuck," Jake said again, loudly. I looked over to see him looking more than a little ticked.

"Damn, Jake, relax, I was apologizing. You know me, I didn't mean to be a dick—" Kase started. Since Jake didn't seem to like people finishing sentences, he was cut off again.

"That's not why she blushed. Is it?" He turned his dark, intense green eyes to me.

"Well, no." I smiled at Kase. "And I wasn't offended, so don't worry about it."

"Ohhhhhkay." Kase looked between Jake and I. "Well? What is it, then?" He glanced at Xavier and Eli who both appeared to be just as confused.

"He wasn't wrong, was he?" Jake asked with a softer voice, though his eyes stayed intense. Scorching.

Get your mind out of your pants! Or, well, in this case, out of his *pants!*

"He was. I'm not a librarian," I said, playing clueless.

"The tats?"

"Oh. About that. Well... I'm not covered."

"No shit?" Warm Eyes asked.

"You can't leave us hanging like that. We gotta see some ink," Xavier said, his smooth voice accented slightly.

"Most of them can't really be seen without me taking off... Well, they just can't be seen right now. I got one I can show." I rolled up my sleeve. On the inside of my wrist was a hot pink star with the word *ROCK* written inside it in a very badass font.

"That is fuckin' rock!" Kase said, complete with sticking his index and pinky fingers out to make the horns. "What else ya got?"

"Uhh, a swallow on each shoulder blade, musical notes down my ribs, shooting stars on the sides of my pelvis, and a heart on my lower back. And, uh, yup, that's it for now."

"For now?" Eli asked.

I lifted a shoulder. "Yeah, well, I like ink, so who knows?"

"Speaking of *work*," Jake growled, though no one mentioned it.

Slamming his pen down, he turned to Eli, Xavier, and Kase. "You mind steppin' back into the fuckin' garage and getting' some shit done?"

This was met with a "Yeah", "Fine", and "Whatever". But it worked and the guys said their goodbyes before heading back through the door.

I turned my attention to Jake, who was watching me intently. "I'm really sorry about that. I didn't mean to get in the way."

"Yeah, sure," he muttered, shaking his head as he sat on a metal stool.

"Pardon?"

"Don't sweat it."

I didn't know what that meant, and was saved from more tense awkwardness when Z came out.

If Eli didn't look like he belonged in a garage, Z definitely did not. He looked like he'd be more at home in a board room. Or a GQ spread. Or on a yacht with a supermodel. The fact he wasn't wearing a custom tailored suit somehow surprised me. Sure, working on cars was dirty work, but still, it just seemed like that would be his casual wear.

Z was what I called 'Rockabilly Dapper'. Around six feet tall, he was lean with compact muscles. I'd guess he was in his mid-thirties, but he didn't look it. He had some ink, was wearing the heck out of a white tee and ass hugging black jeans, and was rockin' a fantastic pompadour.

I seriously didn't know how he could be working in a garage and still have perfectly coiffed hair. I could spend an hour on my hair, and five minutes in the humidity would leave it in total disarray.

I was pretty sure Z owned Hyde, but I'd never had the chance to ask. Our conversations at the few events we'd both attended had always been friendly but short. After a few minutes of small talk, Mommy Dearest would move me along to some boring Ivy League creeper.

I liked Z. And not because he reminded me of a GQ model and called me Doll Face.

Okay, not just *that.*

"I got good news and bad news, Doll Face. The air is working. And I'm pretty sure I froze a ball testing it. But the new speakers didn't work. I hooked your old ones back up."

I smiled at him. "That's okay, the air was the most important part."

"I can get replacements, but not until tomorrow's shipment. Can you come back in on Friday, around eleven?"

I had a clear schedule. I knew it for a fact, not because it was only two days away. I could easily lose track of what day it was.

Or what time.

Or what I'd had for breakfast.

No, I knew because my schedule was almost never clear. When it was, it was memorable thing.

"Yeah, that's no problem. Thanks, Z."

"It's my job. Now let's get you out of here."

I paid for the work on my air, though I got the distinct impression it was less than I owed. A lot less. I also got the distinct impression you didn't argue with Z. Especially if it was about him doing something nice.

"Alright, Doll Face, follow me," Z said as he walked through the door to the garage.

I started following before stopping to look at Jake. "Sorry about being in the way. It was nice to meet you."

Nothing.

Okay, maybe not nothing. He looked at me. Like, *looked* at me, making my heart pound in my throat. I was sure he could hear it, it was so loud. I wasn't entirely convinced he couldn't see it.

I turned quickly, and was almost to the door before I heard him.

"Piper, stop," he said in that firm, bossy voice.

I stopped.

I don't get how those guys can ignore that tone.

"Turn around."

I turned around.

"Fuck," he murmured.

Why couldn't that *be an order?*

That thought required another clearing internal head shake, though they didn't seem to be helping.

"Said it already. Don't sweat it. Come around Friday, bring some dessert or they'll never shut up, yeah?"

"Was already planning on it." I loved to bake and used any chance to. And I had a feeling those boys wouldn't turn away food of any kind, let alone sugary baked goods.

"Of course you were. See ya Friday, babe."

"Yup," I muttered as I took off through the door.

"So, how is it?" Z asked as I slid out from the back of the van.

"Well, if any of you decide to start smuggling penguins, let me know. I can help with transport." It was cold. I was glad my bra had a bit of padding to it because there was a definite tightness in my nipples.

Which of course has nothing to do with the badass, hot guy parade. Grand Master of that parade being Jake.

See? Good at lying to yourself.

"Seriously, though, it's perfect. No more melty cakes. Thank you," I said to Z.

"It's my *job*, Doll Face. I'll see you back here Friday. It might take a while with the speakers, so be prepared."

"Sounds like a plan." I hopped up into the seat and spoke through the rolled down window. "See you then."

As I carefully pulled out, I turned my music up. Singing loudly, and badly, I thought about how I couldn't wait for my new speakers.

Yup, it's the speakers I'm looking forward to.

"Piper!"

I hadn't even turned off the van when my door was opened by a grinning Kase.

"Hey, how's it going?" Looking around, I saw all of the guys were in the garage. I wished, not for the first time, that I was about six inches taller, thereby having the ability to get out gracefully. Instead, I stepped down awkwardly.

I slid open the side door of the van, bending and climbing slightly in to get the goodies.

"Hell, babe, hop out," I heard close behind me.

Standing up, I moved out of the way. "I was just getting the stuff I brought."

Jake reached in and grabbed the containers. He was muttering something, but I missed it over the noise of a bunch of grown men.

Not just grown, but badass, tough guy, hot men, acting like eight year olds over a treat.

"Shit, you were for real?" Xavier asked.

"About bringing dessert? Of course. Who would lie about something so serious?" I asked in mock horror.

I moved to take the cake boxes from Jake, but he just jerked his head and walked away. I took this to mean that I was supposed to follow. Which I did, partially because my brain was mush and partially because I had no clue where to go otherwise.

Mostly, though, it was because he had a *really* nice ass.

We went down a long hallway, giving me plenty of time to enjoy the view. The guys followed me, or, more likely, the cupcakes.

Jake set the boxes down on a table in their break room. "Babe, there are six men that work here. How much did you bring?"

I liked to bake. Really liked it. Which meant I occasionally went overboard.

Just sometimes.

Rarely, really.

It almost never happened.

It totally happened all the friggin' time.

"Uhh, only twenty-four cupcakes." Which wasn't that much. Not really. "And twenty-four cookies." Big cookies. Delicious, chewy, gooey long after they'd cooled, cookies. "I like to bake," I stated, as if it needed to be said.

"Yeah, I kinda figured that one out."

"Hell, Doll Face. Seriously. You made this?" Z asked, cupcake in hand, frosting on his lips.

"Yeah."

"It's good."

The fact he ate a whole thing in two bites had tipped me off.

To be fair, it was a strawberry cupcake with whipped cream cheese frosting. They were my specialty for a reason.

"Yo, Pipe," Kase said from across the table.

"Yeah?"

Kase held up a cookie and winked. "It's fuckin' delicious."

"Thanks, Kase."

"Gotta ask, you cook?"

"Like savory food?"

"Shit, I dunno. Like cook. You know meals. Dinner and shit."

"Yeah, Kase. Not as good as I can bake, but I can cook."

"Run away with me?"

"Christ." Jake shook his head. "Keep it in your pants, Kase. The rest of you, finish what you got and get your asses back to work. Now." After barking out those orders, Jake's voice softened as he looked down at me and said, "Piper, this shit is amazing."

Hellooooooo, jello knees.

"Thanks. I'm gonna head out to the waiting room." As long as my knees could carry me, that is.

"No." His tone was back to bossy. Surprise, surprise.

Oh, I like bossy voice.

Shh, quiet, girly bits!

"What?" I asked.

"You eat?"

"What?"

Where's my brain? I know what eating means. Why am I such a dingus?

"You know, food. Not sugar in cake form. Have you had lunch?"

"No, I was just planning on walking somewhere."

Jake turned to Kase. "I'm takin' Piper to grab a bite. Do your shit, we'll be back." It wasn't an invitation.

Even if it was, I doubt I'd have said no.

I turned to the rest of the guys and waved as Jake grabbed my other hand. "Uh, I'm glad you all like the dessert," I said over my shoulder as he pulled me out the door. It took me a second to wrap my brain around the fact that Jake was still holding my hand as we stepped outside the shop.

My hand? His hand?

Yum.

I looked up at Jake as we walked. "You don't have to do this. I'm sure you're busy."

Shh. Don't ruin it. Lunch. Hand holding! Shut up!

"I'm not letting you sit in there all afternoon."

"Seriously, it's cool. Z warned me it'd be a while. I came prepared."

"No, you didn't."

Uhh, what?

Which, lack of filter meant I said, "Uhh, what?"

My question went unanswered. Though Jake stayed silent, he did it still holding my hand. It was strangely hot. His hand was much larger than mine. I normally hated my petite size, but suddenly I was seeing some major benefits.

We came to a stop in front of a small deli. "You like sandwiches?"

I raised my brows up at him. "Who doesn't like sandwiches?"

"Fair enough."

Jake opened the door and the scent of fresh baked bread hit me.

"I love that smell."

"What one?"

I grinned up at him. "Fresh bread. Regular bread smells good. But the warm, carby smell of *fresh* bread? Unbeatable. Did you know they sell bread scented candles? It isn't like the real thing, of course."

Jake chuckled. "Of course. Figure out what you want, babe."

When we ordered at the counter, Jake paid and I tried to protest. He gave me a look and I stopped protesting. When it was ready, he grabbed our order and guided us to a table tucked in a corner.

As we got settled I asked again, "Why couldn't I sit in the waiting room?"

"You said you were prepared." He shook his head. "You weren't."

"How do you figure that?"

"Your clothes."

I looked down. "I'm not following."

"Too much skin."

What the hell? What century did I unwittingly time travel to?

"Maybe if I was a nun." My thick strapped, black ribbed tank and black cuffed shorts hardly seemed indecent. It was Massachusetts in July, which meant it was *hot*. I could look outside and see a handful of women, and even a couple men, wearing much less.

"Trust me. There were other customers in the waitin' room. Shorts, emphasis on the short, and a tank top. Definitely too much skin."

"Thanks for the heads-up, fashion police," I muttered.

"Eat."

I didn't know what to say. So, I didn't say anything.

I glared.

"Eat," Jake ordered again, immune to my dirty look.

I picked up my turkey sandwich and we ate in silence.

After lunch, I wasn't surprised when Jake brought me to the break room. We hadn't said more than a few words to each other on the walk back, though he'd held my hand again.

So, awkward, silent lunch followed by hand holding?

Meh, I've had worse days.

"I gotta see how much fuckin' around they're doin'. Hang out in here 'til the van is done. One of the men will come get you."

Since I couldn't wait to investigate the break room, I nodded.

Jake started to walk away before pausing and turning back. "Piper?"

"Yeah?" Breathy. Again.

God, I was an idiot.

I'd decided Jake was kind of an ass, though a hot one. Coincidentally, he was a hot ass *with* a hot ass. But he was still an ass.

I was trying to avoid people who made me feel small. Well, small-*er*.

"Just... Help yourself to anything, yeah?"

"Okay. Thanks again, Jake."

"Yeah." With a chin lift he was gone, leaving me to explore.

Their break room was a full blown, restaurant grade kitchen. It had a six burner gas stove and a shit ton of counter space. The countertops were a gorgeous black granite and the appliances a gleaming, stainless steel.

It was what I'd want my dream kitchen to look like. Modern, but comfy.

Tiptoeing like I was breaking the law, I opened the huge walk-in cooler to find a bunch of car parts. "So that's how they make such cool cars." I looked around quickly. "Thank God no one was around to hear that," I whispered to myself.

After surreptitiously taking a few pictures, I settled into a lush couch and brought out my iPad. I'd just started reading when Kase came in and headed straight for the box of baked goods.

"Pipe. Seriously. Did you put crack in these cookies?" Since I'd seen him earlier, he'd pulled his dreads back and lost his t-shirt.

Oh, how unfortunate. I should help him find it and all his other shirts.

And burn them.

It'll be my service to all womankind.

His white tank top and low hung jeans were smudged with grease.

Oh, I see... Golden hued, ripped, flirty, crystal blue-eyed... Wait, where was I going with this again? Oh yeah. So Kase can wear a tank but I can't?

I smiled at him. "Nope, even worse. Loads of sugar."

"They're awesome. You have crazy kitchen skills."

"Speaking of crazy kitchens, what's the deal with this one?"

"It used to be a restaurant-slash-party house before it was Hyde's. Too much work and too expensive to change this room, with the gas line from the stove and all. Plus, kind of hard to disguise a walk-in. So, it was left as is, and made into the break room."

"Gotcha."

"I gotta head back. Thanks for the sweetness, Piper," Kase said with a finger wave.

I couldn't help but laugh at the absurdity of a badass doing a finger wave.

As he walked out, I settled in to read. After about five minutes, I heard a distant and gentle, "Babe."

I blinked. Or rather opened my eyes, and saw Jake looking down at me. I glanced behind him to the clock on the wall and saw the five minutes was more like an hour and a half.

"Damn," I said through a yawn as I sat up and stretched.

Jake leaned back on the table, crossing his arms over his chest. "You good?"

"Yeah. Sorry. Dozed off reading."

"Nah, it's good. I would've let you sleep, but I didn't know if you had to be anywhere. Your van is done."

"Cool. Thanks."

"Yeah," he muttered as he stood. After giving me a chin lift, he left without another word.

I went to the front and paid Z, once again suspecting it was much less than it should have been.

"Ready to rock, Doll Face?" he asked, flipping me my keys.

I followed him back into the garage.

"Test her out. Put something hard on."

I put my current favorite CD on and squealed as the bass pumped. Turning the volume down, I hopped out. "Z, this rocks. Thank you so much."

"Quit with the thanks bullshit."

"Alright. Sorry." I grinned.

"Doll Face," he warned. "Anything else you need?"

"Can you fix a dent?"

His eyes swept the van. "No dent."

"No, it's on my car."

"Got a car?"

"Yeah, this is just for work since my car doesn't have the space to hold cakes."

Before Z could answer, Kase came through the door. "Z, Jake needs help in the office. He can't find the papers for the Viper."

Z lifted his chin. "Be back."

As he left, Kase peeked in at the new speakers. "Damn, that sounds sweet. Fuckin' rockin' a minivan and shit. You like Harington?"

I nodded. "Yeah. I'm totally hooked on this album."

"You know they're playing tonight over at Rye, right?"

"Seriously?"

"We're all heading over tonight, you should come with."

"Sorry, I can't. Crazy busy night with cakes." While I had a ton of homework and some cakes to prep, that wasn't what was stopping me.

"Piper, come on. Live a little. Let your hair down." Kase smiled.

I have no doubt he uses that charming smile to get his way with chicks.

Or have his way with them.

"If it's at Rye, I really can't go."

"Why? Did ya get tossed from there?"

"I'm not twenty-one yet." I headed towards my van. "I can't get in there."

"For real? Not twenty-one?"

"Yeah, not for another couple months. Thanks for the invite though."

"Twenty? Damn, you got your shit together. Good for you. Seriously. But you're still coming with us."

"I can't. It's cool, but—"

Kase pulled his cell from his pocket, touched the screen a few times, and held his finger up to me.

Apparently no one here likes to let people finish a freakin' sentence.

I sighed and climbed into my van.

"Rhys? It's Kase. Yeah? Yeah, I know, your Mom mentioned it while I was eating her last night."

I grinned when he gave me a sheepish smile.

Hot.

I watched Kase walk back and forth as he talked. "Yeah, bud, look, I got a favor to ask. I know, I know. I got a friend that's a big fan of Harington. Thing is, she's only twenty. Ha, I wish. She'll class your fuckin' dump up. She's at the shop. Get this. Getting a boss ass sound system put in a minivan. Nah, not a MILF. She bakes cakes and shit and uses the van to deliver. She brought some today and, I'm not kidding, I'd give up eating pussy for a week to have those cookies every day. Chocolate chip, pure crack. Yeah? I'm sure I can work that. Thanks man."

I was bouncing with excitement by the time he ended the call.

"You're in. Three things, though." He held up a finger. "First, if you drink, don't get stupid shitty."

"Why would you be getting shitty?" Eli asked, startling me as he came into the garage.

I looked to see the rest of the men coming through the door

"She's coming with us tonight," Kase answered for me.

Eli and Xavier both looked happy. Key half smiled, which I counted as a grin from anyone else. Jake looked unreadable, and, at best, disinterested. I didn't care. He was an ass that wasn't interested in me. So what if my panties got wet every time his rough voice got bossy with me. It was probably a coincidence.

Seriously, the way you lie to yourself is deserving of an Oscar. It's such a stellar performance.

"Okay as I was saying, don't get stupid shitty drunk." He held up another finger. "Second, Rhys says he wants some of your crack cookies tonight. That possible if I'm picking you up at eight?" At my nod, he lifted another finger. "Last, wear something sexy. Once again, direct quote from Rhys, though I ain't arguing."

"Fuckin' A, Kase," Jake cursed, tossing a stack of files onto a work bench. "I gotta tell you *and* Rhys to keep it in your pants?"

Kase lowered two of his fingers, leaving only the middle one up and pointed in Jake's direction.

As much as I wanted to see Harington, I didn't want to cause a bunch of drama. "I have a lot of work—"

I almost finished a full thought before Jake broke in. "You're goin'. I'll pick you up since Kase has got a full car already."

Kase shook his head. "Eff that. Key can walk his scrawny ass."

"Damn, why I gotta be the one to walk?" Key said in protest.

"Jesus," Z said, cutting everyone off. He turned to me. "The car with the scratch, drive it tonight. Yeah?"

I nodded.

"Good. I'm all about the wires. Jake's the best with dent skills. Let him see that shit, see what he can work."

Again, I nodded, though this time more hesitantly.

"Good. See ya tonight, Doll Face." With a wink to me, he grabbed the files from the workbench and walked out the door that lead to the hallway.

"Phone," Jake ordered. Shocking.

I didn't get what he was saying. Double shocking. "What?"

"Let me see your cell."

Pulling it from my bag, I handed it over to Jake who had it for a minute before passing it to Kase. When I got it back, I had five new numbers, from five hot guys.

"Text one of us when you get there. Let us know where you park, and wait for us. You got a dent?"

"Yeah."

"Alright, text me then. I'll check it out. Yeah?"

I nodded, because, really, what other option did he give me?

"See you tonight, Piper Skye."

Full name?

Yum.

"Rest of you sorry assholes, get back to work," he said as he walked out.

I said my goodbyes and left in my van with its new, loud ass speakers. Rock on!

Party Hardly

When I got to Rye, I was relieved that I wasn't late. I was usually pretty efficient when I got ready, but for some reason it had taken me forever. Not to impress anyone, of course.

Noooo, not at all.

After leaving the shop earlier in the day, I'd decided to blow off the rest of my plans. It was definitely the right decision.

Since my hair reached the middle of my back, I was used to it taking for-freakin'-ever to blow dry and style. What I wasn't used to was doing, wiping off, and then redoing my makeup multiple times because my nerves were making my hands shake. My usual straight eyeliner looked more like I'd tried to apply it with my left hand while driving on a road covered with potholes in the dark. I still wasn't able to get it precise, so I went heavier on my eye shadow to blend it. Fortunately, rocker glam worked for the night out and made my violet eyes pop.

Now let's hope I don't look like a raccoon by the end of the night.

I'd taken more time than I had available to decide on an outfit. I changed my mind a handful of times before settling on black skinny jeans and a super soft black halter top with hot pink lace trim. Grabbing a matching shrug and black three-inch peep toe heels, I'd run barefoot out the door.

Despite running way behind, I was still able to find some sweet parking at the bar. I texted Jake to let him know where I was. My phone buzzed a second later.

Jake: Be there in a few, babe. Don't get out 'til we get there.

Even on text, Jake was bossy. And, even on text, it turned me on more than I thought was normal.

After a quick double-check to make sure my deodorant was doing its job, my hottie sense started tingling. I looked up to see Jake heading towards me.

Long, purposeful strides while somehow still looking bored... Even his walk is intimidating and undeniably sexy.

During my makeup mini-crises, I'd tried to convince myself that Jake wasn't really *that* good-looking. My memory, imagination, and libido just built him up as the hottest man I'd ever seen.

However, as I watched him walk towards my car, I knew I was *way* wrong. Because, in jeans and a dark colored Henley with the sleeves pushed up his tan and tatted arms, he was somehow even more gorgeous.

I dragged my eyes from Jake and saw that, short of Z, the other guys from Hyde were with him. This included one I didn't recognize, but would be more than happy to meet. My brain, and other parts of my anatomy, were pretty set on Jake but that didn't mean I was totally blind.

Seeing the six of them, I was glad I had a second to do a real headshake to lift the fog. Unfortunately, it didn't work.

Sigh. It never does.

When they got close enough that it'd be rude to just sit and perv on them from inside my car, I got out. I barely stood all the way up when Kase grabbed me around the waist. He lifted me so we were face to face and my feet were about seven inches off the ground.

"Piper, I swear, don't know whether to kiss you or that car. Whose is it?" He carefully set me back down.

I shrugged. "I dunno, hot-wired it." At the guys' looks of

uncertainty, I started laughing. "It's mine! Bo's beautiful, right?" My baby was a gorgeous, teal 1969 Dodge Charger and my pride and joy.

"Babe."

I immediately turned my attention to Jake.

It's like my brain goes on vacation as soon as he says that word. I'm a total Babe Zombie, mindlessly following the hot guy. Goodbye braaains.

Jake chuckled. "You named your car?"

"Yeah, doesn't everyone?"

"Bo?" he asked. "As in Duke?"

"Yeah. I mean, she doesn't look like a Daisy. And I always liked Bo better than Luke." When I got Bo I knew she needed a Dukes of Hazzard name, but she was definitely not a General Lee.

"Right, of course. What was I thinking?" His voice was teasing but amused. "Anyway, this is Rhys." He gestured to Mystery Hot Dude. "He owns Rye."

I extended my hand. "Hey, thanks for letting me come."

Rhys took my outstretched hand and lifted it to his mouth, lightly kissing my knuckles before lowering it but not letting go. Normally a move like that would've had me rolling my eyes and trying not to laugh. Instead, I could feel the heat in my cheeks.

"My pleasure. Once Kase told me about the hot chick who smelled like cake, acted sweeter, and looked even sweeter still, how could I say no?"

I could feel my blush deepen. Nervously, I blurted out, "I have something for you." Rhys released my hand as I turned away and bent back into my open car door, reaching across to the passenger side.

"Gotta fuckin' be kidding me," I heard growled, followed by laughter from multiple people.

I grabbed the container and stood back up, unsure of what I'd missed. I tried not to feel self-conscious as I handed the cookies to

Rhys. "Chocolate chip, as a thank you."

"Well, darlin', you've given me more than a few sweet things tonight. So, thank *you*," he said with a chuckle, deep dimples appearing on his cheeks.

His dimples, while incredibly hot, weren't the only thing he had going for him. Over six feet tall with a muscular build, he looked exactly like the kind of guy that'd own a rocker bar, right down to the kickass beard. His eyes were dark blue with hints of green and little crinkles near them said that he smiled a lot.

His rich brown hair was overgrown and unruly like he spent the day in bed. With someone. And that someone had their hands in his hair, a lot. Based on his boots, I was guessing he owned a hog, which only added further to his appeal.

"Babe," Jake said, his voice impatient. "Where's the dent?"

"It's over here." I pointed out the damage on the passenger door. Even in the dark it was deep and obvious.

"Cryin' shame on this car, for sure, but it looks like an easy fix. We'll get it in soon, yeah?"

"Thanks, Jake."

"Ready to rock, Piper?" Kase asked, throwing the horns.

"Hell yeah."

Rye was the shit.

It was a nice joint that looked like a dive. There was a raw grittiness to it that appealed to a lot of popular bands that wanted to get back to their roots. The smaller venue held more intimate and laid back shows, but that didn't diminish the adrenaline flowing through the air. The place was already alive and buzzing, anticipation running high.

I knew between school and cakes I'd been working a lot. What I hadn't fully realized was that even my rare downtime was consumed with *thoughts* of school and cake. A night out was definitely what I needed.

Jake took off as soon we got in while the rest of us went to the bar. Rhys, who noticed my not very subtle gawking, offered me a tour of the place after I'd gotten my drink.

The walls were covered with framed pictures of all of the bands that had played shows there. Rhys pointed out where they'd signed a hanging picture, the wall, or various signs. Basically anything they could write on.

"This place is *awesome!*" I looked closer at some of the framed pictures.

I wonder if I could sneak some of these out. How obvious would it look if my back was perfectly rectangular and I rattled?

"Thanks, darlin'."

"I can't believe how many bands you've had here." I pointed to a picture of an older group. "I saw them when I was eleven. First show I ever saw."

"Eleven and hittin' up the scene?"

"What can I say? Some girls play dress up in their tutus and tiaras while dreaming of being ballerinas and princesses. I had scarves hanging from my princess microphone and for three months straight I wore my Axl Rose bandanas on my head. Then there was the time I used my markers to color my face like Ace Frehley."

Rhys' deep laughter filled the air. "No shit. Really?"

"Yup. The night before picture day in first grade. My mother was not pleased. My dad, however, had the picture blown up to poster size."

"I'm gonna need to see that."

"I'll see what I can do," I promised before switching topics. "So, did you open Rye?"

"Yeah, about fifteen years ago."

"Wow, you were young."

I didn't know his exact age, but guessed Rhys was somewhere in his mid-to-late thirties. He was definitely one of those lucky people that you just knew got better and better looking as they aged.

"Don't forget wild, stupid, and reckless. I sank every last penny I had into getting this place up and running. I was sick of paying crazy money to drink shitty beer 'cause the joint was wannabe hip. I just wanted to sit in a shitty place and drink shitty beer."

"Sorry." I looked around. "It's obviously not a shitty place."

He leaned against the wall and smiled down at me. "Yeah, fucked that up, too, huh?"

I shrugged. "Little bit."

"So Kase said you run your own business."

"Yeah, it's still in the fledgling stage."

"You like it?"

I nodded, but did it grinning. "It was a hobby that snowballed. It's a lot of work, but it's worth it to do what I love."

"Yeah, I get you. It's the best fuckin' thing in the world. Some days, swear to Christ, I don't even wanna know what fresh hell awaits me. Always some bullshit happening, some fuckin' paperwork to do. But doing what you love? Having the control to do whatever the fuck you want? Wouldn't trade it."

I'd heard all of the horror stories about starting a business so it was nice to hear something positive. "What's your favorite thing about it?"

"Unless you make *really* fuckin' depressing cakes, you'll meet people on the good days. I get to meet them at the high, the low, and everything in between. The ones that come in to drink after they get the pink slip, the divorce papers, the bad news from the doctor. The ones out to celebrate, to party 'cause life's fuckin' awesome. That's what I love, meeting different people."

I jerked my head towards the bar. "Is that how you know the Hyde guys?"

"Kinda. Jake and I go back about ten years. The rest eventually came with him. They're a close group."

"Yeah, I've noticed."

When there was no response, I looked up at Rhys to find him watching me with assessing eyes. I had nothing to hide, but I still fought the urge to fidget. I worked hard at not letting people's opinions matter, but no one wanted to be disliked.

I barely held in a victory dance when his dimples reappeared as he smiled at me.

"I called Jake earlier to find out about you," Rhys admitted.

I tilted my head. "Oh?" I tried to sound indifferent. What I really wanted was a word for word transcript of the conversation.

"Kase... Well, he's got a type, and it isn't sweet, albeit sinful looking, bakers," he said with a wicked smile. "I wanted to make sure Kase hadn't hooked up with another psycho. There are a lot of users and hangers-on. You need loyal people to have your back. When Jake said you were a good chick without hesitation, well, that's like hitting the lotto of approval."

As much as that made me want to bust out the ultimate victory dance, I was more than a little surprised.

Mixed signals much?

"Jake doesn't like anyone, especially women. I mean, he likes them, he just doesn't wanna be around them unless he's getting something, you know what I mean?" He didn't give me a chance to think about what he meant, let alone respond, before he continued. "Anyway, when they were talking, it got me curious. Jake got your text and said he was going to take a look at a dent. When all the men jumped up to go with, I figured I'd come along and take a look for myself. Glad I did, darlin'."

I nudged him with my shoulder. "Aren't you sweet?"

"Actually, no. Not at all. I'm pretty much the opposite. Running this place is more than a full-time job, which means I'm busy. I've gotta make decisions on the fly and trust my instincts. What I don't do is fuck around saying shit I don't mean, especially when I want something. I already asked and know you don't have a man, at least not one anyone knows about."

As my brain was trying to catch-up, I belatedly realized Rhys was waiting for my confirmation. "Nope, no man."

"I want the chance to spend some time together, get to know you better, and see just how sweet you really are. And darlin'? From what I see tonight, I'm betting your sweet comes with a whole hell of a lot of mischievous. Now I'm wondering which one comes out more. Think on it."

I stared up at Rhys, unsure of how to respond. Part of me wanted to ask if he was out of his mind. Who talked like that?

I mean, I got it, I wasn't the best judge of normal. Most of my life had been spent in what I liked to call Repressed Land, a dull as hell place where emotions weren't discussed and faces were so botoxed you couldn't tell how anyone felt.

However, even I knew this was taking blunt to a whole new level.

Which was why another part of me wanted to take Rhys up on his offer. I might not be used to straight talk, but that didn't mean I didn't appreciate it. I'd take blush-inducing honesty over game playing any day. Not to mention, his confidence majorly upped his sexy vibe.

Afraid of what I'd say, I kept my mouth closed and nodded up at him.

Unlike Rhys, I wasn't one to make decisions on the fly. I dug him as a person so far and could see myself spending time with him. However, there was something about Jake that pulled me in. I didn't fully understand it but that didn't matter. I knew it'd be wrong to start something with him when I was lusting after his friend the way I was.

Thankfully, Jake had good timing, walking up to us and saving me from saying something stupid. "Bike has a couple loose wires. Bring it in to Z."

Rhys gave him a chin lift. "Thanks, Brother." He looked back to me. "Alright, darlin', I got shit to take care of. Think about what I said. Alright?" He ran his knuckles across my cheek before leaning in to brush his lips across it. "Fuck, he wasn't kiddin'. She smells like cake," he said quietly, before turning and disappearing into the crowd.

"What're you supposed to think about?" Jake asked.

I looked around to avoid his all-knowing green eyes. "Oh, nothing really."

"Yeah, 'cause you look like someone who just had a 'nothing really' kinda discussion."

"He, uh, wants to spend some time together," I mumbled, pretending to be very interested in the drunk chick dancing to a beat only she was hearing.

"He wants to spend time together," Jake repeated.

"Yeah."

"He said that?"

"Yup." I wasn't sure if I should be insulted that he found it so hard to believe.

"He said those words?" Jake asked. Controlled. Quiet. And scary as fuck for some reason.

"Yeah. Why?"

"No reason."

Before I could push for an answer, an arm was slung around my shoulder. An arm that just so happened to be wearing a very nice dress shirt.

I knew he wore GQ.

"Hey." I smiled up at Z.

His pompadour was fully pomped, his black slacks and gray dress shirt nicely pressed. He didn't fit in at a rock concert in a dive bar, but it was totally working for him.

"Doll Face. Everything good?"

"Awesome."

He dipped his head to my soda. "Want something stronger?"

I glanced back at the unusual gyrating of Drunky McDrunkerson and shook my head. "No, I'm good."

"Damn, it's hot as balls in here," Xavier said, coming up as Z headed to the bar.

Even though my short-sleeve shrug was thin, I was starting to get uncomfortable. I knew my deodorant was doing its job, but I wasn't looking to push it to its limits.

My gaze slid down the bar and caught Rhys' stare. "I'll be right back."

"Make your decision already, darlin'? Or just need a drink?" Rhys teased.

"Refill and a small favor."

"Name it."

"Could you tuck my sweater somewhere safe back there? As Xavier says, it's hot as balls in here."

"Sure thing, darlin'."

I felt someone move in close behind me. Without looking, I knew it was Jake.

His fingers grazed down my arms as he slid my shrug off.

Try as I might, I couldn't hold back a shiver. It would've been impossible for him to miss, but when I glanced back at him, his face showed nothing. I didn't know if it was more embarrassing that he felt my reaction to him, or that he was indifferent to it.

What are you expecting? You're the perv that's getting off on him touching your shoulders. Get it together!

"Thanks," I said to Rhys, grabbing my refill.

He looked down at my wrist tattoo. "Nice tat, darlin'. Got anymore?"

"Not. Fuckin'. Again," Jake muttered.

I ignored him and talked to Rhys. "Yup. Not all visible with clothes on, though."

Rhys' smile turned even wickeder. "Now that just makes me wanna see them more."

Careful not to brush against Jake, I turned around and pulled my hair to the side so he could see the swallows on my shoulders. When I turned back, I lifted my tank top a little so he could see part of the shooting stars on my hip bones. My low rise pants weren't quite low enough to see it all, but I doubted any pants were. Thankfully, my tattoo artist Ray, short for Rayna, was also my best friend.

"There are a few more that common decency and state laws prevent me from sharing."

Rhys put his elbows on the bar and leaned forward. "Darlin', remember what I said to think about?"

I nodded.

"Yeah, I mean that tenfold now. Keep that in mind." He smiled big, his dimples emphasized more.

I could eat cereal out of those dimples.

I felt a strong arm around my waist and fingers digging into my hip. "Time to get back so we can see."

"Yeah, yeah, yeah," I sighed, though I was a big fan of his arm around me.

"Rhys," Jake bit out with a slight nod.

"Jake," Rhys responded with a chuckle.

"Rhys," I bit out mockingly. If Jake was going to be a jerk to everyone, I was going to have fun with it.

"Enjoy the show, darlin'."

Jake moved us effortlessly through the crowd as people hustled out of his way. It took him less than a minute to get us from the back of the room to up near the stage where the guys were.

I'm obviously not the only one that finds him imposing and scary as fuck.

The lights started to go down as they did a quick sound check. When Harington appeared, the small venue roared to life like a packed arena. They jumped into the music and did it hard. Everyone got lost in the sounds. The energy. The whole vibe.

It was amazing.

I danced with all of the guys except Jake. This, surprisingly, included Z. He was stiff and seemed a bit uncomfortable, but he tried.

When I took a break, Jake came up behind me. “Babe, wanna beer or something?”

“No, thanks. I’m gonna grab a water.”

“Don’t drink?”

“Not here.”

“Why, you a mean drunk? Gettin’ wild and startin’ fights?” Jake teased, a smirk changing his face from badass hot to *unbelievably* badass hot.

“You caught me.” I raised my fists. “I’ve got a crazy right hook.”

“I’m thinkin’ that’s not how you do your damage. So, why?”

“I’m only twenty. I shouldn’t be here at all, let alone drinking.”

“Christ. Seriously?”

I nodded.

Jake looked towards the bar then back at me. “Rhys know your real age?”

“Kase told him when he asked if I could come tonight. Why?”

Jake, of course, ignored my question. “And he said he wanted the chance to spend time with you?”

“Yeah. Why’s that so hard to believe?”

“You know he’s pushin’ forty, yeah?”

“Okay… and?”

Jake shook his head, all traces of his sexy smirk gone as he looked ahead at the band. He didn’t say anything further, and I wasn’t going to waste my time trying to read between his hot and cold lines.

There were times, like when he’d held my hand earlier or was being playful, that I thought maybe he was into me. Or at the very least, that we were cool with each other. However, the majority of his responses ran along the lines of disapproval or indifference.

I was way over it.

Without a word, I turned and headed to the bar. I gulped down the water the bartender gave me, happy to break away from the crush of people for a minute.

When I got back to the group, Kase grabbed my hand pulled me next to him. Using his empty cup as a mic, he lip-synced along with the song, his dreads moving wildly.

"I'm gonna get a beer, need anything?" he asked, pretty much yelling in my ear to be heard.

I looked up at him and shook my head, knowing there was no way he'd be able to hear me.

Xavier waved me over to introduce me to some women. I couldn't hear one thing he said, so I just nodded and smiled.

Their response was similar.

The girls moved away from the men to dance, pulling me with.

After a few minutes of dancing and laughing, a hand gripped my hip. I turned to see Jake. He didn't even look at me as he shifted us away from the group. I tried to step away from him but hardly gained any distance before his arm wrapped the rest of the way around my waist.

As much as I wanted to pretend he didn't exist, it was impossible to with his arm around me.

"Uhh, what's up?" I asked when it became obvious he wasn't going to say anything.

Shifting my hair off my neck and onto my shoulder, Jake leaned close to my ear. "The way you were movin'? You want that kinda attention, get it some other time."

It was the shorts thing all over. At his work? Alright, I got that.

At a rock concert in a bar, though?

Yeah, I didn't get it.

I didn't get it so much that I wasn't just upset.

I was pissed.

Quickly twisting my body, I hoped to jerk out of his grasp.

I half succeeded.

I managed to turn around to face Jake, but his arm stayed tight around me.

If he weren't such a giant asshole, I might have enjoyed having his body pressed against mine. Right now, though, a well-aimed punch to the junk seems like a better idea...

"What the hell are you talking about?" I yelled, both because the music was loud and I was losing my temper.

"You were attractin' attention."

"What kind of attention, exactly?"

"The kind that involves every guy gettin' a hard dick watchin' you move. Thinkin' about you movin' like that with them. Naked. You're a fuckin' wet dream."

It wasn't the most flowery compliment I'd received, but it stole some of the wind from my bitch sails until I remembered what an ass he was.

"That's on them, not me. Why should I let what people think bother me? I was just having a good time and dancing."

"You wanna dance, have at it. Just do it back here, yeah?"

"No, I'm good," I snapped, tired of him telling me what to do.

I'd worked hard to not let people's opinions get me down like they used to. Normally, I would keep doing what I wanted. However, it was his friend's bar and, technically, I wasn't even supposed to be there. It wasn't worth ruining my night by getting upset.

Yet, at least.

I spun around to get free, but Jake wrapped his other arm around my chest.

I was torn. Half of me wanted to follow through with the junk punch. I was pretty sure I could position myself correctly to get a good hit.

The other half of me, though, was thinking maybe a *kick* to the junk with my heel would be more effective.

Unable to decide, I went with verbal insults.

"You're kind of an ass."

"No kinda about it, babe," he said, close to my ear.

What good are insults if he just agrees with me?

Instead, I went back to ignoring him, which was hard to do with his arms around me. I focused on the music and people watching, my anger slowly fading.

He was looking out for me in his own bossy as fuck way. He wanted me to be safe. It was kinda sweet, minus him being a jerk.

I wasn't booking us any BFF getaways, but at least he didn't seem to hate me.

I shifted a little and his arm tightened around me again. Moving my head to the side, my cheek slid against his chest as I looked up at him.

"Jake?"

"Yeah?"

"Don't feel like you have to watch over me all night. I'm fine, really. Go have some fun."

Jake looked down at me for a few seconds before looking back at the stage without saying anything. When his arms stayed around me, I sighed dramatically before turning back to the show.

Oh no. Woe is me. I have to watch an awesome show in the arms of a hot guy. How will I ever survive?

When the music ended, the lights came up and brought me back to reality. I pulled away from Jake, his fingers trailing my skin as he dropped his arms. I turned to say goodbye when he unexpectedly grabbed my hand and began walking. I focused on maneuvering through the crowd, but Jake didn't seem to have that problem. He moved with confidence and everyone got the hell out of his way.

I saw the other guys, except Z, with some women at the bar. As we approached, the men were trying not to look at Jake's hand holding mine.

They were also failing.

"Pipe, what'd you think?" Kase asked when we reached them.

I pulled my hand from Jake's and threw up the horns. "That was definitely in my top five shows."

I heard a deep chuckle next to me. "Hey, darlin'."

"Rhys! Your place is the freakin' best!"

"Good to hear," he said, handing me my shrug.

As I took it, I got on my toes and leaned over the bar. I grabbed the front of Rhys' shirt and pulled him closer. I saw a look of surprise in his eyes a second before I pressed my lips to his cheek. "Thank you for letting me come. It was one of the best nights of my life." Releasing his shirt, I lowered myself back down.

Rhys looked down at me, his expression shooting from warmth to pure heat. "I had a few of those cookies, darlin'. I'm definitely looking forward to experiencing more sweet from you in the future." He walked towards the other end of the bar and signaled Jake to follow him.

God, Rhys was sexy. His eyes were such an amazing color, and I was right about his smile coming easy and often. And those dimples? As a woman, I appreciated the view. I liked it even more knowing that his looks weren't the only appealing thing about him.

I just needed to work on transferring some feelings, finding time and energy, and having the nerve to go for it.

That's all? No biggie.

Turning to Kase, I stood back on my toes as he dipped down a bit. I moved his surprisingly soft dreads and kissed his cheek, too. "Thanks for inviting me and setting this whole night up, Kase. It was awesome."

Kase looked down at me and grinned. "Music's to be shared with good friends, hot chicks, and hot chicks who you know are gonna turn into good friends. You leaving?"

"Yeah, I gotta head out. Lots of cakes tomorrow. Let Jake know I said thanks."

"I just experienced how you say thanks, Piper. I don't know if my delivery will be as good as yours. My beard probably tickles."

I laughed. "Good point."

"I'll walk you to your car," he offered, throwing his arm around my shoulders.

"Cool, thanks. See ya guys!" I waved to the rest of the group before Kase and I headed towards the exit.

When we were almost to the door, I heard a deep voice rumble, "I got this."

Looking over my shoulder, I saw Jake had caught up with us.

"Nah, boss, it's cool," Kase said.

"Kase—"

"Fine, fine," Kase interrupted, dipping to kiss my cheek. "See ya, Pipe." He turned and began walking back to the bar.

"Bye," I called to him.

He lifted his hand in a slight wave, bringing it down to rub the back of his neck as he sauntered off, chuckling and shaking his head.

Yum.

Wait.

What just happened?

"Let's go," Jake said, drawing my attention back to him.

"You don't have to walk me. I was good with Kase."

"Yeah, I'm sure you were," he muttered with a slight sneer.

"What does that mean?" I walked as fast as my short legs would carry me.

Quick getaways would be much *easier with long legs.*

"Rhys *and* Kase in one night? Covering your bases?"

When we reached Bo, I opened the door but didn't get in. I turned and looked at Jake. Gorgeous Jake who thought I dressed, and now acted, like a whore. I was hurt and embarrassed. I was also really freakin' pissed.

Since anger was the easiest emotion to deal with, I rolled with that.

"Are you implying I'm a slut?" I gestured up and down my body. "I mean, you think I dress like one. And, apparently, I dance like one. I guess in your mind it's a quick jump to 'covering my bases' with as many men as I can add to my waiting list."

God, I'm so stupid.

"Babe—" Jake started.

"You don't like me. And that's fine 'cause, honestly, I don't much like you, either. I'll stay out of the shop and out of your shit." I quickly slid into my car and slammed the door. I paused and took some calming deep breaths after fumbling with my keys and turning the ignition.

Jake wasn't the first person to be mean to me. He also wasn't the first person to misinterpret my easygoing demeanor and assume I was easy in other ways. I knew the issue wasn't with what he thought. It was that it was *him* thinking it.

I put Bo into drive. Turning to check for oncoming traffic, I saw Jake still standing on the sidewalk. His head was tilted, looking away from me. I held my breath as he took a step towards my car. Changing course suddenly, he headed back to Rye, shaking his head.

I released my breath in a loud sigh as I pulled out and drove home.

Sleep wasn't coming. No matter how many sheep I counted, or how exhausted my body was, I couldn't relax. My brain had decided that the middle of the night was the perfect time to replay and analyze my argument with Jake. Only this time, I had all sorts of snappy and clever comebacks. The Jake in my head was shamed, but also impressed with my biting wit.

My eyes had just closed when I heard pounding on my front door. I jolted up, wondering if I'd imagined it.

It's after two in the morning. Maybe the Sandman is finally here to put me out of my misery.

There was more knocking as I made my way through my small ranch style house. I looked through my peephole, sure I was delirious from sleep deprivation. I opened the door. "What're you—"

Before I could finish my question, Jake's mouth dropped to mine and his hands cupped my face.

He had a thing about interrupting. It irked me. Now? Yeah, not so much.

After the way we'd ended things at Rye I hadn't planned on seeing Jake ever again. I definitely wasn't planning on it being in the middle of the night for a sudden doorway kiss.

I also wasn't questioning it.

Not yet, at least.

Instead, I wrapped my arms around his neck, letting myself enjoy his hot before his cold inevitably came back and pissed me off.

Jake's tongue moved, teasing but persistent.

I opened wider for him, tasting beer, scotch, and something else. Something rich and masculine.

Something Jake.

He groaned, his hands moving behind my head and up into my hair. He fisted it, gently tugging my head back and kissing me harder. He controlled the kiss and me, using his hands in my hair to move me where he wanted. Jake dropped one hand down to cup my ass before easily lifting me.

I instinctively wrapped my legs around his waist, feeling him hard against me.

He carried me into the hallway before stopping.

When I realized he didn't know where my room was, I tilted my head to the right, not wanting to break the kiss.

He walked into my room and I unhooked my legs from his waist, waiting for him to release his hold on my ass to let me down. His grip only tightened as he turned around and fell onto the bed on his back with me on top.

If we kept going, I knew what would happen. What I wanted to happen. What I'd spent an embarrassing amount of time daydreaming about happening. I should've stopped kissing him, but I moved my knees to straddle him, not ready to be done.

I figured a minute or two more couldn't hurt.

Maybe ten more minutes. Thirty, at most.

Jake kept one hand in my hair, his other sliding down my back to my ass and then up again. Moving my head to the side, he brought his mouth to the curve of my neck. His facial hair rubbed against the sensitive skin of my throat, rough and arousing, as he kissed.

I moaned again, rubbing against his hardness, seeking something, anything, to ease the tension I was feeling. My heart started pounding in my chest even harder.

Is it possible to have a heart attack from kissing? Death by make out?

"Oh God, Piper, you taste so good. Fuck," Jake groaned, grabbing my hips and flipping us over so that he was on top. He brought his mouth to mine again, one forearm propping him up, while his other hand trailed along the side of my curves.

Never mind, I'm not dying but I might kill him if he doesn't move his hand to touch me more.

As if reading my mind, his hand moved up my rib cage, inching closer to my breast. I could feel the heat from his hand, my nipples already straining against my top.

My silent pleas for him to touch me turned to silent curses when he abruptly stopped. I was on the verge of a full-fledged tantrum when he lifted his upper body from mine.

"Shit, I didn't mean for this to happen. I came here to explain about earlier. I shouldn't have. I damn sure shouldn't have kissed you."

And there's the cold after the hot.

I've never been kissed like this, ever, and he feels like he shouldn't have done it.

I just want this night to be over.

"It's okay, no worries. About, uh, kissing me or the stuff earlier." I shifted to move out from under him, but his hand tightened in my hair.

"Shit. I'm not good with this stuff to begin with and I've been drinkin' and well... about earlier. I was a dick. I went back to the bar, determined to let you leave and let that be it." He shook his head. "But you were so wrong, I just couldn't stop thinking about how wrong you were. And I couldn't let that slide. So I caught a ride with Eli."

"Wrong?" I asked, trying to decide if I should find the energy to be offended.

Jake rolled to the side and stretched out next to me. He kicked his shoes off before pulling me to him so I was on my side with my head resting on his shoulder.

I moved my hand from being trapped between us, unsure of where to put it. I started towards his stomach, then went up, letting it hover over his chest. When everywhere seemed too intimate, I began to pull it back.

Jake grabbed my hand and placed it on his upper abdomen. "Fuck, you're cute," he whispered, his voice soft and sweet. "There's nothin' wrong with you or how you look. You look... perfect. It's why I didn't want you in the waitin' room at Hyde. Or dancin' tonight. I don't think you know what you do to a man. Still, I was an asshole and I'm sorry."

"It's okay." I was used to being protected and sheltered. It was nothing new. At least his reason was sweet, as opposed to being told what to do so I wouldn't make a mistake and embarrass anyone.

"Tired?"

"No, I'm fine. Do you need a ride home?" I asked, yawning through most of it.

"Let's try again. Tired?"

I nodded, my cheek rubbing against him. "Exhausted."

Jake pulled the blanket over us, still holding me against him. "Night."

Even if I wanted to, I didn't have the energy to question him staying over. I snuggled in and was asleep within minutes.

"Mornin', babe."

I jolted awake as I realized I was not alone in bed. "Mornin'," I mumbled, my mind racing as I tried not to hyperventilate.

Memories of last night came crashing back, including falling asleep with Jake in my bed. I couldn't believe I'd actually been able to sleep. At the same time, I couldn't remember when I'd slept so well.

I was warm and cozy, curled on my side with Jake's body curved against my back and his arm wrapped under my chest. I felt a light kiss behind my ear.

"Your alarm just went off. Gotta be up?"

"Yeah, cakes to do."

"I gotta go, too."

"Alright," I said softly.

Jake slowly loosened his arm as I moved away. His fingertips trailed my skin as he released me.

I rolled off the bed, happy he couldn't see the goose bumps that broke out across my body.

I went to start the coffee maker as I heard the tap running in the bathroom. I got my mug ready and brought out my calendar to plan my day in hopes of distracting myself.

"This is totally no big deal," I muttered to myself. "People wake up with gorgeous men in their beds all the time. Not me, of course, but people. Normal, non-workaholic people. I could pretend to be a people, right?"

Uhh, just sayin', I don't think normal people sit and talk to themselves...

"Shh, quiet. It's not my fault. He hates me, then he likes me, then he's rude, and then he's sweet. There are mixed signals, and then there are signals that are so mixed I'm picking up stations from the other side of the world. How am I supposed to have any clarity?"

"Am I interrupting something?" Jake asked from the doorway, his tone amused.

"Holy heck," I squealed, jumping. "Don't do that! You're gonna give me a heart attack."

"Didn't want to eavesdrop on your conversation with..." Jake trailed off, his lips twitching.

"Sorry, just talking to myself about, uhh, my broken radio! Yeah, damn thing keeps going out. I hate that," I babbled my flimsy excuse, hoping he hadn't heard what I'd been saying. Being caught talking to myself was bad enough.

Luckily, he seemed to believe me. "Bring it to Z, he's a fuckin' magician with that shit."

"I'll probably just get a new one. This one is *way* old," I lied. I had no clue how to break my brand new radio, but if he pushed this, I'd find a way. I'd rather risk electrocution than explain what I'd really been talking to myself about.

Looking around, he thankfully changed the subject. "Cute house."

"Thanks."

Cute was the perfect description of my house. I'd filled the small space with bright, cheerful colors and pictures. There was a plush couch in the living room in front of a big window that let in loads of sunlight. I wanted to live somewhere warm and welcoming, someplace that felt comfortable.

I'd used a huge chunk of my savings, but my dad still had to co-sign for me to buy it. It wasn't a big house or in the best neighborhood. But it was mine and I loved it.

"Come here, babe."

I went to him, running on autopilot and because of the whole Babe Zombie thing.

His eyes searched my face. "We good?"

"Totally." He'd apologized and I wasn't one to hold a grudge. "You need a ride?"

"Nah, I texted Eli. He's already outside waiting for me. I'll see ya, yeah?"

I nodded, walking him to the door and opening it.

I wasn't sure if that was a blow off, and I wasn't about to ask.

My mind's muddled enough for one day, thank you very much.

Jake turned to face me in the doorway, opening his mouth to speak. He closed it again without saying anything. Reaching out instead, he touched my cheek briefly before dropping his hand.

With a small nod, he jogged to Eli's waiting car.

I waved to Eli before closing the door and leaning against it. Taking a deep breath, I did the only thing I could.

I baked.

I was working on frosting cake two of three for the day, when my phone beeped to indicate a text message.

Jake: Hey babe.

Me: Hey, what's up?

Jake: You busy tonight?

Me: Yeah, why?

Jake: We're all goin' out. Thought you might come with.

My phone beeped again with a text from Kase.

Kase: Piper ya gotta come out with us.

Me: Sorry, got plans. Maybe next time?

Jake: What plans?

Me: Huh?

Jake: You told Kase you had plans. What're they?

I chuckled. They were obviously together and talking to each other while they both texted me.

Kase: Next time for sure. Not maybe.

Me: Okay next time definitely. Have fun tonight.

Kase: You got it.

Jake: So what're you doing?

Me: I've got a dinner thing. I told Kase I'm in next time. I gotta get back to work if I'm ever gonna make it out of the house. Have fun tonight!

When I didn't get any response, I shrugged and went back to my cakes.

When my bell rang at six, I opened the door to James.

Twenty-six and on the fast track at my stepfather's company, my mother had been pushing him at me for a couple years. And that's putting it mildly.

I wouldn't have been surprised to find out she'd been meeting with a wedding planner on the sly.

Her efforts weren't going to pay off though. It wasn't that James wasn't attractive. He looked handsome enough in slacks and a pressed shirt. There was just no edge. No badassness. No... anything.

James dipped to press a chaste kiss to my cheek. "Hello, Piper. You look lovely."

I didn't feel lovely. In my conservative black dress, I felt like I was playing the worst game of dress up. Long sleeves and a high neckline ensured my tattoos were covered. The knee length didn't work with my already short legs, and the fit was far from flattering with my curves. My hair was my lone rebellion, worn loose and wild. My subtle makeup was in place producing the world's most boring mask.

"Thank you, James. You look nice, too." It had to be James, never Jim or Jimmy. I wanted to roll my eyes. "Ready?"

"Of course."

After I locked the door, James grabbed my elbow and led me to his car. I wished I could've driven my own.

And kept on driving.

We made small talk until we arrived. Unlike my house, this one was large and in the very best neighborhood. I knew from experience it was neither warm nor comfortable.

A wrought iron gate opened to a long driveway. When we pulled in front of the house, a valet was waiting to park James' car. There was no holding back my eye roll this time.

My anxiety increased as we entered the house, even before an annoyed voice greeted me.

"Your hair. It's down."

I barely held in my sigh as I turned to the displeased woman. Her own shoulder length champagne blond hair was perfectly styled and pulled into a jeweled clasp. Unlike my outfit, her designer skirt and blouse set was flattering on her taller frame. While not my personal choice in fashion, she looked lovely.

"Why, hello, Mother, how are you?"

"Fine, fine. Come with me to double check things. James, please be seated. We'll be eating shortly."

James nodded obediently before walking away.

That's your life if you don't grow a backbone. Mother will keep pushing and you'll keep giving in because it's easier. Before you know it, you'll be Mrs. James, the Obedient Nodder. It'll be a lifetime of business dinners, polite conversation, and...

Oh, sorry, fell asleep just thinking about it.

"I'm so glad you accepted the date with James."

"Mother, this isn't a date. It's dinner at my parents' house. You were the one who insisted James pick me up. I know your address. I grew up here, remember?"

As much as one grew up in a show house.

"Piper, that attitude isn't flattering. Though, with your hair down like that, it's obvious you aren't trying. Ladies wear their hair back."

"So you've often said."

"James is a good man," she continued, pointedly ignoring me. "And you know Thomas trusts him. You should really be trying harder."

I tuned my mother out, smiling wide and rolling my eyes at Anna, the housekeeper.

When Mother married Thomas, Anna had already been working for him for around twenty years. I knew she must be in her sixties, but she looked at least a decade younger and, if you asked, she'd tell you she was thirty-five and a lot of months. She was also one of my favorite people growing up and now.

Mother led me back to the table, still talking about my poor life choices. I kept my smile in place as I pretended to listen. I'd heard it often enough that I had it memorized.

She'd start with telling me how my little cakes weren't going to be enough to support me and that I'd struggle. Then she'd throw in the double punch of my house being too small and in a dangerous neighborhood. She'd end with her finishing move of a guilt trip so extreme I was surprised it didn't require a passport.

I went to the head of the table and kissed my stepfather, Thomas, by the cheek before settling into my seat next to James. I nodded politely at the other ten people at dinner other than myself, James, Mother, and Thomas.

Some people had family dinners.

My mother had family dinner parties.

Through the first two courses, the conversation flowed around me but I hardly paid attention. It wasn't because I was rude.

Okay, it wasn't *just* because I was rude.

I'd learned long ago that the quieter I was, the happier Mother was. I smiled and politely laughed when required, sipping frequently from my glass of wine.

While every place setting at Mother's dinners had wine, my glass almost always went untouched. However, I had a feeling I'd need to numb myself a little to get through the night.

I was grateful I'd trusted my instincts.

About halfway through the third course, one of the women

turned to me, asking, "Piper, what do you do?"

"She bakes dessert," Mother answered. Her words said one thing but her disdainful tone definitely said another. She might as well have been telling them I cooked meth and sold it to school kids.

I'd long ago given up getting overly upset. It was easier to ignore her than to become the bad guy for getting emotional and embarrassing her. Instead, I'd zone out and think about new tattoos, cupcake and frosting combinations, or plan my schedule.

I was finding the wine was a pleasant distraction, too.

Tipping my head back so I didn't miss a drop, I finished my third glass. It was refilled before I could even set it down. I glanced up at Alexander and gave him a small smile as he subtly squeezed my shoulder.

He'd been around for six years so he knew how this conversation would go. Alexander had been hired as chef when I was about fourteen, though he handled more than just cooking. He was in his fifties, a perfectionist, and, although not as coddling as Anna, he was still another of my favorite people.

When Alexander entered the room carrying desserts, I knew I was in the final stretch. I was to have a few bites but no more, which was hard because he made scrumptious desserts. As delicious as they were, it still wasn't worth the lecture about my ample curves.

I might not be able to taste much, but at least I could taste freedom.

Alexander placed an individual Crème brûlée in front of me and I could've kissed him. It was heavenly but also very rich and sweet. He knew I'd only be able to eat a few bites even if I could have more. He winked when I grinned up at him before going back to serving the desserts.

I slowly drank the last of my wine, setting the glass far enough away that he'd know I was done. I savored my three bites, trying not to bounce as I awaited my opportunity to leave.

After the first couple left, I took my opening. Carefully standing, as three inch heels and four glasses of wine could be dangerous, I turned to James. "I'm rather tired."

And rather bored outta my damn mind.

"Please, stay and enjoy," I said, forcing a smile. "I'm going to call for a ride."

"I'm ready to go, Piper." He stood and turned to thank my parents.

I dutifully kissed the air near Thomas' cheek before heading towards the door. Unfortunately, my smooth escape was foiled when my mother stopped me.

"Remember what I said about James. And, for goodness sake, hair back when you see him next," she whispered in my ear as she hugged me.

I'd planned to call Ray to come get me but she lived over a half-hour away. As much as I didn't want to spend more time with James, I was glad I didn't have to wait for a ride. I'd have started walking.

Once I'd moved out, I didn't necessarily *like* returning here but it had been tolerable. The past few visits, however, I'd begun to feel trapped and claustrophobic.

As I walked towards the door, I felt the familiar lack of air, as if the walls were closing in on me.

I need to get out before the house swallows me.

"Piper, are you okay?" James asked. "You look pale."

"Yes, I'm fine. Just tired."

When the valet pulled the car up, I got in, anxious to get home. It hadn't even been three hours since I'd left my house, but it seemed like days.

James chatted as he drove, though I stayed quiet. I couldn't seem to find the energy to pretend to care about his work. I felt rude, but he didn't seem to mind filling the silence.

About two minutes from my house, his tone turned serious. "I know your mother has been pushing me at you. I don't want you to feel like you have to see me but I'd love to take you out to dinner. One not at your parents' house."

Fuck.

"I think you're great," I started, and even I knew it sounded like a blow-off. Which was exactly what it was. "I just don't think either of us is right for the other."

"What makes you say that?"

"I'm not the same person away from my parents. My life isn't just a rebellion against my mother. It's who I am, and, though I can't see the future, my best bet is that this is how I'll always be. I'm not dinner-party-Piper. I'm rock 'n' roll-party-Piper."

Don't forget makeout-and-have-a-sleepover-with-a-badass-Piper.

James nodded. "Maybe I'd like that Piper, too. If you need to think about it, that's fine. All I ask is you give me the chance to decide for myself."

My romantic life wasn't wild but there had always been a decent enough amount of interest. However, two men telling me they were into me in twenty-four hours was definitely a personal record.

On the downside, neither of them were the one that I wanted. Although, Rhys was a whole lot closer to my type than James.

"Okay, I'll think about it," I lied. I knew I wouldn't be putting the thought into him that I would with Rhys. I had zero romantic feelings towards James, and there was no spark between us that hinted at anything developing.

I honestly doubted that his interest in me went much beyond how it would secure his career and future with Thomas' company. My dilemma came from how to tell him without making it tense and weird whenever we saw each other.

Why is it not acceptable to run away from awkward situations, flailing my arms and screaming like a certain green frog puppet does?

I was trying not to giggle as I pictured that when James regained my attention.

"Piper, do you know that man?" James asked, guardedly.

I looked in my driveway to see a sweet hog next to my Charger. Though facing the other way, I definitely knew that man. I'd spent a lot of time trying not to think about him.

I'd also failed miserably at it.

"Yes, that's Jake."

"Are you in some sort of trouble? I know your mother said you were being stubborn about money, but if you're in trouble—"

"No!" I interrupted. I'd have laughed at the obvious presumption and misperception of Jake, if it weren't sad. It was also the perfect example of why James and I would never happen. "I'm definitely not in trouble."

I didn't think I was, at least. However, the look on Jake's face as he watched us pull in made me think twice.

"Are you dating a biker?" James looked at me as if the idea was insane.

"No, James. Jake is a friend."

One that is incredibly hot, makes me think some very un-*friend like things, and kisses me until I forget my own name.*

James put the car in park and opened his door. He got out and hurried to my side.

Jake beat him to it, though, throwing open my door and grabbing my hand to haul me out. He kept hold of me as he closed the door with a bit more force than was probably required.

I turned to face James, but felt Jake close behind me.

James was all soft and safe niceness. Tall enough at five foot eleven, he had plain, sandy colored hair and brown eyes, though his weren't quite as warm as Eli's.

He was safe.

Nice.

Boring.

My mother was out of her damned mind to think that James was who I'd choose. That safe and boring was all I wanted in life. I'd had more than enough of that.

I wanted wild.

"Uh, James, this is my friend Jake. Jake, this is James."

The men gave chin lifts to each other.

Alright, moving on.

"Thank you for tonight, James," I said, lifting just slightly to give him a polite kiss on the cheek. It ended up as an air one when Jake used his hold on my hand to pull me back.

"You're welcome," James said. Hesitantly, he glanced at Jake, then back at me. "Would you like me to stay for coffee?"

If you don't leave soon, I will literally push you into your car. Don't test me!

"That's okay. Thanks."

"If you're sure. Let me know if you need anything. And, please, think about what we talked about, alright?"

"Have a nice night, James."

Jake turned and walked us to my front door without giving me the chance to wave James off.

When I grabbed my keys from my clutch, Jake took them from me, opening the door and pulling me in.

"What's he want you to think about?" he asked when we got inside.

"Hi, Jake. How are you? How's your evening going?"

"Cute. What's he want?"

"Uhh, about the same as Rhys last night."

"He wants time with you?"

"He didn't word it like that, but that was the gist of it. Where are the guys?" I attempted to switch topics.

"Out at The Noise. Why?"

The Noise was supposed to be the best biker bar in the area. One I hoped to visit in a few months when my ID would get me in.

"I thought you were going out with them. Everything alright?"

"Yeah, just makin' sure you got home."

I held my arms out. "Well, as you can see, I did. Go enjoy your night."

"Babe?" I could hear amusement in his voice, and the corners of his lips were twitching, as if he were fighting a smile.

"What?"

"What the fuck are you wearin'?"

"A dress?"

"I got that. But it's fuckin' boring."

"I'm boring."

"No, you're anythin' but."

"I am. I'm totally boring." I opened the door. "Thank you for checking on me, Jake. It was very sweet of you. Have fun tonight."

His arm looped around my waist as he suddenly pulled me to him. "Piper?"

"Hmm?" I mumbled, unable to form words with his body pressed to mine.

"Why don't you kiss me like you do everyone else?"

"What do you mean?" I had no issue with kissing him. I'd totally do it.

A lot.

All over.

Do that now!

"Everyone else gets a kiss when you say thank you."

Going up on my tiptoes, my body slid against his. I pulled him down slightly and pressed a kiss to his cheek, feeling his scruff against my lips.

I couldn't help but wonder if maybe I was focused on the wrong thing. Sure, running my fingers over his scruff would probably feel awesome. Feeling my lips on it, though, was near orgasmic.

"Better?" I asked, happy to sound steady when I felt far from it.

"Not yet," he answered as I yawned. "Tired?"

I nodded. "And tipsy."

"You drank?"

"Yeah, a glass of wine. Or four."

"That'd do it. Go get some sleep."

I nodded, intending to do just that. Giving in to my drunken impulse, I went back up on my tiptoes. I lightly pressed my lips to his before sliding back down. "Thank you, Jake."

His eyes went hooded, his voice huskier. "Now that? That I like."

"Me, too."

Jake brought his hand up to cup my cheek.

I held my breath, silently willing him to kiss me again.

"Sweet dreams, Piper," he rumbled, before turning and walking to his bike.

I was drunk enough to call out to him. Drunk enough to ask him to stay the night with me again. To want him to kiss me, to touch me, to make me feel wild.

I was sober enough, though, to know better.

So I did the smart thing and stayed quiet as I watched him leave.

If only the smart thing was also the fun thing.

Groupie

When I woke up the next morning, I was surprised to see it was almost eleven. It'd been a while since I'd slept in so late. The best part was that I didn't have to jump out of bed in a rush.

There were no cakes to bake or homework to do. I had to sketch some designs, but I already had some clear visuals in my head.

I grabbed my phone and burrowed back into my blankets to enjoy the rare opportunity to be lazy. I reviewed some waiting emails, but all of them were business that didn't need to be taken care of right away. I clicked to check texts.

The first waiting message made me feel guilty.

Dana was one of the only people from my mother's side of my life that I could stand. We weren't close, but we were kind of friends. I'd been so caught up with cakes and school that I'd barely talked to her.

Dana: Wasn't last night your date with the dreamy James? How'd it go?

Only Dana would describe James as 'dreamy'.

Me: It wasn't a date. Just dinner at my mother's. We barely talked.

Dana: Are you seeing him again?

Me: He works for Thomas, I'm sure I'll see him often.

Dana: You know what I mean. You've gotta hook him soon, Piper.

I don't even get how he's still single. He's young, he's attractive, and he's successful. Plus, he seems to tolerate your… you-ness.

Ahh, isn't that what every chick dreams of? A guy who totally tolerates them for who they are. Excuse me while I start knitting booties for all the babies that we're going to tolerate together.

Me: Yeah, he does seem to do that. Anyway, I gotta get in the shower. I'll talk to you later.

Dana: We have to get together, maybe tonight?

Me: Probably not tonight, but soon.

Dana might be a friend, but hanging with her could be draining. She was competitive about everything and constantly needed to outdo everyone. Last time we'd had lunch, she'd switched between badmouthing her other friends, discussing her diet, and making constant mention of her money and shopping.

She wasn't always the easiest person to hang out with but she'd never been quite this bad before. Unfortunately, she was unreceptive when I'd tried to gently broach the subject.

On my rare day off, I didn't want to deal.

I switched to another message and did a giddy bounce when I saw it was from Jake.

Way to play it cool, Piper.

Jake: Mornin'.

Me: Yo.

Jake: Another wine filled date tonight?

Me: I was thinking I'd move up to vodka.

Jake: Cute. Wanna come party instead?

Me: On a Sunday?

Jake: What, you think we take Sundays off?

Me: Ain't no rest for the wicked?

Jake: Rest is for the dead. Life is for the living, Piper.

His words hit me hard. I didn't want to play it safe and live with regrets. I wanted to do what I loved and make the most of the life that I had. It's what I'd been trying to do, what I'd been working for.

While I looked at his words, another message from him popped up.

Jake: So, plans?

As much as life was for the living, it was also for enjoying the rare, peaceful quiet. Especially when that included some chocolate and garbage TV.

Me: Just being lazy tonight, no work.

Jake: So that's a yes then.

Me: No, it's a me saying I'm being lazy, so maybe another time.

Jake: Would you change your mind if I said it was a party at our bud Jet's house?

Me: Uhh, no?

Jake: What if I said that Jet was the X-ers drummer?

Me: No way! I saw them in concert once, they're amazing. How do you know him?

Jake: We went to school together. They're leavin' on tour in a few days. Tonight is a goin' away thing. In?

Me: Oh, I'm so in.

Jake: I see how it is. When it was just me, you were lazy. Now you're goin' for the band. Groupie.

Me: Damn straight. What time?

Jake: I'll pick you up at eight.

Me: Awesome.

Jake: I gotta get some work done. See ya, babe.

Now how am I supposed to be lazy?

"No, I'm sure this sketch would get approved. Who wouldn't want a cake that looked like it was cut with a weed whacker?" I muttered to myself. Tilting my sketchbook to the side, I looked at it again. "Or maybe it was mauled by Satan's cats." Ripping the paper out, I crumpled it up and tossed it on the growing pile.

When it became obvious that my focus wasn't on the badly doodled cake sketches I was working on, I gave up trying. Instead, I decided to make the most of my day off and pamper myself with a soak in the tub and all things girly.

Fearing a repeat of Friday night, I didn't spend too long in the bath. Of course when I gave myself the time, my makeup only took one redo.

Even my hair cooperated when I used a barrel brush to blow-dry it wild. With my luck, I'd expected it to fall flat, become a snarled mess, or maybe even start on fire.

When I finished my hair and makeup, I pulled on dark gray skinny jeans and a thick, hot pink belt. After, I stood, for what felt like forever, staring into my open closet.

Okay, so apparently the perfect shirt isn't going to catapult itself out at me.

Damn.

Jeans and my hot pink wedge shoes were a safe bet. The top was what would make the outfit casual or dressy.

The problem was that I had no clue what kind of party it was going to be. I could safely guess that it wasn't going to be overly formal, but that still left a lot of options.

I reached for a fitted t-shirt when something towards the back caught my eye. Shifting hangers, I pulled out a corset style top.

Dark gray with pink detailing, the halter showed off my tattoos, accentuated my curves, and looked rocker glam. I'd bought it on a whim but had never worn it.

If there was any place to wear rocker glam, I figured a party at an actual rocker's house was it.

I was putting on a gray bolero when there was a knock on the door. Opening it, I was surprised to see Jake.

"Hey, you're early."

Jake didn't say anything, but his eyes swept over me, making me wonder if I should've gone with a more casual look.

"Everything okay?" I asked.

"No, not really."

"What's wrong?"

"Don't suppose I could convince you to go change, huh?"

"Should I? I wasn't sure what type of thing this was."

"Got any sweats and hoodies four sizes too big?"

"Um, no?"

Jake shook his head. "Then don't bother. You look hot, sweets."

Sweets?

"Thanks, so do you."

Which wasn't quite true. He was definitely working a scorching look in motorcycle boots and worn in black jeans. A white t-shirt contrasted with his tanned skin and showed off his tats and strong arms. His hair was pulled back and I wondered again how it looked down.

And how it felt.

I was thinking I might be starting to get a tiny bit obsessed.

Starting?

Tiny?

Full-blown, baby.

"What happened to the other kind of thanks?" he asked, his voice low.

His arms went around me, pulling me closer as he lowered his mouth lightly to mine.

I liked gentle a lot but my body remembered the kiss from Friday night. Without thought, I used my tongue to trace the seam of Jake's lips.

He groaned before deepening the kiss.

Too soon he pulled back, ending the moment. "We gotta go."

"Okay," I murmured from my haze.

"Fuck, really wanna kiss those lips again, but then we won't be leavin' at all."

"Okay," I repeated.

I'm sure there's some appeal to leaving, but I can't for the life of me remember what. Maybe we should stay here until I figure it out.

My face must have shown my thoughts, making Jake kiss me again, hard but much too fast.

"Let's go, sweets."

I locked up and followed him down the walkway, running my hand over the back of my neck. My nerves were on edge about tonight and I couldn't shake my anxiety lately. I was worried about doing something embarrassing and having to avoid Jake and the guys.

As in, I'd be changing my name and moving to a remote town where the moose outnumbered the people.

I caught sight of Jake's Fat Boy Lo Harley, pulling me from my heavy thoughts. I'd seen it briefly last night, but the close-up view was infinitely better. Black with chrome detailing, it was sleek and powerful without looking like a crotch rocket. Not that I minded crotch rockets on occasion, but my love was for cruisers.

As much as I wanted a bike, I figured delivering cakes on one might get a little messy, so I went with the van.

"Awesome," I whispered reverently.

Jake's lip twitched. He grabbed a helmet and put it on me, his fingers lightly brushing my jaw and neck. Straddling the bike, he took care of his own helmet before helping me on.

Under normal circumstances, even in heels, I'd have had no issue getting on the bike. After seeing him on it, however, I was finding myself a little weak in the knees.

As the engine roared to life, I wrapped my arms around Jake's waist. He pulled them tighter, moving me closer in the process.

With my front flush to his back, I could feel each muscle ripple, each tendon tighten, as he moved. I rested my head between his shoulders as we took off.

I was disappointed when we pulled into a driveway. I loved the feel of the ride, the sights flying by as the wind whipped around us.

It was invigorating. It was beautiful.

It was freedom.

Experiencing it pressed tight to Jake didn't hurt, either.

Jake pulled up to the side of the house and cut the engine. Hopping off the back, I set the helmet with his and shook out my hair.

"Damn," someone said from the porch.

I turned and barely contained my fangirl squeal when I saw Jet.

"Hey, baby, I'm Jet. Before anyone else sees you, how about you and I—"

"Too late," Jake said. Curling his arm around my shoulders, we walked towards the steps.

"'Be a drummer,' everyone said. 'You'll get all the girls,' everyone said. Everyone was wrong. Shoulda taken a fuckin' shop class," Jet sighed dramatically.

"You did, you just didn't go. Pretty sure you spent a big chunk of your time in the nurse's office."

"Hey, Nurse Maggie and I had a real connection!"

"She was *fifty*!"

"That doesn't mean she didn't deserve love. Fuck, I still got a thing for nurses. Can't even go to the damn doctor without gettin' wood."

I couldn't hold back my laughter. Rock stars were supposed to be all ego and arrogance, but I'd always heard the X-ers were down to earth and humble.

"You must be the gorgeous Piper," Jet said to me.

"That's me," I wheezed.

I just got called gorgeous by the drummer for the X-ers.

Be cool, Piper. No one likes a screaming groupie.

"Breathe, groupie," Jake whispered in my ear, his voice amused as he proved he could read my thoughts.

I can be cool. I got this.

Right?

Maybe.

Jet lead the way into his house. "Let's go get you two some drinks, huh? The night is young, but the party is already kickin'."

The living room was full of people hanging out and dancing, the loud music traveling throughout the house. There was a drinking game going on in a dining room, everyone laughing and cheering.

I'd never been to a farewell party for famous rockers going on tour before, but this wasn't what I'd expected. The rock 'n' roll vibe was definitely there, but it was relaxed and chill. Instead of a pretentious Hollywood-esque party, it felt more like a kegger.

Freakin' awesome.

When we got to the back of the house, my inner groupie was dangerously close to jumping out and screeching.

The X-ers and some of the guys were casually sitting around a large table in the homey kitchen with open bottles of beer in front of them. Their loud conversation and laughter filled the room.

Sweet baby Elvis, I've died and gone to groupie heaven.

That feeling went into overdrive when Gage, the lead singer, looked up from the table at us. "Aww, you brought me a going away present. Jake, man, you know me so well."

Jet shook his head. "I've already struck out. No way you've got a chance."

"Maybe that just means she's got good taste." Gage threw me his signature bad boy smirk.

I knew from seeing an X-ers show shortly after my eighteenth birthday that he was tall. With lean sinewy muscles, black hair, and dark blue eyes, he always looked dangerous. From what I'd heard, it wasn't a persona he put on to sell tickets and albums. He'd lived a rough life and still had demons that haunted him.

"Hey," Kase said, coming over with a beer in each hand. He handed one to Jake. "Beer, Pipe?"

"Water?"

"Su—" Kase started before Jet interrupted.

"We got a full bar, Piper, and this is our last chance to get a hottie drunk. By the time we get around them on tour, they're already shitty or close to it. Takes the fun out of things when all we see is sloppy, ya know? We miss the fun in between part. Get her something strong."

I shrugged and gave Kase a smile. It wasn't that I didn't want to drink. I just didn't want to get stupid.

I was having enough trouble with my inner groupie while I was sober.

When Kase went to grab my drink, Jet turned back to the table and threw his arm around my shoulders. "Piper, this is Gage, Ryder, Rocco, and Zeke."

As if I needed introductions. As if I didn't know.

Ryder was the guitarist, Rocco, the bassist, and Zeke, rhythm guitar and backup vocals. Zeke was also the baby of the group and the only one from outside of Massachusetts. He was a southern boy, with down-home charm and manners in a rocker package.

Unsurprisingly, he was also first to hop out of his chair and offer it to me.

Jet steered me over, once again not really giving me a choice. And, once again, I didn't really care. Especially when Jake moved to stand close behind me.

When Kase gave me my drink, I took a tiny sip with the plan of making it last.

Reading my mind again, Jake leaned close to my ear. "I'm driving tonight and nursing this beer. Drink up, let loose, yeah?"

I nodded up at him before Gage grabbed my attention.

"So, why no cookies? You brought cookies for Rhys."

"He placed an order for them. Let me know what you want, I'll totally bake some."

"No chocolate chip. I'm thinking oatmeal raisin."

"Dude, no. Fuck no. That's not a cookie, that's breakfast. And a nasty one," Rocco said, his expression making his disgust clear.

"I like them. And the fact that none of you fuckers do means I might actually get some of them."

"I dunno," Kase put in as he set a fresh drink in front of me, making me realize I'd finished the first one. "I'm willing to bet she can make even raisins taste good."

"It's true," I confirmed. "I hate raisins, but even I like my oatmeal raisin cookies."

I forgot about my plan to drink slowly when everyone began debating the best dessert, a surprisingly heated topic. From there the conversation, and the drinks, flowed.

It wasn't long before the nervous tension left my body. Although I was sure the alcohol helped, the band acted like a group of regular guys and that's how most everyone treated them.

I finished my drink and a new one appeared like magic in front of me. Unfortunately, the others I'd had were making themselves known.

When I stood up, Jake's hand went to my waist.

"You good?" he rumbled close to my ear.

"Yeah," I breathed. His hand often had that effect on me, but standing also made me realize I *really* had to pee.

Jake slid his hand down my side before letting me go and stepping back.

"Hey Piper, that your only piercing?" Rocco asked, dipping his head to my bellybutton ring. All the guys were tattooed, but Rocco was pierced multiple times.

"Uh, no, I have a few more." Turning towards the doorway, I stopped when he spoke again.

"Where?"

Looking over my shoulder, I smiled. "Telling would take the fun out of it."

I weaved in and out of couples going at it and pointedly ignored some less than friendly glares I was getting. Not that there were a lot of them here, but still my "Maximum Skank Occupancy Limit" had been exceeded. They were the only ones treating the band differently, and they didn't look too happy about how that was playing out.

When I reached the surprisingly tidy bathroom, I silently thanked the party gods that there was no line. After I was done, I walked carefully, concentrating on my steps so I didn't fall.

Why does walking always mean feeling drunker?

Or is it more drunk?

More drunkerer?

Wrapped up in grammatically measuring my level of intoxication, I got back to the kitchen to see Jake sitting where I'd been. I moved to sit up on the counter with Kase when Jake's large hand engulfed mine. He tugged slightly and I fell back, landing on his lap with a yelp and a giggle.

With my crossed legs hanging over the side of his, I wrapped my arm around his shoulders and settled in happily. That happy became freakin' ecstatic when his hand came to rest on my thigh, his thumb stroking.

"Piper, who did your ink?" Gage asked, watching us closely.

"My friend Ray owns a place called Exxxtreme. She's done all my tats."

"I've gotten inked by her," Jet said, lifting his sleeve to show a Celtic knot covering his upper arm. "We've played shows at her man's place."

Ray, along with being one of the most talented tattoo artists around, was also one of the sweetest women. Her ever-changing hair was past shoulder length on one side and shaved on the other. Her ears were pierced multiple times, she had two lip rings, an eyebrow piercing, plus hidden ones. Both of her tattooed arms were covered in a whirl of designs and colors that showed her inner whimsical and romantic side.

While she wasn't conventionally beautiful, she knew who she was and she rocked it.

Edge was a crazy hottie, emphasis on the crazy. Especially when it came to Ray. He was determined, unrelenting, and totally badass. He fell hard and fast for her.

It would be hard not to.

Ray, however, took her time. Her normally daring attitude flew out the window and skepticism took over when it came to getting involved with Edge. Thankfully he wore her down and her gentle temperament was the perfect match for his hard.

Edge owned Voodoo, a club in the area. Where Rye was known for being laid-back, Voodoo was a venue for high-energy live music.

"What do you have?" Gage asked.

I ran through my list, this time with no growl of annoyance from Jake. I did, however, get a whole different kind of growl when I moved on his lap to show my shoulder and back tattoos.

"Are the notes from a song?" Jet asked about my rib tattoo.

I used my fingers to tap the beat. "It's the opening of Van Morrison's 'The Piper at the Gates of Dawn'."

Gage nodded his head. Putting his elbows on the table, he leaned forward. "As a bona fide rocker hottie, settle a bet… Boring drummer or world-renowned lover and massively hung lead singer?"

"Seriously?" Jake snapped, though his lips were quirked up.

Gage raised his hands and shrugged. "What? It's a valid question. For research purposes, of course."

"So you have the facts to make an informed decision, though, I'm bigger and not boring," Jet said. "Inventive. Imaginative. It's heart-stopping, really."

"Yeah, 'cause they die of boredom," Rocco said, before dodging the empty cup Jet threw at him.

I'm at Jet's house pervin' on rock star hotties! How is this my life?

Shh.

Don't question it.

Go with it.

"Well," I started through my laughter, "as much as I love a sexy voice, and I do, I have a thing for men that work with their hands. So, sorry Gage, this round would go to Jet."

Jet stood up to do a thrusting victory dance. "Ha! Told you. In your face, fucker! I get the best chicks, woo hoo!"

"Damn, that doesn't count then. She's obviously biased. She's here with the master of workin' his hand." Gage used his fist to make an obscene motion.

Jake made his own obscene, one-fingered gesture at Gage.

"Damn me and my voice of a fuckin' angel," Gage sighed. "I even told Jake when he was opening Hyde's that he'd get so much tail."

I couldn't stop myself from momentarily freezing, my body going tight, at Gage's words. Not about how much sex Jake had; that he got laid was not a bombshell. He was hot, smart, funny, and, it was worth repeating, hot.

What was surprising was that Jake *owned* Hyde. The only person I'd seen or read about was Z, which was why I'd thought he owned it. I'd assumed Jake was the manager, just handling the day-to-day stuff of running the place.

I kept a smile on my face and forced myself to relax, hoping it wasn't obvious that I was surprised.

Not one to miss anything, Jake's hands tightened on my waist as he lifted me off of him. "Let's go dance."

I nodded, standing up and trying to think of an excuse. I didn't want to admit I was a dingus, but my brain was drawing a blank.

With a hand at the small of my back, Jake led me to the living room. Looking around, I was able to see how the sound carried so thoroughly throughout the house. Along with the small speakers that were mounted around the room for surround sound, large speakers were set up near the stereo.

All of the furniture was pushed to the side, allowing people a place to sit while also opening up the majority of the space.

I was once again surprised to see how nicely the room was decorated. I wasn't sure if it was more shocking that there were coasters on the coffee and end tables, or that people were actually using said coasters.

Between the music and the crush of people, the noise level was high. There was no way Jake and I could carry on a conversation.

My relief was cut short when the song ended and a quiet one began. I silently cursed the music gods because even with the volume up, we were able to talk.

Jake slid his arms around my waist as we moved. His head dipped down to the side of mine. "Sorry, babe. Gage doesn't think."

"Uh, it's okay," I murmured, confused about why he was apologizing.

"That shit about gettin' tail. I'm obviously not a—"

I pulled back to look at him. "Totally fine. And totally *not* my business."

His eyes searched my face, as if trying to determine whether I was lying. Seeming to accept my answer, he asked, "So what was it?"

"What was what?" I asked, playing clueless.

Just once I'd like to get away with it.

"One minute you're smilin' and laughin'... Christ, even not being able to see your whole face, you're so fuckin' gorgeous I can't look away. Which is how I know that your smile changed."

At his sweet words, my brain went to mush. Thankfully he hadn't asked me anything too personal or embarrassing, because I'd have told him every last secret.

"I didn't know you owned Hyde. I knew you ran it, but not that you owned it. I was just surprised."

"You didn't know I owned Hyde?"

I shook my head. "Nope."

"Fuck me. Seriously?"

"No. Z's always the one doing the publicity—"

"I just hate doing that shit. Z only works part-time in the shop. Interviews, advertising, and all that are the other half of his job. So you really didn't know?"

I shook my head again. "Does it matter?"

Some people took it personally when others weren't aware of their accomplishments, as if it was an insult to their giant egos.

Jake seemed to have the opposite reaction.

His eyes warmed as he leaned down and brushed his lips against mine. When the music grew loud again, he moved his mouth back to my ear. "Yeah, baby, it does."

Before I could ask more, Jet approached us with drinks in hand. "It's been a while since you've had a drink."

"What is it?" I sniffed the shot glass. There were fruity undertones, but it smelled boozy enough to make my nose tingle.

"Dunno. Kase just said don't get near any open flames with it."

I shrugged and tossed the shot back, instantly grimacing at the taste. "Blech. Tastes like burning."

"That face just screams you want another."

"It actually isn't bad after a minute. It tastes like fruit. If said fruit was soaked in lighter fluid, but still."

"Since I'm pretty sure that beer was evaporating quicker than you were drinking it," Jet said, handing the larger cup to Jake, "water."

"Thanks." Jake gulped some back.

Even the way he drinks is sexy.

I've officially lost my mind.

Jet grabbed the empty shot glass from me and handed it to a guy walking by, to their startled surprise. "Here, my gift to you."

"Uh, thanks?" the guy said, before recognition dawned. A smile split across his face as he held the glass close like it actually was a treasure.

"Pretty sure you just lost that." I watched the guy move away slowly, trying to look nonchalant as he slipped the shot glass into his pocket. "Yup, gone."

"Meh, that's okay. I stocked up at Target. I'd have signed it for him if he was gonna steal my shit, though. Anyway, now that you're hands are free but Jake's aren't, looks like it's time for me to steal you for a dance."

Jet pulled me to him, moving us closer to the crowd and further from Jake.

I knew it wasn't about trying to get a better spot to dance. It also wasn't about trying to hit on me without Jake hearing.

Which was why I wasn't surprised when he said, "You really didn't know he owned Hyde."

It wasn't a question. Still, I answered him. "Nope, no clue."

Much like with Rhys, Jet held my eyes with his searching ones. And again I fought the urge to look away. I had nothing to hide, and as a smile spread across his face, I was glad he reached the same conclusion.

I held my breath as his smile faded and he opened his mouth to speak. Unfortunately, or maybe fortunately, a roaring loud song started up, making any conversation impossible.

The party had grown, a steady stream of people coming and going. The air, already thick and sticky from the humidity, grew increasingly warm as more people started dancing.

For tonight, please let me be one of those women that looks sexy and dewy when I sweat. We can return to my regular, splotchy faced sweating tomorrow.

Before the song finished, Jake snagged me around the waist and pulled my back against his chest. Reaching over my shoulder, he handed me his ice water before sliding his hands down to hold my hips.

Amped up and unable to stay still, I swayed and bounced as I drank.

Work and school may have temporarily taken over, but I'd still had some seriously awesome nights in my life. I grew up sheltered, but that didn't mean I didn't venture outside of that bubble.

Tonight was right up there as one of the best of my life.

Considering how awesome Rye had been, and ignoring Jake's previous asshole attitude and dinner at my mother's, the whole weekend was kickass.

It wasn't about hanging out with a band. It wasn't about the hot guy parade. Hell, it wasn't even about Jake.

Okay, it wasn't *just* about all that.

It was about being with fun people. *My* kind of people. No one was eyeing tattoos or piercings with distaste. No one was avoiding eye contact and moving away from anyone, their fear and judgment easily readable.

Hanging out with a rock band that I loved was cool.

The fact they were so chill and friendly was what made it *awesome*.

That said, being with Jake took the night from awesome to seriously freakin' *awesome*. Especially since he wasn't being a dick about what I was wearing or who I was talking to. Instead, he was casually affectionate with me in a way that cleared up any of the mixed signals he'd previously been sending my way.

When I finished drinking, Jake took the cup from me and set it on the window ledge. Pushing my hair to the side, he leaned down. "How drunk are you, sweets?" His mouth touched the skin behind my ear, sending goose bumps across my body.

"I'm not. A bit tipsy maybe. Why?"

"You ready to go?"

I was having a blast and knew the party was not even close to slowing down. Staying would mean playing hooky from classes tomorrow, which I was okay with. As long as I had copious amounts of caffeine, it would probably even be worth the rushing around I'd have to do to stay on schedule with my cakes.

However, I wasn't stupid. Jake wasn't asking because he wanted to get home and get some shut eye. I also seriously doubted he was asking with the intention of taking me home, giving me a chaste kiss on my porch, and then leaving.

I was willing to bet a dozen of my best cookies that if I said I wasn't ready to go, Jake would be cool with that. He'd been focused on making sure I was having a good time the whole night. I'd never really had that before.

But, like I said, I wasn't stupid.

I nodded. "Yeah, I'm ready."

Jake's grip tightened on my hips before he released me. He jerked his head towards the door at someone, but I couldn't see over the crowd.

Using a hand at my back, we moved through the room, and once again Jake had no trouble maneuvering us around the crowd. We stopped in the entryway and I saw Jet coming our way.

"Taking off?" he asked when he reached us.

"Yeah." Jake pounded his shoulder in a man hug. "Good luck, brother. Stay safe, yeah?"

Jet laughed as he returned the shoulder thump before stepping back. "Takes the fun out of being a rocker, but I'll do what I can."

"Good luck on tour, not that you'll need it." I ended on a yelp when Jet grabbed me, lifting me in a full hug.

"Holy shit, she smells like cake."

"I know. Now put her down," Jake said.

"But she's so little."

"I am not!" I huffed.

"Okay, you're fun-sized."

"That I'll accept."

"Great, we're in agreement. Now put her down," Jake ordered, his voice losing some of its amusement.

"Damn, Jacoby, cool your jets! Get it? Jets? I'm hilarious."

"Yeah, *Shamus,* a laugh fuckin' riot," Jake grumbled sarcastically, clearly no longer enjoying the humor.

I, however, was amused enough for the both of us.

So, Jet's real name is Shamus? Hot, and explains the giant Celtic knot. And Jacoby? Double hot.

"It was cool to meet you, Piper," Jet said, ignoring Jake.

I grinned up at him when he set me down. "You, too."

"I know, I'm awesome."

After our goodbyes, Jake grabbed my hand and turned to leave.

"Don't forget about those cookies!" Jet yelled.

"I'll drop them off at Hyde's on Tuesday," I called over my shoulder.

Fifteen minutes later, we pulled up to a nice condo complex and Jake cut the engine. I got off the bike and removed my helmet, handing it to him.

"Jacoby, where are we?" I asked, unable to resist using his real name. He looked down at me with a brow lift, one side of his mouth quirked up. "What? It's a hot name."

"Fair enough."

"So, where are we?"

He opened the front door. "My place."

I walked in first, stopping as Jake punched his code into the beeping alarm.

Minus a coffee mug and a small stack of mail, the room was clean. As in, *really* clean. It was dominated by a plush looking couch and large flat screen TV on the wall. That was it. There were no personal effects. No framed pictures or hanging sports memorabilia. None of the write-ups about Hyde or any of the awards they'd won.

Before I could look around more, Jake grabbed me and pulled me to him, his mouth covering mine. Light and teasing, his tongue danced with mine.

I pushed myself against him, needing more.

His hands traveled down my back to my ass, cupping it as he lifted me. I wrapped my legs around his waist, gasping at the hardness of his *very* evident arousal.

He carried me through a doorway and set me down on a soft bed. His mouth left mine, kissing down the curve of my neck as he pushed my bolero down my arms.

I pulled it the rest of the way off and tossed it to the side before reaching behind his head. Gently tugging the hair tie, I freed his hair and finally, *finally* ran my fingers through the softness of it. It was better than I'd thought it would be, and I'd put a *lot* of thought into it.

He lightly kissed the top of my chest. An intense pleasure grew low in my gut, taking my breath away.

"Jacoby."

"Hmm?" The noise vibrated against me.

"Please, I need more," I pleaded.

"More what?"

"More of you, touching me."

Jake sat up to pulled my shoes and pants off, throwing them to the side.

I grabbed the hem of his shirt and yanked it over his head, exposing tan skin and defined muscle. An intricate tattoo of gears, pistons, and other mechanical parts covered his shoulders and down one arm, giving the illusion that his skin was split open to show a robotic inner. The left side of his stomach was covered in a colorful swirled design that I wanted to explore with my tongue.

The definition of his pelvic muscle leading into his pants would require a month, at least, to explore.

Drawing my attention from the ink to something much better, Jake went up onto his knees and undid his belt. Opening the button and zipper, he pushed his pants partway down. A pair of dark blue boxer briefs covered, but did nothing to hide, his hard cock, though I'm not sure anything could have.

I knew my face gave away my thoughts when Jake's voice grew rougher. "Shirt off." Shifting to his side, he kicked his jeans the rest of the way off.

I sat up and undid the tiny hooks down my side, peeling away my top.

"Fuck, you weren't kiddin'." He covered my body with his.

"What?" I asked hazily as I laid back.

"You show up in my shop lookin' good and wholesome in an outfit that should've turned me off but made my dick hard, thinkin' of ways I wanted to corrupt you. Now I know under all that prim and proper was rock 'n' roll. Ray?"

"Yeah. She was nervous about doing them. Her hands are solid and she never shakes, so I knew she could do it. It was our awkward and very personal bonding experience."

He leaned down to lick around the barbell in my nipple.

"Please, I need more."

His mouth closed around my nipple, his tongue and teeth working together to torture me. Stretching out on his side next to me, he trailed his long fingers down my stomach.

A shiver of anticipation ran through me.

Jake's large hand covered me over my panties, his middle finger firmly tracing up. He released my nipple and sat up, taking his hand away from my aching pussy.

I whimpered at the loss, raising my hips to follow his hand.

He hooked his thumbs into the side of my panties and slid them down, kissing as he went. He positioned himself between my shaking legs.

I tried to close them a little, but his hands on my inner thighs pushed them further apart.

"Perfect, baby." Jake moved his eyes to mine before returning them down. "Everything about you is perfect."

This is why I'll never settle. I deserve someone who thinks I'm perfect, not someone who tolerates me.

He bent low and licked slowly up, his groan vibrating through me. My hips moved unconsciously as my hands fisted in the sheets.

"Please. More."

Ignoring my pleas, Jake added his thumb to my torment, rubbing my clit. When the tension had built to near unbearable levels, he went up on an elbow, pulling his mouth and thumb away.

My whimper of protest turned into a gasp when his finger began to enter me.

"Fuck, you're tight," he growled, working in a second finger.

My body tightened, the discomfort of being so full turning to flat-out pain. I flinched and instinctively pulled back.

Before I knew what was happening, Jake abruptly sat up and moved away.

Far away.

He clenched his jaw, his whole body tight. "Why didn't you tell me?"

"Tell you what?" I tried, and failed, to play clueless.

"You've never done this before, have you?"

I sat up, staring at the unconcealed anger, and what looked like disgust, on his face.

"Answer me!" he roared.

I jumped at his outburst. "Uhh, no," I stammered, freaked out and confused.

"What have you done?"

"Not... much."

Growing up the way I did, it was hard enough to sneak out for a backseat make out, much less anything more. Even if I'd had the chance, there weren't many people I wanted to spend regular time with let alone naked time. Once I moved out, school and trying to get Piper's Cakes off the ground took over my life.

Everything else just seemed like it could wait.

It wasn't like I'd never had an orgasm. There was a reason my showerhead was so high-tech, and why I happily paid my steep water bill every month. Coffee might be my lifeline to get me through the day, but it wasn't what woke me up in the morning.

That's not even counting the drawer of assorted sized Battery Operated Boyfriends.

I wasn't unknowing. Just unpracticed.

"I can't do this," Jake said, moving further away to sit on the side of the bed. His long, muscular body bent as he put his head in his hands.

Of course he wouldn't be interested in my inexperienced fumbling.

Maybe he thinks if he fucks me, I'm gonna get clingy and follow him around. Like I'm holding onto my virginity while I wait for Prince Charming and a happily ever after.

If that was the case, it would be me, my virginity, and my showerhead for life.

Whatever. All I know is I need to go.

Now.

I got up and started looking for my discarded clothing. I picked up my panties. "I'll just... I'll call a ride."

Smelling him, seeing him, still *feeling* him everywhere, I wanted to curl up and hide. To curse my upbringing and my virginity. Most of all, though, I wanted to scream in severe sexual frustration.

How could someone turn from so hot to so cold that quickly?

"No." Jake stood up, pointedly not looking my way as I scrambled around trying to locate my clothes. "I'll give you a ride home. I'll just be..." He turned towards me while I was getting my shirt on, his words trailing off.

I'm sure there was a time in my life when I'd been more embarrassed. Like in third grade when I kissed Billy Mason and then threw up on his brand new sneakers. They were the expensive ones, with the pump on the tongue and everything. After that, all I wanted was a new school.

Or when I grew boobs before anyone else and Mandy Plose started a rumor that I stuffed my bra. It was bad enough to have everyone analyzing my chest, but when a bunch of kids filled my locker to overflowing with tissues and toilet paper, I'd put some serious thought into changing schools *and* my name.

However, standing in the middle of Jake's room in my panties, my chest bare as I awkwardly fumbled with the tiny hooks on my top, I couldn't remember ever feeling so mortified.

I'm never wearing anything but t-shirts again. Ever.

Jake cleared his throat. "I'll just be in the other room," he muttered as he left.

Blinking back tears, I quickly finished dressing.

I thought riding on the back of Jake's bike again would be torture. As we started towards my place, though, it became obvious how preferable it was to taking his car. There was no uncomfortable silence, or worse, awkward conversation.

I'm sure the conversation would've been awesome. He'd probably just grunt at me while I discussed my vow to maintain a monogamous relationship with my showerhead and plans to adopt a cat.

Or ten.

Unlike the ride to Jet's, I didn't hold on tight or enjoy the view of the city passing by. I let the cool air whip around my overheated face as I blocked the world out.

When we arrived at my place, Jake still walked me to my door even though I didn't want him to. I bit my lip to stop myself from saying something stupid to break the tense silence.

Thankfully, Jake spoke first, though we both knew there wasn't anything to say.

"Piper, I—"

"Just... don't."

"Yeah." He shoved his hands in his pockets. "I'll... I'll see you around."

Unlike last time, I knew his words were a blow off.

I gave him a small, tight smile. "Yeah, Jake. Bye."

I hurried in, locking the door behind me. I leaned my back against it, listening as his bike roared to life. A minute later, he took off.

Dropping my head back, I couldn't help feeling like there was more wrong than I knew.

Changes

"Maybe a penis tattoo would've been a better idea."

Looking around the packed club, I was relieved no one heard me talking to myself.

Or, if they had, they were pretending they hadn't.

As much as I wished I was sitting at home in my yoga pants, watching mindless TV and eating Chinese food delivery straight from the carton, I knew I needed a change of scenery.

I was in a rut. And not a minor one.

Ray must've known, too, since she'd threatened me with an obscene face tattoo if I didn't come out.

For almost two weeks straight, I'd been swamped with school and cakes. I'd also started pouring over my financial books. The bank had been in contact quickly to tell me that my loan had been denied. I'd researched everything in hopes that there was an obvious cause but I hadn't found any.

It was easy to not dwell on Jake ending things when I barely had time to think.

Can you end something that never even began?

Well, I didn't dwell *too* much, at least.

When I'd gotten home that night, I was mentally drained and physically exhausted. Even still, I'd forced myself into the shower to wash away the smell of him. Skipping all of my usual nighttime routines, I'd collapsed into bed though sleep was hard to find. My mind wouldn't settle as it replayed the night, once again filling in all of the things I should have said.

I'd wondered if he would try to clear the air again.

He hadn't.

I wasn't sure how the situation with Jake was going to affect things with the other guys. I'd hoped it wouldn't, but knowing he was their boss, I'd understood if they didn't want any weirdness.

That didn't mean I'd like it.

My worry was for nothing. The guys texted and acted like nothing was different.

Unfortunately, I couldn't say I did the same.

The day after my epic crash and burn with Jake, Kase texted to invite me out with them. I was so swamped, I couldn't have gone even if I wanted to.

For over a week, every time one of the guys invited me out, I used my schedule as a crutch. I was busy, definitely. But I could've found time if I tried hard enough.

After flopping on the bed one night, too exhausted to even pull the blanket up, I couldn't fall asleep. Instead, I found myself wondering what the guys were up to. I hadn't wanted everything with Jake to change things between me and them, but it had.

And I was the one responsible for the change.

Waking with the sun the next morning, I began baking a giant batch of donuts in three different flavors. I texted Kase when it reached a suitable time and asked him to come pick them up to take to work.

"Hey, these were on your porch," he blurted out quickly as he handed me a giant vase of Stargazer Lilies.

I looked around for a card, but there was none. It wasn't uncommon for me to get flowers from clients but I liked to know who sent them. Knowing that something I did made someone happy and that they appreciated it was a thrill that never lessened.

I took the flowers before handing him two big containers of donuts with instructions to freeze them at the shop. I also gave him a box to be eaten right away.

Since Kase seemed perpetually cheerful, I was surprised when he leaned against the open door frame and his expression turned serious.

"Jake's being a real dick around the shop. Barking at everyone over stupid shit."

"So it's business as usual?" I joked.

"This is worse than Jake's normal warm and snuggly personality. I don't know what happened and I'm not asking you to share. All I know is you two looked tight at Jet's. Next day you're suddenly too busy to do anything and Jake's a major prick."

"I really have been busy."

"I don't doubt that. I'm just saying that there's more to it. I know Jake can be a little… controlling."

Yeah, and a hurricane is just a little windy.

"It's not that, Kase."

"But if there was something he said to make you end things or—"

"I appreciate this. I really do. But I'm not the one that ended things."

"Jake did? Shit, we'd all just figured…" Kase shook his head. "Well, it doesn't matter what we figured. Really?"

"Yup."

His brows lowered. "What the hell is wrong with him?"

"Sometimes people just want different things. Doesn't make either of us right or wrong." I smiled up at him. "Now get going. I have cakes to bake."

"Yeah, yeah, yeah." Kase began walking off my porch towards his car before stopping. "Don't think any of that means you can get rid of me and the guys." Though his voice was teasing, I was pretty sure his words were more of a warning than a joke.

"Of course not. Hence the donuts. You're still my boys."

"Boys? Hell, woman, we're men!" he yelled back as he got into his car and drove off with a wave.

When Eli had texted to tattle on Kase for hoarding donuts and ask if I was coming out with them, I again declined. This time, though, it was because of my plans with Ray.

A Friday night with the boys would be a chill time.

I needed more than that.

Shaking off my kind of funk definitely called for getting decked out and partying with my girls.

Blowing off my last class of the day, I'd caught up on my baking before getting ready.

Using hot rollers and enough spray to be personally responsible for a sizeable hole in the ozone, I'd styled my hair in a wild tumble of curls. I went heavy on my eyeliner and mascara, but offset it with a simple nude gloss on my lips.

While my makeup had balance, my outfit was all-out. Pairing a black mini skirt with a fitted, dark purple, scoop neck top, I was showing more than a hint of leg *and* cleavage. I'd even dusted shimmer on my legs before putting on matching purple, strappy heeled sandals.

I felt good. I was ready to party.

Until I walked into the club.

It wasn't anything against the place itself. Voodoo was kickass, and I wasn't just saying that because I knew the owner and was best friends with his woman.

I was just in a rotten freakin' mood.

"You can do this. Be normal for once," I whispered to myself as I made my way around people. "Okay, not talking to yourself is probably the first step in being normal."

I reached the bar and saw that Ray was already there with Marcy and Lily, two other tattoo artists from her all female studio.

Lily was a little taller than me and more rounded, with an angelic face framed by blond hair. Her innocent looks contradicted with her far from heavenly interests. She was constantly on the hunt for a partner that understood that. She also had rotten luck finding one.

Marcy was almost six feet tall with smooth brown skin that glowed, hypnotic light brown eyes, and a love of weaves in bright colors. She was also a self-proclaimed nerd with an anti-possession symbol tattooed around her bellybutton. She even dressed up as Star Trek's Uhura for Halloween.

Every year.

Hugs and greetings were given, everyone talking over each other before Ray interrupted.

"Honey, there's time for chatting later. Right now you need a drink."

"That obvious?" I asked.

"Uh-huh. You look totally hot, of course. But if you climbed on the bar, not to dance but to sleep, I wouldn't be surprised."

"Yeah, it's been a long few weeks."

I hadn't told Ray much about what had been happening. She knew there was a guy I dug, he didn't end up being into me, and I was a bit bummed out.

Right after Jake halted things, I wasn't ready to analyze and dissect everything with her. Once I'd made the decision a few days ago to put on my big girl panties and get over it, I didn't feel like revisiting it all.

Jake and I were *kinda* friends on the way to *maybe* more. Things not working out was hardly a great romantic tragedy, even if the end was a bit of a fiasco.

The girls and I tossed back a couple shots and were already on our way to tipsy by the time we hit the dance floor. We danced, laughing and yelling over the music to talk.

"I'm getting thirsty. Anyone else want another drink?" Ray asked.

I opened my mouth to agree when I felt the hairs on my neck stand up, something that seemed to happen often.

"Hellooooo, handsome. Isn't that Jake Hyde?" Marcy asked.

Of course. Seriously, of fuckin' course it is. And next in will be Billy Mason with a new pair of sneakers for me to throw up on.

"Oh, damn. If I weren't in Edge's bar right now, I would say something very obscene regarding what I want to do to him, and which of his tattoos I want to lick," Ray said with a laugh.

I didn't bother to turn around to look. I figured that, based on his magical ability to know and see all, he'd already noticed me. I didn't want to see him with what I assumed would soon be a harem of women flocking to him.

So I went with pretending he didn't exist.

It wasn't the most mature reaction, but it was the best one I could think of.

"Okay, eye candy gone," Lily said. "Let's go get a drink."

We headed back to the bar, throwing back a shot as the bartender mixed up some fruity, but dangerous, concoction.

Wincing, I looked at Ray. "God, that tasted awful. Like ground up cinnamon potpourri and antifreeze. What was it?"

She opened her mouth to speak when her eyes went beyond me and a smile spread across her face.

I turned to see a familiar pair of sexy blue eyes looking down at me.

"Rhys!" I squealed in delight.

"If it isn't my very favorite hot baker. Hey, darlin'."

Ray looked between us. "You two know each other?"

"I had the great pleasure of eating Piper's cookies."

Am I just super horny, or did that sound filthy?

"So good, I licked every crumb."

Okay, yeah, totally filthy.

"I saw a show at Rye recently. I made him cookies to make up for the whole *law-breaking* thing," I told Ray, using finger air quotes.

Her bottom lip jutted out in an exaggerated pout. "You didn't make Edge cookies tonight. I want some cookies."

"I'll hop on that this week." I turned back to Rhys. "What're you doing at the competition?"

"Edge and I are old friends. We try to plan events that would draw similar crowds on different days. How do you know Ray?"

"Old friends. She did all my ink."

"I knew it was quality when I saw it," he said with a wink to Ray. "Let's dance."

"Well, I'm here with my girls, so—"

"Yes!" all three girls said behind me as they pushed me towards Rhys.

I shrugged and smiled, taking his outstretched hand as he led me to the dance floor. We danced and talked as much as we could over the music.

When he turned me so my back was to his front, his hardness was impossible to miss.

So, owning a kickass bar is far *from the only thing Rhys had going for him.*

His mouth pressed close to my ear to be heard over the music. "Do you know how old I am, Piper?"

"Uh, Jake said you were around forty," I confessed, feeling like I was caught gossiping.

"Of course he would. I'm thirty-seven."

"Cool." I wasn't sure what else to say.

"Does that bother you?"

I shook my head. "Does it bother you I'm twenty?"

"No. You don't act it. You don't even really look your age."

Tilting my head, I fake glared up at him. "Are you saying I look old?"

He grinned. "No. I'm saying you look confident. You know who you are, and you own that. You aren't desperate or needy, all things I see nightly. So, you don't look your age, unless you look closer." He stood up straighter as we danced.

I reached back to put my hand on his neck and pulled him down so he could hear me. "And then what happens?"

"Then you see how soft you are. Totally unhardened by life. You're not an act. You're not a mask you put on to manipulate people. You don't want anything, you aren't scheming, and you aren't cynical."

I smiled, liking that someone saw me that way. I was glad he couldn't see my face because I knew my smile wavered when he continued.

"You're almost, I dunno, innocent. Makes a man want to protect you even more."

Innocent. I wonder how he'd feel if he knew just how innocent I really am? Would he drop out of my life, too?

I gave a nervous laugh. "I really don't know what to say to all that."

"Say nothing. Just know it's true."

I nodded, deciding to focus on the positive things he'd said.

We danced a minute more before he leaned down. "I gotta get back to Rye." He kept his arm wrapped around me as we headed to the bar.

"It was cool seeing you."

"Yeah, you too, darlin'. Call me?" He phrased it like a question, but didn't wait for my answer. Leaning down, he brushed his lips slowly across my cheek. "Ladies," he said with a chuckle, giving a glimpse of dimples before he walked away.

I turned to my girls and saw what he found so amusing.

Sitting at the bar, they were attempting to look casual. Since this involved looking anywhere but where Rhys and I were, all while whistling jaunty tunes, they were also failing.

All pretenses dropped once he got far enough away and they let out a collective girly screech and squeal.

Lily grabbed my arm and pulled me closer. "What was all that?"

"And what was with that kiss? How does he make a cheek kiss look obscene?" Marcy asked.

"We were just continuing a conversation from before," I said, not sure how much detail I wanted to go into.

"About?"

"What do you think about? He obviously wants more of her *desserts*," Ray said, using finger quotes as she wiggled her eyebrows.

"Is that what the kids are calling it these days?" Lily asked, giggling.

"From the looks of it, he wants some more of Piper's glorious cookies." Ray grabbed her own chest for emphasis. "So, what's the story?"

"He wants to go out but I don't want to jump into anything," I admitted.

All three made various noises of disbelief.

Ray shook her head. "No, no, that's understandable." Lowering her voice, she leaned in closer. "From what I hear, jumping in with Rhys is like diving into the deep end of sex. It's intense for one night and then that's all she wrote. Or, I guess in this case, that's all he humped!"

We all burst out laughing, which reminded me how badly I had to go.

"Alright, I've had to go to the bathroom for the past three songs. I'll dish when I get back!" Their girly talk and giggles faded as I walked away but still left me smiling.

When I finished in the bathroom, I turned in the hall towards the bar. I let out a startled yelp as I found myself suddenly pressed up against the wall.

I pulled my fist back and was ready to swing when I looked up into a pair of intense, green eyes.

"What the hell?" I put my hand to my chest. "Are you trying to give me a freakin' heart attack?"

"I said your name. I thought you were ignoring me."

"No, I just wasn't paying attention. Lesson learned for both of us."

Jake tilted his head. "Both?"

"Mine is to not zone out. Yours is to stop sneaking up on me or I'll open a can of whoop-ass on you. Maybe even a case of it."

"I'll try to remember that."

"Good, be sure you do," I said, distracted at the way his eyes lightened with humor before going dark again.

"Havin' fun?"

"Yes I am. You?" I was proud of how even my voice sounded since I was feeling anything but with the way he was pressed close.

So close.

You should touch his hair!

"Don't be cute."

"Sorry, I don't know how to do that."

Jake chuckled though this time his eyes didn't lighten. "No, I guess you don't. Where'd your dance partner go?"

"Work."

"Little old for you, isn't he?"

"No."

He wasn't. All of my close friends were older. The only guys I'd seen my age had been horrible. Some were so dull that the only desire I felt was to take a nap. Others were slightly less boring but skeeved me out, like I needed a scalding hot shower *with* my clothes on.

"You're supposed to be with someone your own age. Closer to it, at least. Some nice kid."

"Why? I'm an adult. I can pick who I want. If I wanted someone my age, I'd be with them. Now excuse me." I shifted to get past him.

I barely moved when his mouth was on mine, hard and insistent. My hands went to his chest as I began to lose myself in the kiss. Before my brain could go to total mush, the pain of his rejection resurfaced.

At the reminder of what he'd said and how he'd acted, I pushed his shoulders hard. Though he only went back an inch, he did bring his head up enough to look at me.

"This is fucked up, Jake. I don't play games."

His eyes narrowed. "That's not my name."

"Everyone calls you Jake."

"Yeah, everyone *but* you. You called me Jacoby when you found out it was my full name. I like hearin' my name from your mouth."

"Okay, whatever. I've gotta get back." I tried to move away again but he put his forearms flat on the wall and pinned me with his body. If he were anyone else I'd feel panicked and caged.

He wasn't just anyone, though.

"You don't get it."

"No. I do get it 'cause you made that message *very* clear." Inhaling deeply, I tried to calm my temper. "It's fine."

"I'm trying to do the right thing. It isn't you."

And there goes my Zenful calm.

"Oh, God, Jake, don't give me the 'it's not you, it's me' bullshit."

I heard Ray calling my name from down the hall, but Jake's body blocked my view.

"Dammit, Piper, just listen. Hear where I'm comin' from and give me a chance to explain," he murmured in my ear, his gravelly voice coaxing.

I wonder what else that voice could get me to do. Oh wait! Been there, done that, got the emotional burn. Where was my chance to talk last week?

That thought pissed me off to Hulk-like strength.

Or so I imagined.

I pushed away from the wall, giving Jake no choice but to move.

Getting free, I turned and got toe-to-toe with him, once again wishing I was taller.

"Don't pull that shit with me. I'm not a toy you can throw away and then get cranky about when someone else picks me up to play."

"Fuck." Jake lifted his hand to spear into his hair. His movement stuttered when his fingers tangled in the pulled back strands. Instead, he ran his palm down his face, exasperated. "I swear that isn't it. I was here to talk to you already. You told Kase you were comin' here, he told me. I just want to explain what happened. That's all. You wanna walk away after that, I can't force you to stay."

"Jake, seriously, there's nothing to explain. It's fine."

"It's *not* fuckin' fine." I sensed his control was close to snapping before he stepped back and took a deep breath. "Look, I'll leave and you go have your fun with your girls. Just... call me tomorrow, yeah?"

I nodded, but I wasn't sure if I'd call. My mind was in no place to make a decision right now.

He brought his head down and pressed a light kiss to my lips, though I stayed still. He raised his head to look down at me, searching my face. Lowering his mouth to mine again, he kissed me harder.

Fisting my hands so hard my nails dug into my palms, I resisted the overwhelming desire to return his kiss. I refused to open myself up again. Instead, I stepped back and pulled away from him.

His grip on me tightened briefly before he dropped his hands.

I started walking down the hall with a thoughtfully silent Ray. I needed a second to get my head together, and I knew she got that. When the hairs on the back of my neck stood up, I tilted my head to look behind me.

All I saw was Jake, his back against the wall and his head turned away. Even from a distance, I could see the rigidness of his body as he bit out a curse.

I knew my reprieve was over when we returned to the bar and

Ray ordered a round of stronger booze.

"So, what the fuck was that?" she started as soon as we got our drinks.

"What was what?" Marcy asked, looking to Lily who shrugged.

"Piper has been holding out on us. Big time."

"It's no big deal, really." I took a couple large gulps of my drink.

"Oh, yeah, totally. I go to see if you fell into the fuckin' toilet, and instead find you with Jake Hyde."

"Dude, were you hooking up with Jake?" Lily asked, her face an almost laughable mix of interest and envy.

"No, not our Piper. She had him flippin' in a way that was tortured hero hot. And she's getting all feisty instead of her usual sweet."

Marcy's eyes went wide. "What? Why? I need details. Like what was he wearing? Was he shirtless? Can we pretend he was?"

Because my drama was more interesting than dancing, we went to a quieter VIP area so they could hear the goods while we drank.

"So, Jake was your mystery man?" Ray asked.

I nodded. "Yup."

"Well, that explains why you were the only woman in the place that wasn't looking at him when he walked in."

"When were you together?" Marcy asked.

"We weren't. We were, I dunno." I moved my hand around, spilling some of my drink as I tried to find the right words. "Friends who made out a few times?"

"Whoa, whoa, whoa. You kissed Jake Hyde?" Lily screamed.

"Jeez, Lily, hop on the MC mic and announce it to the bar."

"Hell, if I kissed *the* Jake Hyde, I would totally be on the mic announcing it. I'd tweet it, status it, Instagram it, whatever I could. I'd probably even take out a full page newspaper ad or get a billboard," she declared, to the nodded agreement of the other two.

"Okay, so were you friends with benefits with him?" Ray asked.

"We weren't even that. We hung out a couple times." I looked around to see them all wearing the same shocked expression.

"What?"

"Honey, Jake doesn't do long term."

"I never asked him to. Sure, I've been bummed, but I know he did the right thing."

Ray shook her head slowly. "No, you aren't getting it. Hanging out a couple times with Jake is the same as spending a couple months in a relationship with a regular man. To him, that *is* long term. Only thing crazier would be him spending the night."

My face must have given something away because all three screeched.

That seems to be happening with them a lot. I wonder if they get together to practice synchronized screeching?

"No fuckin' way. Having Jake fuckin' Hyde spend the night is like hitting jackpot. Honestly, if the hype is true, it's way better. It'd be like hitting the jackpot every time, all night long," Marcy said.

"Nothing really happened. We kissed a little and then went to sleep. He only spent the night because he'd been drinking."

Ray held up her cell. "I texted Edge to ask if he's ever heard of Jake spending the night. Of course, he asked why I wanted to know. He said if I get sucked into the whole sexy, smart, and successful thing Jake has going that means no more free drinks for us. But, according to Edge, Jake rarely has sex with the same girl more than once. He hasn't heard of him staying the night since his last serious girlfriend and she was eight years ago. I think he must be into you."

"I don't know what the deal is. Hell, I don't think he even knows if he likes me half the time. He can be a *serious* asshole. It doesn't matter now anyway, it's done."

"What happened that made it done?" Lily asked.

I looked around and saw the three of them were on the edge of their seats.

It seems when I decide to do something out of the ordinary, I really go for it.

"He just said he wasn't into it and that was that. I haven't heard from him in almost two weeks."

"There wasn't more to it?" Marcy pressed.

"Not really. There's just a... barrier between us."

Ha. Barrier.

"What was tonight about then?" Ray asked.

"I think he feels bad. We had a... tiff before and he ended up coming over late at night to apologize. That's when he crashed with me. He was being nice."

"Jake Hyde is not nice. He's an asshole. And, if you asked him, he'd unrepentantly say he was much worse than that. He can be great. He's loyal as hell, smart, and somehow a good guy. But he's still an asshole. There's no way he'd go out of his way *twice* to try to clear up any 'tiffs'."

I was beyond ready to be off this topic. My mind was already muddled, and the conversation wasn't helping. Neither was the booze. "Well, it doesn't matter. The barrier between us isn't just going to disappear anytime soon. Well, maybe. I mean I *really* hope it does."

Okay, the puzzled faces mean I'm not making any sense. Moving on!

"By that time, though, it'll be too late. I'm not mad. I like him and will probably see him around. Maybe he just doesn't want things to be weird if we run into each other?"

"Jake isn't the type to care if things are weird. He definitely isn't the jealous type. I've seen girls he's slept with make it really obvious they're with someone new. I'm talking going at it with another guy against a wall. It's not even a blip on his radar. You moving on with Rhys shouldn't faze him one bit. But from what I caught in the hallway, he was plenty fazed."

"There's more to it. More to him. He's hot—"

"Hell yeah, he is," Lily muttered.

"Well, obviously in that way. But I mean he runs hot and cold. One minute he looks ticked at me. Then he looks bored. All of a sudden he's so sweet that I swear I'm never going to stop smiling. But then he's back to being an ass. It's like he has male PMS that comes every twenty minutes instead of once a month."

"Maybe it would be better if you started at the beginning," Ray urged gently.

With some liquid courage courtesy of vodka, I began what was supposed to be a quick sum-up of what had been happening. I hadn't planned on sharing much, but once I started talking, I couldn't seem to stop. I hadn't realized how badly I needed to get it out, or how awesome it would feel to finally unload.

Because my virginity was personal to me, I still didn't get into the specifics of why things ended with Jake. But I did share everything else, including what had gone down tonight with both Rhys and Jake.

"Edge said this is all unheard of," Ray declared as she looked up from her phone. "Jake even hinting at wanting to talk again is major. Edge also said Rhys left with a big smile on his face. Rhys doesn't do weekends, repeats, anything more than a 'wham, bam, thank you, now get the fuck outta my face'. All of that normally takes place in a backroom at Rye."

"That sounds… unpleasant," I murmured, scrunching up my nose. I liked Rhys. I didn't like that he was that kind of guy, though.

"If the lore is to be believed, it's far from unpleasant. Chicks know what they're getting. After the way he spends those few hours, though, most want more."

From what I felt on the dance floor, I can definitely believe it.

"Wait, you're still texting Edge?" I asked, needing to get my mind out of Rhys' backroom. "He's a room away, go tell him in person."

"And miss these bombs you're dropping? Anyway, back to what he's saying. This is all unheard of territory. Both men, both of them owning successful businesses, they're obviously smart. They know they're getting someone they can have and leave with no second thought when they hook up with some club hopper or biker bitch. They're both honest about it, though, and upfront from the beginning. If a woman moves forward with stars, or more likely money signs, in her eyes, thinking she'll be able to fuck a commitment out of them, that's on her."

I looked longingly at my glass and wished it were full for the truth bombs Ray was dropping.

"Even with all that, I genuinely like them both. They have their reasons for holding back. I don't know all the details, and even if I did, it isn't my place to share. But either one of them decides to settle down and focus that energy, loyalty, and badass hotness on one woman? I love Edge. Absolutely, to the bottom of my soul and back. He's my very own hot, loyal badass. So I know from experience whoever gets one of them is in for a life of beauty."

"It's not that I don't agree, but—"

"No excuses, Piper," Ray interrupted, holding up her enviously full drink. "Just listen. See what Jake has to say. Don't dismiss him as being nice, though, 'cause that just isn't him. He doesn't say shit he doesn't mean. If he wanted to talk just so things weren't awkward, he'd have said that. More likely he'd just let it go. If you wanted to make a scene, that'd be on you. So, just *listen*."

"Yeah, maybe."

Cluck, cluck, chicken.

"Okay, too much heavy. Piper looks like she needs a drink, and as her doctor, I'm saying she gets one, stat," Lily said.

"You aren't a doctor," Marcy pointed out the obvious.

"No, but I have a naughty nurse outfit, and that's basically the same thing. Now, booze, stat!"

I might not have many, but the few friends I had were *the best*.

It was well after two in the morning when the taxi pulled in front of my house to drop me off first. I didn't even need to grammatically calculate my level of intoxication.

Tipsy was a memory.

I was drunk.

"Night, honey!" Ray whisper-yelled out of the window.

"Don't forget to figure out what scent you're putting out and bottle it for me! I need men like that all over me!" Marcy yelled as the taxi pulled away.

If I wasn't so drunk, I'd have been mortified. Instead, I laughed as I carefully climbed the stairs.

"Sweetness," I heard from the side, startling me and making me drop my keys.

"Holy hell!" I looked over to see Jake lounging in one of my porch chairs, like it wasn't the middle of the night. "You're lucky I'm all out of whoop-ass. You scared the bejeezus out of me. What're you doing here?"

Jake ignored my question as he stood and walked towards me. Gracefully dipping as he moved, he grabbed my keys before standing with his body *way* in my space. "The scent you put out? It's your sweetness. Your looks might catch their attention but it's the soft, sweetness that keeps them hooked."

His words reminded me of Rhys. Rhys' words reminded me of Jake.

These dudes are confusing.

"Good to know. Now I can start the process of extracting and bottling it for Marcy." I tried to keep from falling over. Being drunk was one thing. Being wasted with Jake in my space was another.

"Have fun tonight?"

"Why, yes, yes I did. I danced *so* much. And drank. Just a little," I lied, giggling up at him.

"Yeah, just a little," he said with a chuckle, putting his hand on my cheek. "I miss you, sweets. Have you missed me?"

"I really have. I'm not just saying that because I'm very slightly drunk. You could've asked me earlier and I'd have said the same thing. I don't play games, Jake. And I don't like people that do."

"I'm learnin' that."

"So, why are you lurking on my porch?"

"I wanted to see you again, make sure you got home okay."

"How did you know I was coming home?"

"I didn't."

"How did you know I was coming home *alone*?"

"I didn't." His fists clenched and released. "I thought about that, wonderin' how I'd handle it. I can tell you now, for fuckin' sure, it wouldn't have been good. Now, let's get you to bed. Yeah?" He reached around me to unlock the door and push it open.

I heard Jake throw the lock back into place as I started towards my room. When I went into the bathroom, he stopped in the hall outside the door.

"Don't stand out there!" I ordered.

Or giggled.

Most likely giggled.

"Why?"

"I have to do something and I don't want you to hear."

I heard Jake's deep laughter. "You gotta pee?"

"Nooooooo!" I vehemently denied. "Now go away!"

"Alright, but only 'cause I can't resist you when you're bossy. I'll be in your room."

"Okay, baby," I mumbled.

After taking care of my nightly routine, I walked back into the bedroom, still in my clothes and heels.

"These shoes might do wonders for my legs and ass, but my feet freakin' hurt. I need comfy," I muttered to myself, opening up a dresser drawer. I pushed aside nighties and pajamas but couldn't find what I wanted.

Jake cleared his throat next to me. "Colorful."

"Shh. They're my rebellion," I whispered

"Panties are your rebellion?" Jake's head tilted to the side. The angle drew my attention to his strong jaw.

With no impulse control in my drunken state, I reached my hand up. My eyes followed the motion as I ran my fingertips lightly along his jaw.

So soft and so hard, much like another part of him that I wanna touch.

I giggled and then sighed as I dropped my hand to continue my search for pajamas.

"Remember that awful black dress I wore when I was with James?"

"Yeah," Jake clipped, sitting on the edge of my bed.

"That's what my mother likes me to wear. Conservative, tasteful, and most definitely covering. A lot of neutrals and muted colors. When I was around fifteen, Anna, our… a friend of our family, introduced me to the wide variety of lace, satin, and silk. It's all I've worn ever since. I might have on a dull beige dress but I'm Technicolor underneath. It's my rebellion. Well, that and my hair."

"Your hair?"

"Mother says ladies wear their hair up. I say ladies need to let their hair down. They need to get wild. They need to *live*. You know what I mean?" I didn't give him a chance to answer before going on. "I'm too tired for all this nonsense." I closed the drawer.

With no thought to the fact that I had an audience, I pulled my shirt off and removed my bra before pulling my top back on. I slid my skirt down my legs and stepped out of it, kicking it in the general direction of the hamper.

When I turned towards the bed and caught Jake's gaze, I belatedly realized what I'd done. There was no mistaking the heat in his hooded eyes.

I was drunk, but it wasn't the booze that was making me feel brave. It was the way he was looking at me.

Like I was sexy.

Desirable.

Perfect.

I took in all that was Jake, every inch of him gorgeous. That someone like him would look at me the way he was? I realized I wasn't feeling brave.

I was *fearless.*

Walking to where he sat, I stood in front of him and slowly lifted my left foot to the bed next to him. I undid my sandal and returned my foot to the floor, repeating the process with my other one.

I pushed Jake's shoulders, relieved when he leaned back on his elbows. I put my knees to the bed and straddled his legs, letting my shoes fall to the ground before I moved.

"Baby, what're you doin' to me?" he whispered hoarsely as I crawled up his body.

"Feeling you." I felt every hard inch of him pressed against my ass. I leaned down and lightly pressed my lips to his throat, jaw, and lips.

"I wanna feel you, too. But not like this, when you've been drinkin'. And not 'til we talk about shit, yeah?"

"Yeah, I know." I let my lips trail across his jaw again.

"Fuck, you're killin' me," he whispered hoarsely. "Call me when you wake up."

"Okay," I agreed with a yawn, letting myself fall to the side off of him. I curled up on my bed, my eyes getting so heavy that moving to get under the blanket seemed like way too much work.

Further proving he could read my mind, Jake got up and pulled the blankets out before covering me with them. The bed dipped as he positioned himself behind me with the long length of his body pressed to mine.

Mmm, hot guy cocoon.

Wrapping his arm around my stomach, he pulled me closer to him and pressed a kiss behind my ear. "Night, sweets."

"Mmm, hot guy cocoon," I murmured as I fell asleep.

Creeper on a Creeper

I woke up the next morning with clarity.

Unfortunately, that clarity was that I *really* freakin' needed coffee.

Other than that, I was still confused.

It was a safe bet that Jake wasn't just worried about there being drama. No one waited on someone's porch in the middle of the night on the off chance of awkwardness.

That didn't necessarily mean I wanted to pick back up where we'd left off. There was a big difference between things evolving naturally and making the conscious decision to explore whatever it was that we had.

It was a risk, and one I wasn't sure I was willing to take.

I knew I wanted to at least talk, otherwise the 'what ifs' would drive me crazy.

After I did my bathroom stuff, I put on white shorts and a pink flowing tank top. I grabbed my pink wedge sandals before heading to find my phone.

I was startled when I turned the corner into the living room and saw Jake.

Sleeping shirtless, his arms were under his head, making the definition of his chest and abs more pronounced. His height and muscular build dwarfed what I'd considered to be my massive couch, his feet even hanging off the end. The button on his jeans was undone, and a trail of light hair disappeared into what I could only assume was heaven.

I should go get the cereal and milk, and eat breakfast out of the vee of his pelvic muscles.

The sun's rays came in through the big window behind the couch, streaming directly to him as if Mother Nature herself wanted a touch. If a heavenly chorus suddenly rang out, I don't think I'd be surprised.

His tanned skin glowed in the light, making him look like a god.

A tattooed sex god, but still.

I tiptoed quietly into the kitchen to start coffee, wondering about the presence of the half-naked sex god in my living room. I'd woken at some point in the very early morning alone in bed. I'd assumed Jake had taken off.

I hadn't guessed that my couch was as far as he'd gone.

Zoned out in my thoughts, I jumped when Jake wrapped his arms around me from behind. "Jake, sheesh!"

"First, Jacoby. Second, I wasn't even being quiet."

"Uh huh. Want some coffee?" I stretched up to grab a mug.

"Yeah, but not that cup. The other, bigger one further back."

I stood on my toes to reach into the cupboard. "This one?" I turned my head when there was no answer and saw his eyes on my ass. "Ha ha. Very funny."

Jake raised his gaze to mine but his smile was gone as he pulled me closer. "I thought so, too. Now I'm not laughin'. How're you?"

"Good."

"Hangover?"

"Nope, never."

"Must be nice. Do you have work to do right away?"

I shook my head. "I rearranged things when I knew I was going out with the girls last night. I just have to start stuff this afternoon to stay on schedule."

"Do you want breakfast? I could run out for something or we could go out."

"Breakfast here would be fine."

"Anythin' you don't like?" he asked as we walked through the living room.

"No, not really."

Jake opened the door and turned back to me. Bringing his hand up to cup my face, his thumb stroked my cheek. His eyes followed the movement, a thoughtful expression on his face.

"Jake," I began before his mouth opened. "Jacoby, what's wrong?"

"Nothin'."

Before I could call him on his lie, he kissed my nose and then my mouth. He turned and headed down to his bike without giving me the chance to react.

I stood in the open doorway after he'd gone, thinking about everything and nothing at once. The kiss had been a surprise, but not an unpleasant one.

"It was barely a peck," I whispered to myself. "Totally didn't even affect me."

It wasn't until I turned to go back inside that I realized I was holding my fingertips to my smiling lips.

I sighed as I closed the door, unsure of what to think. I didn't get how someone could go from not talking to me to... whatever this was. A kiss goodbye before he left to get us breakfast didn't seem like a peace offering.

Seems like an offering of something much *better.*

I shook my head to clear my thoughts, an exercise in futility. I fixed my coffee and sat down to try and compose my thoughts without overthinking.

It wasn't going well.

Jake seemed to be trying hard. Until I knew what he was working for, though, I couldn't decide if the effort was going to pay off.

When I heard the rumble of Jake's Harley, I went to let him in.

Before I got there, he came in without knocking, lightly kicking the door closed behind him.

"Hey," he said, quickly kissing me before heading into the kitchen.

I stood frozen, watching him move through my house.

The whole scene felt intimate in a casual and natural way, as if it was a daily occurrence. Like he had free rein of my house, coming and going as he pleased.

It was disconcerting, but only because it wasn't.

I liked it.

I'd been on my own for a long time. Even before I had my house, I'd spent most of my time by myself. Truth be told, even when I wasn't alone growing up, I often felt like I was.

I liked my own company. I laughed at my own jokes, I was a good listener, and I never had to compromise about what to have for dinner or what to watch on TV. I could have ice cream at eleven in the morning or coffee at nine at night without judgment.

I had awesome friends who were always there for me. Work and school kept me busy in a rewarding way.

I was honestly happy.

That, however, didn't negate the fact that I was also lonely.

Not the heartbreaking loneliness of a little girl that just wanted time with her mom and dad.

Or the confused loneliness of someone trying to figure out who they were when everything about them went against their surroundings.

Or even the exhausting loneliness that came from pretending to be someone they weren't, in order to fit in with a room full of people they didn't even like.

I was the kind of lonely where I was just… alone.

I wasn't going to be with someone just for the company. But as I watched Jake, I knew I wanted someone to walk casually through my house more often.

Even if it wasn't him.

In order to have that, I needed to drop the walls I'd built around myself. It wouldn't be easy to juggle school, work, and any semblance of a personal life, but it was possible.

As long as I quit making excuses, at least.

"I wasn't sure what you wanted." Jake lifted the overstuffed bag and pulled me from my thoughts.

"Well, I'm sure it's in that bag."

Or holding it.

God, how could he look so good all the time? If I slept on the couch, my hair would be one giant snarl and I'd have fabric indents all over my face.

Jake set the bag on the counter and began pulling out pastries, spreads, and juice.

I fixed a bagel with cream cheese and grabbed a juice before going to sit on the couch. I almost sighed in relief when Jake sat down and launched right in.

"I gotta tell you where my head was at. Yeah?"

"Okay."

"When you came into Hyde that first day, you looked so fuckin' good. When you finally looked me in the eyes, you were all innocent and wide-eyed like you didn't know how fuckin' sexy you were when your tongue licked across your lips. Then you started talkin' and you were sweet. But when you started talkin' about tattoos and music, I was sure you were an act."

I frowned, experiencing a weird mix of turned on and pissed. "I've always been me."

"I didn't know that. I thought you were just out to get with one of us. You had the men eatin' out of your hand. No way could any chick, let alone one that looked like you, be so perfect. Not without fakin' it to try to get somethin'."

Pissed off began to take the lead. "That's not what I was doing."

"Exactly. You just kept bein' you. You weren't tryin' to get with me 'cause of who I was. Hell, you didn't even know me or that I owned Hyde. You're so far from connivin' and schemin', it'd be funny if it weren't so fuckin' appealin'. You make a man face the internal battle of whether he'd rather protect you so you never lose that sweetness or corrupt you so he could enjoy your wild side unleashed."

I looked down at my shorts, picking at an imaginary thread. "Which do you want?"

Jake curved his hand around the side of my neck. Using his thumb on my jaw, he tilted my head up so I was looking at him. "I wanna bring you down low to my level. I get off picturin' makin' you so dirty, so wild, so fuckin' bad that it has to be good," he rumbled.

Holy.

Fuck.

I want that.

Badly.

"I see your lips part, and I know you like what I'm sayin'." Lowering his hand, he sat back. "Which just makes me want to go further. To show you every fucked up thought I have, the ones that make my dick go hard picturin' doin' it all with you. To keep pushin' and pushin' and pushin' until you want nothin' to do with me."

"Why?" I breathed. It was safe to say I was a bit freaked out. I was also more than a little turned on.

As in *a lot* more.

"Fuck, Piper, I'm thirty-four and you're twenty. Every time I think about you, I feel like a dirty old man. I've never made excuses for the life I've lived—"

"I've never asked you to. There isn't anything wrong with it."

"Fuck yeah there is. I'm dirty, baby. If you knew what was in my head you wouldn't look at me the way you do. You wouldn't believe how much longer I'm spendin' on the creeper under a car, feelin' like a fuckin' creeper, 'cause I have a hard dick from thinkin' about you. Or how many cold showers I'm takin'. Or when the cold showers aren't workin'…" His voice trailed off with a shoulder lift.

It's a good thing I'm not a dude or I'd need a car to hide under right now.

"Let's just say you wouldn't want me on your couch, in your house, hell, in your life. That's why I thought you should be with a guy your own age who's good. But when I think about you respondin' to someone else the way you did with me, of them tastin' that sweetness and gettin' your wild it feels like I'm losin' my goddamned mind. When Kase came into my office yesterday and I bit his fuckin' head off about some stupid shit, he started yellin' back."

"What'd he say?"

"He knew what was in my head. He told me someone else would get you soon and I'd regret it. After I fucked up, Gage and Jet would've been all over you but they're on tour. Rhys goes for what he wants and he isn't gonna back down. I knew I had to do some—"

"Is that the only reason you're here?"

"What?"

"You're just trying to stake your claim before someone beats you to it?"

"Fuck no. I just had to pull my head outta my ass."

"And you were successful in your head-ass-ectomy?"

"About this at least. That's why I came out last night. I missed you, and wanted to see you. When I saw you dancin' with Rhys, I tried to remind myself you could do what you wanted. I know if you would've pulled up here with him or anyone else, though, it wouldn't have mattered what I was tellin' myself. I'd have thrown the fuck down. Someone touchin' you? No. Rhys? I love him like a fuckin' brother but *fuck* no."

I was surprised by how vehemently opposed to the idea he was. "Just, you know, out of curiosity, why not Rhys?"

"I'm dirty but compared to him I'm clean as you, Piper. All I could think about was what it would be like seein' you together. I'd either lose a brother, or I'd have to see you and know how shit was between you."

"So," I started slowly, my voice deceptively calm. "In the planning of my life, have you thought about what I want? Or who I'd want and how I'd like it? Just because I'm inexperienced doesn't mean I don't know things." I gestured to my laptop. "One look at my internet history would clear that up." I knew I was blushing but I didn't care.

I'm a woman, damn it! I need to get rid of my innocence, in more ways than one.

"I grew up sheltered and didn't go through the typical rebellion when I was young and stupid. Now I'm old enough to know better than to jump into bed with someone just to say I've done it. I know what I want. I wanted you and that was my choice to make not yours, Mister… Bossy Pants!"

Okay, so my smack talk needs work. Moving on.

"If you don't want to go there with me, that's your decision. But don't try to take away my choice by telling me I can't want you. Or what I should want."

"You wanted me?" Jake asked quietly.

"Well, me and probably half the city of Boston, yeah."

"You said want*ed*. Are those feelings in the past?"

"I wished they were, but no."

"I really thought I was doin' the right thing by lettin' you go so you could be with someone better for you."

I opened my mouth to argue but he interrupted.

Shocking.

"I was already feelin' like I shouldn't be havin' these feelings about you. But when I discovered how innocent you really are—"

"You act like there's something wrong with me, which, I gotta say, is killer for my ego."

"I'm not—"

"My virginity isn't something to be ashamed of."

"I didn't—"

"Yeah, I don't have a ton of experience. And, thanks to you, what little I have now involves you being an asshole."

"I'm s—"

"And, honestly, that whole situation was beyond fucked up. You didn't want to have sex? Fine, but be cool about it. You wanted to slow down, talk, hammer out the details? Also fine. But what you did? Fucked up, Jake, seriously." I slammed my juice down with enough force that some spilled. "I still don't even know what your fuckin' problem was!" I lifted my hands in exasperation, flinging the crumbs off my napkin.

"If you'd stop interruptin'—"

"Now you know how it feels," I snapped, my eyes narrowing as I glared at him.

"And stop throwin' your breakfast at me," he continued as he used his napkin to wipe off. "I'm sorry. I shouldn't have yelled that night and I'm a dick for that. Truth? I was pissed at myself, not you. There's not a thing wrong with you bein' a virgin. I just felt like it confirmed that I was a dirty old man who had no business makin' you dirty too."

"Sex isn't dirty."

I lost my breath as his eyes darkened with a new intensity and his rough voice deepened. "It is the way I do it."

Holy hotness. I don't care what that means exactly, I just know I want it. Now.

"Especially what I wanted to do to you," he added, making me sure I was about to pass out.

"Wanted? Are those feelings in the past?" I asked breathily, using his words.

"No, that is actually a very current want." Reaching over, his hands spanned my hips and he pulled me towards him.

With no other choice, not that I'd want one, I shifted my legs to straddle him. Facing him, I settled in on his lap and felt the current-ness of that want.

Jake's fingertips dug into my hips for a moment before he loosened his grip. "Can we give this another shot, see where things go?"

"I meant it when I said I don't play games. Are you gonna push me away again and say I deserve better?"

"No, I'm gonna be selfish as fuck."

"While we're talking about all this, I like calling you Jacoby. But you aren't Jacoby, the owner of Hyde, to me. You're just... Jake." I reached out and ran my fingertips on his jaw. "Okay?"

"Yeah. We good?" he asked softly.

It wasn't lost on me that there'd been no talk of hearts and flowers. He wasn't promising a future and I wasn't asking for one.

I hadn't believed in fairy tales when I was a kid and I sure as hell didn't now.

I wasn't walking into things wide-eyed in my rose colored glasses. There were no stars in my eyes as I tried to fuck a commitment out of him. That wasn't him and, for all I knew, it wasn't me either. I just wanted to spend time with someone I liked and have some fun without getting tripped up by unrealistic expectations.

Hanging out with a sweet, funny badass and having, hopefully, awesome sex for a while?

Yeah, there are worse ways to spend my time.

We were going to enjoy each other for however long it lasted. When one of us ended things, we'd move on and hopefully do so on civil terms. I wasn't planning on inviting him over for a slumber party where we gossiped and braided each other's hair, but I hoped that some amount of our friendship would remain.

Instead of answering, I closed the distance to kiss him. The little kiss, one that was supposed to let him know things were alright, quickly spiraled out of control.

Jake slouched down on the couch so his head was resting against the back of it and his long legs were spread in front of him. The position gave him better access to my mouth, neck, and chest.

Access that he took liberally.

His mouth was hot, his stubble scratchy, and his body so hard. Even being almost overwhelmed with the different sensations, I wanted more.

He gripped my hips and pulled me to him as he lifted his pelvis off the couch.

Feeling him so hard, pressed against where I wanted him most, I moaned into the kiss.

His hand slid under my shirt, my nipples tightening in anticipation as his rough skin trailed up my ribs. His other hand went into my hair and held me, as though I were about to jump off and run away.

Leaving was the furthest thing from my mind, especially since my brain was no longer functioning. I was focused on what I was feeling, and while it was amazing, I wanted more.

No, I *needed* it.

My hands went in between us, shaking as I worked at the button on his jeans. When I finally got it undone and was reaching for his zipper, a ringing filled the air.

Holy hell, do his pants have a security system?

Did I just trip his dick alarm?

Realizing it was his phone, I pulled back to get off of him.

"Ignore it," Jake growled, grabbing my hands and moving them back to his zipper, before taking my mouth again.

I slid my fingertips into the waistband of his boxers when his phone stopped ringing just to start again.

I pushed back and fell to the side onto the couch.

He cursed, pulling his phone out and touching the screen to answer it. "This better be fuckin' good. Yeah. Yeah. You're fuckin' kiddin' me? It's for a fuckin' eighty year old car. Who the hell else would need that part? Alright, yeah, I'm on my way. No. No. Fuck no. Yeah, bye." He touched the screen to disconnect before putting the phone, and other better things, away.

Boo.

Jake cursed under his breath as he stood. "I'm sorry, sweets, I gotta go."

"Everything okay?"

"Some shit's been goin' missin'. Lots of little stuff mostly. But now a part I need to finish a job, that's gotta get done like yesterday, is gone. Havin' to stay on a creeper for 'Inappropriate Hard-on Time' is seriously makin' me run behind schedule."

"Oh no, woe is you. I'm so sorry, I'll try to be less desirable," I joked, trying to ease the stress I could see settling on his face.

"Somehow I don't think you'll be successful. Especially now with your lips so swollen. Fuck. Okay, I have to go. Right?"

"Oh, I dunno, it's just your livelihood and your company. Who cares if it goes under."

"Good point."

I backed up against a wall as Jake stalked toward me. "Ah, I was kidding! Go, go, go. I hope it goes okay."

"I'll figure it out. Come in later and see your boys. See me. Consider that an order from Mr. Bossy Pants." He pushed against me and kissed me hard, hot, but way too short.

Oh yeah, some risks were way *worth taking.*

Two days later, I walked into Hyde through the garage. I was greeted with loud catcalls and whistles because of my outfit. These turned into proclamations of everlasting love when they saw the homemade cinnamon rolls I was carrying.

When I didn't see Jake, I went into the break room to put the thick layer of cream cheese icing on the rolls. I was finishing up when I heard someone approaching. I glanced over anticipating one of the guys. Instead, I saw a woman looking just as surprised to see me.

Wearing a cropped tank top that strained across what I was fairly certain were fake boobs, a pair of almost indecently short jean cut-offs, and motorcycle boots, she was obviously a biker. In fact, if they ever made a Biker Barbie she could be the model it was based on.

Her blond hair had crazy volume, making me think she was responsible for a much larger ozone hole than I was. Her face was heavily made up and looked very rock 'n' roll night time.

I was all for rock 'n' roll at any time, and had been known to push the limits of acceptable glam, but even I knew this was not the best look.

Even still, she was a definite biker babe.

I had a meeting at the bank later that morning, so I was dressed almost the complete opposite of Biker Barbie. I was wearing a tailored black pinstripe skirt with a matching short vest and a fitted red button down tucked in underneath. I'd added some rocker flair with my favorite pair of back seam black stockings and a pair of shiny, black sling-back pumps. The front of my hair was up in victory rolls and the back was down in soft waves.

What're they gonna do, re-deny my loan?

My eye makeup was more subtle since I'd gone with a bold red lip stain. It was all a trade-off. Otherwise I'd end up looking less 'rocker' and more 'Krusty the Clown'.

"Sorry, didn't know anyone was back here. Jake," she said, drawing out his name while her eyes swept over me, "said I could come back and use the bathroom,"

"It's down the hall to the left," I said, going for polite.

"Oh, trust me, I know. I've been here a few times with Jake. After hours, of course..."

In addition to one's hair always being worn up, my mother had other clear ideas on how a lady should act. Most of the time I tuned her out. Today I was grateful that something actually stuck.

Never let your emotions show.

"Okay then. Have a nice day." I turned back to finish the cinnamon rolls.

"So, whose are you?" She moved into the room just enough to lean against the counter in the corner.

Because of the size of the room, there was still distance between us. Even so, when I caught the calculating look in her eyes, I had the overwhelming urge to step back.

Way back.

"Excuse me?"

"Well, you're in here making breakfast for the guys. I assumed you were one of their *current* pieces."

"I'm not anyone's."

"Who you after then? I'm just sayin', I don't think whatever this play is," she said, flipping her hand out to gesture to me, "will work with any of them. Best bet, though? Focus in on Kase. It's a long shot, but more likely than getting with Jake. He'd be more than you could handle anyway."

Try as I might, some reaction must have shown.

"Oh, hon, really?" Her tone was condescending as she slowly shook her head. "Jake doesn't date. I've known him a while and I've never seen him with a woman more than once. It'd be a few hours and then she'd be gone just like that." She threw out her hip and her hand to snap with attitude. "He goes to great lengths to avoid commitment. Nothing happens at his place, no sleepovers, and he only uses condoms brought by him. I'm pretty sure he even got the big snip," she added, making a scissor motion with her fingers.

Well, that was oddly specific. Guess if I ever wanted a definitive answer, I could ask Jake whether Biker Barbie's boobs are fake. Pretty sure he'd know from experience.

"Jake's the big leagues, baby. You gotta learn to handle a bat before you try stepping up to that plate. You wanna make breakfast and play house, you're playing a whole different ballgame. Jake isn't about wining and dining. He's about fucking."

"Thanks for the heads up." I feigned boredom and indifference as

I frosted the last roll.

"Plus, no offense hon, you're cute, but that's not his style. Some guys get off on teaching barely legal but Jake isn't one of them. He likes a woman with enough experience that she's gonna be down to get it exactly how he likes to give it."

I was used to bitchiness. Biker bitches might be good but rich bitches were better. It was just that what she was saying was a little too spot on. I couldn't help but wonder if that was part of why Jake had originally ended things.

Was he worried about me, or that I wouldn't be able to do what he wanted?

I worked hard to not show the response she was looking for. As I cleared the clutter, a genuine yawn came over me.

Her eyes narrowed and her face got tight at my lack of reaction. I knew things weren't over when her face smoothed out and her lips quirked up in a snide smirk.

She looks like something smells nasty.

Makes sense, I get the feeling there's about to be some bullshit spewed.

"I'd just hate for you to be embarrassed if he came back here and saw you with your little baked goods. Why don't you just hurry and scamper out with them? I'm sure you'll have no problem eating them yourself." She placed her hands on her tiny hips for emphasis.

"What the fuck did you just say, Rachel?" Kase snarled.

He moved towards the corner where Biker Barbie still stood, getting *way* in her space as he stared down at her. Anger radiated off of him, filling the room and making me tenser.

I'd never seen Kase mad and hoped to never see it again. He looked way scarier than I'd have thought possible.

When I'd asked, Kase had told me that his easygoing personality was courtesy of his Hawaiian heritage but his temper was 100% from his Colombian half. He'd said it was good he was so chill all the time since his pissed was off the charts.

I hadn't believed him at the time.

I believed him now.

"Hon, I was just trying to warn her. Us girls gotta stick together," she said with such a fake smile, I had to bite my lip to keep from laughing. "You know how Jake can be."

"Yeah, I do. You don't. You only know how he can be when it comes to you," Kase spat out.

I opened my mouth to call him off when Jake came through the doorway. If Kase's reaction was bad, I knew Jake's would be explosive. I was hoping Biker Barbie was smart enough to haul ass, but I couldn't tear my eyes away from Jake as he stalked towards me.

When he reached me, I realized that not just had he not overheard anything, he hadn't even noticed our audience in the corner of the room.

His hands cupped my ass, his fingertips digging into the cheeks, as he kissed me hard but quick. "Christ, I missed you, sweets. It's been fuckin' forever."

"Baby, it's been a few hours."

"Well, it felt like forever."

I couldn't help but laugh, the tension leaving my body.

"So," Jake whispered against my lips, "what's under that hot outfit? Fuck, please tell me garters. The mental image will get me through the day until I can get home and see for myself." His voice was husky as his grip on my ass tightened and he pulled me closer.

Before I could answer, Kase loudly cleared his throat and drew our attention. Jake turned slightly, though his hands stayed on my ass.

"A word," Kase clipped, his face thunderous.

Biker Barbie, proving she had no sense, stood next to him as she avidly watched Jake and me.

"Yeah, gimme a minute," Jake muttered, his brows lowered as he looked between them and tried to figure out the vibe of the room.

"Jacoby," I interjected, purposefully using his full name.

So sometimes I stumble off the high road. Sue me.

"Did you get everything figured out?" I asked.

Jake's organization system sucked and another part had gone missing. He'd been working late the past couple nights to try and get things in better order. They'd been finding parts that had rolled under things or been set down and forgotten about.

He left work well into the night, came to my place to crash, and then would wake up at dawn to start again.

"Not yet. I had to secure a replacement to get the car done. Now I'm dealin' with tryin' to sort shit."

"I hope you figure it out." I went up on my toes to kiss him. "I gotta go. I'm gonna be late."

"Okay, babe," he murmured. "Come back here when you're done. Yeah?" He looked down, his face soft as I nodded up at him.

I didn't want to be in the same county, let alone the same room, when Kase inevitably told Jake what he'd overheard. An angry Kase was bad enough. I'd been on the receiving end of Jake's temper and, according to him, he hadn't even been mad at *me*.

Even still, I forced myself to walk away calmly when all I wanted to do was run.

I felt deflated when my meeting ended. It'd been like talking to a robot that was programmed to give predetermined, generic answers. I left with the promise that I'd hear soon regarding any other available options.

I wasn't holding my breath.

Rehashing the meeting as I walked back to my car, my frustration grew the more I thought about it.

"You are a valued bank customer," I said to myself in a robotic voice.

"That's good, but what about my loan?"

"You are a valued bank customer," I repeated in the robot voice.

"Cool, cool. But my loan?"

"Loan reviews are a lengthy process and can be denied for any number of reasons."

"The reason for my denial was…"

"Any number of reasons."

"But my specific reason was…"

"You are a valued bank customer. Bee boo bee bop bop."

When my phone beeped in my purse, I laughed at the timing.

"Dude, I think that hot chick thinks she's a robot and her phone just told her a joke," a teenager in front of me said, drawing my attention to the fact I was talking out loud.

"Yeah, man, the hot ones are always fuckin' nuts," his friend put in.

I pulled out my phone to find a message from Jake.

Jake: What're you doing?

Me: Definitely not talking to myself. Why?

Jake: You coming back? We gotta talk.

That's never good.

Me: Yeah. Guys want anything for lunch?

Jake: No.

Yeah, this was not *good.*

Me: Okay. See you soon.

When I got to Hyde, I parked in the back and walked through the garage. My apprehension was cemented when the boys expressed their appreciation for the cinnamon rolls in a polite way, and not one filled with proclamations of everlasting love.

There wasn't even any bickering about someone taking more than they were supposed to.

Wild stab in the dark says that Kase shared about the drama-rific morning.

Shit.

I'd spent the drive to the bank going over what had happened. As I thought about it, I just couldn't believe the level of stupidity on Rachel's part. She invited the wrath that was Kase, and most likely Jake, for no reason.

I'd bet dollars to my best homemade donuts that Rachel was just hoping I'd flip out on Jake. Even if I was going to, I would've refrained just to throw a wrench in her catty plans.

I had no intention of bugging out at him, though. It wasn't like he could go back in time and undo anything… or anyone. I wasn't a big fan of his past coming in and insulting me. Other than a lack of judgment on his part regarding the quality he hooked up with, though, that wasn't really his fault either.

When I walked into the waiting room, I saw Jake in a conversation with an older man. Both of their frames were tight and Jake's jaw was clenched.

As I moved to sit and wait, I wondered if it was regarding the missing car parts.

I didn't even make it to Jake before he reached out and gently grabbed the back of my neck to pull me close.

The older man's words trailed off as he watched the intimate gesture with undisguised shock.

"Wasn't expectin' you gone so long. You okay?" Jake asked, his voice soft as he searched my face.

"Yeah, great. The meeting at the bank went longer than I'd expected."

I hadn't told him about the initial loan denial, only that I was still in the process of meetings and interviews. I wasn't holding out hope that I'd be able to share better news anytime soon.

"Kase told me what Rachel said to you. Care to elaborate on that conversation?"

Looking off to the side, I shook my head. "Not particularly, no."

"Babe, I talked to Rachel and let her know, straight up, she isn't welcome here anymore."

"Oh, Jake, this is your business—"

"Damn straight it is. That's my name outside and that means I say who can and can't be here. Even if I hadn't, Kase filled the men in about what he overheard. I walked into the back and each of them said they wouldn't touch her bike."

"Jacoby Hyde, this is a business. How're you supposed to run it if you're banning customers? Huh, Mr. Bossy Pants?"

"She had no right to say any of what she said to you. Rachel and I—"

I held up my hand to stop him. "Trust me, I don't need to know. Not just don't need to, I don't want to. You owe me no explanations. I'm not your keeper. Honestly." I looked up at him, hoping he believed me and didn't drag this out.

I might be cool with everything but there was a limit to that. Hearing any details about him and Bitchy Biker Barbie was *well* beyond that limit.

Jake opened his mouth to say something but was interrupted by a low chuckle. I looked over at the other man who still looked serious, though there was some amusement in his eyes.

His sharp and intense green eyes.

I knew who he was even before Jake introduced us.

"Piper, this is my father, Gregory Hyde. Dad, this is Piper Skye."

I extended my hand to meet Gregory's outstretched one. He took mine in his big, soft hand.

You could tell a lot about someone by their hands. Jake's were large and calloused. They were strong, hard worked hands. I didn't need to see his dad's expensive, tailored suit to know he didn't work with his hands like his son.

"Pleased to meet you, Mr. Hyde. Why don't I go see the guys and leave you two to talk." As I inched away, Jake's hand released my neck in favor of this idea.

His father, however, held my hand tightly. "Please call me Gregory." Not Greg. Gregory.

Don't roll your eyes at Jake's father!

"I just stopped by to take my son to lunch. I'd be honored if you'd join us."

"Oh, Mr… Gregory, that is very kind of you. I couldn't possibly—"

"Nonsense." He guided me to the door. "Are you joining us, Jake?"

Jake grunted an unintelligible response, though he did follow.

Lunch went well for the most part. Jake stayed quiet but it wasn't his usual intimidating silence.

Key's brooding could make a girl want to hold him and heal his wounded soul.

Jake's brooding would make anyone run and hide.

Gregory was polite as we made small talk, but he watched me with a critical eye and it was hard not to fidget. He grilled me about my business, asking loads of unexpected and thoughtful questions. I wasn't surprised when he told me he was an ADA.

As the lunch wore on he seemed to warm up and drop the interrogation. Unfortunately, he moved on to something worse.

For the second time that day, I was grateful for my mother's lesson on not showing a reaction.

When Gregory began telling me about Jake's time in law school before he'd dropped out, I easily hid my surprise. As he continued talking, though, I had to work hard to hide my anger. I'd heard the tone often enough to know that, much like mother, Gregory was disappointed in his son's choice of career.

"I'm sure your parents are very proud of you." Gregory smiled at me. "It sounds as though you're doing quite well in such a lovely business."

I didn't get it at first. Hyde was a huge success. Jake had accomplished much more than I could ever realistically dream of.

It finally clicked that his dad was disappointed in the *type* of work he did.

"Actually my mom is dreadfully disappointed in me. My stepfather is Thomas Scalding, of Scalding, Inc.," I revealed to the surprise of both Jake and Gregory. "My mom wants me to work a cushy job at Scalding until I find a husband and have children. She wants me to be happy, and, in her eyes, that means doing what she thinks would be best. If I did what she wanted, though, I'd be miserable."

Gregory quietly looked at me for a minute, though it felt like much longer. His eyes, much like his son's, seemed to be all-knowing.

Oh hell, he can see into my soul. He knows all the things I think about his son. He knows that in eighth grade I let David Ramber touch my boob to prove I didn't stuff. He knows about that night when I told my mom I had the flu but I was really drunk and had held the thermometer near the light bulb.

Okay, he knows I'm lying and it was multiple nights.

He knows everything!

Abort lunch! Abort lunch!

"Hmm," he interrupted my panic. "Well, Miss Skye, that's an interesting point."

Thankfully, we moved on and finished lunch on a lighter note. Gregory told endearing stories that gave me a glimpse into what Jake was like as a child. He told me about how he would try to fix anything and everything, even if that meant he had to break it first.

"I can't really picture Jake as a kid. I just see this mini-badass trying to boss everyone around and caveman grunting."

Gregory chuckled and nodded. "Yes, that is actually about right. Sarah, his mom, is going to be very relieved to hear about you. She's been a bit worried about his ability to hold a conversation since he was little. From the time he was about seven and all the neighborhood girls would come flocking around, he'd ignore them or growl at them to leave."

Well, nothing has changed there.

When we got back to Hyde, Gregory surprised me by pulling me into a hug as we said goodbye.

"Make sure Jake brings you to dinner soon."

"It was nice to meet you," I said noncommittally.

"Jake, can I have a moment?" he asked as they moved towards the door. They stood close and began talking again. Though, thankfully, this time Jake didn't look like he was going to throw something.

Okay, he looked *less* like it.

Walking to the break room, I thought about how much Jake looked like his father. Jake's build was bulkier with muscle and he was, in general, rougher, but their frame and body language was the exact same.

I'd anticipated Jake feeling the same sense of freedom that I felt when I left my mom's. But when he walked into the room a few minutes later, he looked pissed.

"Hey, what's up?"

Ignoring my question, he grabbed my hand and pulled me from the room into his office.

I opened my mouth to ask again, but the words and my brain flew out the window as he prowled towards me.

Pushing me against his desk, his hand went into my hair and fisted as he kissed me. His hips ground into me, the long, hard length of his cock pushing against me and making me ache for him.

Almost every kiss we shared was intense but something was different about this one.

I was breathlessly disoriented when he suddenly pulled back. I quickly got my head together when I saw the look on his face.

"What's wrong?"

"This shit is what I was wantin' to protect you from. You have your own stuff goin' on and you come here and get shit. Here? Fuck that. I know you don't wanna talk about it, but fuck what Rachel said. That was fucked up bullshit. But you just smiled up at me, so fuckin' sweet. You didn't even give me shit and I would've deserved it for dippin' my dick in that."

"Why would I give you shit about something you can't change?"

"That's just what's happened before. I figured, at the very least, it'd be the silent treatment."

"I've already told you I don't play games. I'm still not getting why you look like someone scratched the Harley."

"After that shit with Rachel, I figured you weren't comin' back. You shouldn't have had to be in the same room as that bitch. Then my dad showed up and, I'm sure it didn't escape your notice, I'm not his favorite person and he's not mine. But you charmed him. You not only made him smile, you made him fuckin' laugh."

"I'm not gonna drag your past up and throw it in your face. And your dad obviously cares. He was nice and I see where you get your charm from when you want to," I joked, wanting to ease some of his agitation.

"Kase said he only caught the last bit of your conversation with Rachel. Now that my dad isn't watchin', you wanna fill in the rest?"

"Once again, not particularly."

"How about you do it anyway."

I sighed. "He didn't miss much. She was just asking who I was... seeing."

"Yeah, I'm sure she phrased it so nicely. Anythin' else?"

"Uhh." I hesitated. Talking about anything to do with kids seemed a little too... relationshipy.

"Yeah?" he prompted when I didn't continue.

"She also said you don't want kids."

"No, I don't," he affirmed with no hesitation.

"Did you get a vasectomy?"

"That what she said?"

"Yeah, and that you only use your own condoms."

"That part is true. I didn't have a vasectomy, though. But, Piper, I'd be lyin' if I said I hadn't given it serious thought and consideration. Or that I'm not still thinkin' it over. I know I don't want kids. Do you?"

"I hadn't thought much about it." In my mind, kids were just another step somewhere in the future. It wasn't that I didn't like kids, I loved them. Kids' cakes were my favorite to do since they were more creative than most adults put together.

But did I want my own?

That I didn't know.

As much as I wanted to ask Jake why he didn't want kids, that question felt way too personal.

Cluck, cluck, chicken.

Instead, I grinned up at him. "I gotta get going, I'm behind schedule."

"Alright, sweets. I wanna take you out tonight, just us. You gonna be done in time?"

"Definitely," I breathed.

Jake and I are going out just us. Not a hanging out with everyone thing. Not a climbing into bed too exhausted to move thing.

Breathe, Piper, breathe. If you pass out you won't have time to get ready.

"See ya at seven, yeah?"

"Yeah."

Jake's mouth dropped to mine. I moved away before things got too heated and my brain went to mush.

I tried not to skip with giddy excitement as I headed to my car, but there was a definite bounce in my step.

Finally

Even though the clock said nearly seven, I was fairly certain a week had passed since I'd left Hyde.

I had a good feeling about how the night would go. Or, at least, how I hoped it would.

Surprisingly, I wasn't nervous. I wasn't obsessing and doubtful as I overanalyzed every last detail. I didn't even have my usual indecision about what I was going to wear.

Remembering Jake's words earlier, I slipped on blue lace panties and a garter with back seamed thigh highs. When I put on my favorite dress, I loved the way it felt and knew I'd made the right choice.

With its retro rockabilly vibe, the dark blue dress stopped above my knees and fit like a second skin. A thick, black halter strap led down to its square neckline and a matching wide black band went around the waist.

I put on my black heels and sat carefully on the edge of my bed to tie their blue ribbons around my ankles. I moved slowly as I tried not to fall over, smother myself with my cleavage, or split the dress apart in a girly impression of the Hulk.

I hummed softly as I applied my makeup with steady hands, using lavender and gray eye shadow and a few coats of mascara for romantic smoky eyes. I left my hair down but added soft waves to it.

As I walked into the living room, I congratulated myself on having my head together.

I'm so steady I'm a rock. I'm a woman that has it going on. I can have my cake and eat it too. I'm like one of the ladies in feminine product commercials. I can play tennis, go swimming, ride a—

A knock at the door interrupted the inappropriate ending to my thoughts. When I opened it to Jake, I was no longer a rock.

I was mush.

Instead of his usual t-shirt, he was wearing a tailored black suit coat with an untucked dark gray button down. The jacket did amazing things for his already broad shoulders and the colors made his eyes more vibrant.

His dark wash jeans were a slimmer fit than he normally wore, but still hung low on his hips. I knew if his shirt was lifted, the indentation of his pelvic muscles would be on full display for me.

Not that I have sex on the brain or anything.

Piper, you're gawking. Say something!

"Hi," I breathed.

"Fuck," Jake growled, pulling me to him.

His mouth crashed down on mine. I could feel his hard cock, sending a fresh wave of arousal through me.

I didn't care that if we kept going I'd need to change my panties. Or that I was making out with a guy in my wide, open doorway for the neighbors to see.

I just didn't want to stop.

Which was why I whimpered when he pulled away and handed me a bouquet of semi-crushed flowers.

"Think it goes without sayin', sweets, but I'll do it anyway. You look fuckin' gorgeous."

"Thanks," I panted, still breathless.

I walked into the kitchen to grab a vase and tried to think of something to say that didn't sound like corny small talk.

As I arranged the flowers, Jake pressed in close behind me, his arms going to either side of me as his hands gripped the counter's edge.

"Who're those from?" he asked, indicating the other bouquet.

My breath hitched as I felt his rough scruff on my shoulder. "A thank you from a client."

"Hmm. Gotta leave for dinner," he whispered in my ear, his lips teasing as they grazed.

"Mmhhmm."

"Don't wanna go. I'd rather stay here and eat you 'til you scream."

I made a soft whimper from deep in my chest, my knees nearly buckling.

"Let's go before I change my mind," he said with a wicked grin as I turned around.

Dinner for one coming right up!

Or would it be going down?

Jake held my hand as we walked outside. He paused on the porch as I locked the door behind us.

We drove to the restaurant in his blue 1977 Camaro. It looked sweet and rode like a dream. Jake told me about all the changes and customizations he'd made since restoring the car. I told him about some that had been made to Bo, though I didn't do the work myself.

When we arrived in the city, we parked and walked to the restaurant. It was a hole in the wall kind of place that was known for its beer selection and typical bar staples with a gourmet twist. I'd been holding off on going until I turned twenty-one.

I was hoping I'd be able to actually eat some of the highly praised food with the way my stomach was twisting and turning.

"Have you been here before?" I asked when we sat.

"A few times. Z's a beer snob. This is always his choice when he comes out with us. You?"

"No, but I've heard good things."

"It's better than good, which is part of why we don't put up a fight when he drags us here every time."

"Part?"

"Z's... not a fan of typical bar rowdiness."

"Is that why he didn't stick around Rye?"

"Yeah. He can do Rye in small doses, but not places like Voodoo or Jet's." Putting his elbows on the table, Jake leaned forward and lowered his voice. "Which is why it's important you don't spread the word about what is some seriously good food. Otherwise, it'll get popular and he'll start draggin' us to some place new. I'm doubtin' we'll strike gold twice."

"Your secret is safe with me," I whispered as the server approached to take our order.

A silence settled between us when she went to get our drinks.

Say something witty and charming.

Okay, say something alluring and enticing.

Ohhhkay, say something brainy and intellectual.

Fine, how about just say something? You know, make the mouthy do the talky.

Or just keep staring at the bar and looking like a deer caught in the headlights. I'm sure that's a good look, too.

"What cakes are you working on?" Jake asked, taking me out of my awkward panic.

"A few different ones," I began as the server dropped off our drinks. As I looked down at my soda, I wished I'd gone with something a little stronger. Something straight out of the vodka bottle.

Jake continued to ask me about my work and soon enough, the conversation began to flow effortlessly.

He told me about the recent work he'd been doing and about the extreme things people had requested, which made me laugh so hard my sides hurt.

I told him about some of my favorite cakes that I'd done and some of the crazier ones, which resulted in Jake throwing his head back and his rich laughter filling the air.

We talked, we ate, and it was, by a long mile, the best date I'd ever had.

After we finished dinner, Jake put his arm around me as we walked down the street. "There are a couple places around here that have concerts nightly or the movie theater is close by. What do you want to do, babe?"

I stopped walking and turned to face him. Bringing his other arm around me, both of his hands dropped to the top of my ass as I looked up at him. "Anything?" I licked my suddenly dry lips.

His eyes followed the movement of my tongue and his grip on my ass tightened. "Anythin'."

"Hmm," I started slowly as I pressed myself against him. "If I could choose anything to do, I choose... you."

"You sure?"

"Yes."

I felt Jake's growl in his chest as he lowered his mouth to mine.

All of the city sounds faded, every thought I had fled, and all I could do was feel.

I wrapped my arms around his neck, both to hold him close and to support myself. We lost control as the kiss became hot, intense, and incredibly inappropriate for a city sidewalk.

"Let's go," Jake rumbled as he lifted his head and broke the kiss, leaving me swaying slightly on trembling legs.

We walked in silence to Jake's car, as if uttering one word would break the tenuous hold we had on acting like civilized adults. The air around us was filled with tense anticipation.

The ride went faster than when we'd been heading to dinner as he pushed the speed limit.

When we got to his condo, Jake let us in and locked the door. He turned to face me, though he didn't close the distance between us.

Like a pause button had been hit, we just stood and looked at each other.

Moving slowly, Jake kept eye contact as he slid his jacket off, revealing pure, masculine beauty. His every movement was rigid and controlled, but I could sense it was fading fast.

I knew he was giving me space to breathe. Time to think or change my mind.

I needed neither.

His eyes stayed locked on me as he dropped his coat to the floor.

My hand released my purse at the same time, letting it clatter to the floor as its contents spilled out.

I didn't see what went where and I didn't care.

Just like that, the standstill was done. Instead of just pressing play, though, someone pressed fast forward.

Before I could blink, I was against the wall with Jake's mouth hard on mine. Our movements were frantic and urgent, a race to touch and feel all we could. His hands trailed my body, making every nerve ending come to life. I touched every part of him I could reach and felt his muscles flex and ripple in response.

I whimpered and my arms tightened reflexively as Jake moved back slightly to look down at me.

"I'm not walkin' away, Piper. I tried to but I couldn't. But say the word and we'll stop. If you don't like somethin', if you want me to stop, even if you just wanna slow down, just say so. Yeah?"

"Okay." Even as I said it, I knew there was no chance I would want or need to stop.

"Fuck." He pulled me from the wall and led me into his room. "You deserve soft and sweet for your first time, but that isn't me. I don't know if I even have that in me, but as bad as I want you? I don't think my control could hold for me to make love to you."

"I didn't ask you to. I know what I want and it isn't soft and sweet." I began unbuttoning his shirt.

He dipped down so I could push his shirt off his shoulders, then repeated the action so I could whip his undershirt off. I traced the gears in his arm tattoo, feeling his bicep muscles tighten under my fingertips.

"What do you want?"

"I want to taste you," I blurted out.

"No one's stoppin' you."

I felt his hardness straining against the zipper. My fingers shook as I tried to unbutton his pants. When Jake's large hands covered both of mine, I stopped and looked up at him.

Grasping my hands, he lifted them to his mouth and kissed my palms. A small, sweet smile pulled at his lips as he placed my hands back at the button.

My hands were steadier as I undid his jeans and let them fall.

Jake kicked his shoes and socks off and stepped out of his pants. He sat on the bed and positioned himself against the headboard. Lacing his hands behind his head, he stretched his legs out in front of him.

He almost looked relaxed and indifferent, but I knew better. I could feel the tension emanating from him. The strain from holding back was evident on his face though he tried to hide it.

I climbed up the bed between his legs.

Jake's arms went behind my neck to unhook my dress and push it down.

Sitting up, I let the dress pool around my knees before kicking it the rest of the way off.

On my knees in between his spread thighs, I ran my fingers along the edge of his boxer briefs. I felt a thrill as his abdominal muscles clenched and his cock jumped and strained. I hooked my fingers into the waistband, feeling his rough hair as I freed him.

Wrapping my hand around the base of him, Jake's loud moan startled me and I quickly pulled my hand away.

"Good noise, baby. So fuckin' good. Keep goin'."

I curled my fingers back around him, feeling coarse hair on the side of my fist. I ran my hand up, gliding gently up the smooth skin of his length.

"Harder, baby. Tighten your grip."

This is definitely an area where I appreciate the bossy voice.

Feeling his cock through layers of clothes was much different than having nothing in the way. It looked bigger, thicker, stronger, and, it's worth repeating, bigger. Even still, I knew how sensitive it was. I didn't want to do anything wrong, especially if it resulted in pain.

"You're not gonna hurt me, promise," Jake continued, proving again he could read my mind.

Hesitantly, I held him tighter and rubbed up.

His head fell back as his hips rose from the bed.

I released my grasp and lowered myself to run my tongue up his length before taking the tip in my mouth. Going slowly, I pressed my tongue against him and felt the veins and ridges as I moved.

"Oh, fuck, that feels good," Jake quietly groaned. He used his hands to hold my hair back, allowing me to look at him. "You're so sexy. Christ, so fuckin' sexy."

I took him as deep as I felt comfortable, which wasn't much. Drawing on my smut knowledge, I added my hand to work his remaining length and found a good rhythm.

Jake's hips rocked slightly. "Fuck, fuck, fuck."

Hearing his moans, I felt incited, ignited, inspired. I shut out the doubt and just *felt* him.

It might not be the most artful blow job, but what I lack in finesse, I can make up for in enthusiasm.

"You gotta stop or I'm not gonna last." His hand fisted in my hair and tugged back gently.

I pushed down against his hold, moaning around his cock at the pull of my hair.

"I'm gonna come, baby," he warned on a guttural groan as he tried half-heartedly to pull me away. When that didn't work, he switched and used his hand in my hair to guide me. His hooded eyes heated as he watched me. "Fuck. Perfect. So fuckin' perfect." His cock surged and grew harder still. He cursed, the sound somewhere between a groan and a shout, as he came.

I wanted to experience everything I could, but I hadn't thought I'd enjoy it like I had. I definitely hadn't expected to feel so turned on and powerful.

This gorgeous sex god just got off because of me. Because of what I did to him.

His hand gently pulled me back. I sat up, unsure of what to do, but I didn't have to think long about it.

Jake gave me a wicked smile. "Your turn."

His hands gently cupped my face, at odds with the roughness of his mouth as it took mine.

The force pushed me onto my back and my legs spread to allow Jake's hips to fall between them. I could feel his semi-hard cock pressed against me as his mouth lightly trailed my jaw down to my throat. He moved lower and used the tip of his tongue to circle around my nipples without touching them.

"Please." I arched myself closer to him, adding a silent plea to my verbal one.

I moaned as his mouth covered my nipple, his teeth biting down around the barbell before he sucked hard. The pad of his calloused thumb grazed across my other nipple, the tender touch a stark contrast with the roughness of his mouth.

He softly kissed across my chest, the coarseness of his facial hair adding yet another maddening sensation as he brought his mouth to my other nipple.

Every touch was a contradiction. With no way to know what was coming next, no rhythm to settle into, the sweet, unpredictable torture kept my mind and body on edge.

I lifted my hips in anticipation as Jake's hand lowered with ache inducing slowness.

He tugged my garter. "Wear these for me?"

"Yeah, you mentioned—" I started.

His fingertips brushed against my wetness as he pushed my panties to the side and stole what limited ability I had to speak.

"They look even hotter than I could've imagined. Which is why it's so hard to do this." He looped his fingers around the garter and pulled it down, taking my thigh highs and panties with it.

I waited to feel shy. To have the urge to hide myself, or to feel my cheeks heat with embarrassment. The feelings never came, and instead I spread my legs wider, needing more. The cool air hit my overheated body but did nothing to soothe me.

Jake's fingers went between my legs, leisurely gliding up over my clit then back down again in a slow torment. His mouth roamed down my jaw, neck, the base of my throat, my chest, and back up again.

While he seemed content to drive me crazy, I arched my hips up, needing him to enter me.

I've never felt so empty in my life.

I breathed a sigh of relief when he *finally* began to ease his long finger into me. My breath caught as he worked me while his tongue flicked across my nipple.

Keeping his movements slow, he cautiously pressed a second finger in. He bit down on my nipple, the pleasurable sting helping to distract me from the pain of my body stretching to accommodate his fingers.

As his mouth and fingers worked at me, I felt coiled tenseness grow. My hips began to undulate as I tried to find release.

"Please, Jake, I need more. Harder. More," I mindlessly begged.

His groan vibrated against my nipple, his teeth tugging harder.

I was close, and I was pretty sure I was going to die if I came. It was too much, too big, too intense.

But I knew, without a doubt, I was going to die if I didn't come soon.

Jake put his thumb on my clit and applied just the right amount of pressure. Moving it in small circles, his fingers thrust shallowly in and out.

White exploded behind my eyes as the tension broke and I came harder than I thought possible.

I died. I must have. I'm a puddle of nothing. There's no way I'm moving again. Ever.

"God, baby, so wet, so tight." Jake's deep voice rumbled against my chest, his fingers gliding. He leaned back and the hard length of his cock pressed against my thigh.

Hey, what do you know, I'm ready to move. More than ready.

I need to.

Now.

"I want..." I started, losing focus as Jake's mouth teased across my collarbone.

"What do you want?" he whispered in my ear, pressing his lips to the side of my neck.

"I need you in me."

"Fuck." He sat back.

My heart clenched as I watched him pull away.

Shit. This is it. This is where his mood changes and he's back to being an asshole. I'm never getting laid. It's just me, my smut, and my showerhead.

Instead of his face twisting in anger or disgust, Jake smiled sheepishly. "I have to go run to the car and grab... Well, the thing is, I didn't want to assume. And I don't bring girls here. So, I have to go to the car." He bent to grab his jeans, almost tripping himself as he talked.

The fact that he didn't have a Costco sized box of Magnums within reach was surprising. It was even more shocking that he really didn't bring girls here. Seeing Jake so uncharacteristically ruffled was what touched me most. It was charming, but also reassuring.

I had no doubt I wanted him and this, but it helped to know he wanted me just as much.

"Jake, well, I mean, I'm on the pill, so you know," I blurted out.

I'd been on the pill since I was sixteen as a precaution. Every time I went to pick up a new prescription I'd contemplate if I should even bother. I was happy I had. I knew how Jake felt about having kids, and I wanted him to know that there was an added layer of protection.

"I was tested after my last thing ended and it's only you. Do you get what I'm sayin'?"

"Yeah," I whispered, telling myself that the relief I felt at knowing he wasn't going to be sleeping with anyone else was just about the safety aspect.

Jake distracted me from deeper analysis when he continued, asking, "Do you trust me, Piper?"

I nodded immediately.

"Fuck, such sweetness." Jake dropped his jeans back down and returned to the bed, positioning himself between my thighs.

"You can still go get the condoms. I wasn't telling you so you wouldn't. I was just telling you so you'd know."

He fisted his cock, rubbing it up and down my slit. "I don't want anything between us when I finally get to feel you. I've wanted this since I saw you at the shop, and haven't stopped thinkin' about you since. Strokin' my dick in the shower just isn't cuttin' it, baby. But you tell me to stop, I will. Swear it. You sure?"

I felt myself grow wetter at the mental image of him stroking himself. "I don't think I've been surer of anything. Ever."

Jake gripped his cock and guided it into me.

I spread my legs further, not feeling shy. Not feeling embarrassed. Just feeling him.

My body stretched to accommodate him as he used short thrusts to ease in. The twinges of pain weren't surprising, but they were there.

"Want me to stop?" Jake asked, his concern evident as he paused his movements.

"No. God, more, please," I said breathlessly as I lifted my hips.

When he began moving again, he pushed further until he was in all the way. He stopped, allowing my body to adjust as his eyes searched my face.

It was indescribable, being so full, feeling so connected.

"Mine," Jake rumbled, as looking into my eyes. "You understand, baby?"

I shook my head.

"This pussy, squeezing' my dick so tight, is mine. No one else's. No one touches you but me. You're mine, Piper. Got it?"

I lifted my hips, urging him to move. My mind was so occupied with what my body was feeling that I barely processed a word he was saying.

"Say it, Piper," Jake demanded. He pushed his hips down to pin mine to the bed so I couldn't move them.

"I'm yours. Now, please, I need you." I ended on a moan as Jake started moving.

His shallow thrusts served only to tease and torment me. I tried to move against him again, urging him to go faster.

"I don't want to hurt you," he grit out, his restraint etched on his face. His arm muscles were taut and shook with the effort to hold back.

"You're not and you won't. But if you don't give me more, I'm gonna hurt you," I threatened as I dragged my nails down his back.

"Fuck." His pace increased, more force going into his thrusts.

"Oh, God, *finally.*"

Jake lowered his forearms to the bed, his body sliding against mine as he pushed into me. The hair on his chest was rough against my overly sensitive nipples and his pelvis rubbed against my clit.

The angle took him deeper, hitting areas that I'd never

experienced on my own with my Battery Operated Boyfriends.

Jake pressed so deep, so *fucking* deep, into me.

Even if I wanted to, there was no way I could've held back. My body tightened around him and then there was nothing but unimaginable pleasure as I came.

The speed and power of Jake's thrusts increased, and I knew the control he'd been holding onto was gone. His green eyes blazed into mine as his movements became more frenzied.

"Oh God." My hands, which had been moving up and down his back and shoulders, became nails scoring as I felt another orgasm building inside of me.

The books and movies did not *do this justice.*

"Fuck." Fisting one hand in my hair, his other held my hip down as he moved.

Had he not been holding me, I'd have moved up the bed from the force.

It. Felt. *Glorious.*

"Harder. Please. Don't stop," I begged just before I came again.

I wasn't sure if I was wake the neighbors screaming or barely whispering. Beyond thought, my world was reduced to this moment, this wave I was riding. My moans were met with his as he came.

As Jake dipped low to press light kisses to my face, I could feel his heart pounding against my palm. Our hands moved leisurely in a slow exploration of each other as we caught our breath.

Just as his weight was becoming too much, he slid out of me and collapsed to his side.

"You okay?" He wrapped his arm around me and pulled me close.

"I'm more than okay. So good, Jake, that felt so good." I tilted my head and pressed a kiss to his jaw.

"Stay the night."

"Just because we've fucked doesn't mean I think I have to—"

"You don't have to, no. But you're gonna."

"Fine," I sighed like it was a hardship.

Oh no, woe is me. I have to sleep next to a tall, built, sexy-as-sin man who I am now ninety-nine point nine percent sure is actually a sex god.

Poor me.

Reaching over, Jake turned the light off and pulled the covers over us. He stretched out on his back and pulled me so that my head was resting on his chest.

I yawned as he pressed a kiss to the top of my head.

"Sleep, babe."

"Okay, Mr. Bossy Pants," I muttered as I snuggled into him.

His fingers followed along the tattoo on my rib cage, going slowly as if to memorize the notes. Stilling, his breathing evened out when he fell asleep.

Though I was exhausted, sleep was slow to find me. Middle of the night thought sessions were rarely a good thing. It was the time when I'd remember everything I forgot to do. Or when I'd think of everything I'd done but wished I could change.

As I replayed the night, all I could think of was how perfect it'd been. I hadn't been waiting for my Prince Charming or marriage. I just knew I wanted better than a hookup at a frat party or on some guy's dirty futon.

I wasn't going to jump into something just for the, well, fuck of it.

From what I'd heard, even with experience, the first time with someone new could still be an awkward disaster.

I'd always expected my first time to be a catastrophe of epic proportions.

What happened tonight surpassed anything I could've imagined, and I'd imagined it quite a bit. The Jake holding me tight in his bed was *much* better than the Jake that had been living in my fantasies, and that was definitely saying something.

Breathing in the smell of Jake, the smell of us, I exhaled in a quiet rush. With a smile, I fell into a deep sleep.

"Baby, I gotta take my shoes off."

"No, leave 'em," Jake grunted as he reached behind his head and pulled his shirt off in a move that would have left me tangled had I attempted it.

Watching Jake do it, however, only left me close to panting as I enjoyed the view.

My show improved when he shoved his pants and boxer briefs down just enough to free himself before dropping his body back down to mine.

"I'll go gentle next time. Gentler, at least. But I can't right now."

"Don't." I rubbed my hands down his back, letting my nails drag. "You know how I like you, baby."

"Fuck, Piper, I need you. So bad. I've never needed anyone like I need you."

I knew he wasn't just talking about sex. Had I repeated the words back to him, I wouldn't have been, either.

However, any thought other than feeling him left my mind when his hands moved up my thighs and he hooked his fingers into the gusset of my panties to pull them to the side. He fisted his cock in his other hand before positioning it at my entrance.

I moved against him. "Please."

Going achingly slow, he pushed into me while his hands trailed down my legs. "Give me your feet, baby."

"What?"

"Bend your knees."

When I did as he said, Jake gripped the heels of my shoes and bent my knees further back. The position lifted my ass slightly, changing the angle he entered me and the places he hit. Everything felt more intense and each inch felt bigger.

And there were already a lot of big inches.

"Christ, I can't hold back."

"Don't. Fuck me, please."

I knew he loved it when I begged, but even if he didn't, I'd still do it. I couldn't help it.

His body moved just where I needed before I even knew that I needed it. I cried out as my orgasm hit fast and sudden.

I knew what this was all about and that Jake was losing patience with me. In this way I'd let go, get wild, and come hard every time. I had no choice.

And, call me crazy, I liked that.

You're crazy, perv.

"My sweets, so fuckin' perfect," Jake whispered in my ear, his lips skimming my neck as his thrusts slowed.

A moan of protest escaped me as he pulled out and sat back.

Grabbing the sides of my panties, his eyes followed the progress as he slid them down my legs and tossed them over his head to land wherever. "On your hands and knees."

When I moved, Jake positioned himself behind me, his hands tenderly running down my sides before he gripped my hips. In one powerful motion, he entered me, lifting me off my knees. "You drive me crazy, Piper. So. Fuckin'. Crazy," he grunted, his thrusts a staccato as he punctuated the words. He settled into an intense, continuous rhythm, building the tension in me. "Work your clit. Now."

"I can't. Too much," I panted. I could feel him so deep, filling me so full, and I knew I couldn't handle anymore.

I jumped when his hand came down on my ass, warmth radiating from where it landed, and my fingers went instantly to my clit. Not because he'd told me to, but because now I *had* to come again.

His hand rubbed gently over my ass, continuing slowly up my spine and into my hair. He fisted it and turned my head to the side using just the right amount of pull.

Just the right amount of everything.

"I wanna see you. I love watchin' your face," Jake groaned as his speed increased.

His words and the way he looked down at me were enough to send me over the edge. My pussy gripped and released him, greedy as always, as I came.

"Mine." His voice was thick as he found his release.

Using his weight, Jake pushed me down on my belly and pinned me with his body, keeping us connected through the movement. The scruff on his jaw tickled as he nuzzled his face into my neck.

"Stay with me tonight," he whispered, a shiver running through me as his lips grazed my skin.

"Okay," I agreed as if he'd given me a choice.

Jake moved to the side to grab the blanket, pulling it over us before stretching out next to me. He held me close, warming me in a way that no blanket ever could.

I started to doze off when he murmured, "You're gonna give me what I want. And soon. Now sleep."

"Okay," I agreed, though in my mind it was only to the sleep part.

Jake's low chuckle traveled through me as he pressed a kiss behind my ear. "Smartass."

He so knows me.

"Takes one to know one," I whispered back before falling asleep.

In the two and a half weeks since we'd gotten together, things with Jake had been going well. I'd expected there to be a steep learning curve on both of our parts, but our limited time together was awesome. Better than awesome, really.

Almost... perfect.

Even though I'd never been happier, I still hadn't fully let myself go. I should've known, like most everything else, that wouldn't slip by Jake.

Everything had come to a head when I'd stopped at the shop earlier that day to drop off cookies. I'd been in the break room talking to Key when Jake had come in.

"Hey, I was just about to call you. Got a minute?" Jake asked.

"Sure." I said my goodbye to Key before following Jake into his office.

"What's up?" I asked after he closed the door.

My question went unanswered as Jake walked to the front of his desk. Turning towards me, he leaned back against it and crossed his arms over his chest while his eyes searched my face.

When his gaze shot to my hands and his body tensed, I realized I was twisting my ring on my thumb. I dropped my hand and tried to appear casual when Jake finally spoke.

"What was up before was that I was hopin' to convince you to fool around before you had to get back to work. What's up now is I'm wonderin' why half the time when I talk, you're bracin' like I'm about to tell you that your cat died?"

"I don't," I denied.

And lied.

I *totally* did that. Not always consciously, but I did it.

"Babe, you do."

"No. I don't even have a cat," I joked.

"You can't cute your way out of this."

"That's not what I'm trying to do."

That's soooo what I'm trying to do.

"What're you scared of?"

"Nothing."

"You can't even talk to me without doin' that." He dipped his head to where I was twirling the ring again. "Or somethin' like it."

"That's not entirely to do with our conversations, though."

"Then what is it *entirely* to do with?"

"You."

"Me?" he asked in a rough, quiet voice as hurt slashed across his face.

Realizing what I'd said and how he'd taken it, I rushed to explain.

"You're hot." I watched as Jake's eyes widened in surprise. "Like unbelievably, scorching hot. But you're also smart and, despite what you say, sweet. You make me smile and laugh all the freakin' time. Plus, you're a total badass and that's crazy sexy in and of itself. When you look at me like that," I said, gesturing to his eyes that had gone more than their usual intense, "like you can see into my soul and you know all my secrets, I don't know whether to hide or jump you."

Nine times out of ten, though, it's totally jump him.

Do it, do it now!

I'd always heard that to keep a man you should act disinterested and mysterious.

I was obviously never going to be the aloof siren since I was pretty sure that babbling my enthrallment with all things Jake *to* Jake was the exact opposite of that.

The look in his eyes as he stalked towards me both affirmed my choice to lay it out and scared the hell out of me.

Even more so when, as soon as I was within reach, he wrapped his arms around me to cup my ass.

I was damn near hyperventilating when he used his hold to pull me close, dipping his face down to mine.

"I can't see into your soul, sweets," he admitted, his gravelly voice rougher than usual. "And I don't know all your secrets. But I will. And you'll be the one tellin' them to me."

His words and how he said them warmed my chest even as I panicked.

They weren't a threat. Not even a promise.

I wasn't a challenge he was set on besting.

It was simply that he wanted to know about me, to know my secrets, and he wanted me to trust him enough to share.

And I would. If he asked, I'd answer.

And that was part of the problem.

"That still doesn't explain why you look like I'm about to drop bad news on you."

I opened my mouth to speak, though I wasn't sure what I was going to say. Thankfully, a knock at the door interrupted us and kept me from embarrassing myself by babbling more.

"Hi, Kase!" I greeted when he came in, my relief evident even to my own ears.

"Hey, Pipe," he said with a quick smile, though he was clearly distracted. "Jake, we've gotta problem. The parts order is totally fucked. We're missing more than half of our shit."

"What're we missin'?"

"It'd be quicker to tell you what we did get." Kase tossed a stack of papers on Jake's desk. Leaning over, he began pointing out different things as they riffled through the pile.

With their attention elsewhere, I began moving slowly towards the door. I knew I was a coward. I also knew that if I stayed, Jake would turn my brain to mush.

I'd spill every last secret I had.

Just as my hand closed around the doorknob, I heard Jake's amused voice call out. "Babe?"

Damn. Must work on my stealth ninja skills.

"I figured you guys need to focus. I've gotta get going anyway."

"Of course you do." His lips tipped up as he shook his head. "At least kiss me before you make your escape."

He so *knows me.*

"No problemo, Mr. Bossy Pants." I moved close and pressed a kiss to his lips before backing away quickly, lest my getaway be thwarted. "Good luck, baby."

"I'll figure it out, Piper." He held my gaze and lowered his voice. "I always do."

When we'd met up for dinner, I'd expected him to start with the questions right away but they never came. We had a fun night that turned into a whole different kind of fun. He didn't press for answers, which was good because I didn't want to go there.

I was doing what I had to do to protect myself, and that meant holding back. I hadn't been lying when I'd told Jake what I thought of him. Being the happiest I'd ever been made it hard to keep that distance.

It made it hard to remember why I'd even want to.

Connections

'Operation: Keep My Freakin' Distance' was a fail.

No, it was an epic, colossal fail.

Considering what little time we'd spent together the last couple of weeks, this either said something about my fortitude or how awesome Jake was.

I blamed Jake.

With school in full force, I was out of the house in the morning before seven. I'd get home sometime midafternoon and launch right into cakes, my studies, and whatever else needed to be done. I didn't stop going until after nine most nights.

Thankfully, I loved what I did or this would've been a *major* pain in the ass.

Jake was even busier at work. His nights often went later than mine, but they always ended with us in bed together.

I popped in to see him when I could, and he broke away to have dinner with me most nights. While it wasn't much, we were making it work. That didn't mean I wasn't looking forward to a weekend together.

Every year, Hyde participated in a growing charity auction. Loads of businesses, politicians, and even some local celebrities came to downtown Boston to attend.

I'd heard of it, but I hadn't known many of the details, including the fact that Jake had started and organized the event. It was only recently that his and the shop's involvement was becoming common knowledge.

When I'd tried to find out more, Jake dodged most of my incessant questions. The gist, from what little I could get out of him, was that Hyde had started out donating to groups for at risk kids around the holidays. It had snowballed from there.

Since he hadn't been able to give me much notice, Jake insisted that I take his credit card to have lunch with Ray and shop for a dress. My days had been so busy that I hadn't even thought about what to wear, much less about shopping.

If the Girl Card was a real thing, mine was in danger of being revoked.

While a day with Ray sounded awesome, Jake paying did not, and I told him so.

I told him again when I found his credit card in my purse.

And again when he left it on my desk at home.

When he slipped the card into my back pocket while we were kissing in the break room, I told him there was absolutely no way I was using his card.

Then he told me why he was paying, and most of that was done nonverbally.

In the end, when my brain was mush, I somehow agreed to it.

My head eventually cleared enough to realize how he'd played me and I decided to use his tactic against him.

Grabbing his hand, I pulled him into his office. I nudged him towards his chair as I locked the door. Walking over to him, I watched as he sat, his eyes never leaving me.

When I stopped in front of him, Jake slid down in his seat, bent his knees, and looked up at me. It was a move he'd made countless times before so I could straddle him.

This time, though, I didn't.

He was rough. Scary. Powerful.

His faded and worn jeans were stained from the day's work. His dirty t-shirt stretched across his broad chest as he weaved his hands behind his head. The defined muscles of his arms, covered in tanned skin and colorful ink, added to both the beauty and the edge of him.

He looked dangerous, intimidating, and every bit the badass he was.

And then he smiled.

It wasn't cocky because he knew he was gonna get some.

It wasn't gloating because I'd given in.

It was just happiness. It was the smile of someone that was exactly where they wanted to be with who they wanted to be with.

I recognized it because I wore a similar one.

To everyone else Jake might be gruff, but to me he was sweet.

Bossy as fuck, definitely, but sweet, nonetheless.

In that seemingly inconsequential moment, I knew things would never be the same. Whatever distance I'd tried to keep, whatever piece of me I'd tried to hold back, was pointless. Jake wasn't going to let it happen and I was tired of fighting it.

There were no guarantees in life, but there were sure as hell regrets. It was time to strap in, hold on tight, and enjoy the ride.

With that decision made, I dropped slowly to my knees.

Jake's eyes darkened and went hooded as he watched me.

All plans of retribution were long forgotten.

Instead, I unzipped his pants and took him in my mouth simply because I could.

Along with giving me his credit card, Jake suggested I check out a boutique, Ella's, since he knew the owner. I was grateful for the idea because I didn't know enough about the event to know what to wear.

When I'd asked him whether it was cocktail or more formal, Jake's answer had been a shrug since he had no clue what the difference was.

It wasn't helpful.

After lunch with Ray, I opened my wallet to pay.

"That ratfink!" When I realized that everyone was looking at us, I lowered my voice before continuing. "He's a thief, that's what he is. I mean, can you be a thief if you're replacing money with money? Either way, he's a sneaky thief."

"What're you talking about?" Ray asked.

"This is what I'm talking about." I held up Jake's card and a scrap of paper. Those two things, along with my license, were all that was left in my wallet.

"'Nice try, sweets,'" Ray read out loud. "Yeah, I'm still not following. Is that Jake's card?"

"Yeah, he insisted he pay for lunch and my dress. I tried to fight him on it, but he... well, he can be pretty persuasive." I blushed, making it obvious how he'd persuaded me.

She nodded knowingly. "I'm sure he can be."

"I figured I would compromise and use his card for something, but I'd pay for everything else. As you can see, that thief bastard stole my card!" I slammed my wallet onto the table, drawing glares from those around us.

"How did he know?"

"'Cause he always does. He swears he doesn't know my secrets, but he lies. And steals!" I added, shaking my nearly empty wallet for emphasis.

"I don't know if that's sweet, hilarious, or scary."

"Yeah, you basically just summed up Jake," I muttered as I took out my phone to text him. "I thought I finally got one past him."

Me: Huh, I feel like my wallet is a little lighter.

Jake: Funny, I feel like mine is a fuckuva lot heavier.

Me: That's what you get for taking my stuff.

Jake: I was just gonna grab your cards 'cause I know you. But your wallet was such a fuckin' mess I couldn't find them, so I took everythin'. You carry around a lot of shit, babe.

Me: No I don't! It's all necessities.

Jake: All these frequent shopper cards for coffee places are necessities?

Me: Hey, I'm close to a free coffee on a lot of those.

Jake: Half of these places went out of business long ago.

"What's his excuse?" Ray asked.

"He's making fun of how much I carry in my wallet."

"Sweetie, he's right. You don't need a wallet, you need a portable filing cabinet."

I stuck my tongue out at her before sighing as I texted Jake.

Me: Fine, I might need to do a small amount of cleaning. Stop looking through my stuff.

Jake: Too late, baby, I saw *that* card when I was grabbin' it. And I'm gonna need to see the eight purchases you've made.

Of course he honed in on the one card I didn't want him to see. That's what I get for keeping a punch card from an adult store in my wallet.

Me: Only those eight purchases? What about the stuff from the other three cards I've filled?

It wasn't true, but he didn't need to know that. He deserved a little torture for taking my stuff.

"What're you saying to him?" Ray asked, startling me.

"Huh? Oh, nothing. You know, typical things."

"Really? 'Cause you're smiling like the cat that ate the canary *after* dipping it in the cream."

"No, no. Just boring stuff," I lied when my phone went off again.

Ray laughed. "Go ahead and look. Don't mind me, I'm enjoying the show."

Rolling my eyes, I picked up my phone only to almost drop it when I read his text.

Jake: You're a fuckin' tease, Piper. I'm not gonna be able to leave the office all afternoon, I'm so fuckin' hard right now. Get your ass over here.

Me: Sorry, can't. I've gotta use your card and shop, or you'll keep stealing my stuff.

Jake: Guess I've gotta go think baseball stats while I'm a creeper on a creeper. Miss you.

Me: Miss you, too.

Jake: And, baby, make sure you don't tire yourself out today. I'm feelin' hungry *and* energetic.

Time to go! Who needs anything else when you can have hungry and *energetic?*

"Miss, can I take that away for you?" The server drew my attention as she reached for the bill.

"Oh, yeah. Sorry." I handed it off before looking at a smiling Ray.

"You know, I like Jake and I liked him for you. But now I love him for you."

"Because he steals my stuff?"

"Your smile. I'm sure half the conversation was obscene, but I've never seen you smile like that. I love it, and I love that he gives that to you."

I leaned forward, dropping my voice like what I was saying was a secret. If I'd been trying to hide it, I was failing. Epically. "I don't think I've ever been so happy."

"You deserve it."

I grinned at my friend. "Have you been to Ella's?"

"No, you?"

"Nope. Jake recommended it."

"Badass likes to window shop boutiques?"

"No, he knows the owner."

"As in—"

I held up my hand. "Don't know, don't wanna know. I'm assuming since he's not a huge douche, he wouldn't send me to the shop of someone he's... known."

"That's true."

"I'd mentioned that I wasn't sure what kind of dress to wear. I wasn't about to ask my mom. She'd have probably taken it as a sign I was asking for a wardrobe makeover."

"Oh God, could you imagine?"

"No. Beyond no. Could you picture me in a sweater set and khaki slacks?"

"No, but now I wanna see that!"

I pretended to look thoughtful before grinning and shaking my head. "Not gonna happen."

"So are you excited about this weekend?"

"Yes, but also nervous. I wish you guys were able to be there. I'd feel more comfortable."

"Me too. But we've had this vacation booked for months. You know how hard it is for Edge and me to take time off."

"Yeah, I know."

"Seriously, though... Are you okay with the card situation? I know how Jake can be, but I also know how you are with money."

"It's hard to be mad when he's doing it to be thoughtful, not controlling. Plus, my real issue is with the strings that are usually attached to the money. If I took some from my mom, she'd use it as a way to manipulate me. With Jake, there are no stipulations. I mean, he's buying the dress with the expectation that I'm going as his date. But if we ended before then, he wouldn't use that to guilt me into going." I was surprised at the ache that grew in my belly at the thought.

"Have I mentioned that I absolutely love him for you?"

"Me, too." I polished my voice to sound like my mother before continuing. "Now that we've lunched, darling, let's shop."

It was a short walk to Ella's. The boutique was small but everything was high quality, and most of it was gorgeous.

A tall brunette that looked like she'd just walked off a runway was waiting for us when we arrived. Her hair was cut in a severe bob that accentuated her high cheek bones and upturned eyes. Her clothes fit so perfectly they looked like they were specifically made for her.

"You must be Miss Skye," she greeted, fake polite with a forced smile. Still, it was better than outright hostile. "I'm Ava, I'll be assisting you this afternoon."

Please don't let this be the owner that Jake knows. I can compete with Bitchy Biker Barbie but I'm not sure about Catty Catwalker.

"Ms. Ella sends her apologies that she can't be here, but an emergency came up at her other location." Before I could reply, she turned and started walking towards the back. "Follow me, I've got some ideas."

Ava might not have been the friendliest, but it was clear she knew her stuff. It only took three dresses before she handed me the one.

As in, the most beautiful piece of clothing I'd ever seen.

The dress I wanted to wear until it disintegrated off of me.

The dress.

The deep plum color contrasted well with my hair and made my violet eyes brighter. The haltered back dipped to an almost indecent level and a slit went past the middle of my right thigh. It showed a lot of skin but the quality of the dress made it look elegant rather than cheap. There was little adornment which made it appear almost plain. When I moved, however, the nuances in the color, the slit, and the fluidity of the dress all came together.

The result was sultry with a definite edge.

After I changed back into my clothes, I came out of the dressing room to find multiple pairs of shoes waiting for me near a plush chair.

"Uh, I already have shoes. Actually, I have a lot of shoes," I said.

"That's the understatement of the century," Ray muttered.

"Ms. Ella said Mr. Hyde instructed we get you everything you need, and that includes shoes." Ava added three more pairs to the already impressive stack.

"Also, side note, there are no khakis or sweater sets," Ray told me, clearly disappointment.

"Well, of course not. Plus, why would she wear khakis or a sweater set to a formal event?" Ava asked.

"She wouldn't." Ray lowered her voice, though we were the only three in the store. "It's a fetish thing Mr. Hyde has."

"She's kidding! Totally kidding. Hey, those shoes are nice!" I gestured dramatically to a random pair of shoes on a display.

Ava looked distracted as she glanced over. "I'm not really sure those will work, but we'll see."

"You're evil," I hissed at Ray, as Ava went to get whatever I'd pointed to.

"Yeah, I know. Twenty bucks says there is a *major* increase in suburban gear at the bars, though."

Before I could respond, Ava returned with a pair of black, shimmery, very high-heeled sandals. The intricate black wrappings around the toes and a thick ankle strap added just the right touch of wild to compliment the dress.

"They look like little bondage devices for your feet!" Ray giggled as I took them off, passing them to Ava.

She tilted her head to the side and looked down at the shoes in her hands. "I wonder how that fits with the khakis," she muttered to herself.

Ray burst out laughing, startling Ava from her beige S&M thoughts.

I followed Ava when she walked to the register, leaving a still laughing Ray behind.

After I paid, I dropped Ray off at her parlor and went home to carefully put my purchases in the guest room closet.

When I caught myself peeking at my dress for what had to be the twentieth time, I knew I needed to find something else to do. I decided to get ready to see a hungry and energetic Jake. I wasn't sure which I was looking forward to most, and I'd been putting a *lot* of thought into it.

As I was getting changed, I heard my cell in the living room ring with Jake's tone. I hurried in to grab it before it went to voicemail.

"Hey," I breathed, partially because of where my thoughts had been and partially from running like a dingus through my house.

"Fuck, sweets, what were you doin'?" Jake's low whisper rumbled through the phone and straight through me.

"I was getting changed."

"Tell me you're naked right now. No, don't. That'll make things harder."

I giggled. "Yeah, baby, that's kinda the point."

"Not when I gotta cancel for tonight."

"Oh."

"Shit is fucked to hell here." One of the boys in the back called his name at the same time another phone started ringing. "Fuck, I gotta go. Sorry, sweets."

"No biggie." I hoped I kept the disappointment out of my voice. It was never particularly quiet there, but I could tell it was even more chaotic than usual.

"It's gonna be a long night. I'm just gonna crash here or at my place, yeah?"

"Yeah. Good luck," I said before we clicked off.

Instead of spending my night getting energetic, I got ahead on whatever baking I could before starting schoolwork. When my eyes got bleary and I'd begun answering accounting questions in baking measurements, I decided to call it a night.

I climbed into bed and tried not to think about how empty it felt. Since it was the first night that we'd slept apart since Jake and I became 'us', I failed miserably.

"'Ello?" I mumbled into my cell, answering it before I was fully awake.

"Come open the door, babe."

I yawned. "'Kay." I tossed my phone onto my side table and saw it was after three in the morning. I padded into the living room and opened the door for an exhausted looking Jake. "Hey. Everything okay?"

"Tired," he said as he moved into the room.

I relocked the door and turned to face him. I was surprised when he didn't move to kiss me. It was something he always did no matter where we were or who was around.

When I'd gone to the shop a couple days before, Jake had been talking to Z. As soon as I got within reach, he'd stopped midsentence to kiss me.

It hadn't been just a little peck, either.

"Okay. Wanna head to bed?"

"Yeah, that cool with you?" He glanced towards the bedroom, looking dead on his feet.

"Of course."

I climbed back into bed as Jake stripped. I avidly watched as each inch of his impressive body was revealed. Seeing him naked worked like a triple shot of espresso and I wasn't feeling nearly as tired as I had been.

Unfortunately for me, Jake belly flopped on the bed and his eyes were closed before he landed.

"Night," he murmured as he folded his arms under his head.

Seems I'm not the only one feeling these long hours.

Careful not to disturb him, I leaned over and kissed him softly. "Night," I whispered back, but I knew he was already asleep.

Over coffee the next morning, Jake and I talked for a few minutes about what was going on at Hyde before he pulled his phone out to check his messages.

"Shit. Sorry, gotta go." Jake walked to where I was sitting on the counter. When he moved between my legs, I instantly wrapped them around his waist.

"It's okay. I know you're busy."

"Can you do me a favor?" he asked against my neck, kissing as he went.

"Sure," I breathed. As long as his lips were on my neck, I'd agree to just about anything.

Who are you kidding? He just has to look at you.

"I'm supposed to pick up gift certificates at Serenity Spa for the auction today. Can you grab them?"

"Of course, what time?"

"Around eleven."

"No problemo, Mr. Bossy Pants."

"I gotta go," Jake whispered against my lips.

"I know."

"Don't wanna go."

"I don't want you to either, but I know you have to. And now I do, too." I unlatched my legs from around him.

"I'll pick you up tonight, yeah?"

At my nod, he dropped a quick kiss to my lips and started towards the door.

"Jake?" I called out impulsively.

Jake stopped as I spoke, though he didn't turn around. "Yeah?" he prompted when I didn't continue.

"I hope your day goes smoothly. I miss you," I blurted out.

Turning his head, he looked at me over his shoulder. My nipples tightened instantly when a wicked grin spread slowly across his face.

"Hungry and energetic, Piper. Hungry and energetic," he rumbled before continuing out the door and leaving me a pile of mush.

As I walked into Serenity, I fell in love and began mentally calculating how long I'd have to save before being able to visit again.

The décor was a mix of contemporary and comfort with smooth, clean lines and plush furniture. The smell of vanilla and citrus filled the air, immediately giving me an idea for a new cupcake flavor.

The whole place screamed relaxation. Maybe not screamed. More like whispered it in a soothing, lulling voice.

"May I help you?" an older woman asked. She was dressed similarly to my mother, including her strawberry blond hair being pulled back. Her whole vibe, however, was genuinely open and pleasant.

"Hi, I'm Piper Skye. Jake Hyde sent me."

"Miss Skye, welcome! We've been expecting you. My name is Alicia. I have the certificates ready for you when you're finished."

"Pardon?"

"I see Mr. Hyde is good at keeping surprises to himself. He's booked you for a full afternoon. Isn't that romantic?" She gave a wistful sigh.

"Yes. Very. I'm sorry, could you hold on a moment?" I asked, though I was already pulling my phone out.

When the call connected, it rang once before an amused Jake answered.

"How did I know this call was comin'?" he asked through his chuckle.

"Jake." I'd wanted my voice to be a warning, but I couldn't stop the warmth from seeping in.

"I knew if I offered, you'd have said no."

"Of course I would have."

"So, I didn't offer. You've been workin' hard. Relax and let me take care of you, yeah?"

How could I say no to that? "You didn't have to do this."

"Just makes me wanna do it more. Miss you."

"Miss you, too." I let out my own wistful sigh as I hung up.

"Surprise!" Alicia said with a broad smile and jazz hands.

I bit back my laughter at her unexpected silliness, not wishing to disturb the tranquil setting.

"If you'll follow me, we'll get things started." She led me to dressing rooms that were larger than my bedroom. "This room will be for you during your time at Serenity. When Mr. Hyde scheduled your visit, we asked a variety of questions in order to plan the best experience for you. If there is anything that doesn't work for you, please let us know and we will tweak things accordingly."

"I'm sure that won't be an issue." I doubted there was much he didn't know.

"Jake said that you normally wax," Alicia said nonchalantly, confirming my internal thoughts. "He wasn't sure if you would need that at this time, but we like to start with the most unpleasant thing and move on from there."

My hand began to move towards my eyebrows before the look on her face clued me in that I was heading in the wrong direction. "Um, yes, I actually could use that."

"Perfect. There are robes in the armoire to change into and I'll be waiting out here when you're done."

I walked in and closed the door behind me. Setting my purse down, I opened the dresser and pulled out the lushest robe I'd ever felt. Lifting it to my face, I breathed in the same citrus and vanilla scent that lingered in the air.

Hurriedly, I undressed and pulled it on.

I opened the door and Alicia walked me to another room to be waxed. When *that* was done, she returned to guide me into a different area for a facial and body scrub.

My skin felt and smelled awesome, and I kept trying to

inconspicuously sniff my arm.

When Alicia returned, there was a smile playing at her mouth. "Miss Skye, if you'll please follow me, it's time for your massage. You have a choice between a male or female masseur. I promised Mr. Hyde I would inform you that he would greatly, and I must put the emphasis on how greatly, prefer you chose the female. However, the choice is yours."

"Female, please," I said through my laughter, picking what would have been my choice anyway.

"That's probably a wise choice." Her small smile grew wider. "Jake's a good boy, but if he's like Gregory was with Sarah, well... let's just say I like my staff without broken fingers."

"You know Jake's family?"

"Yes, we went to school together. Though, as you can see," she said, gesturing around her, "I wasn't made to be a lawyer. Instead, I opened Serenity and Ella's."

"Oh, I didn't know you owned Ella's! I had a hard time not staring at my dress all night."

Try as I might to deny it, I was secretly freakin' *thrilled* to hear that the owner of Ella's hadn't been an old hookup of Jake's.

His past was his past, but that didn't mean I wanted to buy a dress from it.

"That dress is a favorite of mine, I'm glad you picked it. Don't you just love the way it moves?"

"It changes the whole dress. It's kinda miraculous."

"Yes, it is," she agreed as we reached a new room. "Enjoy."

After a peaceful massage that left my body feeling so loose I was afraid I'd fall asleep, I got redressed for my time in the salon.

My fingers and toes were painted an iridescent violet. When they were done, I shuffled over in my foam flip flops to meet the stylist, Jonathon.

"Mr. Hyde had a request, but he said it's up to you. I, on the other hand, am saying that the choice is *not* up to you, and we're just doing what he said. 'Cause, sweetheart, your man might be fine with a capital 'Fuck Yeah', but he's also scary as a broken condom on prom night."

"Understood."

"So no up-dos."

I lowered my brows. "Really?"

"I said the same thing. You're going to a formal event, an up-do would be fitting."

"I have no clue—"

"Oh, and no product that would make your hair stiff. He said something about being able to put fingers through it easily," Jonathan said with an exaggerated eyebrow wiggle.

Oh, well, yeah, that does solve that mystery.

"Anywho, let's start with a gloss, shall we?"

Jonathon put a deep conditioning gloss in my hair, leaving it to sit before rinsing it out. He trimmed my hair and put in some flattering layers, telling me hilarious stories the whole time. When he finished, he put my hair in big rollers and sent me to makeup with Kamani.

Kamani's looks were exotic, and, like everyone else, she was genuinely nice. She was also a goddess with a makeup brush. She made my skin look smooth and dewy with just a hint of blush. She deftly created a smoky eye with gray and purple shadow, perfect liner, and multiple coats of mascara in no time flat, with no mistakes. It looked dramatic, but felt like I was barely wearing any makeup at all.

I'd thought I was efficient when I got ready, but I was *centuries* behind her.

When Jonathan came back to get me, he pulled the rollers from my hair and applied a small amount of product. My hair fell in a tumble of loose curls with the bottom piecing out this way and that. It was a simple look, but in perfect balance with my makeup.

By the time he finished fussing with each little strand, I was running way behind. After thanking everyone, I almost left without the certificates. I stopped to hug and thank Alicia as she handed them to me, even though I needed to be gone.

When I got home, I began stripping off my clothes as soon as I closed the door, leaving a trail as I walked to my guestroom. I pulled on barely there panties before cautiously removing my dress from its garment bag.

Mindful not to smudge my makeup or ruin my hair, I slid the dress on and fell in love with it all over again. I stepped into my shoes and carefully hooked them before moving in front of the mirror on the door.

My chest tightened and I forced myself to take deep breaths as I tried not to cry. Instead, a giddy laugh bubbled out as I looked myself over.

I was right. I could never settle for just being tolerated.

What meant the most to me, what had me fighting back tears, was that Jake hadn't sent me somewhere to pick out a conservative dress. He hadn't suggested I tone down my makeup.

He'd shown that he knew me, and that, most importantly, he liked me as I was.

I was headed towards the living room when I heard a knock at the door.

"Hey, I'm..." I began as I opened the door, my words trailing off when I saw Jake.

I couldn't imagine ever finding Jake unappealing. I'd just figured that I'd eventually grow accustomed to his level of attractiveness. That my body wouldn't always react so strongly every time I saw him. At the very least, I wouldn't keep losing the ability to think and speak.

As I looked at him, his hair pulled back into a messy knot and face unshaven, I knew that time would never come.

Because just as he liked me, I was *way* into him exactly how he was.

Wearing a tailored black tuxedo jacket and gray vest over a black shirt that he'd left open at the throat, Jake looked beautiful. Pairing it with dark jeans and his motorcycle boots, though, he was beyond scorching.

He looked like Jake.

The combination does look sexy, though. Who knew formal badass was such a good look?

Jake pulled me close and kissed me in an entirely inappropriate way in my open doorway. "You look un-fuckin'-believable, Piper," he whispered against my lips, before letting me go.

"You look hot. Is that how guys are supposed to look in a tux? Regardless, you look badass hot," I babbled, more than a little flustered as I closed and locked the door.

As always, when Jake threw his head back and laughed, deep and rich, it made being a dingus worth it. I was a dingus often, which meant I got his laugh often.

That didn't mean I didn't treasure it every time.

"Glad you think so. Remember that when I'm fightin' for your attention tonight."

I laughed. "I don't think you'll have to worry about that." Other people might want attention, but the idea that they'd be any competition for Jake was hysterical.

When I looked up at him, the humor on his face was replaced with warmth and I knew he was thinking the same thing about my laugh.

"Trust me, Piper, I do worry about that." His hand slid up my bare arm to my neck, his thumb sliding against my jaw as his eyes followed the movement. "I can't think of an appropriate way to tell you how you look. I can think of a lot of inappropriate ways to show you, but seein' as I actually have to be at this shindig, that'll have to wait."

Before I could pull Jake inside for some inappropriate behavior, he curled his arm around my shoulders and started walking us towards a seriously kickass limo.

I'd consulted my good friend, Professor Google, about the event, and learned everyone's arrival was met with photographers and press. I was on edge about doing or saying something wrong.

When we reached the limo, Jake opened the seriously, *seriously* kickass angel wing door and moved aside.

I bent low to get in, stopping when I felt Jake's hands on my hips and his hard cock pressed against my ass.

"Didn't see the back of the dress 'til now. Like it, baby." He pushed harder against me as he bent to lightly kiss behind my ear. "Not too fond of other people seein' you in it. But I like it."

He slowly released my hips, his fingers trailing as I moved away to climb in. I sat to one side, Jake getting in and sitting across from me. The door closed behind him, and a few moments later we were on our way.

"Are you excited about tonight?" I crossed my legs, the slit moving to expose my thigh.

Jake's eyes moved slowly over my calf, his gaze like a physical caress. He sat quietly and stared for longer than was appropriate, not that I was complaining.

He left my question unanswered. "Who chose the shoes?"

"We all pretty much agreed they were perfect."

"Good choice. Though they're givin' me thoughts that're gonna make bein' in front of people pretty fuckin' awkward."

"Wonder if they're the same thoughts I had." I laughed softly.

"Really doubt it. What'd you think?"

I looked to the side. "Ray mentioned that they look like little bondage devices for my feet, and, well, I agree."

Leaning over suddenly, Jake took my hand and pulled me onto his lap. His arm wrapped around me, his hand resting on my exposed thigh while his thumb stroked back and forth. "And what, might I ask, do you know about such scandalous matters?"

"It comes up a lot in books. Then there's the movies, of course," I teased back.

At my words, Jake's playful expression was replaced by heat. "We aren't goin' to the auction. Fuck that. We're spendin' the whole damn weekend in bed. You'll tell me, in great detail, everythin' you've read and watched, and we'll reenact it. The guys can handle tonight."

"Really, baby? You wanna leave Kase in charge of talking to a whole room?" I started laughing as I pictured Kase ordering all of the men out and then making his rounds to hit on all the women.

"Yeah. Guess that wouldn't work," he muttered, looking disappointed.

As another car drove by, the interior of the limo was briefly illuminated. "I love the chrome and black look."

"You can probably get something like this in the Charger. I know a guy."

"I don't know. I think dudes that work with their hands like that are crazy hot. You might not want me around him."

"You do, huh?" Jake slid his hand further up my thigh as he bit down gently on my ear lobe.

"Oh yeah. Especially ones that are so thoughtful to their..."

Shit, what am I supposed to say?

We still hadn't put labels on anything, and I didn't want him to think I was forcing one. We were together and neither of us were seeing anyone else, and that was what mattered. I knew enough to know that labels didn't equal fidelity or respect.

"Sweets," I finished.

"As much as I'd love to stay in here doin' this, we're almost there and I need a few minutes of baseball stats. Maybe a book to hold all night."

"Baby, that's why you have me."

"I'd *really* fuckin' love to have you, but we'll be there in less than five."

I glanced at the closed partition before lowering myself to my knees in between his legs. "Well, I'll just work extra hard." I unzipped his jeans, pulling them and his boxers down just enough to have room to work. Skipping any teasing, I went straight for the good stuff, taking him in my mouth as far as I could.

"Fuck, baby, your mouth feels like heaven, but you don't have to do this," he rumbled, though his hand stayed at the back of my head as he rocked his hips.

I looked up at him, unsurprised to find his eyes on me.

He always loved to watch. It didn't matter how many times I'd gone down on him, he watched each time with the same rapt attention. There'd been a new intensity when he looked at me lately, and even in the dim lighting, I could see it.

"So gorgeous, so fuckin' perfect. Dressed up so beautiful, but down on your knees for me," Jake groaned, his voice thick.

His words warmed me, making me ache to give him all he gave me. He made me indescribably happy, and I loved the chance to make him feel that, too.

Jake rocked his hips as I went faster, no longer worried about hurting him. I knew that no matter what we were doing, he liked it hard, fast, and rough.

I felt his cock pulsing in my mouth as it swelled, and I knew even before his warning that he was close. His groans filled the small space as he came.

When he was finished, I eased my mouth off of him and sat back, looking up into his hooded eyes as I slowly licked my lips.

Jake growled as he tucked himself away, his gaze locked on my tongue.

Leaning forward abruptly, his hands spanned my ribs as he lifted and settled me back onto his lap. I barely had time to process the movement, when his mouth lowered to mine, cutting off any chance of my brain functioning. With one hand stroking my thigh, his other trailed tenderly up my side, stopping at my neck as he pulled away and ended the kiss.

I stared at his mouth, silently willing him to kiss me again, when he applied pressure to my jaw with his thumb. I tilted my head back to look up at him, though my brain was still mush.

"You could do that a million times, and, baby, I hope you do," Jake said, his lips tipping up before his expression turned thoughtful. "Still don't think I'll ever get used to how perfect you look and how fuckin' good your mouth feels."

"I like that you like it."

"Fuck, Piper, I love it." Jake moved his thumb, slowly sliding it across my bottom lip as his eyes followed the movement. "Now I wish we were headin' home since I'm feelin' hungry."

"Okay," I breathed my agreement. I'd been looking forward to the night, but a hungry Jake would win every time.

A hungry Jake meant that I was winning every time, *multiple* times.

I jumped when the door swung open, not having realized we'd even stopped.

Jake's low chuckle rumbled against me. "Ready, sweets?"

I nodded my head, though I was feeling anything but. I carefully moved off of Jake's lap, facing away from him as I took a second to try to prepare myself.

With the noises and lights from outside surrounding me, I couldn't settle my nerves. My stomach churned and flipped as my heart pounded in my chest. I was seconds away from passing out or running, screaming into the night. I honestly didn't know or care which at this point.

I just knew that I wasn't leaving the limo.

Nothing is getting me out these doors. I'll live in here if I have to. There is no *way I'm doing this.*

My inner freak out was interrupted when my hair was pushed to the side and Jake's strong arms wrapped around me. He pulled me back into him, kissing the spot behind my ear before whispering, "I love that you're here with me."

Time to get out these doors. What're we waiting for? I'm so *ready to do this!*

Back Against the Wall

"Fuckin' hate that shit. Thank fuck it's only once a year," Jake muttered after we got into the event.

The press line had been more extensive and time consuming than I'd anticipated. Not to mention, intrusive. I wasn't sure how celebrities put up with it. The thought of someone watching every move I made skeeved me *way* out.

Jake spent most of the time politely, and occasionally impolitely, ignoring personal questions.

Though he didn't verbally respond about us, he was his usual openly affectionate self with me. It spoke volumes that his touch was casual and familiar, not forced or awkward. He'd wrap an arm around me, kiss me, or talk softly to me, whispering something naughty if he could get away with it.

Every time I tried to shift out of his way, his grip would tighten and he'd pull me close.

In the middle of being asked a question, Jake turned to kiss my shoulder and the spot behind my ear. When he'd gently tugged the back of my hair, I'd tilted my head to look up at him.

I'd been fairly certain I could hear the subtle whoosh of women's panties dropping around us. I was absolutely sure I heard more than a few wistful sighs.

"You doin' okay, sweets?" he'd asked, his voice soft and tender. At my nod, he'd smiled down at me and moved his hand from my hair to my neck. He kept his hand there, his thumb rubbing the spot behind my ear, as he went back to answering questions.

As much as I loved all of that, my favorite part was when Jake actually answered a question. It was baffling to me that he didn't handle more of the publicity for Hyde.

He'd told me how much he hated interviews, which was why he let Z handle it all. Since Jake wasn't always great at communicating, I'd assumed that it leaked into his public speaking, too.

I was *way* wrong.

While Jake's confidence and roughness came across in an appealing way, he also simply had a way with words. It made people want to listen. His dad was half right because he probably would have made a successful lawyer.

However, his passion as he spoke came from his work now, from doing what he loved. That was what made his words so compelling.

Within moments of walking inside, I yelped as strong arms wrapped around me and lifted me into the air.

"Damn, Piper, lookin' fuckin' good," Kase said, setting me back down. His bogus, innocent smile grew into a grin at Jake's growl.

It didn't matter that I wasn't Kase's type, or that he flirted with almost any woman, it still irritated Jake.

Which meant, of course, Kase kept doing it.

"Hey, Pipe," Eli greeted, rolling his eyes at Jake and Kase's usual routine as he dipped down to kiss my cheek. "You look great."

Jake pressed a kiss to the top of my head. "I need a fuckin' drink after all that shit out there. Wait here, I'll go get us somethin'."

"Seriously, though, you look beautiful," Kase said after Jake was out of earshot.

"Thanks. You both look very handsome." Wearing traditional tuxes, both men cleaned up well.

"I know. I feel like James fuckin' Bond, yo."

"What about me, Doll Face?" Z asked from my side, startling me.

"You scared me. I didn't see you sneak up. You're also looking quite dapper."

His dark slate gray tux complimented his eyes and hair, which he wore in his usual pompadour. He looked more in his element here than he did at the garage.

"Perfect. Just what I was going for. You look lovely as always."

I scanned the quickly filling room. "Thanks. There are a lot of people here. All of your work has paid off."

"You're giving me too much credit. I should just say, 'Tax deductions. Open bar. Hot chicks.' It'd probably draw more people."

"No way. I think the longer you talk, the more likely those hot chicks are to show up. Otherwise it'd be a big sausage fest in here."

When conversation took the inevitable turn to the shop, I felt Jake behind me. He handed me a drink, his hand going to my back as he leaned close to me.

"I gotta go up and talk. Stick with the men."

"Why?"

"Peace of mind. I'll be back as soon as possible, yeah?"

Before I could ask what that meant, Jake pressed a kiss to my head and walked away.

I tried to figure out why he wanted me to stay with the boys. When the only reasons I could come up with were bumming me out or pissing me off, I decided to focus on his ass rather than him possibly being an ass.

I love the way his loose jeans hang from his hips, but I could seriously get used to the way the slimmer fit ones look.

I pulled my thoughts out of his pants when the room quieted as Jake's voice came across the sound system. It was easy again to forget how much he hated public speaking as he thanked everyone for coming and introduced the charity.

When Jake stood back so the representative from Tools for Teens could speak, I took the opportunity to use the ladies room.

As I was returning to the main room, I heard my name called. I was surprised to see James heading towards me.

"Hey," I greeted. "How're you?"

"Good." He shook his head slightly, smiling. "Wow, Piper, you look stunning."

"Thanks, you look great, too."

"It seems like it's been forever."

"Yeah, it's been a while."

We often saw each other at Mother's, but I'd used my schoolwork and cakes as an excuse to bow out of her last few dinner parties. She'd been her own version of understanding since the only thing worse than a baker for a daughter was a *failed* one.

"I didn't realize you'd be here. Thomas sent me in his place, but he didn't mention…" James trailed off, looking around.

"Oh, I'm not here with Scalding. I'm with Jake Hyde." I glanced towards the stage where Jake stood while the representative still talked.

"As in his date?"

"Yeah, we've been seeing each other."

"Interesting. I was under the impression that the two of you were just friends." James reached out and tucked my hair behind my ear.

I moved away when, for the first time since I'd known him, I began to feel uncomfortable. "We were. Now we're more."

"Does your mother or Thomas know?"

"About Jake? Why?"

"You never know someone's intentions."

"Yeah, you never can be too careful," I murmured, taking another step away. "I should get back. Goodbye, James."

"James, there you are," a familiar voice called out. Dana approached, stopping *way* in his space. "Oh, hello, Piper."

"Hi, Dana. How're you?"

"Wonderful. We can't seem to get our schedules lined up for that dinner, though, can we?"

I tried to sound appropriately disappointed. "No, sorry, things have been crazy."

"Well, the last couple of weeks James has kept me very busy, haven't you, darling?" Dana looped her arm through his.

James looked uncomfortable as he nodded. It appeared to be more of a noncommittal gesture than an actual agreement.

"Well, that's fantastic," I said with genuine enthusiasm.

Maybe this will get my mother to stop pushing him at me.

"This isn't your normal crowd. Are you helping bake for the event?" Dana asked, eyeing my outfit.

It was obvious that I wasn't dressed for work. I knew it and she knew it. Any idiot could see that. Just like any idiot could see that she was trying to make a jab when there wasn't one to be made. I'd have been proud to bake for a function like this.

I was always careful about keeping my walls up with Dana, and this was the perfect example of why. There were times when we'd have such a blast together that it made me forget the times like these.

Those good times were coming few and far between.

Instead, she'd become focused on climbing the social ladder.

Even if it meant using her friends as rungs.

"No, not working. I'm actually here with Jake Hyde. So if you'll excuse me, he should be done soon. Enjoy your evening."

"Goodbye, Piper," James replied, his face and tone not matching his polite words.

I nodded as I turned from them.

My progress was halted a few steps later, when a vaguely familiar man stepped in front of me and blocked my way.

I couldn't place where I recognized him from. His chestnut hair was styled to look casual and wild when I'd put money on a hairdresser spending ages getting it just right. His brown eyes weren't warm, and his smile was more of a sneer.

He was definitely attractive, but it was obvious that he knew it.

"Hey, gorgeous."

"Hi," I replied politely, moving to walk around him. He shifted his large frame to block me again.

Uhh, ever hear of personal space? 'Cause you're all up in my bubble right now.

"And what might your name be?" His voice was condescending as he looked me over.

"Piper. And what might yours be?" I asked, using the same tone.

"You don't recognize me?"

"Vaguely."

"I would've guessed with the tattoos and rocker thing you're workin' that you would. Kind of refreshing that you don't, actually," he lied, obviously ticked off. "I'm Blake Green."

That explains the off the charts reading on my Douche Radar.

Blake Green was the lead singer of Static in the Sun, a popular rock band, though I wasn't a fan. They were constantly on the verge of breaking up.

The weight of the egos alone must weigh down the tour bus.

"Nice to meet you." I turned to walk away.

Blake grabbed my wrist and twisted me back facing him. "Oh, gorgeous, don't go breakin' my heart by leaving me with these bores." He rudely tilted his head towards the people who'd been talking to him. "Are you here with someone?"

"Yes."

"Who?"

"Jake Hyde." Though it wasn't any of his business, I hoped dropping Jake's name would be enough to get him to back off.

"Sweet young thing like you? You aren't anywhere near his type."

Huh, seems like carrying around that giant, egotistical head of his means there's no room left for some common sense.

"Well, you know what they say about variety. Enjoy your night." I fake smiled, trying, and failing, to pull my arm from him without making a scene.

Jake had been working hard to make this evening a success and I didn't want to do anything to ruin it.

That said, I had a limit and it was quickly approaching.

"Stay," he said, talking to me like I was a dog. "Chat. I'll tell you what it's like being a world famous rock star. Ever spend time with a rock star?"

"Here and there. I really should get back."

"Little girl, Jake won't even notice you're missing. More than once he's left his date here and left with someone else. Usually someone else's date."

"I'll take my chances with that." I attempted to shift again, this time managing to move an inch before his grip tightened.

Reaching out, he sifted my hair through his fingers. "Trust me, little girl," he said, pausing to watch the strands fall through. "You wouldn't have to worry about that with me."

I jumped as an arm wrapped tightly around my waist. "Not gonna happen, Green," Jake snarled, pulling me back against him.

"Since when do you care about your dates, Hyde?" Blake sneered, proving he was a moron. Even so, he had the sense to finally release my wrist.

"Back the fuck off."

"Wow, Hyde, never thought I'd see you get all possessive over a piece." I fought back a skeeved out shudder as his eyes slowly trailed my body. "Makes me wanna get a taste of what must be a very, *very* sweet cunt."

Before I knew what was happening, I was behind Jake and Blake was on the floor. Someone else's hands held my shoulders, steadying me before pulling me back.

"Let's go, Pipe," Kase whispered in my ear. "He'll be good, but he'll be fuckin' pissed at me if I don't get you outta here."

I glanced over my shoulder and saw the other guys were positioned to block the scene. I knew they had Jake's back, which meant letting him handle things his way and keeping everyone out of his path while he did it.

The air went wired as Jake leaned down. "Get up, fucker," he growled. His voice was barely above a whisper, yet it felt like he was yelling.

"Go fuck yourself. The great Jake Hyde really is pussy-whipped, huh? Gonna get all bent outta shape about some piece? She really must be honey," Blake taunted unwisely, blood dripping from his nose.

Jake pulled him back up before his fist viciously connected again. The gruesome sound of flesh hitting flesh was audible over the noises of the party. Blake fell back on his ass, blood beading from a tear on his lip.

Luckily, almost everyone was either at the bar, on the dance floor, or looking at the auction items. Only a few people in the immediate area were aware of what was happening, though no one jumped to Blake's defense.

"I said get the fuck up, motherfucker. We'll head outside, I'll show you how bent outta shape I can get."

"How about we finish here?" Blake asked, standing up and brushing himself off. "You know, that way I can take your piece outside and bend her."

When Jake stepped forward, Blake swung hard and fast. Jake was faster, though, dodging the punch and using Blake's momentum against him. Jake brought his fist up, slamming it into Blake's jaw with a sickening thud and sending him back down on his ass.

Before things could get any more out of control, I pulled free of Kase and got in front of Jake. "Enough. It's done, let's just go enjoy our night."

"Gotta know I'm not lettin' that slide, Piper," Jake rumbled, not taking his eyes from Blake.

"Jake," I whispered, putting my hands on his chest and getting up on my tiptoes. "You've been working hard on tonight. Don't let him take away from that."

"I don't give a fuck. No one says that shit about you."

"I know, baby, I know." I rubbed my fingertips over the stubble on his jaw. "But I do care. I'm thirsty, let's go get a drink, okay?"

Jake finally pulled his eyes from Blake to look down at me. "You thirsty, sweets?" Bringing his hand to the side of my neck, he rubbed his thumb along my jaw.

I closed my eyes for a second, his touch tender and calming. "Yeah."

"Get his ass outta here," he grunted, jerking his head towards Blake. "I'll be back."

Jake slid his hand to the back of my neck and guided me towards the bar. When we reached it, his steps didn't slow and we walked past it. He kept going, turning and walking us down a long hall.

"Jake, what're we doing?"

My question went unanswered. Anger rolled off of Jake in waves, and it finally hit me that he wasn't just pissed at Blake Green.

But that's just crazy. Well... okay, I didn't exactly listen to his Mr. Bossy Pants order, but why would I? And, yeah, he ended up kicking ass at his meticulously planned party because of it. But how was I supposed to know that would happen?

I braced when he stopped us near the end of the hall, boxes and miscellaneous buildup around us.

"I asked you to stay with the guys," Jake growled.

I shuffled backwards as he advanced. When my back hit the wall, his hands went to the wall on either side of my head.

"I had to use the bathroom."

"You should've had one of them go with you."

"I can't go to the bathroom alone? What, worried I'll get lost?" My voice dripped with sarcasm.

Don't poke the bear, Piper.

"No, I don't want you talkin' to anyone."

"God, Jake, I wasn't gonna embarrass you. I don't need a sitter, especially not to go to the freakin' bathroom."

"Is that what you thought this was?"

"Isn't it?"

"No. Actually, fuck no."

"Then why?"

Jake ignored my question. "Who was that first guy you were talkin' to?"

"James. You met him at my house before."

"Why were you talkin' to him?"

"He stopped me to say hi. Why?"

"He touched you."

"He tucked my hair behind my ear. It isn't like it was obscene."

"Not like what Green wanted to do to you. Why the fuck were you talkin' to him?" His jaw clenched as his body tensed further.

"He stopped me. I was politely excusing myself and trying to get away from him."

"That didn't seem to be workin', did it? You like what he was sayin' to you, babe? Like hearin' him talk about your sweet cunt? Were you thinkin' about how it would be?" Jake asked crudely, his voice low and rough.

"No, what? How what would be?"

"Fuckin' a rock star. Slummin' it with the lowly mechanic not doin' it for you anymore?"

I stared up at him in wide-eyed disbelief.

Fuck it.

Poke the bear.

I glared at him, my temper rising. "Why are you being a jerk? I'm here with you."

"Oh, so if I wasn't around? I could leave if that'd make it easier for you to work the room." He lowered his hands and stepped back. His shoulders were tight as his fists clenched by his sides.

"You're being an ass. Come find me when you calm down." I shifted to leave but Jake moved back into my space.

"James," he sneered, "tucked your hair behind your ear. Do you know how intimate that is? How it felt to watch that? And Blake? I can't even go there again. You stood there and let them touch you, Piper. Why?" His hands slammed back on the wall, punctuating the word as his body pressed close to mine.

"Jake, I didn't—"

"You don't care when we don't see each other. I called you yesterday, fuckin' hatin' that I had to cancel, but you were totally fine with it. Christ, you couldn't even call yourself my woman on the way here. Obviously, you're still free and available to do what you want."

Oh yeah, poke the bossy bear with a sharp fuckin' stick.

"Are you serious? No, are you *fuckin'* serious? You've never said you were my boyfriend or anything, either," I pointed out.

"I told you it was only you for me."

"What? When?"

"Before the first time. I said it was only you and asked if you knew what I was sayin'."

"I thought that meant you were only gonna be having sex with me."

"No. It's *only* you."

"I'm not a mind reader, Jake. How was I supposed to know that?"

"I showed you—"

"Wait! Was that what all that shit was last night? You're more than a replaceable dick to me. I missed *you*, not just hungry and energetic. But you're busy, and I get that. I'm not gonna bug out on you about your job. That's not cool."

"You're—"

"We are... well, *were* awesome. I didn't need a title to make it official because I was already there. You wanna put labels on us, we'll put labels on us. I'll buy a freakin' label maker and label the hell out of us. But you know I'm yours. I've told you that over and over."

"When?"

"During sex."

"Yeah, exactly. While my dick's in you and I'm makin' you come. Even then I'm promptin' you to say it. Not once have you said it on your own. And then you wonder why I'd think I was a replaceable dick to you. I'm not a mind reader either."

As much as I hated to admit it, he had a point. Just because he seemed to know all my secrets didn't mean he actually did.

My shoulders slumped as I lost some of my anger. "Oh."

"Yeah. Oh."

"You're right. I guess I just thought you knew how I felt. That you'd figured it out because of... well, everything."

Just like that, I could feel the tension leave his body. His eyes went warm and soft, though no less intense. "You're my woman?"

I stayed silent, staring beyond him, unseeing, as I worked through my anger and hurt at what he'd said.

Blowing out his breath, he ran his palm down his face before bringing it up to rub the back of his neck. "Shit. I really fucked up. Let my temper get to me. I'm sorry."

"You're an ass."

"Yeah," he agreed. "I'd never be embarrassed by you. The way I see other guys lookin' at you? Them talking to you as soon as I walk away? That's why I wanted you to stick close to the guys."

Who knew a badass could be so vulnerable.

Because Jake was so experienced in other ways, it was easy to forget that a lot of the relationship stuff was as new to him as it was to me. We needed to learn to communicate better so things didn't build up and explode.

"No one else has me. You do."

"You're my woman?"

I nodded.

"Say it."

"I'm your woman, Jacoby."

He didn't like anyone else calling him by his full name and it was rare that even I used it. Each time felt like a gift and I savored it.

Watching his eyes close slowly, I knew he felt the same way.

"Fuck yeah, you are. Pull your dress up."

I brought the skirt up enough that, when Jake's hand on my ass lifted me, my legs were able to wrap around him.

Shifting me higher, he reached under my ass to free his cock from his jeans. Pushing my panties to the side, he ran his fingers through my growing wetness.

"Fuck. Soaked."

"Always." I bit my lip to muffle my moan when he lowered me onto his cock.

"I gotta be inside you. Need you, Piper, more than I've ever needed anything. More than I need my next fuckin' breath." Fisting his hand in my hair, he tugged my head back and kissed me hard.

There was no thought to the hundreds of people a short distance away. In that moment, as the slow burn built, the world fell away. It was only Jake and me. With my back against the wall, his cock gliding slowly in and out, it was sweet torture.

"Baby, I need it," I said, breaking the kiss.

"Need what?" He moved slower, building my orgasm but keeping it out of reach.

"You. Always," I panted. "But right now I need you to fuck me harder."

Jake's low growl vibrated against me, my slow burn turning to an inferno as his momentum increased.

I arched my neck, and his hand in my hair cushioned my head from hitting the wall. Biting my lip to muffle my moans, my legs tightened around him as I came.

"Christ, my woman looks so hot when she comes," Jake murmured, his words making the pressure build again. "Sweet pussy, squeezin' my dick so hard."

"Oh, Jake," I whimpered.

"So fuckin' perfect. God, Piper, I love you. So fuckin' much," Jake groaned, pounding on each word as he came.

Tell him you love him.

Okay, catch your breath and then tell him.

Alright, fine, panic and be a coward on the off chance he said it in the heat of the moment and didn't mean it.

Cluck, cluck, chicken.

When I undid my legs from his waist, Jake slowly loosened his hold on me and slid me down his body to stand. He stepped back to tuck himself away and arrange his clothes.

"Don't wanna go back in."

"Neither do I." My heart was pounding in my near bursting chest as my stomach flipped wildly. "I've gotta go get cleaned up."

Jake pressed in close, his hands going into the back of my dress to grab my ass as he kissed me hard.

He backed away. "I'll be waitin'."

We walked into the main room a few minutes later and stopped at the bar. With drinks in hand, Jake wrapped his arm around me. We'd barely taken a step when he was stopped.

"Hyde, how's it hangin'?" a man greeted.

I was with the hottest of the hottest. I knew this without a doubt. However, I had to admit this man was good-looking.

Raw with a sharp edge, he was tall and thickly built. His dark hair was closely shaved and his eyes were a deep, midnight blue. Skipping over the traditional tux, he was wearing slate gray slacks and a shirt that matched his eyes.

"Long and strong, brother, long and strong." Jake released his hold on me long enough to give him a back thumping hug before he put his arm back around my waist. "Piper, this is Lars. Lars, this is my girlfriend, Piper."

I'd thought the label was silly. What we had was good. Perfect. There was no way that something so small and insignificant would make any difference.

I was *way* wrong.

Hearing Jake call me his girlfriend was *awesome.*

"Nice to meet you," Lars said.

I knew I was grinning huge, but I didn't care.

"You, too." I took his outstretched hand.

"Happy for you," he said, still holding my hand but looking at Jake. His voice was deep with meaning when he continued. "Truly, brother. Fuckin' thrilled."

"You and me both."

"Alright, I'm gonna go catch up with Kase. See you both around."

From that point on, every time Jake introduced me to someone, he referred to me as his girlfriend. I knew my cheeks would hurt by the end of the night from smiling, but I didn't care.

We eventually made our way over to the tables and sat for a while with Jake's childhood friend Liz and her partner, Sammi. They owned a restaurant together where Liz handled the business side and Sammi was the head chef.

"I gotta go talk again," Jake said, kissing me.

As he walked away, Sammi and Liz burst out laughing.

"Boy, you both have got it B-A-D, bad! I've never seen Jake like this. Not even with Chloe," Liz said.

"Chloe?"

"Jake's ex. She was years ago, but basically the only real girlfriend he's had. Well, until now."

"I gotta say, I'm totally diggin' this change in him," Sammi put in. "He looks happy. Like really happy. And he isn't even around a car."

"Which makes me curious what happened earlier when he looked like he was ready to kill someone," Liz said.

"Someone was talking to me that Jake doesn't get along with." I didn't want to go into detail, mostly because I didn't want to think about it. It was done, Blake was long gone, and what followed was what I wanted to focus on.

"Who was it?" Sammi asked.

"Blake Green."

"Oh yeah, they're not fond of each other. Blake thinks they're competing for chicks. They aren't; Jake's not like that. But if they were, Blake's record would be dismal."

"That also explains the growl," Liz put in.

"Growl?" I asked.

"Yeah, he stopped in the middle of what he was saying, growled, and was already on the move when he told us to have a good evening. He jumped right off the front of the stage, not even bothering with the steps."

"You're kidding."

Jake's voice came through the speakers as he let everyone know that there was a half hour before the end of the silent auction.

When he returned to our table, he bent down and kissed the spot behind my ear. "Gotta make the rounds some more."

"Okay. It was great meeting you both," I said, standing.

"You, too. Stop into the restaurant soon," Sammi told me.

"I will."

Jake put his hand on my back, his thumb rubbing across my spine as he brought me over to another group of people.

As everyone chatted, he leaned close to my ear. "Havin' fun?"

"A ton."

Moving in front of me, his hands went to my neck and he ran his thumbs along my jaw. "I love you. I've been tryin' to think of when to tell you, but it just came out earlier. I know I've fucked up, and I get it if you don't feel the same way, I just—"

"I love you, too, Jacoby."

I barely finished saying his name when he kissed me, soft and sweet.

Jacoby Hyde loves me.

Keep it together, Piper.

Don't squeal. Don't even do Jet's thrusting 'in your face' victory dance.

"Jake?"

Jake tensed at the interruption, pulling up but wrapping his arms around me so tight that I almost couldn't breathe.

I turned towards the voice and saw a tall, slender woman. Her blonde hair was cut in a fringed, shoulder length bob that highlighted her pretty features. She was wearing a black cocktail dress that showed off her porcelain skin and long legs.

"Chloe," Jake replied.

Chloe? As in the heretofore unknown ex-girlfriend?

And she's the exact opposite of me.

Awesome.

"I'm here with Frederick, he just went to get drinks. I thought I'd stop and say hello." She turned to me, her eyes critical as she looked at me. "Hi, I'm Chloe. You must be the Piper I've heard so much about."

"Chloe, go find your man. We're in the middle of somethin' here."

"Sorry, Jake, I didn't mean to interrupt you acting like a teenager."

"Well, you did. And I'd kinda like to get back to it."

"Baby, don't be rude," I laughed playfully up at him. "I'm sorry, Chloe. He can just be *so* greedy when it comes to his time with me." I rubbed my fingertips across his jaw, forgetting for a second that I was supposed to be returning some bitchiness. "Anyway, it was nice to meet you. I'm gonna go get my man a drink." I turned, dismissing Chloe altogether. "Beer, baby?"

Jake leaned down and kissed me. I knew his touch wasn't to provoke a reaction, but just because he wanted to do it. "Yeah. I'll come with. Don't want to have to punch anyone else."

A shiver ran through me when he placed his hand on my bare back.

As we walked away, I subtly looked to the side. Unsurprisingly, Chloe was glaring at us with her arms crossed. What caught me off guard was also seeing Dana staring us down with envy darkening her face.

She's always had a thing for James. Shouldn't she be dancing on a table or something?

The animosity was a physical feeling that hit me hard.

I took a deep breath and exhaled, letting everything go. I couldn't control how other people felt. I could, however, control how I dealt with it.

And, tonight especially, I'd deal with it by enjoying time with my man.

When we got to the bar, Jake looked down at me, eyes searching my face. "You good?"

"Yeah, why?"

"Chloe. Sorry, babe, her man works for one of the companies that we invite. She never comes. I don't know why she's here."

Oh, I know why she's here. And it isn't to bid on the theater tickets.

"Do you love her?"

"Fuck no. What the hell would make you ask that?"

"Do you want to take her home tonight instead of me?"

"No."

"Then I don't care."

Jake backed me into the bar, his arms at my sides holding onto the ledge. "I love you."

"I love you, too."

"I like hearin' that. A lot."

"Good, 'cause I like saying it."

"Remind me never to piss you off, though. The way you handled that? Sweet as fuck, but you made it clear if she was gonna be a bitch, you'd outdo her. Instead of being pissed at her interruptin' us, I was tryin' not to get hard at your sweet version of attitude. So, never mind what I just said. Expect me to piss you off."

I laughed up at him, but did it while pushing my body closer. "Don't you have some official business to handle that would be hard to do if you were, well, hard?"

"Yeah, shit, I gotta go finish up."

We walked towards a table near the stage where Xavier, Key, and a couple other people were sitting.

"Who's that next to Key?" I whispered to Jake.

"Everett. They're... complicated."

"Wait, you mean that's his date?"

"If Everett had his way. Like I said, complicated."

I looked back at the table. "He looks familiar..." Suddenly it dawned on me where I recognized him from.

"What?"

"That first day in the shop, you called me babe but I didn't know if you were talking to me. I looked around, saw a couple bikers, and figured you must've been talking to me because I couldn't see any man calling them babe."

"I take it Everett was one of them?"

"Yup. That's what I get for judging a book by its cover. I've seen him with women, so is Key..."

Jake raised a shoulder and said, "Key is Key."

When we got to the table, I sat as official introductions were made before Jake walked towards the stage.

I watched as a few women tried to stop him to talk. Based on their body language, it wasn't the charity they wanted to help.

Xavier jerked his side towards Jake. "Piper, don't let that shit get to you."

"It doesn't. He's freakin' hot, no woman could resist."

"Too bad for them there's only one woman he can't resist," Key said, his smile shy but loaded with affection.

I love my boys.

Jake reached the microphone and began his closing speech for the evening. As he talked, a few men approached me and asked if I wanted to grab a drink. I was polite in declining, and they were polite with the rejection.

Jake introduced the representative before returning to the table.

"Damn, be nice if I could leave my woman for five minutes," Jake said with a smile in place, though it didn't quite reach his eyes. "Piper, you ready to go?" His fists were clenched so hard his knuckles were white, though he was trying to look calm.

"Yeah." The day had caught up with me long ago and I was running on fumes.

I stood and said my goodbyes. Jake did a jerky chin lift to the table.

As we walked towards the waiting limo, Jake, silent and tense, kept his hand on my lower back.

As soon as the car door closed, he pulled me to him and kissed me so hard it almost hurt. After unfastening the halter, he pushed the dress down.

I lifted my hips from the seat so he could drag it the rest of the way off, letting it fall to the floor in a pool of dark purple.

Grabbing my waist, he pulled me to him. I swung a leg over his thighs to straddle him. Burrowing his head in my neck, he used his tongue, teeth, and lips to drive me wild.

"Oh God, Jake." I pushed myself against the hardness in his jeans, wishing for nothing between us.

"I lose my fuckin' head when it comes to you."

"There were just as many women trying to talk to you, trying to get in your pants. Which, by the way, make your ass look awesome. If you have twenty or so more pairs, that'd be great."

Jake sat back and smiled at me, his hands still cupping my ass. "You gotta know there's no one I'd rather have been with tonight. Especially right now with your sweet ass on my cock. But seein' another man tryin' to be in my place right now, with you on their dick? Fuck that."

I rubbed my fingertips on his stubble. "But you're the only one whose lap I want to be on."

"You cool with the condo tonight?"

I nodded my answer. I was fine sleeping anywhere as long as I was with him.

He picked up a phone and told the driver where we were going. After hanging up, he pulled me closer and kissed me again. His hand lifted from my ass and moved up to rub my nipple. Rolling it between his finger and thumb, he tugged slightly at the barbell, making me moan into his mouth.

When we pulled in front of the condo, Jake grabbed my dress and handed me his tux jacket to put on.

I fought a moan when the cool, softness of the fabric rubbed against my sensitive nipples.

Stepping out of the limo, he leaned back in and took my hand to help me out. With my hand still in his, I hurried to keep up with Jake's long strides.

After closing his door, he turned to say something to me but I didn't give him the chance. Instead, I pulled his mouth to mine, putting everything I was feeling into the kiss.

He stood frozen for a second before his arms closed tight around me.

Jake picked me up with little effort. His ability to do that was one of the few reasons why I did *not* wish I was six inches taller. Carrying me to his bed, he placed me gently on it before following me down.

"My lips," he whispered, his lips brushing against mine as he spoke. He brought his mouth to my neck before continuing, "My neck." His mouth moved to the spot behind my ear. "My sweets."

His lips traveled down as he opened the tux jacket. My back arched when his mouth covered my nipple and sucked hard. He went agonizingly slow as he worked his way further down. When he finally, *finally* settled between my thighs, his tongue lightly teased, licked, and flicked through my panties.

I heard a tear and my panties were gone, a shred of torn, expensive fabric in his hand. His mouth covered me, devoured me, as he lifted my legs over his shoulders. Gripping my hips, his tongue was relentless. Even when I cried out as I came, he didn't ease up as he drew out my orgasm.

When I finished, I pushed Jake up onto his knees. I unbuttoned his vest and shirt, the process taking entirely too long. He worked at removing everything from the waist down while I leaned to the side to unhook and kick off my shoes.

Dropping between my spread legs, he eclipsed all else, his face all I could see. The feel of his hardness sent a fresh wave of arousal through me.

Jake lowered his strong body to mine. His forearms went under me and his hands wrapped over my shoulders. Entering me, his fingertips dug into my collarbone as he thrust up.

There was so much sensation, pleasure, and intensity that it took my breath away.

"I can't go back to no sweetness in my life, Piper," Jake groaned in my ear. "I can't not have you."

"You have me, baby."

Jake shifted his hips, his pelvis grinding against my clit.

I moaned at the friction, my orgasm barreling through me. My nails clawed into his back as his mouth found mine, swallowing my cries.

Pushing up onto his knees, Jake went slowly, teasing me as he coasted in and out with shallow thrusts.

"More." I lifted my pelvis and tried to move faster.

Grabbing my hips, he held me still as he continued his leisurely pace. "Tell me what I wanna to hear."

"I'm yours."

"Fuck yeah," he growled. "Never leave me, Piper. Never take away the sweetness."

Before I could respond to his words, his movements sped up and became more forceful. His head fell back, exposing his angled jaw and the strong column of his neck. The power in his thrust increased and his hold on my hips was all that kept me from flying up the bed.

It was frantic. Frenzied.

It was desire, lust, passion, obsession.

It was *life.*

I awoke in the middle of the night to moonlight streaming through the window. After we'd finished, Jake had rolled, keeping us connected as I straddled him. I'd snuggled into him as I tried to work up the energy to fall to the side.

As I woke up fully, I realized that I was still sprawled on him. I snuggled my face deeper into his neck.

"Piper?" he whispered.

"Hmm?" I kissed his neck and then his jaw.

I didn't know jaws could be so damn sexy.

"Good, you're awake."

Jake rocked his hips and entered me in one smooth motion. Feeling playful, I sat up and leaned back to stretch. I brought my hand down to my nipple, pulling my barbell and cupping my breast.

Jake growled as he bucked up, and the teasing didn't last long.

Luckily what followed did.

Settled

"A mechanic, Piper? Really?"

Crap. Leave it to my mother to try to sweep the confetti from my happy parade.

"And a happy Monday to you," I returned, wishing I'd let the call go to voicemail. Since it was before eight in the morning, I was worried that there was something wrong when I saw her name on the screen.

"Why did I have to hear from Elaine that you were seeing someone? Oh, and you know she must've loved that. Not just who you're dating, but that she knew before me."

"Sorry, Mother."

For once I actually was. I'd been dreading this conversation, but no one should have to deal with Dana's mom.

If Dana's recent behavior was any indication, she was learning from the best.

Or worst.

"Mechanic?"

"Not that it matters, but Jake isn't a regular mechanic. He owns his own business."

"But I thought you and James were getting serious?" she whined.

"Nope. Never have been, never will be. From what I saw, he's with

Dana," I revealed, trying to change the subject.

"Oh. Well, that is an... interesting choice for him, I suppose."

"I have to go. I'll call soon."

"You know," she said, ignoring my attempt to end the call. "With your father and Thomas' money, you're going to attract certain individuals who want to take advantage and use you."

I sighed in frustration. "If you're referring to Jake, have Thomas look into him. I'm sure you'll be more than reassured. His garage is very popular, especially with celebrities."

"Celebrities?"

"I've got to get to school. Talk to you soon." Without giving her the chance to respond, I hung up.

The call didn't get to me the way it normally would have. It could have been because fall was in full swing and it was beautiful outside. The smell of crisp leaves was in the air, but the sun was shining and birds were singing.

Maybe I was just finally growing and learning to brush the negatives off.

Or it might have had something to do with the orgasms Jake had given me when he'd insisted we conserve water and shower together.

Either way, I was in a good mood.

Thank the sex god for those orgasms.

I was used to a hectic schedule. Mondays were always busy, and that was without taking the weekend off. The phone call with my mom had made me run late, and I was beyond frazzled. I'd been counting down the minutes until my lunch break.

I sat outside at a table with some people from my accounting class, including my friends Melanie and Gia.

In the middle of talking about her weekend, Gia stopped and

looked past me. "Oh, wow. Who's that? He doesn't look like a student." She pushed up out of her seat to see better.

"Oh, please tell me he's a professor. I'll go sign up for his class right now, even if that means switching majors," Melanie said, dramatically fanning her face.

"Unless they teach a course on badass, I doubt he's a professor."

Without turning around, I knew who she was talking about. A wide smile spread across my face.

"Oh God," she frantically whispered. "He's heading over here."

When I turned around with a grin, it was Jake's turn to smile as he continued toward me.

And if you listen carefully, you can hear the subtle whoosh of panties dropping and *bras unhooking themselves.*

I couldn't blame any of the women craning their necks to do a double take. Wearing black jeans, a black t-shirt with the Hyde logo on it, a very worn leather jacket, and his scuffed up motorcycle boots, my man looked *good*. His hair was pulled back, but I knew he must have come on his bike because the front had come loose.

"Hey, sweets," he greeted, dipping down to kiss me.

"Hi, what's up?"

"Nothin'. Just brought you lunch." He placed a bag from my favorite sandwich shop in front of me. It was where we'd gone on our unofficial and very awkward first date.

Is there something more than love?

I mega love him.

"Thanks. Do you wanna sit?"

"No, I gotta get back to the shop. Plus, I might not have left the bike in a 'parkin' spot'." He lifted his hands to make air quotes. "Miss you."

"Miss you, too."

He fisted his hand into my hair and kissed me. "Love you."

"Love you, too. Have a good day."

Jake chuckled, deep and low. "I'll be done with work early tonight.

Want takeout?"

"Nah, I've gotta go to the store. I'll pick up something to cook."

"Sounds good. Let me know if you change your mind."

Jake dipped his chin to the girls before walking away. I stared at his ass as he went and knew I wasn't the only one. I also knew I'd be the only one with my hands on it tonight.

"Hellllooooooo! Earth to Piper!" Gia yelled.

"Sorry, what?" I reached into the bag and pulled out my favorite turkey, Swiss, and cranberry mayo sandwich, a drink, and a triple chocolate chunk cookie.

"Seriously, girl, spill."

"About?"

"About? About? Sorry, did I fall, hit my head, and hallucinate a god delivering tasty sandwiches?"

"Oh, that." I flipped my hand, sandwich crumbs flying. "That's my boyfriend."

"What's his name? How long have you been together? How is he in bed?" Melanie grilled.

"A couple months. His name is Jake." I ignored the last question.

Yeah, there's no reason to rub it in that your god is actually a sex god.

The cute-as-a-button redhead sitting next to Melanie looked at me closer. "You really are that Piper, aren't you? I thought so, but I wasn't sure."

"Yeah... Do I know you?"

"I'm Harlow Cooper. We have economics together. You always work so hard and don't socialize, so I thought you were half robot or something."

"Nope. I do a mean impression, though."

"What?"

"Never mind. Anyway, what were you saying?"

"I saw your pictures in the paper and online yesterday. Well, I thought it was you. But then I figured what are the chances?" she chattered on in an equally cute-as-a-button voice.

"Pictures?" I asked at the same time as Gia and Melanie.

"Well, yeah, from the Tools for Teens thing in the city. The article was so sweet, too."

"Article?"

"You know what, I was reading it while I was grabbing coffee. I might still have it." She began digging through her giant purse. "Woo! Here we go!" She smiled as if she'd just found the Holy Grail.

Given the size of that bag, it's possible the Holy Grail is in there hanging out with Jimmy Hoffa.

When she pulled out a newspaper, Melanie and Gia grabbed it before I could. "No, that's cool guys. Not like I wanted to see. It's only about me, no biggie."

"So did he really stop in the middle of an interview to kiss you and ask if you were okay?" Harlow asked.

My brows went up in surprise. "Did they talk about that in the article?"

Harlow nodded. "Oh yeah. There was even something about how you two seemed to forget there were other people around."

Oh, there was definitely a big chunk of time in the hallway where we forgot there was even a world around us.

Gia, Melanie, Harlow and the rest of the women at the table stared at me as they passed around the paper.

When it was within reach, I snatched it and studied the largest picture of Jake and me. His fist was in my hair and I was smiling up at him with my hand on his abs as he looked down at me.

We looked happy.

Also, very much in love.

Next to that was a picture of Kase and me laughing after I'd made some goofy joke. The focus of the picture, however, was Jake watching me.

If he hadn't told me that night that he loved me, this would have.

"He seems so sweet. I guess he isn't a badass," Gia said.

"No, he totally is. Trust me, I've seen him pissed. Not at me, of course."

Well, not much.

My phone beeped, and I saw a message from Jake.

Jake: Lunch okay?

Me: Of course. This sexy dude delivered it to me.

Jake: Lucky dude.

Me: You're so gettin' laid later.

Jake: Fuck I hope so. Been half hard since seein' you. After reading that I'm gettin' laid, I'm gonna have to spend some time at my desk 'til things calm down.

Me: Wish I could be there to help but I gotta get to class. Love you.

"Seriously. Does he have a twin brother? A cousin? Anything?" Melanie asked. All the girls nodded.

"No brother. Don't know about the rest but I'll find out. I've gotta get going." I grabbed my bag and headed to class, no longer frazzled.

"What's up?" I asked as I got out of Bo.

Since Jake brought me lunch the week before, we'd only seen each other at night. Because of the publicity, I'd had a rush of new business. My schedule was completely full for months and I was turning away more orders than before.

Hyde was even busier.

Jake had texted when I was in class and asked me to come see him when I was done. I'd been trying to get him to tell me why all afternoon, but he wouldn't spill.

"It's a surprise."

"What is?"

"Come here." Jake grabbed my hand and pulled me through the shop.

"Hi, boys! Bye, boys!" I said with a wave as I hurried to keep up with Jake's long strides.

Coming to a sudden stop in the hallway, he turned to me. "Close your eyes."

"No problemo, Mr. Bossy Pants." I played along and shut them. Surprises weren't normally my favorite thing, but I knew if anyone could change that, it was Jake.

Grabbing my hands, he guided my steps. I heard a door open and then close. "Okay, you're good."

Opening my eyes, I closed them again, sure I was seeing things. We were in the break room, only it wasn't the one I remembered.

The walls had been repainted. There was a new stand mixer on the counter that was similar to mine at home, but much bigger and a higher quality. Next to it were mixing bowls, spatulas, measuring cups, and just about everything needed in order to bake.

I was speechless.

"We cleaned the walk-in and it's up and functional. The health inspector was in and, as long as you use the side door and not the garage, it's legit. I also had someone come in and double check the walk-in and the oven. Both are good to go."

"Jake..." My voice trailed off, unsure of what to say.

I'd never told him about my loan getting denied. Dwelling on it wasn't going to change anything. I'd handled the rejection by putting on my big girl panties and moving on. I had a business to run, with or without the help.

"I wanted to save it for your birthday, but I'm sick of barely seein' you. I thought it might be easier for you with more space and stuff. The men were on board when I brought it up. Though I'm sure they wouldn't say no if you baked them somethin' every once in a while."

I looked around the room, my mind going off in a million different directions.

Jake had done this for me.

I didn't ask for it.

He thought of it to make my life easier.

To see me more.

It's only me.

"Sweets, if you don't like it, it's cool. I should've talked—"

I grabbed his hand and began pulling him from the room.

"What's wrong?" Jake asked.

"Nothing. I just wanna thank you in a way that wouldn't be appropriate in a health inspected kitchen."

"God, I freakin' love it when you do that." I stood up from being bent over the front of Jake's desk. I stretched before bending down to pull up my pants.

"And I love when you do that. Got a killer ass, sweets."

"Are you sure you want it hanging around every day?" The gesture was touching, but I was a little worried that the reality of seeing me every day would get old. Fast.

"Will you let me do what I just did?"

I nodded. "Definitely."

"Then, yeah. I'm sure."

"Jake, for once I'm being serious."

"So am I. I've seen you bake before. You zone out and you're in your own world. It isn't like we'd be steppin' on each other's toes."

"Good point." I buttoned my pants and turned towards the door.

Then I froze.

Hung on the wall opposite his desk were five framed pictures of us.

"Like them?" I jumped as Jake's voice rumbled close to my ear. His arms slid around my waist and he brought his chin down to rest on my shoulder.

"Where'd you get them?" I whispered

"One of the photographers."

"I saw that one in the paper." I pointed to the picture of us smiling at each other.

"Didn't know you'd seen that."

"Yeah. A friend from school showed it to me after you dropped off lunch last week."

"You freak?"

"Nope. I mean, it was a little weird to know someone was interested enough in what I was doing to take pictures."

I looked closely at the other four pictures. One was Jake behind me with his arms around my waist and his lips on the spot behind my ear. There was a close-up of me smiling. The third was him kissing my shoulder when he'd interrupted the interviewer to check on me.

My favorite, by far, was of us from behind. Jake's hand was on my ass and I was leaning into him. His lips were pressed to the top of my head and his face was in profile.

"How'd you get them?" I asked, unable to look away. The lighting and composition of the pictures gave them a magical look.

"I called the photographer after I saw the ones in the paper. He sent me over these five prints."

"Why?"

"Gives me somethin' to look at while I'm workin'."

So badasses can be vulnerable and romantic.

Good to know.

I tilted my head back and kissed Jake's jaw. "If I'm right across the hall, you can come look at me while I work."

"And thank fuck for that. Though, if I'm in there, I'm doubtin' you'll be gettin' much work done."

"And thank fuck for that." Stepping away, I put my shoes on and turned back to him. "I've gotta go. I'll work from my place today, but I'd love to try out the kitchen tomorrow. That okay?"

"Why would I set this up if it wasn't?"

"Good point."

"Do you wanna go shopping tonight and get anything else? When

I went to get the stuff, there was all sorts of fancy shit at the store."

"That's okay. I have plenty I'll bring."

"Gotcha."

I could tell from the look in his eyes that he did get me.

What he'd done touched me in a way that I knew would stay with me forever, but it was still my business. My pride in working hard and doing things myself meant a lot to me.

He so knows me.

The next morning, I got up early and left Jake sleeping so I could get to Hyde's before it opened.

Before bed, he'd given me the key and alarm info, which made me feel warm all over again. To show him how much it meant to me, I'd given him something else that made us both hot.

After packing up my supplies and laptop, I stopped at the grocery store for ingredients. Once I got everything settled at Hyde, I made a batch of scones and whipped up some sweet cream.

Huh. Who'd have thought a bigger mixer and oven would make things so much easier? It's almost like those are imperative to baking. Nah. Just like I'm sure the extra million feet, give or take, of counter space won't come in handy.

My first hiccup of the day came when I'd opened the bag of flour.

I knew my day was going to be hectic so I'd come up with a genius idea to save time by wearing my delivery outfit of a black wrap skirt with a purple camisole and black cardigan. Proving I was a daredevil that lived on the edge, I was also in strappy heels.

Since I had the tendency to wear half of my ingredients, this was not a smart idea. I was also forced to move at a snail's pace to prevent spills, which meant it wasn't even a time saving idea.

Note to self: Wear junk clothes and bring nice ones to change into. No one wants a cake delivered by someone covered in so much flour they look like they're reenacting Scarface.

After making a pot of coffee, I sat down with a cup and started planning my cakes for the day. I was roughly sketching some ideas when I sensed someone watching me.

"What're you doing here?" the voice accused, as if I'd broken in.

"Hi, Chloe. How're you?"

Mother's lessons have really been coming in handy. Who knew?

"Does Jake know you're here?"

No. I like to break into random businesses and leave baked goods as my calling card. I call myself the Reverse Santa.

That sounds like a weird sex position. With the sack...

Never mind.

Chloe stepped into the room and looked around. "It looks different in here."

"Yeah, I changed it," Jake rumbled as he entered the room. Walking to me, he bent and kissed my head. "Couldn't sleep once you left, sweets. You get up too fuckin' early."

Key, Kase, and Z all walked in, looking between the three of us.

"Hey, dudes," I greeted, keeping my voice light. "Scones are on the counter. There's sweet cream in the bowl next to them. Have at it."

"Hello? Am I invisible?" Chloe asked, looking one step away from stomping her feet and throwing a tantrum.

Which was why it probably wasn't a good idea for Kase to say, "Ah, a man could wish. As long as invisible also means silent."

"Like I care what *you* think. At least I'm not a—"

"Chloe, why're you here?" Jake interrupted.

"Well, I figured after our conversation last night, we should talk in person."

Last night?

I didn't miss the smug look Chloe shot in my direction. More importantly, I didn't miss that Jake wasn't denying anything.

Instead, he avoided my gaze.

When Jake and I went to dinner the night before, he'd left in the middle of the meal to take a call. By the time he got back, I'd already finished eating. He was distracted as he picked at his cold food. When I'd asked him if everything was okay, he told me that something had come up at the shop.

I wonder what else has been coming up…

"Let's go to my office, Chloe."

Chloe smiled triumphantly at me again before turning on her expensive heels to follow Jake.

"Don't let her get to you. She's far in Jake's past," Kase said.

I nodded, standing to refill my coffee. I wasn't going to jump to conclusions until I talked to Jake.

He better have one hell of a freakin' answer, though.

The men sat down at the table and began looking through my cake drawings. Within minutes there was a loud crash as glass shattered.

"Don't get too fuckin' comfortable!" Chloe shouted at me from across the room.

"I said get the fuck out," Jake bellowed from behind her.

As Chloe approached me, the men stood. I held out my hand for them to stay back.

"You think you're so fuckin' special, but you won't last. You may be here longer than most, but that isn't hard since no one is around more than a day."

"Chloe. Out."

Ignoring him, Chloe's hate spewed on. "Enjoy his big fuckin' dick. Enjoy his tongue. Take the fuckin' ride of your life. 'Cause you'll put *everything* into this, but good, hard fucks is all you're gonna get out of it. You'll bend over backwards, literally, just waiting for him to tell you his feelings. But he never will."

"Too late for that," Z said under his breath.

Just not quietly enough.

Chloe whipped her head around to look at Z, who decided a little too late to keep his mouth shut. "What did you just say?" Turning her head, she looked between Jake and me. I saw the flash of pain in her eyes before it was replaced by anger.

When she stepped closer to me, I held out my hand again as the men shifted. Even with my heels, she was still four inches taller. I wasn't afraid or intimidated, though. I'd been around enough mean girls to know what she was.

Sad.

"Enjoy the wild ride while you have it. You can't give him what he likes. And since he's been talking to me all week, he obviously knows that. Once he gets bored of you, he'll be back with me where he belongs, doing what he should be doing. No more being stupid. No more wasting his life with these losers and this fuckin' bullshit."

I punched her. Right in the face.

She crumbled to the ground with a pained cry.

Bending down, I got in her space as I vibrated with anger. "Don't you ever, and I mean *ever*, talk shit about *my* man or *my* boys," I bit out, my voice low and raspy. "You wanna lash out at me? Fine. But if you ever talk like that about them again, you'll regret it. And that's a promise."

I rose up as Chloe stood and then took a tiny step towards me. "Who—"

"You wanna keep going, feel free. I used my last shred of control not pulling you up so I could hit you again. Since *Jake* went through all the work of setting up this spot so he could see me more, I'm thinking it wouldn't be a good idea to get blood all over the place. But if you'd like to push this, I'll be happy to."

Stepping back, she turned to face Jake. "I hope you're happy with your choices, Jake. Not only is she too young for you, she's crazy. You can't seriously want to be with someone like this."

"Fuck yeah, I do," Jake rumbled. "I told you to leave. Multiple times. I should call Frederick and have him come remove you, includin' tellin' him why you're here in the first place. But if you're like this when you've got a man, I hate to think how you'd be when he dumped your ass. Now I'm more inclined to let my woman remove you herself."

"You're making a huge mistake, Jake." Chloe looked my way, her eyes going wide as I stepped towards her. Turning, she rushed from the room.

"I'm gonna make sure she leaves without making another fucking scene," Z said, following her.

Jake came over to me but I turned away.

Placing the scones and sweet cream on the table, I asked, "Anyone want coffee?"

"Sweets, come here."

"Now is *not* a good time, Jake."

"Piper, what she said about you—"

Putting my hands on my hips, I let out a humorless laugh. "I don't care about that, Jake. Biker bitches might do it well, but rich bitches do it better. Her running her mouth? That was nothing. That was white noise. I didn't care 'til she started talking shit about my boys. *No one* does that." There was a fierceness in my voice that I hoped they heard. "I've gotta get to work. I'm running behind schedule."

"Okay." Jake lowered his lips to mine.

For the first time since we became us, I let him without returning the kiss.

Like most everything else, Jake didn't miss it. Pulling back, he looked down at me. "I'm... I'll... See ya, babe," he muttered. His body was stiff as he turned and walked out the door.

Key grabbed a scone. "Thanks, Piper. These are my favorite."

"I know." I attempted a smile. "That's why they're here."

He gave me a wide smile before heading to the garage.

Best compliment ever.

"You okay, Pipe?" Kase asked when we were alone. His eyes searched my face.

"Yeah, I'm good. The adrenaline wearing off means my hand hurts now, though. How do people do that all the time?" I wiggled my fingers to try to ease the tightness at my knuckles.

As I pulled ingredients out, I began second guessing my decision to bring so many of my supplies.

First day working in the kitchen here and I already wish I had an exit strategy?

Awesome sign.

Coming up next to me, Kase fixed himself a cup of coffee. "Didn't know he was talking to her this week, did ya?"

"Nope."

"Jake's a dumbass sometimes but he's nuts about you. He wouldn't do anything with anyone else, especially not Chloe. You know that, right?"

"I wouldn't be here if I thought differently."

If I honestly thought Jake was cheating on me, I'd leave behind everything I had. Even if that meant going to my mother for a loan to replace it all, I wouldn't bother sticking around to pack a single box.

Still, he'd lied to me. So while I wasn't making a run for my car, I also wasn't happily skipping across the hall to fool around.

"Nah, didn't figure you would be." Kase headed for the door before pausing. "Hey Pipe?"

"Yeah?" I looked over at him when he didn't continue.

His dreads were pulled back and up for work. His work stained jeans were loose and hung way low from his hips. A white undershirt tank top accentuated his golden skin, colorful ink, and the strength in his body.

Rougher around the edges than most, he was blatantly male. There was a raw power about him that was impossible to miss.

But in that moment, I could almost forget he was the man he was. With his crystal blue eyes gleaming with feeling and vulnerability, I saw a kid, long ago lost.

A feeling of grief hit me as I looked at him, but I didn't know why.

Kase cleared his throat. "What you said about us? The way you said it? *Mahalo nui loa, me ke aloha.*"

"That's beautiful, but I don't know what it means, sweetie."

"Thank you very much, with love." His voice was low, the feeling in it so immense that it was physical, like the tightest hug.

Before I could respond, Kase's face lit with his usual playful smirk and his eyes glittered with humor. "And, Piper? You ever punch someone again, especially if you're wearing killer heels and a short skirt, make sure I'm there to watch. That was hot!"

"No problem. That being said, don't plan on it being anytime soon. My hand still hurts and it's going to make cake decorating more painful than the usual cramps."

He shook his head as he left the room. "A man can dream."

A few hours later, I loaded my van with cakes and one birthday pie, then left to make my deliveries. When I arrived at the first drop-off, I noticed my phone was blinking. I looked to see a missed call and an unread text, both from Jake.

Jake: Babe, where'd you go?

I was tempted to let him sit and wait, but games were never my thing.

Me: I'm making my deliveries. I'll be back in a couple of hours to clean up.

Jake: You didn't come say bye.

Me: You were working. I told you I wasn't gonna be constantly around. I gotta get this cake in.

As I made my deliveries, I thought about the morning. I was fine with Chloe talking shit about me. The sooner she got it all out, the sooner *she* was out. I could handle it because I didn't care about her or what she thought of me.

Obviously, her talking shit about the boys and Jake was a step too far.

I should've punched her again.

Felt freakin' awesome.

I trusted Jake, but he'd lied and I didn't know why. Maybe I was naive, but I just couldn't picture him messing with her.

When I returned to the shop, I went straight back to tidy up for the day. As I entered the room, I saw Jake sitting on the couch waiting for me.

He held out his hand. "Come here."

"I've gotta get cleaned up."

"Just talk to me."

"Like you talked to me yesterday?"

My stomach dropped as I watched him flinch.

That kills the illogical sliver of hope I had that maybe he hadn't lied.

"Fuck." Jake ran his palm across his jaw as he shook his head. "It wasn't how she made it seem."

"I know. I'm not an idiot."

"Then why're you mad?"

I threw my hands into the air. "You're hiding shit and flat-out lied last night." The implied 'duh' went unsaid.

"She called on Monday and said she wanted me back. I told her I'm not interested. Literally, I said two words and hung up. I ignored her followin' million fuckin' calls. Last night I'd had enough. We were havin' a good night, and she texted a few times. Not... Not appropriate texts. And then she called. I was done. I didn't say jack fuckin' shit that would encourage her. I told her I was with someone, and to stop with all the shit."

"Why didn't you just tell me?"

"I should've. I just worry you'll get sick of my bullshit. I didn't want to add any more to the pile."

"What bullshit?"

"How many hours I put in here. The stupid shit I say."

"I work just as much. And I put my foot in my mouth all the time, too."

"Sweets, c'mon. Come here."

"Fine, Mr. Bossy Pants." When I got within reach, Jake grabbed me and pulled me onto his lap.

"I can't lose you, Piper." His words were muffled as he buried his head in my hair and neck.

"You won't unless you lie. And that includes lies by omission. You've gotta trust me and know I'm not gonna leave at every bump. I don't brace anymore, Jake," I pointed out. "And neither should you."

"You're right."

"Of course I am. So what's the deal with Chloe? Why is she showing up all of a sudden?" I moved to straddle him, the side of my wrap skirt opening to show almost my whole thigh.

He sighed, looking and sounding annoyed. "I've got no fuckin' clue. We split a long time ago and I haven't seen her much since."

"Why'd you breakup?"

"There were a lot of reasons."

"Such as?"

"When Chloe and I got together, she was a different person. She seemed down with my life, the shop, all that. She just fit so even though we weren't serious, we also were. You know?"

I laughed. "Not even a little."

"It was more that she was there and I was there, and so we were together. Not that we were *together*. Now do you get me?"

"I think so."

"Anyway, she started changin'. Dressin' different and tryin' to be someone she wasn't. All of a sudden she wanted to go out all the time to upscale restaurants. Then she was buggin' me to take her to my folks' dinner parties. She's a biker bitch pretendin' to be a rich bitch," Jake said, using my words.

"The worst of both worlds."

"Fuckin' tell me about it. When business picked up, she started naggin' me about the time I spent here. But she'd turn around and want me to take her places or buy shit with the money I was workin' so hard for. When my dad would get on my case about going back to law school, she was right there with him. It didn't matter that the business was a success; my title wasn't good enough. I'd heard it enough from my folks, I didn't need to hear it from my supposed woman."

"I still don't get that."

"You wouldn't, 'cause you're not a bitch."

"Well, yeah, there's that. So what happened to finally end it?"

"She wasn't fun. It wasn't like the good times were good and the bad times were bad. There were no good times. She'd just been doin' what she had to do to try to hook me. It wasn't even like she'd been very stealth about it. I was just so caught up in gettin' shit up and runnin' here that I didn't notice her most of the time."

Ouch! Harsh.

Well-deserved, but still.

"Honestly, it was one of the reasons I kept you at a distance. I'd always wanted someone like you, but I'd never found anythin' even close. By the time I met you, I was jaded. I kept waitin' for you to change."

I opened my mouth, but he kept talking.

Shocking.

"You aren't gonna. I know that now. Still, I don't wanna give you any reason to leave."

I leaned against him to whisper in his ear. "You know I won't leave you. I'm yours." I ran the tip of my tongue over the edge of his ear, eliciting a groan as he raised his hips. "Alright, I've gotta get cleaning."

"No, you don't."

Holding my ass, Jake stood and carried me across the hall to his office.

After some hardcore making out while I straddled him on his chair, I stood up, much to Jake's dismay.

"Don't you have work to do?" I asked, breathlessly.

"Nope, that's why I started my own business. Let them handle it."

"Well, I've gotta get stuff done. Why don't you go help them out, Mr. Bossy Pants?"

"Not really in a position to go out there. Unless somethin' needs to be hammered." Jake grabbed the bulge in his jeans to emphasize the point.

And what a big point it is.

I focused on his hand there. I'd never... Well, there was a lot I'd never seen or done before Jake. But that?

That was hot.

Licking my suddenly dry lips, I looked back up to meet his eyes. "Well, I gotta get those dishes done." I started unbuttoning my cardigan, easing it down my arms and off. "Don't wanna get my sweater wet."

"Baby," Jake croaked before clearing his throat. "That skirt looks nice. Best to be safe and take it off too."

"You're so smart, Mr. Hyde." I untied the bow at the side of my skirt. Pulling it off carefully, I held it in front of me and blocked his view.

"You can't do the dishes holdin' that skirt, Miss Skye."

"Very true." I folded it, gradually exposing more skin.

Jake leaned back in his chair and put his boot clad feet on the desk. Watching me intently, he slid his zipper down and freed his hard cock. "Don't wanna get dirty water on your shirt either. Take it off."

"Yes, Mr. Hyde." Using my fingertips, I traced the lace trim at the top of my cami and grazed over my cleavage. Goosebumps broke out across my skin and my nipples tightened in my bra. Running my hands down my chest and torso, I crossed my arms and gripped the bottom hem. I pulled the shirt up over my head and folded it before putting it with my skirt.

Jake's fist tightened around his cock.

My plan was backfiring. *Badly*. I'd wanted to tease him, and yet I was so turned on my thighs were slick.

Better step it up a notch.

"Oh no. There's a problem, Mr. Hyde. This is my very favorite bra. See how good it looks on me?" I leaned over to show off my cleavage. "I would hate for it to get ruined."

"Then take it off, Miss Skye," Jake's deep voice rumbled, his hand working himself more.

I nodded, arching my back to unhook my bra. I crossed my arm over my chest and slid the strap off. Switching arms, I repeated the process. I pulled the bra down but kept my arm in place, blocking my naked breasts.

"Much better."

"How're you plannin' on gettin' work done usin' only one hand?"

I dropped my arm. "Is this better?"

"Fuck yeah."

I watched Jake's hand move faster, mesmerized at the wickedness of it.

"And what about your panties, Miss Skye?"

"Oh, I don't think we have to worry about those."

"Why not?"

My voice was thick with lust. "They're already soaked. Ruined, really."

"Take them off." Jake's voice was equally thick, his eyes heavy-lidded as he watched me.

I hooked my thumbs into the side of my panties and pulled them down, bending at the waist to remove them. "Better?"

"Come here, Miss Skye."

"I've gotta go across—"

"Now."

"Yes?" I asked, walking to the side of his desk.

Jake stayed lounged in his chair. "You have work to do."

"You're correct. I'll just head across the hall now."

"Try it." The sound of Jake's boots hitting the ground echoed in the room as he dropped his legs from the desk.

Taking his challenge, I began to slowly inch backwards. I wasn't going to open the door, but I figured touching it would make me the winner. I shifted to take off, but I was too late.

I burst out laughing when Jake easily reached out and hooked me around the waist. Lifting me, he sat my ass on the edge of his desk and stood between my spread legs.

"Not fair. Your arms and legs are longer," I fake pouted.

"Doesn't matter."

"Yes it does. Otherwise I'd have totally won."

"Sweets, you kept lookin' in the direction you were gonna go."

"Just part of my plan to throw you off." My breath hitched as Jake moved closer to cup my breasts, his thumbs skimming my nipples. The feel of his cock pressed against me stole any other teasing words I might have had. "Please," I whispered. Biting my lip to muffle my cry, I dropped my head to his chest as he roughly pushed in.

"For the rest of my life, Piper. You'll be mine for the rest of my fuckin' life. And I'll be addicted to this pussy 'til the day I die."

"Oh, God, Jake," I moaned, his words going straight to my heart and continuing lower. I pressed my lips to his chest, panting as he moved faster. My legs tightened and trembled as the delicious pressure built.

Before I could let go, a loud knock sounded at the door.

"Whoever it is, go the fuck away," Jake snarled, his movement slowing.

"Sorry, brother, but we need you out here," Kase yelled back.

I was so freakin' close. Now I'm gonna have blue balls.

Wait, what's the chick equivalent of blue balls? Hot pink vulva?

That sounds like all girl metal band. Or a bad car knockoff.

"No. Now fuck off."

"You mean so we can fuck on?" I whispered. I heard Jake's chuckle, but I felt it in some *very* good places.

"Fine, it's your business. Let it go to hell. Never mind about your loyal employees or anything," Kase said dramatically.

I giggled and moved my ass back to separate our bodies.

"Stay here," Jake ordered, kissing me roughly. He pulled his pants back up, adjusting himself with a groan. "Kase, get the fuck away from the door."

"Why? Is Piper naked in there? Pipe, you naked?"

"Yes. Gloriously. I'm thinking of becoming a nudist," I yelled back.

Jake scowled at me, shaking his head.

"I think that's a good idea. As tempted as I am to sneak a peek, I don't think my heart could take it. I'll be in the garage."

I laughed, which got me a deeper scowl from Jake.

"Don't encourage him."

"Can't help it that I'm adorable."

Jake's scowl lessened as he left the room muttering, "Don't I fuckin' know it."

Despite his bossiness, as soon as the door closed, I got dressed. Going to the break room, I made quick work of cleaning up. When I finished, I was surprised that Jake hadn't returned.

I walked out to the garage and found him talking with Kase and Z. They looked tense as they stood around a sweet Corvette.

Jake looked up and smiled when he saw me. "Sorry, babe."

"No biggie. I'm done for the day here, so I'm gonna take off."

"You and I have some work to finish."

"No can do, Mr. Bossy Pants. I've got errands to run. I'll meet you at home later." I lifted up to kiss his cheek.

"Sounds good, sweets." His eyes were soft as he brushed a kiss to my lips.

I put a little extra sway in my hips as I walked away. When I was almost to the door, I looked back over my shoulder and saw Jake's eyes on me. "By the way..."

"Yeah?"

"I hope you don't mind, but I couldn't use that thing that got ruined while we were working earlier." I saw his eyes drop to my ass. "I left them in your office."

"Piper, get back in there. Now!" He stepped towards me.

"Nope. See you at home," I called over my shoulder as I hurried out the door.

Jake wasn't kidding; Inappropriate Hard-on Time can totally screw with the schedule.

When I got home that night, I began working on the two frostings that I hadn't been able to make at Hyde's. I put in my earbuds, cranked my music, and went to work.

I turned around to grab something and jumped when I saw Jake leaning against the wall.

No big deal. I was just dancing around like a dingus and singing into my whisk. Not embarrassing at all.

Liar.

"I didn't realize you were..." I started, pulling my earbuds out only to realize I was yelling. "Home," I finished on a whisper.

"Just got here. Was enjoyin' the show."

"Oh, you mean things like this?" I grabbed a spoon with frosting on it and dipped my finger in it. Putting my finger in my mouth, I sucked it clean.

"Such a damn tease," Jake growled.

I laughed and turned back to pack up for the night. "Crap, I didn't realize how late it was."

"Ready for bed?"

I turned to Jake, laughing again at the tone of his voice. My laughter died when I caught sight of the bulge in his jeans. "Oh yeah."

I took care of my nighttime stuff and put on one of my sexier nighties with no panties. When I got to my room, I paused at the door and looked at Jake. Leaning back against my headboard, his arms were behind his head, the blanket pulled up to his waist. I knew from experience that he had nothing on underneath.

"You comin'?"

I plan on it.

"Just enjoying the view." I walked to my side of the bed.

"Tired?"

"Not exhausted. Why?"

"Just wanted to make sure before I did this." Flipping back the blanket and sheets, Jake leaned across the bed to grab my waist and yank me down to him. "You know how hard it was to get any fuckin' work done when all I kept doin' was picturin' you strippin'?"

I threw a leg over his lower abdomen to straddle him. "Try working with frosting. I kept thinking about where I wanted you to lick it off of me." Holding his cock, I positioned him and slid down until he filled me.

"Christ." Jake held me as he kept the rhythm slow. "Payback."

"No. Faster. Harder." I pushed down, but Jake's fingertips dug into my hips. I was ready to explode and he'd barely touched me.

Jake pulled my hips down and thrust up. I cried out, my release just out of reach. My pussy contracted, pulsing and needing more. Greedy for it.

He stilled. "Fuck, did I hurt you?"

"Good. So good. Baby, fuck me hard like that."

"Wild," he murmured, running his hands up my sides. He cupped my breasts, the pads of his thumbs tracing my nipples.

I arched my back, pushing my chest into his hands.

"More." My voice was a husky, demanding rasp.

"Grab the top of the headboard."

I straightened to follow his direction.

"Hold tight, yeah?"

I nodded, grinding against him, desperate.

"Perfect," he groaned.

Gripping my hips, he lifted his off the bed and drove into me. Rising and falling, I met him thrust for thrust as I came powerfully. Grunts, screams, moans, and growls filled the room.

"Fuck, baby, I can't hold out." Jake's pelvis lifted and his hands brought me down harder. Going faster, we kept a frantic pace, though our movements stayed synchronized.

Continuous.

Perfect.

Jake's hand cupped the back on my head and pulled me to him, my mouth crashing down on his. His kiss was savage as he came.

After catching my breath, I tried to fall to the side. Jake rolled with me so he was on top and still inside me. I wiggled my hips a little, enjoying the feeling.

"Christ, Piper. I just came so hard I thought I'd die, but I can't bring myself to pull out."

When he nuzzled into my neck, I wrapped my arms around him, wanting him to stay.

Wanting it forever.

Birthday Infatuation

"Tell me about your heart tattoo," Jake said at dinner Friday night.

It'd been less than a week since I'd started using the Hyde kitchen, and it was awesome. My work got done quicker, I saw Jake loads more, and we got to fool around during the day.

It totally kicked ass.

Which was why it was unfortunate that he'd pissed me off.

"I'm not talking to you."

"Why?"

"You know what you did," I huffed.

"It's your birthday dinner, we gotta celebrate."

"It's not even my birthday yet. I thought we were going out to dinner tomorrow?"

"We are." He smiled wide. "This is a pre-birthday dinner."

"So you lied to make people sing to me."

"All I did was mention it was your birthday, which it basically is. Don't control how the restaurant operates, Piper."

"They put a candle in my baked potato. That poor candle was probably looking forward to one day being in a delicious cake. Instead, it ended up in a spud."

"Sweets," Jake said through his laughter. Putting his forearms on the table, he leaned closer. "Tattoo?"

"What about it?"

"What's the deal?"

"Just a tattoo I liked."

"Liar."

I shrugged.

He was right, there was a lot more to my tattoo. I'd always wanted all of my ink to have meaning. Sometimes, though, the meaning conveyed more about me than I was comfortable sharing.

"It's interestin', a heart and an anarchy symbol intertwined. Why?"

Drop the walls, Piper.

Inhaling deeply, I avoided his eyes as I focused on cutting my steak. "Love's anarchy. There are no rules, no rhyme or reason. You can't control it. You can fight to keep it and lose. Or fight to keep it away and lose. Or win, depending. Love's chaos. It's mayhem."

Jake's lip quirked up.

"So, yup, that's it."

"When'd you get it?"

"On my eighteenth birthday."

"Most chicks get a butterfly or some Chinese symbol that they think means 'peace and love' but really means 'parkin' in the rear'. Why'd you pick that?"

"My mom grew up on the wrong side of town. Her parents weren't shining members of society and she suffered the consequences. When she was old enough to realize how that life was, she swore she'd have better. And eventually she did. But before that happened, she hooked up with my dad. Nine months later, I was born."

"Were they married?"

"Nope. He wanted to marry her, but she always turned him down. Eventually, he stopped even bringing it up. And when I was seven, he left her."

"He left?"

"Yeah. It was heartbreakingly romantic." At Jake's inquisitive and sexy as hell eyebrow raise, I elaborated. "She wanted more. Dad is fantastic. I can't wait for you to meet him when he comes up next month. But, as kickass as he is, he wasn't the image in her head. She loved him but not the way either of them deserved. Though she would've stayed, he told her he couldn't be selfish and let her settle."

"Is she happier now?"

"She's with Thomas. She loves him in her own way, which is pretty much the opposite of how she loved my dad. There's no worrying about the bills or people looking down on her. But there's no passion."

"What about your dad?"

"That's the funny thing. My dad's loaded. He lives out in California, shacked up with his longtime girlfriend, Natalie. He owns a bar that's insanely popular since he's a skilled chef. Even in a biker bar, his stuff is gourmet."

"So, if your mom would've waited..."

I shook my head. "I don't think it would have worked out the same way. Years ago, Dad took off on a cross-country bike trip. He stopped in a town in California that he said felt like home. So he moved and opened the bar. He wouldn't have taken the trip, made the move, or followed his dream if he and my mom were together."

"Him movin' must've sucked for you."

"They knew I'd have more stability here. It was hard, but it made the times I visited him better. I still saw him a ton. Once the bar was up and running, he flew out for *everything*. Graduation, prom, stuff like that. Even little things. Like when I did a few baking competitions, he'd come watch. They weren't any of the major ones, but he was always there, cheering me on like I was in the Olympics."

As I spoke, I saw an expression I couldn't figure out cross Jake's face. Before I could ask about it, he continued, stating, "So it worked out."

"Yeah. Mom and Dad might've lasted a while longer, but I think they still would've split eventually. And by then they may have missed out on Thomas and Nat. Timing can change your life like that."

"Don't I fuckin' know it."

"How so?"

Jake's gaze heated as he looked at me. "Wasn't supposed to work but had shit to do."

My brows lowered in confusion. "What?"

"Planned on just stayin' in the office but couldn't find some papers. Went out to the lobby and saw this woman. Fuckin' gorgeous. Fuckin' classy. Fuckin' *perfect*. If I'd stuck with the plan? Even an hour later, and my life would be completely different."

That he felt that and told me? I didn't just love it.

I freakin' *loved* it.

I closed my eyes and let the warmth seep in. Opening them, I reached across the table and grabbed his hand. My lips tipped up. "Glad something awesome came out of your crappy organization system."

"And thank fuck for that. Excited about tomorrow?"

"Eh. It's just a day. Birthdays have never really been a big thing for me."

"But tomorrow you'll be twenty-one. You gonna wanna be with me now that you won't need me to get you booze?"

"Are you gonna wanna be with me now that I'll be so old?" I shot back.

"Oh, good point." Jake made an exaggerated thoughtful face as he stroked his jaw.

I threw the rest of my dinner roll at him, laughing as he caught it easily and popped it into his mouth. "You know I'm crazy about you, right?"

"Makes me the luckiest man in the fuckin' world. Do you wanna do anythin' tonight?"

"Today was insanely long. I kinda just wanna chill. Are you cool with going home and watching a movie?"

"Let's go." Jake stood and dropped cash on the table before guiding me to his bike.

"Couch or bedroom?" Jake asked as he punched in the code for his security system.

"Bedroom."

"Okay. Pick a movie. I'm gonna grab a shower real quick, yeah?"

I started browsing through his collection, pulling some DVDs out to look at the descriptions on the backs. As I went to return one, I noticed a few other movies hidden behind the rest. I pulled out his small stash of porn and looked them over.

Good to know my man likes it wild but not too crazy. I like kink, but it would've seriously sucked to find a stash of leather unicorn fetish videos.

Or worse.

I felt my body heat up as I imagined watching one with Jake. Taking the one that looked best, plus a regular movie, I hurried into the bedroom.

Listening to the shower going, my stomach flipped with giddy nervousness as I got the DVD started.

Stripping down to my bra and panties, I stretched out on top of the covers. I lowered the volume of the movie so I could hear when the water turned off.

As I waited for Jake, I started watching the people who were *very* fond of each other.

"I wanna come home to this every night," Jake said from the doorway, startling me. "You look fuckin' hot."

Oops. Distracted much?

Already overheated, the look on his face as his gaze travelled across my body turned me into an inferno. "Thanks," I rasped.

Jake moved into the room. "Beer?"

Before I could answer, a loud, moaning scream came from the TV.

Jake's eyes went wide as he turned and saw what was on before snapping back to me.

"What? You told me to pick a movie."

"Yeah, I did. Just wasn't expectin' this." His eyes stayed on me as he approached the side of the bed. The towel around his waist did nothing to hide his reaction.

Getting up on my knees, I moved towards him and rubbed my palms over his chest. "You want me to put in the real DVD?"

"Hmm. Dunno. Lemme check, yeah?" Sliding his hand into my panties, his finger glided easily through my wetness.

"Oh God." My hands shot up to clutch his shoulders.

"Nah, I'd say we're good with this one." He pressed his thumb against my clit, pleasure shooting through me as my hips jerked up and my nails dug into his skin. "On your back, baby, but keep your ass on the edge of the bed and your legs hanging off it. Yeah?"

Releasing my grip on him, I laid down. I lifted my pelvis so he could pull my panties off.

"Pull your tits out. I wanna watch you play while I taste sweetness." Dropping to his knees on the floor, Jake grabbed my hips and pulled me closer to the edge. Putting my legs over his shoulders, his mouth covered me.

"Yes!" I cried out, tugging at my nipples.

Jake's growl of approval vibrated through me. His mouth worked me relentlessly, but still I wanted more.

Digging the heels of my feet into his back, I ground myself against him as I moaned through my orgasm.

I'd barely finished when Jake stood. "Flip over onto your knees."

When I rolled over, he held my hips and kept me at the side of the bed while he stayed standing.

I cried out, my head shooting back and my hair flying wildly, as he entered me forcefully.

"Sorry." Slowing down, his fingers dug into my ass with the effort.

"No. Harder. Now." I didn't just love him unrestrained, I craved it.

I needed it.

"Piper." Jake's voice was surprisingly soft and warm. "Love you."

"Love you, too. Now harder," I demanded, pushing back into him roughly.

"Yes," he said, thrusting so hard it took me off my knees. "Dear."

After sleeping in the next morning, I woke up to an empty bed and the smell of fresh coffee. I tried to enter the kitchen but was banished to the bedroom.

"Happy Birthday." Jake grinned as he brought me breakfast in bed.

"Pancakes?" I questioned, bouncing on the mattress with excitement.

"Maybe."

"My favorite!" I squealed, hopping up on my knees to hug him.

Jake chuckled, lifting the plate up before I knocked it over. "Are you talkin' to me or the pancakes?"

"The pancakes, of course."

"Smartass. I dunno. I don't like being jealous of food." He brought the plate closer to his chest. "Maybe I should eat them myself."

"You can't do that, it's my birthday."

"So?"

"So, hand them over!"

"Fine." Sighing dramatically, he handed me the plate with a napkin, fork, and knife before leaving the room. He returned a minute later with a mug of coffee and set it on the bedside table next to me.

Taking a bite of the buttery, fluffy pancake, the sweetness of the maple syrup hit my tongue. I closed my eyes. "Mmm, these are so good."

"Sweets, they're pancakes."

"Exactly. Cake that's acceptable to eat for breakfast. What's better than that?"

"Of course. What was I thinkin'?"

As I ate, we planned what time we needed to leave for dinner.

"Wanna finish this?" I held out the half eaten plate of pancakes.

"You sure?"

"Definitely. I'm gonna go shower."

"You missed a spot."

"I did?" I looked over my shoulder at Jake standing near the sink. "Is it here?" I used my shower loofa to rub my ass cheek. "Or maybe here?" I turned to the side and began rubbing my chest. "Oh, I bet I know. It's here, isn't it?" I spread my legs slightly and bent at the waist to scrub my foot.

Before I could stand back up, Jake was in the shower with me, his hand on my spine.

"Tease. You, Piper, are a damn tease."

"You're fully clothed! Get out of here!" I tried to straighten, but his hand on my back held firm.

"Not fully. No socks. Now stay bent over." His index and middle finger eased into my wetness while his thumb worked my clit.

I rocked my body against his hold to get more.

His zipper slid down before he pushed into me. "Can't resist you."

"Thank God for that," I moaned, as he continued not resisting me.

After his pleasant interruption, I finished up and got dressed.

When I went into the room, Jake was sitting on the bed with his back against the headboard and his legs stretched out in front of him. There was a present on his lap.

Biting my lip, I smiled at him. "I'd make a joke about the placement of that gift, baby, but the box is *way* too small."

Jake threw his head back and laughed as he moved the present onto the bed.

Watching him, hearing that laughter, *feeling* it, my heart felt like it was going to explode in the best possible way.

This man, my man, was so damn sexy. Gorgeous. Hell, even beautiful. His blond hair was down and slightly wavy, thanks to the impromptu shower. He was all angles and edges, including his personality, but he was soft for me.

Sweet.

Romantic.

Loving.

I ran across the room and jumped, landing with a bounce next to him on the bed. I threw my leg across his thighs to straddle him and weaved my hands into his hair. Pulling his lips to mine, I put everything I was feeling into the kiss.

"I love you, Jake," I whispered against his lips.

"Love you, too, Piper. So damn much," he whispered back. Leaning over, he snatched the present up. "Happy Birthday."

"Oh, Jake," I murmured while opening the light blue Tiffany's box. "It's..." I tried to take a calming breath, but it still shook. "Baby, it's perfect."

Inside the box was a beautiful charm watch. Dangling from the chained band was my birthstone, a coffee cup, a music note, a high heel, a cupcake, a car, a baseball, and a heart. Each charm was special to me. To us.

"I love it. Thank you."

"I know you don't wear jewelry often. So if you don't—"

"You're kidding, right? First of all, it's gorgeous. Second, I'd wear anything from you."

"Good to know. Next time I'll make sure it's somethin' wild and sexy."

When Jake went to get ready, I grabbed my bag and set up my laptop on the island in the kitchen. Opening and booting it up, I began sorting emails when I felt his lips behind my ear.

"What the fuck is that?" he snarled, standing up quickly.

"Prank emails. I just delete them."

Because my email address was on my website and social media, it wasn't unusual for me to get fake requests from assholes messing around. I'd even gotten the occasional dick picture or dirty message.

Lately, though, the frequency of junk messages had increased. They weren't always outright vulgar or harassing. They were more…

Skeevy.

Instead of generic messages, they'd become more complimentary of my appearance. Since there were a few pictures of me on my site, plus the ones that had been in the paper, it wasn't surprising that someone would know what I looked like.

It was still creepy as hell, though.

I always blocked the addresses, but it was easy for the pranksters to get new ones.

"That's far from a fuckin' prank, Piper. That shit is sick. Why haven't you said anythin'?"

"It happens all the time. It's probably some kids pretending they've got giant balls behind a computer screen."

"Piper, there are a lot of these."

"I know," I admitted, crinkling my nose. "I think maybe from all the publicity after the Tools for Teens event. Increased publicity has meant more orders coming in, but also more of this crap. It's nothing."

"It's somethin'. That shit is fucked up. You should've told me." With his clenched jaw and rigged body, Jake looked mad. But behind his anger was fear.

"Baby, my work email is public. I get offers for hot and horny local ladies, instant money transfers from Nigerian princes, and tips to make millions from the comfort of my own living room. I even get emails for penis enlargement, which would come in handy if I decided to look up those local ladies. These things happen and it's harmless. But I'll make sure I tell you now. And I'll be extra cautious, okay?"

"I'm gonna talk to my dad, see what he thinks."

"If it'll make you feel better."

"It's a start. I've gotta go to Hyde for a few hours. Wanna stay here or go to your place?"

"Mine." I wanted to finish up some work and then get ready for tonight with enough time that I wasn't rushing around.

"I'll drop you off on my way, yeah?"

After an intense goodbye kiss, I plopped down onto my couch with my laptop. Tucking my legs under me, I dealt with emails, stopping throughout to answer birthday calls and texts.

When my phone rang again, I picked it up without looking. "What's up?"

"Piper, is that any way to answer the phone?"

Gah. Caller ID was invented for a reason, dingus. Use it!

"Sorry, Mom. I wasn't expecting a call from you."

"Well, why in heaven wouldn't I call my daughter on her birthday?"

"I just meant I wasn't expecting it right now. How are you?"

"As fine as one can be when they're continually blown off by their only child."

"Sorry. I've been busy with school and the business."

"And your young man? Are you still seeing him?"

"Yes, Jake and I are still together. So, how's Thomas?"

"Piper Skye, don't try to change the subject. However, he is right here and wishes to speak to you."

"Happy Birthday, Piper," Thomas greeted me.

"Thank you, Thomas. How're you? Mother driving you crazy yet?"

"Yet? You mean *still*, correct?"

I laughed at the rare joke. "Yes, exactly."

"So, your mother told me you're involved with Jake Hyde."

"Yup."

"At your mother's request, I looked into him. His company is extremely successful. So much so that he could have multiple shops. Word is he chooses to stick with just one so he can be as hands-on as possible."

And he is very hands-on at work, indeed.

"Yes, he does great work," I said, trying not to think pervy thoughts.

Trying, but failing.

"He's known for his skill and work ethic. His mother is a well-respected attorney and his father is an ADA. Good choice, Piper."

It's a mother friggin' birthday miracle.

"Thanks, Thomas. Make sure you tell my mother that."

"Already done. Here she is."

"As you can imagine, I was very reassured to hear things checked out well. You'll still have to stop making excuses and bring him over."

"Yes, Mother."

"Did he get you anything special for your birthday?"

"A beautiful watch."

"A watch?" Obviously, the appeal of a watch was lost on my mother.

"From Tiffany."

"Oh. That is special then."

"Yeah. I have to go get ready. We're having dinner in a few hours."

"Enjoy your birthday. I love you."

"I love you, too. Goodbye."

As I hung up, I realized just how far behind I was. I cranked some music up and went to plug in my hot rollers.

While I waited for them to warm up, I crouched by the bed in my room and began pulling things out from underneath. Finding what I was looking for, I pushed everything else back and set up my surprise for Jake.

Well, mostly for me. After all, it's my birthday.

When I got back into the bathroom, my phone was lit up with a new message.

Jake: Did you start gettin' ready?

Me: Just did.

Jake: There's another present in the spare room closet.

Me: When did you put a present in there?

Jake: Couple days ago. I figured even if you looked, you wouldn't see it. That closet is worse than your wallet.

Me: Hey! Actually, you know what? I've got no come back. You're totally right.

Jake: I was hopin' to be home already, but things are taking longer than planned.

Me: That's okay, I can wait.

Maybe. Possibly.

Unless I go in there for something else. Then I might trip and have to grab the knob to stop my fall. That might accidentally open the closet door.

Oops.

Jake: Go look, yeah?

Woo hoo!

Walking into the room, I turned on the light and opened the closet door. "Oh, Jake," I whispered to myself.

In front of me was a gorgeous green dress with a bag from Ella's looped around the hanger.

I jumped when my phone started ringing. Checking the screen, I answered immediately. "Jake."

"Like it?"

"I love it, but the watch was enough. Actually, I was happy just waking up in your bed."

"I'd give you the fuckin' moon, Piper. Honest to God, lay the whole fuckin' world at your feet," Jake said, his voice low and gravelly. Before I could respond, someone called his name. "I gotta go. Love you."

"Love you, too."

After hanging up, I grabbed the dress and bag from the closet and brought them to my room. I peeked into the bag to see a pair of black pumps, a glitter clutch, and the world's tiniest thong.

Returning to my hot rollers, I put them in and started on my makeup. Because the dress was so bold, I used a neutral cream colored shimmer shadow, black liner, and dramatic mascara to do my eyes. I went light on the blush and skipped the lip gloss altogether.

When I got changed, I knew I'd made the right decision.

The soft, jersey dress was completely off my shoulders. Black lace detailing around the edges gave glimpses of more skin, but also made it a softer, more feminine look. The material was clingy, which explained the miniscule thong.

No matter how extensive my underwear collection was, I didn't have any that wouldn't leave visible panty lines.

I pulled a shoe out and set it on the bed carefully before picking up my phone to text Jake.

Me: These shoes are Jimmy Choo.

Jake: The purse thing is, too. I still have no clue what that means. Alicia picked them out. I just agreed they looked hot.

Me: Alicia?

Jake: Went into Ella's and she was fuckin' ecstatic to help me out. Mostly 'cause that means I'm still with you. She likes you, sweets.

Me: I like her, too. But you don't have to do this stuff.

Jake: I know I don't have to. I like it.

Me: How do I argue with that?

Jake: You don't. On my way in a few.

From the first time I saw his sexy, broad back in the shop, I'd been *way* into Jake. There'd been a pull to him that had nothing to do with his status or what he could give me.

Well, except for the orgasms I'd been sure he could supply. Thank the sex god himself I was right about that.

It wasn't what he was buying me that made me so happy.

Okay, they were Jimmy Choo's, so it wasn't *just* that.

It was him.

I set the phone aside and picked up the pumps again. After I put them on, I walked to my dresser and added my watch. As I latched it, I noticed the time and knew Jake would be here soon.

I quickly unraveled the cooled rollers from my hair and tossed them on my dresser. Bending over, I shook my head to loosen the curls.

"Fuck."

"You scared me. How was the shop?" When I got no response, I straightened and looked over at Jake.

I smiled when I saw his hair was down. Wearing dark jeans, a black fitted button down shirt with the sleeves rolled up, and gray converse, my man looked good.

He also looked tense.

"What's wrong?" I began walking towards him.

"Stop."

I did, my brows lowering in confusion. "What?"

"We have to go. Like *have* to."

"I know, I'm ready."

"If you get any closer before we're out of this house, we're not goin' anywhere."

"I wouldn't mind that." I smiled wickedly. "In fact, why don't we order in and I'll let you eat off of me?"

"Tease. You're a cock tease. Out."

"Fine, Mr. Bossy Pants."

Turning and walking away, Jake didn't stop until he was on my porch.

I locked up and followed him down to his car.

Jake shifted the Camaro into reverse and turned to back out of the driveway when his phone started ringing. "Yeah? Uh huh. No, it's cool. See ya." Jake hung up and turned to me. "We gotta stop back at Hyde for a minute."

"Everything okay?"

Though his organization and filing was better, they were slammed with customers. With the amount of work they were doing, it was inevitable that things would fall between the cracks.

"Yeah, I've gotta log into the computer system to check something for Kase. How was your day?" Putting his hand on my leg, his thumb absently caressed my inner thigh, which made me mindless.

"Huh?"

"Your day?"

"Oh. Good. I got a lot more done than I thought I would."

"Anymore emails?"

"Nope. I told you it doesn't happen much."

"Once is more than enough," Jake grumbled.

"If I thought it was something to be concerned about, I'd tell you."

"I'm still gonna talk to my dad."

"I figured as much, Mr. Bossy Pants."

A short while later, Jake pulled into the front parking lot of Hyde and cut the engine. Coming around, he offered his hand and helped me out.

"Hold up." Curving his hand around the side of my neck, his thumb stroked my jaw and tilted my face up. "You look fuckin' gorgeous."

I pushed myself closer to him. "Thanks for the outfit."

"Love you, Piper."

"Love you, too. By the way, we have to stay at my place tonight."

"Why?"

"So I can thank you properly."

"Christ. How're you plannin' on doin' that?"

"It's a surprise. Ready?" I rubbed my fingertips across his stubble.

"No. I wanna go back to your place."

"Hey, I offered to stay home and let you eat off me."

"I'd rather eat you off," he growled. "Fuck." His curse echoed around us as he pulled away and unlocked the entrance. The lobby was dark with only a glow coming from the garage. "I've gotta see if Kase is still back there." He put his arm around me as we walked.

Maybe this will be fast and I can still convince him to just take me home. At the very least, maybe we'll have time for a desk quickie.

"Surprise!" I heard several voices scream, scaring me as they pulled me from my incredibly inappropriate thoughts. I burst out laughing and my heart pounded as I looked around to see a lot of my favorite people.

With everything hidden away and decorations in their place, it barely looked like a garage. The work benches were overflowing with food and a thrown together, though very well-stocked, bar was in the corner.

"Happy Birthday, sweets," Jake whispered, squeezing me to him.

"Can I get a hug from the birthday girl?" a voice behind me asked.

"Daddy?" I whipped around to see my dad and Nat.

"Happy Birthday, Lil' Rock," Dad said, calling me by the nickname some bikers had given me when I was younger.

I threw myself at him and hugged him. His arms wrapped around me just as tight.

I pulled away and looked at Jake. "Jake, this is my dad, Floyd, and his girlfriend, Natalie. Dad and Nat, this is my boyfriend, Jake." Without giving them the chance to say anything, I turned back to my dad. "What're you doing here? I thought you weren't coming until next month."

"When I got a call from Jake, how could I resist the chance to see my girl?"

"So I guess those introductions weren't needed," I muttered up at Jake.

He winked at me before looking to the side and giving someone I couldn't see a chin lift.

"Happy Birthday, Piper!" Nat said, her valley girl lilt more pronounced in her excitement. She grabbed me in a hug. "You look gorgeous. The wild hair is totally rocking."

"I'm so happy to see you!" I squealed, bouncing as I hugged her. "You look fabulous, as always."

At five foot eight, with gleaming, chocolate brown hair and hazel eyes, Nat was gorgeous. Dad introduced her to me when I was twelve and I'd been sure she was a model or actress. Almost ten years later, she still looked like she could be.

He was my dad and all, but I knew he was good-looking. Even if I hadn't noticed, enough of my friends had had the hots for him to clue me in. He was six feet tall and still fit from being on the go at work all day. There was a lot of gray growing into his black hair, but it worked.

From the stories I'd heard, Nat had come into Dad's restaurant on a date. Dad had taken one look at her before literally jumping over the bar to talk to her. Fifteen minutes later, the other guy was out the door and Nat's ass was planted on a bar stool. That was the power of my dad's looks and charm. A week after that, Dad moved Nat in with him. And now, almost a decade later, they were still going strong.

"And, oh my God, those shoes!" Nat nudged my leg so I'd stick my foot out.

I did, twisting it slightly so she could see the pumps better. "They're Jimmy Choos. Jake's surprise. Well, one of many, apparently. But he has no clue what a big deal that is."

"It's *killer*. And, oh my goodness, look at that watch!"

"I get the feeling now's a good time to go grab a beer. They can talk for hours. You with?" my Dad asked Jake.

"Yeah. Beer or mixed drink, sweets?"

"Beer, please."

"Natalie?"

"Beer sounds good, thank you."

Jake nodded before walking away with my Dad.

"How're—" I started.

"Okay, they're gone. You were way holding out on me, girly."

"I told you about Jake."

"Yeah, making it seem like he was no big deal. That conversation about him should've lasted like three times as long."

I looked over and caught Jake's eyes on me. I smiled at him before turning back to Natalie. "Probably longer than that."

"How serious are things?"

"Very."

"Since he hasn't looked away from you yet, I was guessing that."

I looked over, wiggling my fingers in a wave and watched as his lips tipped up.

"You owe me the full talk. But here comes your man."

Jake handed us our drinks.

"I'm gonna go see what your dad is up to," Nat said with a smile. After giving my hand an affectionate squeeze, she headed towards the bar.

Jake slid his arm around me. "Surprised?"

"That's the understatement of the century."

"Hungry?"

"Not right now. I wanna see everyone."

The next hour and a half passed in a blur of birthday hugs, wishes, drinks, and shots.

While I'd never been big on my birthday or surprises, Jake had worked miracles. He was thorough and everyone I'd want invited was there. My boys, Ray and Edge, plus Rhys, Harlow, Gia, Melanie, Lily, and Marcy. Even Gage and Jet showed up, though they couldn't stay long.

"Where'd you meet these people?" Harlow asked as she pulled me aside. Since meeting officially at lunch, we'd become fast friends. "Everyone is flippin' beautiful. Even your dad is a total D.I.L.F. Dad I'd like to—"

I covered my ears. "Whoa, whoa, whoa. Don't go there. I don't wanna hear it. La, la, la!" I yelled over her.

Ick!

She pulled my hands away. "What? I was just gonna say he was a dad I'd like to be friends with because he seems like a cool guy. Sheesh, perv!" she said as we erupted into giggles. "Seriously though, I feel like I crashed a flippin' Hollywood party. Oh wait. Some of the X-ers are here. So, yeah, total Hollywood party!"

"Hey, my life was boring a few months ago. You know me, half-robot and all," I teased.

"I need my own badass. Is Gage available? No, Jet. No, who's the dude with the dreads? He gave me a chin lift earlier, which I took to mean he was declaring his undying love and inviting me to spend years getting lost in his eyes. Goodness, he's gorgeous!"

"That's Kase. I'll introduce you."

"Maybe later. Right now I'm thirsty, and wow, talk about coincidence; Gage and Jet are over there. I'll just fangirl squeal in my head." She lowered her voice into her version of a whisper. "If I pass out, promise to make one of them give me mouth-to-mouth."

"I promise," I vowed, trying to keep a straight face.

The night progressed with everyone talking, laughing, and drinking together like they'd all been friends for years. Nat and Harlow bonded over fashion and talked at speeds that only they seemed able to understand. My dad, my man, and my boys got into an in depth discussion about cars and bikes.

The only dark cloud in my birthday brightness was Rhys' date.

At first I thought she was keeping to herself because she was shy. After trying to talk to her, though, it became obvious she was just a bitch.

A big one.

I liked Rhys a lot. We were still close and he was genuinely happy for Jake and me because that was the kind of guy he was.

I didn't have the details, but I knew there was something dark he'd been through. The longer I'd been around him, the more I saw the shadows that lurked in his blue eyes and the pain he hid behind a dimpled smile.

He definitely deserved better.

"Happy birthday, darlin'," he said with a hug.

"Thanks. How're things going?" I glanced meaningfully towards... whatever her name was. Something fussy and she'd spelled it out. I was honestly expecting a Batman symbol to be in the middle of it.

"She pissed Damon and Tito off right before we were leaving. Went to grab my coat from my office, was gone all of two minutes. She said something, I have no fuckin' clue what, but it pissed them right the fuck off."

"To upset them it'd have to have been awful."

Damon was six foot five, two hundred and fifty pounds of dark chocolate muscle. He was also one of the sweetest people I'd ever met. His boyfriend, Tito, was a DJ that worked at both Rye and Voodoo.

Damon grew up in a rough area. He'd known he was gay his whole life and had a rough go of it. As in, he barely made it to adulthood.

Tito hid the fact he was gay and ended up hating himself and those around him. He started injecting, smoking, popping, and chugging anything he could to get through the day. His addiction was so bad he'd started selling himself to anyone, including men. In a moment of lucidity, he realized he was doing the very thing he'd been afraid to do. Only now, he was doing it in order to almost kill himself with drugs. He got himself clean and eventually hooked up with Damon.

After all they'd been through, they were both thick-skinned. No one who made it through all of that would bother to sweat the small stuff.

"Yeah. As payback, Damon made sure to tell her that I had feelings for you. Deep ones. She started bitching in the car right away, demanding we skip your party. Like I take orders." He shook his head slightly, an amused smile pulling at his lips.

"What'd you say?"

"I offered to drop her home. Volunteered to get her a taxi. I may have even said that one of the other guys might be willing to give her a ride, in whatever way she might want one. And yet she's still here. Glaring. Yeah, 'cause that's gonna stop me from having fun."

"Did you tell her your feelings aren't like that?"

"Nope. As soon as Jake pulled his head out of his ass, it was clear he's the one for you. He's like a brother to me, so I was fuckin' thrilled he found a good woman to give him what he needs. Never have I heard him laugh so much, or seen him smile so easy. Because of that, my feelings for you might not be romantic, but they're still to the bone deep, darlin'."

"Oh, Rhys," I whispered, hugging him as I tried not to cry.

Hmm. Harlow's single. Oh, so is Melanie. No, wait, maybe Lily?

"I better let you go before Jake throws a beer bottle at me. He might've won, but he still doesn't look too happy."

I pulled away and laughed up at him. "So you know, there's a blond over there—"

"Lily?"

"Yeah."

"Not happening, darlin'."

"I think you two would have a ton in common."

"We do. Which is why it's not happening. Anyway, your dad said he doesn't have your Ace Frehley picture, which is disappointing. He does, however, have one of you dressed as Freddie Mercury."

"Oh God, I forgot about that. I was like eight or nine. That was a fun Halloween."

"I'm gonna go see if I can get him to show it to me." Rhys headed towards the bar, lifting his chin at Z as they passed each other.

"Happy birthday, Doll Face." Z dipped to hug me and kiss my cheek.

"Thanks. Having fun?"

"Yeah. Watching Rhys' date has been entertaining as fuck. Well, until she came over and hit on me."

I burst out laughing. "You've gotta be kidding! That's hilarious."

"Yeah, it was a barrel of laughs. I've gotta head out soon. Enjoy your birthday, Doll Face."

"Thanks for coming." I went up on my toes to kiss his cheek.

"Anythin' for you."

"Sorry, brother, gotta steal my woman," Jake said from behind me as he grabbed my hand.

"What else is new?" Z joked.

Still holding hands, Jake and I walked over to Ray.

"Hey, hot stuff," she said, smiling huge at me.

"Yo. Having a good night?"

"Yup, and the best is yet to come."

"What?"

Instead of answering, Ray jerked her head towards Jake.

"I still have one more present for you." Jake's hands shook slightly as he began unbuttoning his shirt.

"Uh, baby, I'm *totally* liking where this is going. But not in front of Ray."

"Oh no, he promised I could watch," Ray said.

"Kinky." I wiggled my eyebrows at her. "At least let me do some stretches first so I can bust out my best moves."

Jake's shirt gaped open to reveal a bandage on his chest, sobering me instantly.

"What happened?"

"Lift it off," he whispered.

Moving in front of him, I carefully peeled it away.

"Oh my God, that's totally badass."

Under the gauze and tape was a fresh tattoo. Similar in style to the one on his arm, it looked like the skin on his chest was tearing away to reveal a mechanical heart.

"Check out the center gear."

"Oh, Jacoby," I murmured, my eyes filling with tears.

In the middle of the tattoo was a gear that connected the other mechanisms. Interspersed with the regular square ones, were five block letters made to look like gear teeth.

"You've got my name on you."

Cupping my neck, Jake's thumb pushed my jaw up, though my eyes stayed locked where they are. "Sweets, look at me."

I dragged my gaze up to meet his. "Why?"

"It's only you."

I carefully put my hand on his chest to the side of the ink and felt his heart pounding.

"I want your name on me."

His brows lifted with surprise. "What?"

"Ray, I want his name," I declared over my shoulder.

"Already set aside a block of time on Monday afternoon," Ray said, her voice thick. "I'm gonna go to the bar, knock back some shots, and pretend I'm not crying like a girl."

"You don't have to—" Jake started.

"I want to."

"Think it over, yeah?"

"Yeah," I agreed, though I didn't need to.

It was crazy, reckless, and some people might think it was idiotic. It was a risk to ink something that might only be temporary on your body permanently.

Good thing I know risks with Jake are always worth taking.

“What’d you wish for?” Jake’s voice rumbled in my ear after I’d blown out the candles.

“I can’t tell you, that’s against the rules.”

“The rules, huh?”

“Yeah. If I tell you, my wish won’t come true.”

“You’re wasting your breath,” Dad said to Jake. “Every year I’d try to get her to tell me, but she’d keep it to herself like it was a national secret.”

“It’s like the birthday *law*. Everyone knows that. Are you and Nat having fun?”

“Yeah, but we’re gonna head to the hotel and let you young folks enjoy the night.”

“I’m pretty sure you could out party anyone here.”

He chuckled. “Probably, but we’re still gonna go. Walk me out?” I nodded as my dad turned to Jake. “Good to see you, Jake.”

“You, too, Floyd.”

“Keep an eye out for Nat? She went back to use the bathroom.”

“Yeah.” Jake walked towards the doorway to the office.

“Guess I don’t have to ask if you’re happy,” Dad said when we got outside.

“Nope.”

“Don’t have to ask if he’s treating you right either. You’re at your own party, surrounded by friends, and he still watched to make sure you were having a good time. Can’t say I see that often.”

“That’s Jake.”

“I find myself wondering, though, are you in this as deep as he is?”

“I love him, Daddy.”

“It’s easy to see that. But there are levels to that. Your mom? Broke my heart. I thought she was it. Prissy.” A smile pulled at his lips. It wasn’t sad, just reminiscent. “Fuck, even back then she’d walk around, looking down her nose at everyone. I took one look at her and knew I wanted to spend a lifetime bringing chaos to that order. I was happy putting in the effort to break down those walls she'd built around herself. But she was determined to keep that distance, and I couldn't get through."

If I'd forced that distance with Jake and kept those walls up...

Holy shit, I'd almost turned into my mother.

"She loved me, but it was on a different level," Dad continued, interrupting my panicked relief that I wasn't as stubborn as my mom. "How I love Nat? Your mom broke my heart, but Nat would *shatter* it."

"Nat wouldn't leave."

"Thank God. What I'm saying, Piper, is there's nothing wrong with having fun. So if that's all you're doing, make sure you're both on the same page. Now. 'Cause it's clear you love him. But it's crystal fuckin' clear you're it for him."

"It's only him."

"Yeah, that's what I figured. You've worked hard and built a good life with good people. I'm proud of you, sweetheart."

"Thank you, Daddy."

When I heard the door open and close, I turned to see Jake and Nat heading our way.

"Brrr. It's cold." Nat rubbed her arms and bounced like it was negative digits and not the breezy sixty degrees that it was.

"Told you to grab a coat. Not in California, Valley Girl."

"If I brought my own then I'd have no reason to steal yours. Which would mean you wouldn't get that look I love when you see me in your coat."

Aww. And ick. But totally aww.

"Thanks for coming out early," I said before they continued sweetly skeeving me out.

"I'm so glad we could." Nat pulled me close for a hug. "Go enjoy your night. Get wild."

"I plan on it. Love you, guys."

"Love you, girly."

"Happy birthday, sweetheart," my dad said, hugging me tight. "Best day of my life, twenty-one years ago. Always been the best kid a dad could ask for."

"Daddy." My voice trembled.

"No crying on your birthday. We'll see you tomorrow."

I gave Dad and Nat a tear-filled, wobbly smile. Nat returned it with one of her own before they walked towards the cab.

"Ready for another drink, birthday girl?" Jake's deep voice rumbled in my ear as he wrapped his arms around my waist while I waved.

"Oh yeah."

"Why don't we go to my place?" Jake asked, carrying me to the Camaro because my feet hurt.

"The surprise is at mine."

"Maybe it would be better for tomorrow, yeah?"

"Why?"

"Sweets, you're drunk."

"Are you?"

"No. I only had one beer with your dad." Jake lowered me to my feet and I got into the car.

I slid closer to him when he got in on his side. "Then we're good. Trust me, baby. Me drunk is good. Especially for you."

"Oh, really?" He smiled as he pulled me into his lap. "How so?"

"Well, I'm fun drunk. Happy drunk. Most importantly, *horny* drunk. Of course that's not saying much since I'm always horny."

"Always?" Jake's voice was deep, his fingers sliding under my skirt.

I caught his hand, halting its journey. "Nope, you have to be patient." Pressing a kiss to the underside of his jaw, I moved over to the passenger's seat. "Now take me home, Jeeves."

"Yes, dear."

Revelations

"Harder. Faster."

"Where's the fun in that?"

"You're in so much trouble when we're done, Mr. Bossy Pants."

Jake smirked. "Doubt it since I'm pretty sure you're stayin' tied to the bed."

"God, baby. Please?"

"What do you want?"

"You."

"What about me? You want me to go slower?" he teased, barely inching in and out.

I hadn't thought it was possible to go slower. "No, stop!"

"You want me to stop?" Shrugging, he pulled out and sat back. "If you say so."

"No, no, no. I meant stop going slow. Go fast." I tried, and failed, to move.

"And end this? I'm thinkin' I wanna taste some sweetness."

"There are cupcakes on the counter," I muttered flippantly.

"Good idea."

"I was joking!" I pleaded with Jake's retreating back as he left the room.

Me and my big freakin' mouth.

I'd read books with bondage and had always been intrigued. After our conversation in the limo, I'd ordered soft cuffs online and had been working up the courage to surprise Jake with them.

I hadn't planned on him leaving in the middle for a bite to eat. Hell, I hadn't even thought he'd be this good at torturing me.

But that's what it was.

Body tingling, blood burning, every nerve ending in my body heightened, torture.

"Get back here and fuck me!" I yelled, pulling against the restraints.

"Why, Piper, what will the neighbors think?" Jake leaned in the doorway, casually peeling a cupcake wrapper as though I wasn't on the verge of spontaneous combustion.

"I don't care. Throw that out and get over here."

"Throw out somethin' you made? I don't think that's possible. They're near perfect."

"Yes, throw… Wait, *'near* perfect'?"

"See? Imagine your outrage if I tossed it out."

"Fine, okay, whatever," I conceded. "Now, what do you mean?"

"Oh, I just thought of some ways to improve this one."

"Like what?" I glared at him as he came back to the bed.

"Like all this." Jake used a finger to scoop a little of the whipped cream frosting. Dabbing it on the spot behind my ear, he licked it off. "Maybe it'd taste better here." Scraping up more, he rubbed his frosted finger on my hard nipple. He leaned down and took it in his mouth, sucking hard.

"You're right," I panted. "This is better."

"Still not perfect." He positioned himself between my legs.

My head fell back to the bed with a moan as the coldness of the frosting hit my overheated body.

Jake lowered his head to lap up the sweet, sticky topping. His thick finger slid into me, stroking slowly. When my hips rose from the bed, he put a muscled arm across my pelvis and pinned me in place.

"I need you," I pleaded.

Jake groaned, his grip loosening before he regained control.

Bingo.

"Please, baby. You always make me feel so good."

"Piper," he growled a warning, even as his finger inside me picked up speed, rubbing deliciously.

"What? I was just telling you I love what you do to me." I whimpered when he used more force. "It must be 'cause I'm yours."

"Fuck." Jake's body covered mine. Cupping my ass in one hand to lift my hips, he slammed into me. His speed and force increased and the head of his cock hit just where I needed it.

When the tension he built in me broke, I pressed my mouth against his shoulder to muffle my moans.

"God, I fuckin' love you."

"Love you forever." Running my tongue up, I tasted sweat and Jake. I nipped at the strong, thick tendon of his shoulder.

Jake groaned deep, burying his face in my neck and coming.

Unlatching my arms and legs, he rubbed my limbs as we caught our breath. Starting at my ankle, he slowly massaged up to the top of my thigh before switching legs. Shifting to my wrists, the coarse hair on his forearms was rough against my nipples.

Closing my eyes, I let myself feel.

I was undecided about whether I should fall asleep or jump him. I wasn't even sure if he knew what he was doing to me until I opened my eyes and saw his hard cock jump, straining for me.

Reaching up, I sank my fingers into Jake's hair and pulled his mouth down to mine. The tip of my tongue traced the seam of his lips before pushing in. Twirling, stroking, teasing, my tongue moved with his as I let the heat build. The slow burn turned into a blaze and my hips lifted as they sought his.

Sliding in, Jake's hand held my hip to the bed while his other arm stayed straight to support him. "Forever. Right, Piper?"

I nodded my answer.

"Say it."

"Forever," I moaned.

"Marry me." Jake's thrusts stopped as his eyes went wide.

I returned his shocked look. "What did you just say?"

"Marry me. I have a ring at the condo. I can go get it, but I kinda wanna finish first." He pushed his hips as if I could forget he was in me.

"Are you serious?"

"About wantin' to finish? Fuck yeah."

"No, about the other thing."

"You mean the you marryin' me thing?"

"Uh, yeah, that thing." My heart felt like it was going to pound out of my chest.

It's official. I'm dying. Death by incredible, unbelievable, extreme happiness.

And here I thought it'd be the sex that ended me.

His fingers at my hip began to tremble slightly. "I wasn't plannin' to ask you tonight, but—"

"Yes. Yes, definitely."

Jake closed his eyes before burying his face in my neck. "I love you, Piper."

He rocked his hips as our mouths and hands moved in frenzied abandonment. Our need to touch and taste as much as possible was overpowering.

"You'll have my ring, my name. You want that?"

"More than anything." Digging my nails into his shoulders, I leaned up to nip his jaw as my orgasm ripped through me.

"Never lettin' that sweetness go. Never lettin' you go," he groaned as he came.

When Jake collapsed on me, I wrapped my arms around him. Eventually, he slid off of me and padded barefoot into the bathroom.

Pulling the sheet up, I smiled huge as I thought of everything and nothing at all.

When he returned wearing track shorts, a t-shirt, and his converse, I sat up. "Where're you going?"

God, my boyfriend is beautiful.

No, wait. My fiancé.

Don't squeal. Don't squeal.

Okay, totally squeal. Just try to disguise it as a cough or something.

"I'm gonna go get your ring."

"I can wait 'til tomorrow."

Jake put his hands in his pockets and shook his head. "You might be able to, but I sure as fuck can't. I've waited long enough."

I threw the sheet off and hopped out of bed. "I'll come with and we'll just crash there."

"Thought you wanted to sleep here?"

"We did what I wanted to do." I quickly dressed in a pair of yoga pants and a slouchy, off the shoulder t-shirt, going commando and braless.

Reaching into my closet, Jake pulled a suitcase from my set and tossed it on the bed. "Grab some clothes for the rest of the weekend, yeah?"

"No problemo, Mr. Bossy Pants."

"Where do you wanna live?" I heard, and felt, Jake ask.

On his back in his bed, I was half on my side and half sprawled over him. My head rested on his shoulder while my leg was bent over his hips. One of his hands sifted my hair through his fingers.

"What do you mean?" I tried to sit up but his grip tightened and kept me tucked close.

"Do you wanna live here or your place?"

"I really hadn't thought about that." The reality of the changes that were coming made my stomach flip. I was excited. Thrilled out of my freakin' mind. But I was nervous, too.

Jake chuckled. "Of course you hadn't."

"What's so funny?" I again attempted, and failed, to push up.

"Most women's minds go wild plannin' every detail of this kinda stuff from the first date."

I opened my mouth to argue when he talked over me.

"I know, you're not most women."

Seeing as he made my point for me, I closed my mouth but did it rolling my eyes.

"Don't gotta decide tonight, but I'd like to get into the same place with you soon, yeah? Packin' a bag to go back and forth got old long ago. Don't care if it's here, your house, or a new place as long as I come home to you every night."

"A new place?"

"Yeah. That somethin' you might like?"

It was scary as hell, but the good kind. "Yeah. Someplace that wasn't mine then ours, or yours then ours. It will just be ours."

"I like that. Get some sleep, yeah?"

"Yeah."

Within a few minutes, Jake's breathing evened out. Unable to sleep, I opened my eyes to see my new engagement ring sparkle in the moonlight streaming through the window.

I didn't know much about jewelry, but I knew it was exceptional. The unique, platinum band was elaborately intertwined and dotted with sparkling diamonds. In the center was a good-sized, round diamond. It was gorgeous and different.

It was perfect.

"I'm gonna be Mrs. Jacoby Hyde," I whispered to myself as happy tears pooled in my eyes.

"Fuck yeah, you are," Jake said, startling me with his gruff response. After shifting me to straddle him, he leaned up and cupped the back of my head. His mouth took mine savagely, leaving me panting when he sank back into his pillow. Using his hold on me, he tucked my forehead into his neck. "I love you, Piper."

"Love you, too." I kissed his jaw, feeling the stubble on my sensitive, swollen lips.

We lay in comfortable silence for a while until Jake broke it, bizarrely saying, "I'm good at my job."

"Yeah," I agreed. "Though I don't know why you're stating the obvious."

"The kinda work I do is labor intensive and intricate, which means I can charge a shitload. Which I do."

"Okay..."

"Your place? It's a home. This is a crash pad. I picked it 'cause it's close to work and was available. That's it. Barely fuckin' looked at it before I signed the lease. That was seven years ago. Never bothered wastin' time doin' shit with it 'cause it was never gonna be a home."

"Really?" I'd noticed the first time he brought me here that there was nothing personal. I'd wondered if maybe he'd recently moved in. I couldn't imagine living in such a sparse place for *seven* years.

"I went out with the guys. Worked on my car and bike. Normally that'd be a seriously fuckin' expensive habit, but since I get the parts for cost and do the labor myself, it's not.

I sat up and looked down at him. "I'm sorry, baby. I'm not following."

"I got more fuckin' money than I know what to do with, but I still worked seven days a week. I had the kinda fun that meant I spent each night alone in a fuckin' crash pad. I was livin', but I wasn't *alive*. I wasn't breathin'. I was fuckin' color-blind, tastin' nothin' but sour and bitter." Even in the dim moonlight, I could see the intensity in his eyes. "You brought me sweetness. Brought me color and brightness. You've got me breathin' deep and doin' it easy. Lovin' life. Not just enjoyin' it. Fuckin' *lovin'* it."

"Jacoby." Tears stung my eyes as I pushed his hair away from his face.

Grabbing my wrist, he pulled my hand to his mouth and kissed my palm. "I'm gonna spend the rest of my life takin' you places. Buyin' you shit. You tell me I don't have to but you're wrong. I *need* to give it to you. 'Cause I've had nothin' but fuckin' gray. Nothin' but a nasty taste in my mouth. Now the rest of my life will be nothin' but bright and sweet. I could give you the fuckin' moon and still owe you."

"Jake, you give me just as much."

"Thirty-four fuckin' years of that shit, Piper. So I'm gonna keep buyin' you sexy as fuck dresses and fuck-me heels. Bracelets that you smile while lookin' at. A home for us. Yeah?"

"As long as you know you're the only thing I need. Well, and the home with you. But I'll help with buying—"

"Don't finish that sentence."

Unable to work up the fight, I sighed. "We'll talk about it later."

"Never," he muttered. "Long day tomorrow. Get some sleep, yeah?"

"Yeah." I tried to fall to the side, but Jake's hold on me tightened.

"No. Just stay like this a little longer, yeah?"

"Just for a few minutes, then I need to get comfy." I closed my eyes, enjoying his hands rubbing my back and playing with my hair.

Another minute or so.

Five, tops.

I woke up the following morning, still sprawled on top of Jake, and said a prayer to the sleep gods that I hadn't been drooling or snoring.

After a quick shower, I began digging through my bag to find clothes. Realizing I didn't know what to wear because I didn't know what we were doing, I called out to Jake to ask.

"Nothin' fancy. And it's gonna be fuckin' hot," he answered, setting a mug of coffee on the dresser. "Gonna shower. We gotta go soon, yeah?"

I pulled on a pair of dark washed jean shorts and a black tank top. After applying a little eyeliner and mascara, I attempted to tame my wild hair. I was tying my high-tops in the living room when Jake came out of the bedroom.

His hair was still damp and wavy from the shower. He was wearing a gray Red Sox tee with red, three-quarter-length sleeves, a pair of gray basketball shorts, and some sneakers. Pulling his hair into a knot, he threw on a worn and faded Sox hat.

You slept without drooling, Piper. Don't start now.

"Got somethin' else for you." Reaching into the closet, he handed me a white, fitted, Red Sox jersey.

"Baby, I'm sensing a theme with the clothes today."

"I did some work for a guy and got tickets, so I thought we might catch a Sox game. If you wanted." Though his voice was indifferent, his eyes were bright as he watched me failing to contain my excitement.

I grinned up at him. "Totally." I pulled the jersey on, but left it open.

His eyes darkened as he looked me over. "I'm thinkin' maybe I don't wanna go now."

"Too late. Let's go!" I bounced.

"Sweets, that isn't makin' me move any faster. Hell. Want one of my sweaters? A coat? At least throw some damn sweatpants on."

"It's gonna be unseasonably hot today so pants aren't happening. Now, let's *go*."

"You're lucky we're meetin' Floyd and Nat there or I seriously doubt we'd be leavin'."

"Hooray! Now I extra can't wait. Dad used to take me to games a lot." I flung the door open and headed towards the driveway. "You coming or what?"

"Never again. Do you hear me, Piper? Never. Again." Jake stormed through his condo, throwing his hat on the couch as he went.

I trailed after him. "Baby, it really wasn't that bad."

He stopped suddenly and turned to face me. "Are you kiddin' me? You and Nat almost got us kicked out of the game."

"Did not! The security guards thought we were hilarious."

"No, the security guards thought you were hot."

I rolled my eyes. "We weren't even that bad."

"Not even one day." He held up his finger. "Not even one day with my ring on your finger and you were yellin' your love for another man."

"To be fair, Anderson is the catcher for the Red Sox, not some random guy." At Jake's warning growl, I quickly moved on to my next defense. "And that wasn't even me yelling the dirty stuff. That was Natalie!"

"Never again. Not goin' anywhere with the two of you," Jake muttered as he headed into the kitchen.

Following him, I hopped up onto the island and tried to figure out why he was so exasperated. Since I was pretty tipsy, it was a difficult endeavor to focus on.

When we arrived at the stadium earlier and I showed Dad and Nat my ring, neither of them were surprised. I found out that the reason Jake had called my dad in the first place was to ask for his blessing. Though I'd already told Dad, and more so, Nat, about him, that didn't mean a phone conversation was going to suffice. Since my surprise birthday celebration was already in the works at that point, they'd decided the party was the perfect opportunity to meet Jake.

After finding our seats, which were so close I could reach over and touch the dugout, I looked at Jake with raised brows. He returned my unspoken question with a wink and smirk.

The work Jake had done wasn't just for some guy with an extra bunch of bleacher tickets. It was for Jason Pasters, the third baseman.

When he came over before the game to shake our hands and talk with Jake, I barely kept my screams in my head. Nat looked like she was fighting the same battle.

It quickly became obvious that Dad liked Jake. Nat told me that he'd met them for breakfast after their flight landed. According to her, Dad had to work hard to keep a stern face when he was greeted by a guy in scuffed motorcycle boots, well-worn jeans, and a t-shirt, instead of some pretentious yuppie from my mother's line-up of men. It still wasn't until Dad saw Jake and me at my party that he'd pulled him aside to give him his blessing.

While we watched the game and Nat filled me in on everything, we drank. A lot. Which led to us declaring our undying love for Teddy Anderson in the bottom of the ninth when he was going up to bat. I loved him because his batting average was rocking and he went by Teddy, not Theodore. Nat said it was because of his fine ass.

Regardless, he hit a double and got the two RBIs they needed to win.

Nat and I might have also heckled a few of the opposing team's players.

Just a little.

Like hardly noticeable.

Okay, maybe not.

Probably *very* noticeable.

As I silently accepted that maybe Nat and I had gotten a little wild, Jake handed me some pain meds and a tall glass of ice water. "I don't need those, I'm not even drunk."

"Yeah, you are."

"Okay, maybe a little. But not really."

Jake looked up and inhaled deeply. "Piper, take the damn pills."

"Fine. But I don't get hangovers, so it's a total waste of perfectly good medicine. You never know when you might need some and you'll go for the bottle but it'll be empty. And you'll only have yourself to blame 'cause I really don't need these." I stopped talking when Jake's deep laughter filled the kitchen.

"No. You're right. You're not drunk at all. What woulda made me think that?"

"What's so funny?" I asked, hiccupping in the middle and making his laughter start again.

"You. You're also fuckin' cute."

"Yeah?" I smiled as warmth spread through me.

"Yeah, sweets." Jake moved between my knees. "Did you have fun?"

"So much. I never knew I could be this happy. It was the best birthday, but also just the best weekend of my life," I whispered like it was a secret.

"Piper," Jake returned hoarsely.

Leaning up, I pressed my lips to his jaw. "About Nat and I. Maybe we did get just a little crazy."

"Yeah, babe." Grabbing my ass, he lifted me off the counter. "Just a little."

"Sorry."

"Worth it to see you happy."

"Fuck, I love my man."

Did I think that in my head?

"Love you, too. But no more with the love shit to anyone other than me, yeah?"

Nope, I said it out loud.

Okay, so more than a tiny bit drunk.

"Earth to Piper."

I opened my eyes, ready to open a can of whoop-ass on the cute voiced intruder for interrupting my sleep. "Huh, what?" Looking around, I realized I was still at school.

"You went into robot shutdown mode. Class is done," Harlow said, grabbing her backpack.

"Shit. Did Professor Marns notice I was asleep?"

"No. You just looked like you were really focused on your book."

"Thank the Sandman." Standing, I packed up my bag quickly and headed towards the door.

The hallway was loud and chaotic as we tried to weave through groups of people.

"Long night with your sculpted from marble, god of a fiancé?" Harlow put the back of her hand onto her forehead dramatically. "Oh woe is you."

"If by that, you mean elbow deep in fondant drama, then yes."

"God, you guys are kinky."

I laughed. "And that's not including what we do with whisks, oven mitts, funnels, and baking sheets."

"Do you guys really..." Harlow held up her hand. "You know what? Don't answer. The image in my head is hilarious, I don't wanna ruin it. So what's the deal with fondant?"

"I just hate it." I scrunched up my nose. "It tastes nasty and it's so shitty to work with. I was up until way late trying to get it all right. I have no clue how I'm going to get through my last class."

"At least you only have one left. Fridays are my longest days. I'm gonna need an IV of coffee."

"So I take it you can't go out tonight?"

"Nope. I can do Monday, though," she said, her voice hopeful.

"No can do. I've got a fully booked baking schedule for the beginning half of the week and dinner at my mother's house on

Friday. Next weekend?"

Her brows lowered as she thought it over. "Maybe lunch on Saturday. But Sunday is packed with school work. Hooray," she said sarcastically, rolling her eyes.

I smiled at her. "I'll look over my calendar and see."

"Sweet. I'm gonna haul ass to a vending machine for a much needed dose of caffeine. Talk to you soon."

"See ya!" I waved as we went in opposite directions.

As long as there was nothing that absolutely had to be done next weekend, I'd rearrange to make lunch happen.

I felt like I worked all the time, but it was nothing compared to Harlow. She took more classes than I did, worked an internship, and bartended at a crappy place in the city. Even though she must be running on fumes, she was always perky and happy.

If I didn't like her so much, I'd hate her for it.

"I'm so pleased. Just thrilled. I mean, he's a little rough, of course. But the way he looks at you? That thing he does with his thumb and your jaw? Wow. And that ring?"

Seeing my mother flustered by all things Jake, I burst out laughing. When she'd dragged me into the kitchen, I hadn't known what to expect. "I know, he's very *wow*."

"I only wish I hadn't invited Elaine and Dana. I know you like Dana, so I thought you'd want her here." She shrugged. "And, fine, I may have wanted to rub Elaine's nose in your engagement. Sue me."

"Mother! I'm shocked."

"See what it gets me? They're making a scene. James is sulking. And Dana's father is drinking all of Thomas' good scotch."

"At least it's been entertaining."

"Well, yes, there is that." She smiled mischievously. "Speaking of, we should get back so we don't miss anything."

"I'll meet you in a few." I gestured with my head towards the bathroom.

Now that Jake and I were engaged, Mom had put her foot down about meeting him. This meant throwing us a small engagement party with her and Thomas' friends.

How she'd managed to throw it all together in two weeks, I had no clue.

Though Jake wasn't a big fan of my boring dress or my pulled back hair, he was being his usual charming, bossy self. It was no surprise that the women were gawking at him with a mixture of fear and lust in their eyes.

Is that how I look at him?

The worst, by far, was Dana and her mother. Dana was there with James, though they'd hardly said a word to each other. Elaine was blatantly flirting with Jake, and her husband wasn't paying attention since his eyes were glued to whatever legs or chest were in his line of sight.

Mother had told me that Elaine didn't treat James like he was a potential son-in-law. She was also more than friendly with her pool boy and gardener. Then there were the tennis lessons she took, though no one ever saw her play.

With overly processed blond hair, big, fake, stripper boobs, and a baseball mitt tan, she was a walking cliché.

I'd felt bad for Dana until she'd begun hitting on Jake so overtly it made her mom look demure.

I opened the bathroom door to go rescue my fiancé from whatever fresh hell he was facing when I was pushed back into the bathroom and a mouth was on mine.

I jerked away and wiped my mouth with the back of my hand. "James! What're you doing?"

"Just a friend, Piper? Then you were just casually seeing him? And now you're marrying him? *Him*?" James threw his arm out towards the door, his brows lowered and his expression filled with both confusion and contempt.

"Yeah, that's kinda the way relationships progress."

"Don't be stupid. You see the way he's flirting with all those women out there. You want that life? A man like that who's going to fuck around on you and use you for your money?"

"First of all, Jake hasn't done anything wrong. If I were you, I'd be looking at Dana's behavior because he isn't encouraging shit. The fact she didn't sit her naked ass on his dinner plate is surprising. It certainly would've been subtler."

"Don't be vulgar."

"If you think that's vulgar, it's a good thing we never got together. I'd like to get back to my fiancé. I'd suggest you get Dana and leave, or I might have to talk to Thomas about what just happened. Which means in addition to finding a new woman, you'll be finding a new job. Don't pull that shit again, James."

Disgusted, I stormed out, leaving James in the bathroom as I went to find my man.

"Babe, it ain't gonna happen, so get it outta your head now."

"What the hell, Jake? You're being ridiculous!"

"Think what you want, but you aren't doin' it."

"Yeah, I am."

"There's no way I'm lettin' you spend time with Blake fuckin' Green," Jake spat out, crossing his arms over his chest.

I matched the gesture by putting my hands on my hips and mustering up all the attitude I could. "First of all, you don't *let* me do anything."

Okay, that isn't technically 100% true, but that's beside the point.

"Second, it's not a social visit. I'm doing the cakes for his album drop party. I kinda have to know what they want."

"Work through Rhys then. He might want in your pants, but at least I can trust him not to make a move."

"Normally, I totally dig your whole big, badass, possessive thing. I really do. But not now. This is my business and I can't let this kind of opportunity pass by just because you don't like the client."

"He's not a *client,*" he said with a sneer, "because it's not fuckin' happenin'."

"You know what? I've gotta get to class." Grabbing my bag, I left the condo, slamming the door behind me.

It wasn't the most mature thing to do, but it was a small release.

I got in my car and took off without a backwards glance.

It'd been two and a half weeks since my birthday weekend and a few days since the interesting dinner party at my mother's. Much like our transition into coupledom, we'd settled easily into our engagement.

The Monday after my birthday, I'd gone to see Ray. With zero hesitation or doubt, I got a cupcake tattoo on the inside of my wrist. There was a red cherry on the top with 'Jacoby' spelled out vertically to make the stem. Like his ink, the name placement was subtle but fitting.

That night he'd very thoroughly showed me how much he liked it. Since then I'd catch him staring at it, tracing it with his fingers, or pressing gentle kisses to it.

I knew how much it meant to him because seeing my name on his chest still made my breath catch.

I worked in the kitchen at the shop, which came in handy since business was insane. After work, we went back to one of our places, had dinner, and did typical couple things.

It was nice.

It was normal.

And, surprisingly enough, it wasn't boring.

The only dark cloud in all the brightness had been the emails.

In addition to receiving them more often, they were also getting increasingly graphic. Gregory was working with the police to see if it was a legitimate threat that went beyond someone seeking attention.

I tried not to think about them, but sometimes they'd pop into my head and I'd get freaked. The hairs on the back of my neck would stand up and I'd get the overwhelming urge to run.

I'd also had three more anonymous flower deliveries. They only came when I wasn't home, which was most of the time.

After the second delivery, though, Jake called his dad again. Gregory came over with some forensic people who took the flowers and put a logger on my computer.

During the last trip out, Gregory invited us to dinner. And by invited, I mean he laid a guilt trip on Jake so thick it put my mom's to shame.

Jake's mom, Sarah, was a lot like her husband. She was obviously a good lawyer since our conversation started out as more of an interrogation. Eventually, the tension eased and the atmosphere grew more comfortable. Even the vibe between Jake and his dad didn't seem as tense.

The night ended with tentative plans for all of us to get together with my mother and Thomas next time.

On the bizarre side of things, Jake and I had become tabloid fodder. It was weird seeing news of our engagement in local newspapers. While I felt like it was a huge deal, I didn't think anyone outside of our circle would.

I was wrong.

Jake was worried about the increased exposure, but I hoped it would fizzle out and we'd become old news.

Rhys had texted that morning to ask if I'd be interested in doing cakes for a launch party going on at Rye. The event was celebrating Static in the Sun's album release. It would be the biggest order I'd ever done, both in volume and exposure. I wasn't thrilled when he told me Green had some specific requests, but I didn't want to give up my chance to provide cakes for such a high-profile event.

I knew Jake had a point; Blake Green was an egotistical ass and working with him was going to be a headache.

Still, I was confident I could tune him out and make it through one evening. I wasn't going to bail just because Jake told me to.

Huh. Wonder where he got the idea he could do that?

Shut up.

Normally, I gave in to him because I didn't care what he was being bossy about. When I did, we always compromised. We both seemed to know what was worth the fight and what wasn't.

Sighing, I pulled into a spot at school and forced myself to go to class.

"Girl, I don't know what the deal is, but your man is putting out a serious pissed off vibe," Harlow said, looking past me at the table in the cafeteria.

I whipped my head around and saw Jake stalking towards me. I vaguely heard Melanie ask what was going on, but I was already up and heading his way.

As soon as I got within arm's reach, he pulled me to him. Grabbing my ass, he lifted me up and I wrapped my legs around him. One of his hands weaved into my hair as his mouth crashed down on mine.

It wasn't until Jake pulled up and gently lowered me to my feet that I registered the comments, catcalls, and whistles. His hand curved around my neck and his thumb pressed my chin up.

"It wasn't my place to tell you how to handle your business."

"Thank you for that. I'll talk to Rhys about working through him. Next time, though, please ask me, don't tell me. Deal, Mr. Bossy Pants?"

"Deal. But don't leave without kissing me again. Yeah?"

I nodded because the lack of kiss had thrown my whole day off, too.

When we returned to the table, Jake sat, grabbed my waist, and pulled me onto his lap.

I wrapped my arm around his shoulders. "Don't you have to get back to work?"

"Nope. They kicked me out for the day. Out of my own damn business. Apparently, I was making it a 'hostile work environment,'" he scoffed with air quotes. "Where's your lunch?"

"I wasn't feeling hungry."

"Important class next?"

"Not really."

"Let's get the fuck outta here and get you some real food, yeah?"

"You sure you're alright? Maybe we should call your doctor." The concern in Jake's voice made the tears start all over again.

"No. No, I'm fine." I hiccupped, wishing he wouldn't stand outside the door. I didn't like being sick. I *really* didn't like Jake hearing it. "Can you go call Ray and tell her I can't make it today?" I listened to his footsteps fading before I lost more of my breakfast.

When I stood up, feeling wobbly but better, I heard the front door close before Jake's bike roared off a moment later. I was surprised, but grateful, he'd left. I needed a shower badly.

And a gallon of mouthwash.

That'll teach me to never play hooky.

We left school but I ended up not feeling well enough to go for a bite. Instead, we came back to the condo and I slept most of the day and night. Every time I woke up, Jake was holding me close and would try to get me to drink or eat something. Though I sipped at the water he always had waiting for me, I couldn't stomach anything else.

I woke up early and felt worse than I had the day before.

After my much needed shower, I was brushing my teeth when

Jake came into the bathroom. His face was blank as he handed me a plastic bag from the store and my cell. Without a word, he walked back out.

Looking at the phone, I saw it was already connected to Ray. "'Ello?" I croaked.

"Sweetie, are you late?" Ray asked.

"Yeah, I asked Jake to call you. I can't meet up with you today, I'm not feeling well."

"No. Are you *late*?"

"Huh?" I looked in the bag and found bright pink stomach medicine and a pregnancy test.

My fiancé who doesn't want kids went out and bought me a pregnancy test.

Awesome.

Excuse me while I sneak out the window.

"Did you say something to Jake when he called to cancel?" My nervous stomach churned, making me feel worse.

"I kinda blurted it out without thinking. Why?"

"Jake doesn't want kids."

"Are you still on the pill?"

"I started getting the shot. With me spending the night at both places, I didn't want to risk forgetting. I've never missed or been late with either, though," I rambled.

"It'll be okay. I'll pick up a test and be right over."

"Jake got one. I'm gonna take it. Can you stay on the phone? Please?"

"Of course. Where is he?"

"I dunno. He just handed me the pregnancy kit and left." My hands shook as I opened the package and followed the directions.

"Well?"

"It says it takes three minutes," I whispered.

"Okay. I'll wait," she whispered back.

I tried to look at anything but the little white stick on the counter.

After three minutes, I peeked and saw only one pink line. I let out a breath I wasn't aware I was holding as my feelings bombarded me.

"Negative?" she asked.

"Yup."

"You good with that?"

"Yes, totally. Definitely. Maybe."

"Maybe?"

"I'm relieved?"

"Is that a question?"

"No, I am. This is a good thing?"

Ray's voice was soft. "I don't know, sweetheart, is it?"

"Uhh."

"Why doesn't he want kids?"

Ray was asking something I wanted to know, too. I'd been putting the conversation off but I knew, now more than ever, it was one we needed to have.

"I don't know." I picked up the test to throw it out when something caught my eye. "What does it mean when there is a really light second line? Is it still negative?"

"Usually a line is a line. Are there two?"

"Yes." I swallowed painfully over the sudden lump in my throat as my queasy stomach threatened to revolt.

"Congrats, sweetheart. Do you want me to come over?"

"No. I… I have to go talk to Jake."

After I let Ray go, I found Jake pacing in the kitchen.

When he looked at my face, his eyes closed slowly before he dropped his head.

"I'm gonna, uh, go call my doctor." Dazedly, I headed into my room and sat on the edge of my bed as the call connected.

"Doctor Augusta's office," the cheerful receptionist answered.

"Hi, this is Piper Skye."

"Hi Piper, honey. How're you?"

"Good. Well, maybe. I've been feeling pretty run down and sick, so I took a pregnancy test and it was positive."

"Congratulations! Normally Dr. Augusta doesn't see patients until they're nine weeks into the pregnancy. Since you were just in for your shot, though, I'm not sure. Let me put you on hold for a second, alright?"

As I waited, Jake came in and sat behind me. Pulling me to him, he kissed the spot behind my ear.

The receptionist clicked back on. "Piper?"

"Yes?"

"Doctor Augusta would like to see you. Can you come in at eleven thirty?"

"Sure, that's no problem."

"Okay, you're all set. See you then."

I ended the call and leaned back into Jake's chest. "She wants to see me in a couple hours."

"I'll come with you," his voice rumbled in my ear.

"No, that's okay. You left work early yesterday."

"It's cool, I know the guy who owns the place."

"I'll be—"

"Piper." From his firm tone, I knew arguing was a waste of time.

"Fine." I got up and went to the bathroom to get ready, not daring to look at Jake.

"Well, Miss Skye, it was a false alarm."

My breath whooshed out of my lungs. I felt Jake's body shift next to me. "False alarm?"

"After a short period of time, pregnancy tests can develop evaporation lines. Because you said that the line was faint and didn't show initially, I'm assuming that's all it was. It could have also been an indent line and shadow playing tricks. Regardless, your blood test was negative," Doctor Augusta explained.

"So feeling sick?"

"It may be a typical virus. However, since you just had the shot, it could be a reaction to that. It can take a few doses for your body to adjust to the influx of hormones. To avoid this, you can switch back to the pill or try something else."

"What would you recommend?"

"I know you were hesitant when we discussed it last time, but I do think an IUD would work well for you. It lasts for five years and then we replace it."

"But the side effects..." I squirmed just thinking about it.

"You're right, they can be unpleasant. It can fall out, get embedded in your uterus, or change your menstrual bleeding. But, Piper, the majority of women have no problem. There's nothing to remember to take, put on, or put in. You're set for five years."

"What if we decide to have kids before the time is up?" Jake asked, shocking the hell out of me.

As this was the first thing he'd said since we came into the office, Doctor Augusta looked a little surprised, too. "If you decide to start trying, all Piper needs to do is come in and have it removed. Some women get pregnant that same month, but for others it takes a little longer. If this is the way you want to go, we can insert a non-hormonal one today."

"Okay." I felt both shocked and numb.

Jake's cell rang. "Sorry, it's work." Silencing the ringer, he stood and left the room to take the call.

"Congratulations on your engagement, by the way," Dr. Augusta said, looking at my ring.

"Thank you." I smiled as I looked at it, too.

"Alright, I'll go get everything ready and be back." Walking out, she closed the door behind her and left me alone with my thoughts.

"I think we should talk, sweets," Jake said.

Pressed against him in bed, my leg was thrown over his while my cheek rested on his chest. His rough hand rubbed along my spine.

Naked in bed is so not where I want to have this conversation. Let's schedule it for later.

Maybe the seventh of freakin' never?

When the uncomfortable IUD insertion was done, Jake insisted that I go home and rest. I didn't want to relax. If I was alone with my thoughts, I'd obsess and analyze every single thing. I wasn't ready to deal with my feelings.

Cluck, cluck, chicken.

Using the excuse of being behind schedule, I told Jake I wanted to get some work done. Since arguing with him was normally like stapling jello to a tree, I was surprised when he gave in.

After getting caught up on orders, I grabbed takeout and went to my place in case Jake needed time to himself.

He obviously didn't since he showed up shortly thereafter, kissed me, and fixed a plate of food like nothing was amiss.

We spent the rest of the night watching TV and ignoring the baby elephant in the room.

"About what?" I asked hesitantly, hoping in vain that we were just going to keep ignoring it.

"Do you want kids, Piper?"

"I've never had kids, so I wouldn't know what I'm missing out on. I have had you, so I'd definitely know what I was giving up."

"I changed my mind."

"What?" I sat up to look down at him.

His hand gently combed through my hair. He watched the long strands fall through his fingers. "Been thinkin' about it for a while but I didn't wanna freak you out."

"You're the one that seemed freaked. In the kitchen, when you saw—"

"I was already breathin' deep, seein' bright, tastin' sweet. The thought of my baby in you?" He looked me in the eyes, his showing exactly how he'd felt. "Fuckin' perfection."

Seeing the two lines on the test had sent a rush of emotions through me. I was worried about Jake's feelings, but happiness had been a close second.

In a nervous, petrified, excited, and giddy way, that is.

"Why didn't you want kids before?"

Every time I'd thought about asking, I chickened out. I wasn't ready to face the definitive reality of never having kids.

I hadn't lied to him. If the toss-up was between him and babies, I'd pick him. That didn't mean I wanted to have to make that choice.

"I grew up lonely. My parents worked all the time and even when they were home, they weren't really there. Floyd flew across the country to be there for you. My dad missed my high school graduation."

Well, that explains the look on his face when I was telling him about how often I saw Dad.

"Baby," I whispered, rubbing his stubble.

Catching my hand, he pulled it to him and kissed my fingertips. He kept them close, his lips grazing as he spoke. "I got it then and more so now. But it was one more thing in a long list of things they missed. I know it's stupid—"

"No, it's not." I tried to pull my hand away but his grip stayed firm.

At my raised brows, he gave me a half smile. "You smell and," he started, before nipping the pad of my middle finger, "taste like cake."

"Don't distract me. Continue—"

"I was tryin' to." With a wicked grin, his tongue touched my finger.

"With your story. Continue with your story."

"Fine," he sighed. "Workin' with cars was all I'd ever wanted to do. I woke up one mornin' and I was just done. I was puttin' time, effort, and a shit ton of money into a college I didn't wanna go to so

I could start doin' a job I didn't wanna do. So I quit. I started workin' at garages until I built enough of a client base that I could start my own place. My focus has always been on Hyde."

"So you thought if you had kids, they'd have the same life you had?"

Letting go of my hand, Jake went up on his elbows and nodded. "It wasn't a big deal 'cause by the time I'd even be thinkin' about kids, I was already cynical as fuck. I wouldn't trust a lot of these women to hold my fuckin' beer, let alone my baby. The crazy shit some bitches have tried to pull on me is laughable in a fucked up way. And it wasn't just a few women doin' it. There's shit with Rhys, babe, that isn't my story to tell. But what he was put through? If it weren't for the fact I knew you were mine, I'd have been happy for him."

"Since it's only you, thank God your head-ass-ectomy was a success."

His face went soft. "Love you."

"Love you, too." Bending my legs, I wrapped my arms around them and rested my head on my knees. "And?" I prompted again when he stopped his story.

"I didn't wanna date most of the women I fucked. Even with the ones that weren't crazy, it wasn't like that. I had no interest in getting married, so I didn't wanna end up in a jacked situation where I'm only seein' the kid every other weekend or some shit."

"But with me?"

"Without a doubt. You're sweet and silly as fuck with kids when you're workin' up cake designs with them. I can totally picture you with our kids."

"Really?" I hadn't known he'd seen any of my planning meetings at the shop, but he was right. I was a dingus.

"Fuck yeah. The thought of you carryin' my baby? I'm selfish as fuck so I'm happy I get you to myself for a while. But down the road?" His lips tilted up before his expression turned watchful. "You didn't answer me, though. Do you want kids?"

"Badly. I'd be happy without them, Jake. But I want babies with you."

I barely finished my sentence before Jake cupped the back of my head and pulled me down to him. Rolling us, his heavy weight settled on me and his mouth brutally took mine.

"Fuck, shoulda waited to talk to you," Jake muttered against my lips.

"Why?"

"Wanna be inside you." He pushed his boxer clad hardness against me.

"I want that, too." I tried to hook my fingers into the waistband of his boxer briefs but he moved away.

Stretching out next to me, he wrapped his arm around my shoulders and curled me back into him.

"I take it that's a no?" I murmured. Resting my head on his shoulder, my fingertips danced down the contours of his ab muscles.

Jake's hand captured mine and pulled it up. After pressing a kiss to my palm, he rested it on his chest. "Doc's orders."

"You know I'm not good with following orders."

"Don't I fuckin' know it. While we're talkin' about heavy shit, have you thought about when you wanna get married?"

"I'm almost done with classes. I thought we'd wait 'til then."

"What about where?"

"I did have an idea," I said, feeling silly. "Vegas."

"Yeah?"

I nodded. "I just think it'd be kickass. When I've done wedding cakes, the event itself always seems so stressful. People are running around in a panic. Someone's usually crying or ready to bolt. It's supposed to be the happiest day of their lives, but, more often than not, everyone's miserable."

"Sounds like a problem with who's gettin' married, not where."

"I think people just forget that the important part of a wedding is the life that follows it. I'd rather have a fun and easy start to our life together."

"That's what you want, that's what we'll do."

"Awesome," I said through a yawn.

"Get some rest."

"Okay." I could feel Jake's heart under my hand, the beat lulling me. "Love you, Jacoby," I whispered as I fell asleep.

"This isn't up for discussion."

"Oh, so that's it? You say so, and I'm just supposed to agree. Your wish is my command? Should I put on a genie outfit, twitch my nose, and nod my head, too?"

"Fuck. Now I'm gettin' fuckin' hard."

"Jake, this isn't funny!" Though knowing he was getting hard was taking some of the wind out of my bitch sails.

"You're right, it isn't. It's about safety. You heard my dad; you need to be careful. And just you and your girls at a club isn't safe."

"We're only going to Voodoo. You and your dad are both overreacting. The flowers could be from anyone and I'm hardly getting any emails."

Balling his hands into fist, he banged them on the desk that separated us as he leaned closer. "There's more, Piper!" Jake's low voice rumbled. His anger was evident, but fear and frustration lurked under the surface.

"What more?"

"Nothin'." Standing up straight, he exhaled deeply and rubbed his palm down his face. "Edge and Kase are both gonna stick close. I wish I could go, but I'm the only one that can finish this bike."

I crossed my arms. "What more is there, Jake?"

"Nothin'."

"I'm cool with them coming, but you could've just asked me instead of being Mr. Bossy Pants about it. Now what else is there?"

Jake walked around his desk as he spoke. "I got a couple emails at work. Nothin' like what you were gettin' but with the flowers showing up so often, it's suspicious."

"Why didn't you tell me?"

"I didn't wanna worry you."

"I can handle it. I'm strong, but I'd be a lot stronger if I had all the facts. You need to talk to me, okay?"

"Yeah." Jake leaned on the edge of his desk and spread his legs. "Now, bring that sexy ass over here."

When I stopped in front of him, one of his hands went to my ass and pulled me close. "I have to get finished up. And you have a bike to work on," I reminded him.

"Love you."

"Love you, too." Placing my hands on his hard chest, I went up on my toes and pressed my lips to his.

Jake's fingers curved around the back of my head as he took over the kiss.

Neither of us got back to work for a while.

"Time to go, Piper," Jake yelled over the music.

"See what I mean?" I grinned at Ray and Harlow, then giggled as I gestured with my thumb over my shoulder. "He's crazy hot. But he's also crazy bossy. He's Mr. Bossy Pants. Sometimes it's hot. Other times? Yeah, not so much."

When, drunken Piper, is it not hot?

Yeah, good point, girly bits.

Ray burst into a fit of drunken giggles that she was barely able to talk through. "If you don't like full-time bossy, it's a good thing you didn't hook up with Rhys."

I tilted my head. "Why? Is Rhys a Mr. Bossy Pants, too?"

"Don't worry about it," Jake said, shooting Ray a glare.

Since Ray was looking at me and not Jake, though, it was a warning she missed. "He's beyond a Mister. Rhys is a *sir* always, but especially in bed."

We'd been at Voodoo for a few hours. In that time, I'd had a lot to drink. *Copious* amounts. I was toeing the fine line between fun wasted and thinking I could sing karaoke.

Hmm. But if the song was right, I'm sure I could totally rock it.

Since I was drunk, Ray's comments were lost on me. Unfortunately, my filter had taken a trip out the window to make room for my fourth shot.

"Like, he fucks fancy with his pinkies out? Or with a top hat on?" My brows lowered as I shook my head. "I don't think that'd work well. Wouldn't it keep falling off? I mean, I guess he could hold it on. But then how would he move much? I don't think I'd like it if Jake wore a top hat in bed. I couldn't run my fingers through his hair. Hair, by the way, that's so soft it *must* be made of angel wing feathers."

Jake's loud laughter interrupted my drunken babbling. Edge and Kase were laughing even harder.

I made wide eyes at Harlow before whispering loudly, "I think I just put my foot in my mouth."

"I don't think so. You brought up some good points," she whispered back, equally as loud. "Is his hair really that soft?"

"Softer. Which is crazy, 'cause most of him is *so* hard. Especially his—"

"Piper," Jake interrupted.

"What? I was just gonna say your abs. Sheesh, perv."

"Say goodbye, Piper."

"Goodbye, Piper," I said, imitating his deep voice. I wiggled my fingers in a drunken wave.

Jake wrapped his arm around my shoulders as we moved

through the room. The crowd around us parted like the Red Sea.

"You must be a badass Moses. He had long hair and beard, too. And I think a wooden staff. You don't have that, but you do have something long and hard and so much better."

I could feel Jake's body shaking with laughter. "Funny, that's not the biblical name you usually scream."

"If you're gonna make fun of me, maybe I won't scream anything anymore," I huffed.

"That a challenge?"

"Nope. I'm just saying I won't be screaming, biblical names or otherwise."

"No, what you're sayin' is it's a challenge. And I'm competitive, baby. I'd rather wait 'til we get home to win this but if you wanna keep provokin' me, I'm sure Edge will let us borrow a storeroom."

I looked up at Jake with wide eyes, but I did it silently.

"That's okay, we'll be home soon," he muttered, looking vaguely disappointed.

By the time we made it outside, my drunken mind forgot to be freaked about the impending screaming. "Soooo," I sing-songed. "Who ratted me out?"

"Kase about five minutes after you guys got here. Then Edge. Then Felix."

"Felix?"

"Bartender. Apparently, I owe him and Edge money now."

"Why?"

"He had to keep tellin' guys not to bother buyin' you a drink. Actually, a couple girls, too. He said I was costin' Edge money and him tips."

I rolled my eyes. "Guys are so dramatic. And gossipy. It wasn't bad," I assured him as I got into the car. "I was getting tired anyway. I just want to crawl into bed and sleep for a month."

"I'll get you into bed but it'll be a while before you sleep," he said with a wicked grin as he closed the door.

When he got in and started the car, I yawned before resting my head on his shoulder. As he started driving, my hand went to his lap and the sound of his zipper going down filled the car. Jake adjusted himself, allowing me to free his already hardening cock from his pants.

"I'm really tired, though." I fake yawned. "I think I should put my head down."

Jake's voice was soft and sweet. "Okay, sweets."

Lowering my head to his lap, I took him in my mouth. My drunkenness might have messed with my finesse, but I hoped my lowered inhibitions and enthusiasm made up for it.

Jake's hips rose up and down to meet my motions. The sound of his deep groans seemed to echo around the small space.

"Play with yourself," Jake demanded.

My moans joined his as I slid my hand into my pants and panties. Putting pressure on my clit, I moved my fingers in a tight circle. I felt the car jerk to the side before Jake slammed on the brakes and put the gear shift in park.

"Backseat. Now," he grunted as he threw his door open.

"Yes, Mr. Bossy Pants."

Deepest Darkest

The lull in emails was done.

I knew because I was sitting at my desk, frozen in terror as I looked at myself.

Being fucked.

In a car.

The picture was dark and fuzzy, our faces impossible to make out. Based on the positioning, though, it was obvious what was happening.

I knew it was us. Which meant someone else did, too.

Someone who watched us.

With shaking hands, I grabbed my phone and touched the screen a few times to call Jake.

"Hey, babe. I was just thinkin' about you."

"Jake," I whimpered, fear soaking into my voice. Soaking into me.

"What's wrong?"

"I got another email."

Could someone be watching or listening right now?

"I'm on my way. I'll call Dad and we'll be there soon."

"No!"

"What? What's wrong?"

"There's a picture. You can't call your dad, Jake. He can't see it." I was mortified at the thought of Gregory even knowing about the picture. I didn't want him to see it.

"What is it?"

"You and me on the way home from Voodoo. When we pulled off on the side of the road." I heard Jake's breathing change, then something crash. "Jake?"

"I'm here." Jake's voice was thick and gravelly. "I'm leavin' now. Dad will be fine. Call Detective Oscar. Do you still have her number?"

"Yeah."

Gregory had told us he'd specifically asked for Detective Oscar to look into things. When she'd come with him to pick up one of the flower deliveries, I'd been surprised at how young she was.

Since she was a detective at her age, she obviously worked hard. Though she was very attractive, it was her no-nonsense attitude and confidence that stood out.

Okay, so I was completely wrong and there's something going on. At least I have a tough fiancé and detective at my back.

"Call her. I'm headin' out now. Lock the door, yeah?"

"It already is."

"Okay, sweets. I love you. See you soon."

I disconnected and dialed again.

"Detective Oscar," she answered after a few rings.

"Hello, this is Piper Skye."

"Miss Skye, what can I do for you?"

"I got another email." Though I tried to fake strength, the fear once again seeped into my voice.

"I'll be right over. Your door locked?"

"Yes."

"I'm on my way. I'll announce myself when I get there, okay?"

After ending the call, I began to pace the room but stayed away from the big window. The way it let so much sun in had been one of the main reasons I bought this house.

At that moment, though, I hated it.

Leaning against a wall, I took some deep breaths in an attempt to calm down.

I knew I failed when the knock sounded and I nearly jumped out of my skin.

After we got home that night from Voodoo, I took care of my bathroom stuff and got ready to go to sleep. I crawled up Jake in bed and snuggled my face into his neck.

"Jake?"

"Hmm?" he rumbled, his hands rubbing my back.

"What did the emails say?"

"Shit about how hot you are and how beautiful your smile is. Since the flowers have been comin' more and they haven't been able to track down from where, Detective Oscar and my dad think it might be connected."

"What about the email tracking on my computer?"

"The locations are pinging from all over. Either there's more than one person or they've got some serious tech skills. Until we figure it out, you've gotta be careful, yeah?"

I nodded as a shiver ran through me. Not wanting to think about it, I moved on to another subject I was curious about. "So, about Rhys—"

"Not my place to say."

"Please?"

"Sweets, I don't think Rhys even wants you to know. Ray shouldn't have said anythin'."

"But she did. And now I want to know. I don't want to ask him, that'd be awkward. But you know I will," I threatened, even though I totally wouldn't. Not unless I was drunk, at least. "Is he… you know?"

"He's in charge. Of Rye, but also of all areas of his life. I might like to fuck bossy, but Rhys takes it to a whole other level."

"I never would've guessed that."

"Everybody has their own kink."

"What's yours?" I dragged the tip of my tongue along his stubbled jaw.

"Corruptin' and teachin' my woman all the ways *I* like control while makin' her mine."

"How coincidental. My kink is to be corrupted by my man while he teaches me things I've only read about."

"How about we work more on those lessons? Turn around and face the other way on me, yeah?"

I learned a lot that night.

I'd been safe since Jake told me about the emails because he hadn't given me much choice. He'd started coming with me when I had deliveries or errands to run. When he couldn't break away, he'd rope one of the boys into taking me.

Key was my favorite since he was so quiet. Usually I forgot he was even there. Xavier and Eli both liked to chat, which was fun, but not very productive.

Unless I had no other options, Kase was banned from helping. Especially when it came to deliveries. Him flirting with brides wasn't good for business. Not that any of them were complaining, of course.

Of them all, Z was even worse than Jake. He was so alert while we shopped that it put me on edge. When he dropped me off at home, he'd made me wait in his car while he did a walkthrough, saying, "Better safe than sorry, Doll Face."

When I brought up Z's intense surveillance, Jake told me it's because he'd been Special Forces. "Don't know the details. Just know it fucked with his head, the same way it'd fuck anyone. He doesn't talk about it. Ever. Yeah?"

I nodded. I might like to chat, but even I knew not to go there.

Though I was being cautious, it had only been for Jake's peace of mind. I hadn't believed there was a real threat.

Until that email.

"Miss Skye? It's Detective Oscar," I heard through the door.

I threw the locks and opened it to let her in.

Though she was only a couple inches taller than me, her authority made her appear much larger. Her brown eyes were warm but sharp as she looked me over. "How are you?"

"Uh, if I say brave and fierce, can we pretend I look it?"

Her lips quirked up. "Of course. Are Jake and Gregory coming?"

"Yeah, Jake should be here soon. He said he'd call his dad."

"Okay. Why don't you show me the email while we're waiting?"

I brought her over to my laptop and moved my finger on the pad to wake it up. My stomach lurched again as I looked at the picture.

Detective Oscar opened a notepad and began writing in it. "How long ago did this take place?"

"A few days ago."

"Where were you parked?"

"Honestly, I'm not sure. I'd been drinking at a club, Voodoo, and Jake came to pick me up. So somewhere between there and here." My cheeks were hot with embarrassment, but I was also pale and clammy. It was an unpleasant sensation.

"Do you know what time it was?"

"Probably midnight or so?"

"Anyone at Voodoo acting weird, giving you too much attention, making you feel uncomfortable?"

I shook my head. "Edge, the owner, and Kase, a friend and employee of Jake's, were there with me and my friends. I guess they played blocker during the night. But nothing seemed out of sorts. No one made a scene or anything."

I heard Jake's Harley roar up my driveway. Opening the door, he came straight to me and crouched near where I sat on the couch. "You okay, sweets?" His thumb stroked my jaw as his eyes searched my face.

I shrugged. "I've been better."

Jake looked at my laptop and saw the picture of us doing something that should have been private.

Standing, his fists clenched so tight that his knuckles turned white. His body was rigid and a muscle in his jaw jumped.

Reaching out suddenly, he snatched the lamp off the table and side armed it across the room.

It hit the wall with so much force that it looked like it exploded, shattering into tiny shards of nothing.

I couldn't hold back when my laughter bubbled out. Jake and Detective Oscar both turned to look at me, most likely trying to assess if I going into hysterics. "Sorry, sorry. It's just that that lamp was a housewarming gift from my mother. I hated it and wanted to break it just so I wouldn't have to look at it anymore. You did me a favor."

"I'll still buy you a new one."

I shrugged. "We'll wait until we get our own home, then pick one out together."

Some of the tension left Jake's body. "Sounds good."

"So—"

A knock interrupted, making me jump and Jake tense again. He looked out the window before opening the door.

"Sweetheart, how're you?" Gregory asked as he came straight to me. His green eyes searched my face in much the same way as Jake's had.

"I'm better now, thank you. Sorry for interrupting your day."

"Don't even think about it." His expression switched from

concerned to all business. "What's happened?"

Detective Oscar took control and filled Gregory in.

I was grateful to be saved from the embarrassment of telling my future father-in-law that his son and I had been photographed going at it at the side of the road. I'd have preferred he didn't have to know at all, but since he did, I was relieved I didn't have to be the one to say it. My face was on fire from just hearing it.

Jake sat on the arm of the couch and rubbed my neck. As Gregory and Detective Oscar talked about the dead ends they were hitting in the investigation, he got up and paced.

Bet he wishes I had another lamp to throw.

"So, what's the next step?" Jake asked. His patience had clearly run out.

"Vigilance," Detective Oscar said. "Be aware of who's around you. If you get a feeling, Piper, don't try to convince yourself it's nothing. Leave. Call me. Call Jake. Call *anyone* and do it loudly. Don't go out alone. I'd suggest changing your email address, but I know it's your work one. Still, change it if you can swing that. I'd definitely recommend buying a new laptop. Before you even turn it on, though, bring it by the station and they'll put the tracker on it. See about replacing your phone, too. These things are easy to dig into. Most bad hackers barely get in before virus protection or firewalls shut them down. But with some serious skill, they can get in so deep there's no scan that can detect them."

"We'll go tonight," Jake said instantly.

For once, I wasn't going to put up a fight when Jake said he was paying. I kept looking at my laptop and bracing, like it was a viper about to strike.

"Good idea. However, and I'm sure you both realize this now, the threat is real. We'd hoped to track down some punk that saw your pictures in the news, but that's not what's happening here. Stay safe. Don't do anything that would put you at undue risk." She jerked her head towards the picture on the laptop.

Yeah, I don't see any roadside booty happening again anytime soon.

Or ever.

"I'm going to head back to the station and start digging in with the tech guys. Piper, bring by the new computer." With a nod goodbye, she left looking totally badass.

"I need to get home to your mother. She's worried," Gregory said as he headed towards the door. "Call her soon, yeah?"

Huh, that sounds familiar.

"Yeah. Thanks, Dad."

"Anything for you. Call me day or night. Love you." He stepped outside and closed the door after him. "Lock that."

Yup, definitely familiar.

"Here's your computer back, Miss Skye."

"Thanks."

"He with you?" Detective Oscar asked with a head jerk towards Rhys.

"Yeah. Jake's recruiting from our pool of friends for 'Piper Babysitting Duty'."

"Don't be stubborn about letting them help." Her expression softened. "Speaking of Jake, it looks like he's here to relieve the sitter."

Turning around, I saw him stop and talk to Rhys. "Weird. He wasn't expecting to be done at work until late tonight." I looked at him again as he headed towards us. "Shit. Something's wrong."

Detective Oscar's head tilted for a second before her body got tight. "You can say that again." Her face returned to controlled and professional. "Mr. Hyde."

Jake's vibe was dark and tense, his tone short and clipped. "Detective Oscar, a word?"

"What's wrong?" I asked, going up on my tiptoes to try and make him look at me.

Instead, he kissed my forehead distractedly. "I just need to talk to Detective Oscar about somethin'. Go see, Rhys, yeah?"

"Come on, darlin'. Let's get some coffee." Rhys put his arm around my shoulders and guided me towards a small kitchenette.

When Jake didn't even react, I knew something wasn't wrong.

Something was *really* wrong.

After what felt like hours, but was probably only about five minutes, Detective Oscar opened a door and stuck her head out. "Miss Skye, can you come in here?"

My stomach twisted and turned as I made my way to the room she was in.

I hadn't noticed Rhys following until Detective Oscar looked behind me. "Sir, I think it might be best if you waited out here."

"And I think it might be best if I came," Rhys' low voice argued, his easy smile gone.

"Detective Oscar," Jake rumbled from inside the room. "Like you said, the more Piper and those around her know, the better."

"Fine. Miss Skye and..." she paused, waiting for Rhys to introduce himself. When he just looked down at her silently, she continued. "Sir, please take a seat." Detective Oscar walked around her desk and sat down.

Stiffly, I lowered myself into one of the chairs in front of her. My body was taut and rigid as I sat, literally, on the edge of my seat and waited to hear what was going on.

Jake stood behind me and gave my shoulder a squeeze. His thumb ran along the nape of my neck.

I turned to look back at him, but his focus was on a bagged envelope on Detective Oscar's desk.

Rhys leaned against the wall by the door. Catching his gaze, he smiled at me but his dimples were barely noticeable.

Uh oh. Something is really freakin' *wrong.*

"Jake got a package at work today." After putting on gloves, Detective Oscar moved an evidence bag with a manila envelope in it to uncover two more bags. Grabbing one, she carefully opened it and removed a ball of fabric.

As it unraveled, I realized what they were.

"Those are my panties," I whispered.

"Have you worn these recently?"

"A few days ago. When... Oh my God. The night I went to Voodoo." Wide eyed, I gestured with my head back to Jake.

"Did you throw them out? Go to the gym in them? The laundry mat? Anywhere where they'd have been outside of your house?"

I shook my head as I tried to find some excuse for why my panties weren't at my house. My *home*. "No. I have a washer and dryer at home. Tomorrow's laundry day. They were in my hamper."

When Jake began rubbing my arms, I noticed I was shivering.

"I'm going to be honest, this was an extreme escalation. This isn't cyber stalking, or even regular stalking. Someone obviously broke into your house. There was a note included in the package, Miss Skye." Grabbing the other evidence bag, she moved it so I could see.

I leaned down to see the frantic scrawl on a torn piece of paper.

Next time she creams her panties,
it'll be for me.

"Wait, what?" Like my brain was trying to protect me, the words were a meaningless jumble. As realization dawned, I wished I hadn't tried so hard to understand. A strangled sob broke free and my shivering intensified, the chair vibrating and rattling from the movement. "Why?"

Detective Oscar shook her head sadly. "I wish I knew. There's something else. Another reason this is an *extreme* escalation. It appears as though there's fresh ejaculate on these."

Lifting a small table, Jake jerked it up so he was gripping the bottom of two legs. Assuming a batting stance, he stepped into it as he swung forcefully, putting all of his weight into the momentum. Time seemed to slow down as the table hit the wall. Like an explosion in an action movie, the wood imploded as it splintered into pieces.

When the door burst open, I was vaguely aware of Rhys moving to stand in front of me. However, my eyes were locked on Jake.

His fury radiated as he dropped the jagged posts and turned back towards the desk. "Are you sayin' some sicko jacked off on my woman's panties? And then sent them to me in the fuckin' mail?" he bellowed, making the room feel as though it was shaking.

Detective Oscar's face softened again. "Yes, but also no, I'm sorry, that isn't what I'm saying. There's no postage on this envelope. No evidence it's been through the postal service. This was hand delivered."

"You've gotta be fuckin' kiddin' me!"

"Who has access to your office?"

"Anyone. Everyone. I got a safe I keep anythin' valuable in, but the door is unlocked."

"I need any surveillance you have, Mr. Hyde. I'll contact businesses around you to see if anyone has seen anything. We'll also check if there are other cameras in the vicinity that might've picked something up. In the meantime, I'm going to send these off for analysis. In fact, Mendez and Franklin here will take them to the lab." With a nod, she held them out to the officers that had burst in.

"That means you might be able to get the DNA, right? And if there's DNA, he might be in a system? Or it could help when you catch him?" I preferred to look at the one positive thing that could come out of having my privacy so grossly violated.

"*If* it is confirmed that this is ejaculate and there's DNA, it will help. But you need to remember this kind of extreme escalation is a double-edged sword. On one side, he's breaking his pattern. Instead of the occasional emails, and most likely the flowers too, he's increasing both in timeframe and actions. He's pushing for a reaction."

He's about to get one in the form of me losing my lunch on my shoes.

"And he's getting stupid. All of this could make him easier to apprehend. But I need to stress that this level of recklessness could also make him more dangerous." She gestured between Jake and I. "When things were casual, or maybe before you got together, the occasional flower delivery was sufficient. As your relationship is progressing, so is his desperation. His obsession with you is surpassing his desire to not get caught."

"Fuck," Jake cursed roughly.

"Jake, we'll need to swab for your DNA so we can exclude it."

Clenching his jaw, he jerked his chin up.

"How long do the results take to come back?" I asked.

"It's not like on TV. DNA is temperamental and it takes a while for the analysis to come back. After that, there's the additional time to search through multiple databases. In the meantime, keep safe. Continue to have friends go everywhere with you." Her voice softened. "We'll get him, Piper. Just stay watchful and vigilant. Contact me day or night, okay?"

"Yes, thank you, Detective Oscar." My legs shook as I stood and began walking to the door.

"Come on, sweets. We'll head to the condo for the day." Jake's arm wrapped tight around me.

"No. I have so much to do and want to work. It'll help." I felt numb, my mind in a fog as I tried to process everything.

"Okay, we'll go to Hyde's." With a nod to the detective, he guided me from the room.

Rhys fell in step behind us, a silent guard.

Jake touched his pockets. "I ran out of the shop without my phone. Call Ray and get her to head to your place with Edge and some of the security if he can swing it. Have her pack a bunch of your stuff for the condo, yeah?"

I nodded, pulling my phone out as we exited the station.

"You need to cancel that cake," Jake said, storming into the Hyde kitchen a few days later.

I didn't have to ask which one he was referring to.

After our argument about Blake Green, Jake had tried to be cool and supportive about me doing the cakes. More so after our skeevy and upsetting visit to the police station.

I knew it wasn't easy for him. So, making myself a total hypocrite, I didn't tell him any of the shit Blake spewed.

I tuned Blake out and never even showed a reaction to any of the ridiculous things he said. Since I usually wanted to laugh in his face or roll my eyes so hard I'd give myself a headache, it was sometimes tough not to respond. When it became difficult to remain professional, I'd just remind myself how many opportunities this job could bring.

I'd thought things were moving along tolerably. Based on Jake's tone, however, I was wrong.

I sighed and continued washing measuring cups without looking at him. "I'm not cancelling. What's up?"

"You tried goin' through Rhys but Green shot that shit down. Now every fuckin' day he's callin' to talk about the cake. Needin' to get together to change somethin'. I don't trust him."

"Neither do I," I readily agreed. "Which is why Rhys is there. Or Kase is there. Or Z. Or Eli. Or Key. Or any combination of them." Picking up a dishrag, I turned to face Jake as I dried my hands off.

"Well, next time I'll be there."

"No way. Not gonna happen. We don't need a repeat of the Tools for Teens event. He'll poke the bear. The bear will punch him in the face. Then the bear will fuck me up against a wall." The towel in my hand flipped back and forth as I talked. I tossed it on the counter before I accidentally hit myself in the face. Again. “I’m all for the wall fuck, so can we just skip the other steps?”

“I don’t like the shit he says to you.”

“Yeah, what about Chloe? She’s still texting you, but you don’t see me bugging out.”

Jake leaned on the table and shrugged. “I ignore her shit.”

“And I ignore his.”

“Yeah, but he’s in your space. I can hit delete on a message without readin’ it. You can’t mute Green.”

“Yeah I can. He starts talking, and there’s this little black and white cow in a grass skirt that pops into my head. She dances the hula and plays a ukulele, and I don’t hear any of the white noise that comes out of his mouth. I’ve got a handle on this. I’ve gotten this far, and it’s almost done. If I do this, I’ll be a lot closer to hiring help and expanding.”

“You shouldn’t have to deal—”

“I’m dealing with this for my business, for my dream. You’re dealing with Chloe ‘cause you dipped your dick in crazy. It’ll be done soon and we’ll move on. Until then, you have to trust me.”

“Fuck, Piper, it isn’t you I don’t trust. But you’re so fuckin’ naive! You don’t get it.”

“No, I guess I don’t.” Crossing my arms, I looked up at him. “Explain it.”

“Every day that fucker is comin’ up with new shit to say to get you. To try to take my sweetness. And I’m supposed to just sit back? Fuck that.”

“You know what? I’m gonna be smart and bite my tongue right now. I’ve gotta get going anyways.” Storming out of the kitchen, I hopped in my car and drove to lunch with Ray, completely livid.

After all this time, he still didn’t trust me. There was nothing Blake could say that would make me interested in him. There was definitely nothing he could say that would change the way I felt about Jake.

Only Jake could do that.

"Well, well, well. Look who it is. Jake's innocent little bitch. Or should I say *former* innocent little bitch?"

I'll take catty, shrill voiced bitches I don't have patience for, for $800 Mr. Trebek.

Oh look, she's got a friend. Looks like it's a Daily Double.

"Rachel, dear, didn't you hear the news? Oh, I forgot, you're banned and no one is talking to you. Oh, that makes this extra fun then," Ray said, giving an evil smile.

I turned to look at Rachel and her friend who were both overly made up and showing near indecent amounts of skin. It was only two in the afternoon but they looked like they'd already been partying hard.

Like the karma gods were in on it, I held up my hand at the same time Voodoo's door opened. Sunlight streamed through and hit my engagement ring at the perfect angle to make it sparkle brightly.

"I'm going to be Mrs. Jake's Innocent Little Bitch Hyde. Boy, that's a mouthful. I'm thinking I'll just go by Mrs. Hyde."

"That's not what Chloe said," her side bitch said, looking to Rachel.

"Shut the fuck up, Chrissy," Rachel hissed, elbowing Chrissy hard in the ribs.

Chrissy continued on as if nothing happened, giving no indication she felt what had to have been a painful jab. "I'm confused. Chloe said she was with Jake and this chick was gone. Why would he give her a ring if they broke up? I don't get it." Even with the distance separating us, I could see that her eyes were glazed over. As she talked, her hand kept darting up to rub her nose.

"Holy shit, that bitch is high," I whispered to Ray.

"As a fuckin' kite. I already texted Edge, and he and security are on their way. Rachel's been banned for a while. I don't know how she got in, but I'm guessing it had to do with the both of them on their knees. I'm also betting whoever is working the entrance is about to lose their job."

"Chrissy, I said shut up," Rachel hissed again, her face contorting in anger.

"But Chloe said now that she's back with Jake, she's gonna get you unbanned from all the good places. Then you're gonna get one of the guys, and hook me up with one. I thought I was getting a man," Chrissy whined.

Pretty sure my boys would rather cut their own dicks off than dip it into noxious snatch.

"Chrissy, I swear to fuck, I'm gonna beat your ass!" Rachel screeched, stepping to her just as security showed up.

"Chloe said she sends him naked pictures all the time. She said that he has always wanted her back."

Holy fuck.

Jake had kept his promise and told me when Chloe started texting again. However, he hadn't said a word about pictures.

"Chloe's a lying, scheming whore. Don't trust a word outta that bitch's mouth," Ray said to Chrissy.

But I knew she was also talking to me.

"She sent Rachel a screenshot of a text from Jake. Show them."

"I'm really sorry, but she's right," Rachel said with fake sympathy as she reached into her bag. She touched her phone a few times before turning it to face Ray and me.

Jake: Fuck, that picture has me so hard. I can't wait to fuck you again. I have to figure out how to get all of her shit out of my shop and house. Then we won't have to sneak around. I'm going to come over later, get another taste of you to tide me over. I tried to make myself move on but there is no one else for me. You know what I like without me having to teach you every damn thing.

My stomach lurched and my face heated. The restaurant seemed to fall silent as the blood roared in my ears.

Looking around, I saw that Ray was saying something to me. Edge was screaming at Rachel as security forced her out, but all I heard was Jake's voice from that morning.

"But you're so fuckin' naive!"

Was I?

"I have to go," I mumbled as I woodenly stood. I knew Ray and Edge were talking, I saw their mouths moving, but I didn't hear a word they were saying.

Grabbing my bag, I ran to my car and drove to Hyde.

I pulled up to the garage and saw that Jake was already outside waiting for me. When my phone rang, I almost ignored it until I saw Rhys' name.

After what he'd heard at the police station, he'd started calling or texting more often to check on me. I didn't want to leave him hanging.

"Hey, hon, now's not a great time. Can I call you later?"

"Yeah. I just wanted to double check with you about cancelling the cake with Green. I wouldn't blame you. That dude is a half-ass voice with a full-scale ego. But you seemed so determined."

I shook my head as if he could see me. "I'm not cancelling." Looking out the window, I watched Jake pace as his hand rubbed the back of his neck.

"And that's why I was calling to see. Jake texted that you decided not to do the cake. He offered to pay someone else to take over on such short notice."

"I have to go. The cake is still a go. Sorry about the confusion."

"Cut him some slack, yeah? He's used to making the decisions. It comes with owning a business," he explained, knowing it wasn't a misunderstanding that caused Jake to text. "You know he's protective of you. This is all new to him."

"Maybe not as new as everyone thinks. Bye, Rhys." I hung up on him talking.

I'll feel bad later, but right now I'm pissed.

Beyond pissed.

Furious.

I was barely out of my car when Jake started talking. "I talked to Ray. And Edge. I have no clue what the fuck that message was. I haven't sent shit to Chloe."

"Does she send you naked pictures?"

"She could. I delete anythin' from her without lookin'. I swear to you, I haven't seen or texted her."

"Did you cancel my cake order?"

Guilt flashed across his face as he reached for me.

On clumsy feet, I took a few steps back. If he touched me, I'd give in.

I always did.

No wonder he thinks he can just do what he wants.

"Piper." His voice was rough as he looked at my feet. "I kept thinkin' about what Green said to you, all the shit about the trash I fucked. How you fuckin' me made you trash. Then Z told me about some shit he overheard him sayin'. We got enough with the fuckin' sicko out there. You don't need to be puttin' yourself through that."

"You don't always get to tell me what to do!" I screamed, stomping my foot. "I'm an adult."

Minus the foot stomp.

"You need to trust me to know when it's too much. And it isn't. I can ignore him. I don't know where you're getting all your information from, but he barely says shit to me. He's a joke. What's not a joke is you promising to trust me, and then going behind my back to do what you want."

"Piper, just—" Jake said softly as he reached for me again.

And again, I backed away. It was unmistakable, such was the distance I put between us.

Pain followed by anger shrouded his face.

"I'm supposed to trust that the screenshot I *saw*, with *your* name,"

I said, pointing at him, "from *your* number, isn't you. You expect me to believe you, but you won't do the same for me."

"But—"

"I'm not some trashy skank looking to bed hop. Why would anything he says make me change that? What's the point of being together if you think that little of me? I told you, I've got a handle on it. I'm fine!"

Jake raised an eyebrow. "Are you fine, Piper?" His voice was low, his tone misleadingly soft. "How fine? You so set on doin' this cake 'cause you like spendin' time with Green? Hearin' all the things he wants to do to you? I know you email with Jet and the guys all the time, sendin' shit to them wherever they are."

I threw my hands up in frustration. "Yeah, 'cause we're friends."

"Maybe you really are just a fuckin' act. No one's this naive."

"I'm not—"

As he prowled towards me, I backed away until my body hit the side of the building. Not in fear.

In heartache.

"Slummin' it with a fuckin' mechanic gettin' old for you? Does it turn you on to have famous rock stars hard for you? Knowin' they jack off thinkin' about you? Make you wanna go all groupie on their rocker dicks?" Jake's voice was malicious as he fired off his questions in rapid succession, each one hitting like a physical blow.

"Whoa, too far, man," Xavier barked before I could say anything.

"Step back, dude," Kase warned, wedging himself between Jake and I.

After all we've been through, this is what he thinks of me? What he thinks of us?

Ducking to the side, I stumbled as I moved away.

Jake shifted to steady me, but Kase blocked him.

Though I wished I sounded fierce, my voice was small and shaking. "Fuck you, Jake." Tears blurred my vision as I turned and ran to my car as fast as my wobbly legs and heels would carry me.

My fingers shook as I tried to fit the key into the ignition. Involuntarily, my eyes focused out the window to see Kase toe-to-toe with Jake as he got in his face.

I started the car and put it into reverse. Every instinct I had screamed at me to slam the car back into park, but I ignored them.

We needed a break.

Killer Insecurities

"I'm sorry, Jake. I just think it would be best if we ended this now," I said through the crack in the door.

He'd tried to gently push it open to get to me, but that wasn't happening.

It was too late.

"What the fuck are you talkin' about, Piper?" Jake asked, his brows drawn down.

Even Kase looked stunned. Though he was giving us space, he was still there to have his boy's back. He must've given Jake a ride since we'd taken my car that morning.

Has it really been less than an hour since I left him?

"Things just aren't going to work between us. Here." Wiggling my engagement ring off my finger, I held it out to him.

Adding a head tilt to the lowered brows, Jake glanced blankly at it and then back at me, like he didn't comprehend my words or action. He made no move to take it.

My sweat slickened fingers shook so badly that I lost my hold on it. It fell between us, hitting the ground with a ping.

Neither of us looked to see where it landed.

"But you're mine."

"I'm not."

“You are. You swore you wouldn’t take your sweetness from me.”

His words made me regret the promises I often gave him. “Things change.”

“You got my name tattooed on you. Your name is fuckin’ inked permanently on me.” His hand shook as he touched his chest, reminding me of the night he’d first shown it to me.

I looked at him with a bored expression. “Tattoos can be covered. Just blend it in with your other ink.”

“Are you fuckin’ serious?”

I wished I was joking, but I knew there was no going back. I had no other choice. “It wouldn’t have worked, Jake. I… I need to be with someone more my level. Like James. Or Blake. You were right. I need better than a mechanic.”

“I fucked up. That was fuckin’ stupid today. When you asked what the point of us bein’ together was, I just lost it. I’m sorry.” His words were sincere and I knew he’d put the effort in to never act like that again.

It was just too late.

“Don’t apologize. You were right because I do like that stuff. That’s how I know things aren’t going to work between us. Goodbye, Jacoby. Bye, Kase.” I tried again to close the door.

“Sweets… Fuck, Piper. Please, just talk to me,” Jake pleaded, the tortured strain in his voice painful to hear. “I’m sorry I said all that shit. I’ll never say anythin’ like that again. But you can’t leave me, Piper. You promised.” His eyes went bright with unshed tears. Tears I’d never thought I’d see from him, let alone be the one putting there. “You can’t do this. You can’t give me all that’s you, make me so fuckin’ happy for the first time in my life, and then walk away like it meant nothin’.”

I’ve gotta get him out of here. This is too fuckin’ much.

“It *was* nothing, Jake.” My voice was cold and firm so he’d get the point. “I’m too young to settle down. I thought we were just having fun but then things kinda spiraled out of control. I should’ve put a stop to it earlier. It was fun, and you taught me a bunch, but there's nothing else to get from this."

"I've *taught* you a bunch?"

I shrugged. "Even you had to get your experience from somewhere."

Jake threw his arms out. "Are you seriously fuckin' tellin' me you're gonna suck and ride some other man's dick the way I taught you I liked it?"

"Well, yeah." The implied 'duh' went unsaid. "It's not like I'm never going to have sex with anyone again."

"It was supposed to be me. *Only* me." He thumped his chest for emphasis. "You fuckin' said it!"

Balling my fists at my side, I leaned forward. "And I fuckin' *lied*!"

His voice was hoarse as he shook his head. "Piper—"

"I've gotta go."

"Wait." Leaning heavily on the doorframe, a single tear started down his stubbled cheek.

I shut the door in his face.

"I don't fuckin' get it, man. I've gotta go back. She's gotta talk to me." I was ramblin' but I couldn't help it.

"Dude, just give her time. This is Pipe we're talking about," Kase said, trying to calm me, but it wasn't workin'.

"Exactly. Piper doesn't play games. She wouldn't say that shit to me unless she was sure." My gut felt painfully empty and my head was poundin'. "I love her. Fuck, I've never loved anyone *but* her. She's everythin' I've been tryin' to find but so much fuckin' better. I had that sweetness, and now she just wants to take it away? I have her fuckin' name tattooed on my chest." I rubbed the spot where I knew her name was. I smiled every day when I saw it there.

I smile every fuckin' day 'cause *of her.*

"I was supposed to give her my name. She was supposed to be my *wife. Mine.* I know I fucked up, but I've done it before. She calls me out on my bullshit and we move on."

"You gotta relax. The shit you said? That was seriously fucked up, brother. Just give her time. She'll come around. Piper isn't like this. She'll call you, and shit will get straightened out," Eli put in.

Eli didn't know. He hadn't seen her face when she'd told me that we were a mistake. Or when she'd handed me back my ring and just let it drop between us like it meant nothin'.

After Piper shredded me, Kase had to drag me away. I kept hopin' she'd throw open the door and laugh as she explained it was all just a really fuckin' bad joke.

I believed her every time she'd told me she loved me. That she needed me. That she'd never leave me.

I could tell, from a fuckin' mile away, which women were connivin' and tryin' to blind me with biker bitch snatch like I was fuckin' dumb. They wanted to use me for my money, my name, my dick.

But that wasn't Piper.

She'd never been an act. She wanted and loved me for me.

Didn't she?

Fuck.

"Dude, you gotta chill. All the pacing is making me dizzy." Kase pulled out a bottle of scotch and some glasses from the bottom drawer of my desk.

I kept it in there for bad days.

And since Piper came into your life, how many days have you had to dip into it? How many nights have you worked yourself to exhaustion and then drank yourself to oblivion before crashin' on the couch in the break room?

Yeah, that's what you have to look forward to again.

I stared at the dark amber liquid in the heavy tumbler. Liftin' it, I side armed it at the wall and watched the light reflect off it as it exploded into worthlessness.

As incredibly expensive scotch dripped down the wall and soaked into the carpet, I knew I had to go.

"I gotta get the fuck outta here," I growled, reaching for the door as Kase blocked it.

"Give it time. Nothing good will come from you going over there when emotions are so high."

"It's not that. Okay, it's not *just* that. I've gotta get outta *here*." The whole place smelled like her. Her fuckin' pictures were coverin' the wall. All I could think about was the shit we'd done on the desk, what she'd done under it... "I can't fuckin' breathe. I won't go to her. I just gotta get out of here."

Kase moved, allowin' me to throw the door open.

I started for the garage when I turned towards the break room.

No, Piper's kitchen.

I'd often make any excuse to come back here and watch silently from the doorway while she baked, shakin' her ass and singin' louder than she realized. Sometimes she'd be curled up on the couch with her legs tucked under her as she sketched a design. Her focus was so intense that she didn't notice me starin', astonished all over again that she was mine.

Or so she'd said.

A roar left me as I stalked into the break room. Grabbin' anythin' I could, I threw it, breakin' it like she broke me. I reached out to snatch up the next thing, only to come up empty-handed.

As I stood in the middle of the destruction, I saw my life without Piper.

An empty fuckin' mess.

"Uh, sorry to interrupt."

I glanced to the doorway and saw Rachel.

"Hey. I just..." She looked around, her lips tipping up slightly. "Have you seen Chloe? She isn't returning any of my texts or calls. I thought maybe you might know."

"I've got no fuckin' clue."

"Are you okay?"

"I've got no fuckin' clue," I repeated.

"You wanna go somewhere private to talk?" She tentatively approached, like I was a wild animal that might attack.

She's right.

We'd fucked once years ago. It wasn't meaningful, but it'd been semi-effective.

I looked down at her again, this time actually seein' her. She was pushin' her fake tits out and there was a hungry look in her eyes. I knew talkin' wasn't what she was offerin'.

"C'mon, sweetie, let's get outta here."

I let her grab my arm and pull me from the room.

I fucked up. Shit, did I fuck up.

We were supposed to be having dinner at my mother and Thomas' house with Sarah and Gregory that night. The parents hated the Vegas wedding idea, and were pushing to discuss alternatives.

Since Ray hadn't packed anything from the conservative side of my closet, I needed to grab a plain dress. I was even going to pull my hair back again. I wanted to try to make the dinner go as smooth as possible.

So I'd gone home alone. I'd thought it'd be fine. I was just going to grab a couple of things and then I'd meet Jake at the apartment to talk.

What was there to worry about in the middle of the afternoon?

A lot, as it turns out.

After arriving home, I kicked the front door closed behind me and tossed my purse onto my junk table. My thoughts were consumed by my fight with Jake and I wasn't paying attention.

I wasn't being vigilant.

"Piper!" James yelled as he ran into the room from the kitchen.

My doors are locked and James is in my house.

My mind flashed back to James' reaction to Jake and me together. Then I thought of the way he'd pushed himself on me at my mother's, kissing me and saying all those awful things.

I started to back away in fear when he yelled again.

"Piper, run!" His last word seemed to boom and then he crumpled to the ground. Red spread across the floor.

Was he holding a Kool-Aid?

No, wait, that's blood.

Someone shot James.

"Hey, there, Doll Face."

"Z, what're you doing here?" I forced out.

My mind raced for any excuse to explain why he was in my house. I wanted to believe he was protecting me. James could be a dick and lately he'd been seriously creeping me out. But Z? He wouldn't hurt me.

Looking into his eyes, though, I knew I was wrong. He didn't look like the same handsome, should be GQ model. He looked crazy.

Crazy as fuck.

As Z came towards me, he casually stepped over James as though he were nothing more than a mild inconvenience. Like there was a puddle of rain, and not blood, in his path. When he got closer, I saw the glint of the gun in his hand.

"Sorry about the stain on your carpet."

"That's okay." I tried to keep my voice level. "Things happen."

"They do, but they shouldn't. Things should go according to plan. Always!" he suddenly roared, spit flying from his mouth.

"What—"

At the sound of car doors closing, Z's head snapped to the side. Unmistakable loathing took over his face, twisting it. The gorgeous man became a memory replaced by ugliness. "Speaking of, it's the man of changes. The man who couldn't stick with a plan. Even now, he's fuckin' shit up. You were supposed to break things off at Hyde and he was supposed to move on. Why don't we help him out with that, huh?"

Please, turn away Jake. Just cut your losses and go!

"How should we do that?"

"Crush him. Tell him you need someone different, someone better. Oh," he said with a maniacal, humorless laugh. "Tell him you want to be with James here." He nudged James' shoulder with the tip of his shoe. "No, I've got better. Tell him you want Blake. Say you want someone closer to your own age, working a better job. He's so insecure about that shit."

"Why do you want to hurt him?" I asked, but Z talked right over me.

"He's talked to us before about how he worried you'd change your mind about slumming it with him. Classy chick like you with a glorified mechanic? Young, beautiful, *clean* woman with a dirty old man? He thought you'd wake up one morning and regret everything. He's used to bitches wanting to fuck their way up the food chain. It's all he's ever known. But you? No, not his *sweets*," he said with a sneer. "Won't that fuck with his head, huh?"

"Z, why are you doing this?" I tried again. My heart was breaking just thinking about what he was asking me to do.

I'll just figure out some way to signal to Jake that there is something wrong. He'll fix it. He always does.

"That doesn't matter now. Open the door, Doll Face. And if you say anything, I swear to fuck, you'll regret it." He raised the gun and shook it. Like I could forget it was there. "If I even catch a hint that he thinks something's going on, I'll shoot Jake and Kase and make you watch. Got it?"

There goes that plan.

I nodded, deep breathing.

I was again thankful for my mother's lessons. They prepared me to act as though my heart wasn't being ripped out and shredded to pieces.

After putting on what had to have been an Oscar worthy performance, Z pushed me to the window. His fingertips dug into my jaw painfully as he forced me to watch Jake and Kase outside.

When they finally left, he used his hold to move me towards my bedroom. Panic gripped me and I screamed inside.

Once in my room, he let go of me. I stumbled and almost fell to the ground as my legs threatened to give out.

Z grabbed my suitcases from the closet and threw them on the end of my bed. Opening my dresser drawers, he dumped clothes in one handed while his other gripped the gun.

"Sit. I'm just gonna pack you some stuff and then we'll be on our way, okay? Then things will be like my plan. I said sit!" Z barked, his face back to harsh.

I jumped and scurried up my bed. Pressing my back against the headboard, I tried to put as much distance between us as I could. The bed shook from the force of my tremors.

As I watched him pack, I wished I was cool and calm. I tried to think of ways to escape, but I had nothing. Short of throwing the lotions and vibrators I had in my bedside drawer, there were no weapons within my reach.

I'm thinking dildos flying at his head wouldn't be enough to make him drop the gun and run for his life.

"Why?" I asked again, trying to keep my voice upbeat as if I were simply curious.

He stopped rifling through my drawers and turned to me with a smile. His grin made his handsome face near breathtaking. He almost looked like the old Z, except his gray eyes were crazed and his movements erratic. "'Cause you're mine, Doll Face. That was the plan. I saw you and knew right away you were mine. When you needed work done, I knew it was fate. Jake wasn't even supposed to be in that morning. He wasn't supposed to see you but he did. I thought he didn't like you much. But I saw the way you were watching him. I couldn't tell you that you were mine then. Not when you were practically presenting!"

Terrified, I pushed against the headboard until it squeaked in protest. My heart pounded in my chest as I worked to steady my breathing.

Z's face went soft as he tamed his crazy. "I could've done your speakers the first time, but I needed you to come in again. Jake was supposed to have a meeting with the parts distributor, but he cancelled. He never cancels anything. Hyde is his life. We all knew he did it to see you. I figured he'd move on after a couple days. But he didn't, Piper. Why did he have to change the plans?"

I curled into myself further when his thundering voice filled my room.

"I don't think he knew the plans, sweetheart," I said. "Why don't you tell them to me?"

The contempt he has for Jake, the deep hatred? I can't believe how well he's been able to hide it.

"See? I knew if I just got you away from him, you'd be so sweet to me. You'd look at me like you looked at him. You'd love me and I'd protect you. And I did, Piper. James came here to tell you that he loved you and to make you feel bad. And I stopped him. I did that for you, Doll Face."

I nodded my head. "I know. Thank you," I lied through the lump in my throat.

"I'll always protect you. I'll die for you. I'm sorry you had to see me hurt him but you weren't supposed to be here. You weren't supposed to see what I have to do to protect you. Why were you here? Why? Answer me!" he demanded as he ran his hand over his head. His hair was in disarray, no longer the perfectly coiffed pompadour.

For some reason, seeing that hit me hard.

How symbolic.

Down to his fucking hair, he's not the same guy I thought I knew.

"I don't know. I'm sorry." I had no clue what I was apologizing for, but it seemed the best choice.

I knew I was right when, just like that, he was back to soft Z. "It's okay. I kept you safe this time. I'll always keep you safe."

"I know, sweetheart. What're the plans? I don't want to mess them up."

"You're so good to me. I love you so much, Doll Face. That's why I did all of this. I needed you to need me. Not Jake. Not the bank. *Me*!"

I flinched when his hand that was holding the gun hit his chest for emphasis.

"What about the bank?"

"That's another way I knew it was fate. Imagine my good fortune when I found out you did your banking at the same place I did. I followed you in all the time. You were always in your own world, so oblivious." He crossed his arms over his chest as he shook his head. "You need to pay attention, Doll Face."

Ain't that the fucking lesson of the century?

"I let it slip a few times to the bank manager about how irresponsible you were with money. I told him you kept baking after partying so everything was burnt and that I was surprised you hadn't started a big fire yet. Now you need me and I can take care of you, right?"

That solves that mystery.

"Right," I agreed softly.

"I'll always take care of you." He smiled at me lovingly before his lips curled in disgust. "That's why that bitch Chloe had to die."

I never thought I'd say this, but poor Chloe.

"That's why James had to die," he continued nonchalantly, as if killing two people was no biggie.

Definitely poor James.

A sob wracked my body, but Z didn't notice. Completely absorbed in his rant, he didn't seem to even know where he was.

I braced in the bed, waiting for any opportunity to make a run for it. I barely scooched when his eyes snapped back to me, cutting off my escape before it'd even begun.

"Chloe went off plan. She tried to fuck me like I wasn't already yours. She called me over today and said she was horny. Things weren't working with Jake and she thought she could get me. When I turned her down, she said she'd run to Jake and tell him *everything*. Just like that, months of work would be for nothing. I couldn't let that happen, could I, Doll Face?"

"No." My hands clutched the sheets as I watched the gun move haphazardly as he started grabbing things from my closet.

"She didn't want Jake to be happy with someone else. Her pride couldn't handle him giving someone else what he'd never given her. She just wanted to be back in the circle. To get invited to the parties and bars without everyone ignoring her. She didn't even care who she was fucking to get her there. And she thought she'd get me? That bitch was insane," Z muttered, shaking his head.

Uhh, psychotic pot meet batshit crazy kettle.

"I'd told her the plan when we walked out of Hyde that day she got in your face. Fuck, she was a stupid bitch. Jake wanted sweet, not a bitchy ballbuster. All her fuckin' scene did was make him want you more. I told her to be sweet and offer him everything he liked. She'd get him, I'd get you, and everyone would be happy. But he didn't go. He didn't even acknowledge her. I had to grab his phone to send that text."

Yet another mystery solved.

"But she got cocky and ran her mouth. She had to brag to that stupid bitch, Rachel. No one fuckin' believes Rachel. And then she wanted to hurt you. As payback, she'd said, for stealing her man and then punching her in the face. She wanted me to record her and Jake fucking and force you to watch. Then while you were held down, she wanted her chance to hit you. Like I'd let anyone hurt you. I protect you!"

I'd known Jake hadn't sent that text. If he hit his head, got all sense knocked out of him, and decided to cheat on me, it would never be with Chloe.

Thinking about the screen shot I'd seen, I realized the message had to have been sent when we were at the police station. I'd called Ray because Jake didn't have his phone. We were leaving, shaken and upset, because of what he had gotten in the mail.

As if on cue, Z's packing stopped as he opened my underwear drawer. "I can't even tell you how good it felt covering your come with mine. When I did the walkthrough of your house, I'd passed by your hamper and there they were. I wanted to be in your bed, smelling you, but I didn't want you to worry about me. You always worried when I was gone too long."

What? Since when?

Before I could ask what he was talking about, he kept ranting.

"So I pocketed them, knowing what I was going to do. I was there, you know, when Jake opened the package. I got to watch him feel what I felt seeing you two together. Rhys told us later that Jake hadn't even noticed the special addition that I'd made to the panties. He said that Jake broke a table." Z's gleeful expression quickly turned angry again. "But you let him fuck you, Doll Face. All the time.

His office *reeked* of it. We could hear you sometimes. We'd get to the hallway and you'd be in there, moaning and screaming for him. I needed to see what you were letting him do to you. How you were a whore for him. I needed to know what to punish him for. I couldn't protect you if I didn't watch you. That's why I wired cameras in his office and the break room."

Holy fuck. I was right that something felt off. Why didn't I listen to my instincts?

Oh yeah, 'cause they also demanded I jumped Jake.

Which crazy ass Z watched, like the fucking creeper he is.

"I loved to see you in the break room. You looked so fragile when you curled into yourself and drew. You were pure. Then you'd walk across the hall, and instead of being my *good* girl, you were Jake's whore. But I had to watch." He pulled his phone out of his pocket. "In fact, let's see how *Jacoby* is taking things."

He touched the screen a few times and turned it for me to see when Hyde appeared. The men, *my boys*, were sitting in Jake's office, but he wasn't with them. Z touched the screen again to switch to the break room.

Jake was standing in front of the couch, and he wasn't alone.

Standing close to him, Rachel held his arm. She turned and pulled him out the door, though he didn't look like he was putting up any kind of fight.

I gulped back tears, the pain of seeing him with someone else stabbing through me.

"It's about fuckin' time, am I right?" Z chuckled as we watched Jake and Rachel leave the room, *my* kitchen, together. "Finally he goes with the plan but it's too late. He's already made things get this far. I tried to end this earlier because I didn't want you to get hurt. That's why I started stealing parts."

Another mystery solved.

This is like the world's creepiest freakin' episode of Sherlock.

"They were expensive, custom parts that set him behind and cost him a fortune. I thought he'd break things off nicely 'cause he needed to focus on Hyde. It was his business, his pride, everything he'd worked for. But he didn't give a shit. He just kept fucking you at work, as if shit wasn't going wrong. As if the answers to all of the shop's problems were hidden in your cunt. So I kept messing shit up while no one was looking. I thought you'd get sick of him working long hours, but you didn't. You were so sweet. And do you know what Jake did?"

"No," I whispered. My chest ached as I thought of what he was most likely doing at that moment.

"Nothing. Not one *fucking* thing. He worked with a smile on his face as if everything was perfect. Instead of putting in more hours to try to fix things, he started leaving earlier to go see you."

Hearing that was bittersweet, warming me even as it eviscerated me.

"I sent Rachel after you. I made sure Chloe went to the Boston event. I thought if you saw the trash he normally fucked, you'd realize you were too good for him. But you were sweet about that, too. When nothing else worked, I started telling Green about the way you fucked Jake. The way you're such a whore for him, screaming and begging. Green wanted you anyway, but after he heard about that? I hated to see him try to touch you, touch what's mine, but I already knew my good girl wouldn't fall for it." His expression darkened. "He'll pay for every sick word that came out of his mouth."

Even though he's a douche and an asshole, no one deserves Z's version of payback.

"I overheard him and his friends talking about how they pictured you when they jacked off. Being the good friend that I am, I told Jake today."

Z fell silent as he grabbed another suitcase and started throwing random lotions and creams from on top of my dresser into it.

I had no plan. I knew he wasn't going to let me just walk out of here. If I had any chance at getting away, I needed to stall.

"Why?"

"Jake's fuckin' crazy when it comes to you. I knew he'd be a dick and push you away. He couldn't help himself. You were so sweet, so forgiving, but even you'd have a breaking point." He looked at me over his shoulder and smiled. "Now you'll be sweet to me, right?"

Before I could answer, his face clouded as anger took over.

"You didn't notice me. You didn't care when the pervert's date was hitting on me. You laughed. You were supposed to feel what I felt. But you didn't. Now you'll love me. You'll need me. You'll listen and stick to the plan!"

Watching Z walk around with his gun bouncing, I swallowed down my panic and tried to stay calm.

His mood was mercurial, his expressions changing rapidly between fury, disgust, crazy as fuck, and obsessive love.

It was the love that was scaring me the most.

"I tried to be patient," he started again, staring into my dresser drawer before looking back to me. "I tried to wait. But all the while, you were letting him fuck you wherever. Like up against the wall in Boston. Anyone could've seen you. Heard you. You let him fuck you in a car at the side of the road. That's what whores do, Piper. They suck dick and fuck in cars at the side of the road. And that's what you did." He picked up a fistful of my panties and nighties. "You were a fuckin' whore! Why, Doll Face? Why'd you do that?" he screamed as he pulled at the delicate fabric, tearing it apart.

"I don't know. I'm sorry."

"I tried to save you from him. I tried to remind him how young you are and how much more experience he had, wanted, needed. The trash he usually fucked talked about how he liked it. At least he wasn't as bad as Rhys. Thank Christ you didn't get with that pervert. Still, I thought even if Jake did go for it, you'd run from him when he did that stuff. But you couldn't get enough. You were fucking begging for it. I heard you. Literally begging. Like his dick was magic. Like you needed it to breathe."

It's not his dick I need to breathe.

It's only him.

"And, fucking *Jacoby*." The hate twisted his face again. "All of a sudden he couldn't get enough. He wasn't jumping to anyone else. Girls, exactly his type, would come on to him, but he brushed them off like they were pests. Nothing more than annoying gnats. He wasn't even tempted."

Based on him leaving with Rachel, I'm guessing that's done.

"He didn't go with the plan. What's so addicting about that pussy, Doll Face?" he asked softly. As his eyes travelled my body, his arousal became evident. Dropping the tattered panties, the scraps fluttered uselessly to the ground.

I knew what was going to happen if I didn't find a way to distract him. "You never told me the plans. You started packing 'cause we're going, right?"

Z walked towards the side of my bed, his eyes bright with twisted pleasure. "You hurt him so badly, he's not coming back, Doll Face. He's probably fucking Rachel already. You told him how you really feel, didn't you? You were over him. No one could fake being that mean, that cold. Tell me you don't love him. Tell me!"

Even in the face of his crazed rage, I couldn't force myself to say the words.

A pained yelp burst out instead when Z pulled his arm back and backhanded me. The force slammed my head back to collide with the headboard. Lights burst behind my eyes, and a dazed nausea followed.

"I told you to say it. We need to stick to the plan. You weren't supposed to love him. He wasn't supposed to love you. And now he's hurt you. It's his fault and he'll die, Doll Face. Just like Green. Just like James. You weren't supposed to be here. I have to do things to protect you. You weren't supposed to see."

I couldn't keep up with his tirade. It was a safe bet that no one but the voices in his head could.

I tried my best to appease him. "Tell me the plans. Please. I want to make sure I'm doing the right stuff."

"I love you. I knew you'd love me, I just had to get you away from him. He had you blinded and fooled. But it'll be fine now. We're going to disappear together, anywhere you want. Just the two of us at first, but we'll start a family soon. Jake didn't want kids, but you'd make such a good mother. That's another way I'm protecting you, by giving you everything you deserve. Where do you want to go?" Sitting on the side of the bed near me, his hand rubbed my tight cheek.

Holding back the urge to scream and move away, I clenched my fists until my nails dug into my palms. I could feel my blood dripping down my fingers.

I forced a smile. "Somewhere far. If we're going to be together, we need to go now. Just the two of us, we'll leave all this behind."

If I can't get away, I'll make him take me far from here. To keep Jake and everyone safe, I'll do anything.

I jolted back, hitting my head again, when Z lowered his head and sloppily pressed his lips to mine as he climbed on top of me. I could feel him hard, thrusting against me. Tears pooled in my eyes as I battled to control my retching stomach. My mouth filled with saliva.

"I have to feel you again, Doll Face. I have to see what made Jake go so far from the plan."

Again? What the hell is he talking about?

"We should leave. Please, before someone shows up. We'll just go," I begged, trying to prolong what was clearly an inevitable.

When Z set his gun down on the side table, I lurched up in a feeble attempt to get it.

His hand closed tightly around my throat. Using his hold, he pushed me down onto my pillow.

My stomach heaved as I tried to breathe around the pressure.

"We'll leave when I'm done and my scent is on you. After it's me you're screaming for." Getting up onto his knees, his hand pressed harder against my throat while he focused on undoing his pants.

As my head started pounding and my lungs burned from lack of air, I fought hard.

Not against Z, or what he was trying to do. His grip was too tight and his body pinned me in place.

I fought against instinct.

When the black around the edge of my vision started creeping in, I welcomed it. I knew what was going to happen, whether I was awake or not.

I chose not.

I heard a final muffled noise. Then blissful nothingness.

Jake

"I gotta grab my keys from the office," I said to Rachel as she led me from Piper's kitchen.

When we entered the room, the men were still in there.

Probably discussin' the best way to handle me losin' my damn mind.

At the sight of Rachel hangin' on my arm, they looked ready to physically take me down.

"Brother, I know you're hurting but are you out of your fuckin' head?" Eli asked.

"Rachel, believe me, I mean *all* the offense in the world when I say this because I truly do think you're a cock-juggling thundercunt," Kase started before lookin' at me. "Dude, if you're wanting what Rachel's gonna give you, you'd be better off dipping your dick in honey and sticking it down a fuckin' fire ant hole. You'll still get that burning sensation, but it'll save you the embarrassing trip to the doctor for a large dose of penicillin." He looked back at her. "Once again, Rachel, I mean that in just the absolute *worst* possible fuckin' way."

"Fuck you, Kase. You're just jealous we never hooked up," Rachel spat, movin' closer to me.

"Damn, you've figured me out. I'm totally heartbroken." Kase sighed dramatically. "My secret fetish has always been to fuck a chick with fake titties. Especially one whose snatch is probably so loose by now that it'd be like throwing a hot dog down a hallway."

"Are you gonna let him say that shit?" Rachel asked me, crossin' her arms under said fake tits.

"'Course not. Kase, there's nothin' wrong with good fake tits." I watched as she started to smile smugly at Kase. "That bein' said, Rachel's are seriously jacked up. But don't lump all fake ones together. Plus, man, if you think I'm dippin' my dick in anythin' but Piper, you're outta your mind. Rachel's only here 'cause my gut's sayin' Chloe and her are up to somethin'."

"I don't know shit," Rachel denied, clearly lyin' as she moved towards the door. Xavier and Eli were already positioned in front of it, no doubt to block me from leavin' with her.

"I know you're a bitch, but that doesn't mean you're not smart about this shit. No way would you go along with anythin' unless you were sure you'd get somethin' out of it. Edge and his woman already said you were spoutin' shit about Chloe hookin' you up with someone. What made you think she'd be able to pull off that miracle?"

"Even if I knew anything, why the fuck would I tell you?" Her lips curved up as she put her hands to her waist. "Especially after all this?"

"See? You just proved my point. You won't do shit unless there's somethin' in it for you. And I've got somethin' to offer you that I know you'll want. But you have to tell me what Chloe's plan is, and I mean every detail."

Her eyes lit gleefully. She'd happily rat out her girl for whatever she could get. "What is it?"

"I won't call the cops."

Rachel rolled her eyes. "Why would I care? You can't prove I know anything."

"True," I agreed. "However, you either took a fuckin' bath in vodka or you're drunk, 'cause it's honest to God burnin' my eyes just breathin' in. Plus, I'm doubtin' that white powder under your nose is makeup. And, if you drove here on your bike, my security cameras recorded it."

Rachel's eyes went wide as she brought a hand up to rub at her nose. "I don't know much, but I'll tell you what I do. Just don't call the cops, okay?"

I glanced at Key who already had his phone out.

He looked up and gave an almost imperceptible nod.

I nodded at Rachel.

"Promise. Before I say a word, swear it."

"I promise no one will call the cops."

She'd driven drunk and coked out in the middle of the afternoon. There was no way we'd turn a blind eye to that shit. While no one was callin', I knew Key was textin' Detective Oscar. I'd given everyone her number, just in case.

I tensed at the reminder of the detective and why everyone needed her contact information. "Fuck! Someone give me their fuckin' keys." I moved to my safe as Xavier tossed me the keys to his bike.

"What is it?" Kase asked, all humor gone from his face.

"I left Piper alone," I pointed out. I heard the men curse but I turned back to Rachel. "What the fuck was Chloe up to?" Opening the safe, I pulled my gun out and checked it. Grabbing the shoulder harness, I slid it on and holstered the gun.

"Is that real?" she asked, a mix of fear and lust in her eyes.

"No, it's a squirt gun." I turned away and pulled on my leather jacket.

"Why do you have a gun?"

"I own a multimillion dollar custom garage near a major city. What part of this isn't obvious? Talk."

"*Multi*million?" she breathed.

"Bitch, fuckin' talk!"

Rachel jumped before she started talking so fast I was having trouble following. "Chloe said she was working with some dude that wanted your bitch. A lot. She didn't tell me who, just that he was positive he'd get her. She made it seem like it was someone you were close with 'cause he easily fucked with you all the time. That's all I know, I swear."

"Keep her here 'til the cops pick her up," I said as I opened the door.

"You said you wouldn't call!" I heard Rachel screech just before it slammed closed behind me.

"He *texted*, you selfish..." Kase said, the rest of his words trailin' off as I ran to Xavier's bike.

I fucked up. Shit, did I fuck up.

Weavin' in and out of traffic, I went as fast as I could. I knew somethin' was wrong. I felt it in my fuckin' gut.

I'd fucked up.

Piper was right when she'd said I didn't trust her. Now she could be in danger and it was my fault.

I was missin' some link between today, the shit with Chloe, and Piper's stalker. If Rachel was tellin' the truth, that connection was someone we knew. My mind worked as I tried to figure out who'd do this.

Not just who *would* do it, but who *could*.

Sweet as she was, there was no way Piper would've stayed and let things between us continue because they'd spiraled. If she'd wanted out, she would've been gone. She definitely wouldn't have said she loved me and agreed to marry me if she thought we were just havin' fun.

Thinkin' of Piper with anyone but me made my gut clench and temper rise. I breathed in deep and tried to think it through logically.

Even if she was endin' things between us, there was no way Piper would go with James. Maybe she'd be into Gage or Jet, but definitely not Blake Green.

She didn't even like his music.

But they were meetin' often and with everythin' Z told me...

No.

Not Z.

No way he'd do this to me. No fuckin' way.

It's gotta be someone else.

It's gotta be.

Even as I tried to convince myself otherwise, the pieces fell into place like a fucked up puzzle.

The men liked their jobs and they worked hard. I never had to babysit any of them, but I knew where they were most of the time since we worked side by side.

Except Z.

He did the wiring in a different room at the shop. He'd had access to Piper's phone and computer. More importantly, he'd know what to do with them.

I asked her fuckin' stalker to protect her from himself.

I'd been grateful when Piper told me he'd gone into her house to check things out. I'd thought he was bein' a good friend.

That was probably when he grabbed her fuckin' panties.

At the reminder of the package he'd probably just fuckin' set on my desk, I accelerated the bike faster.

Parkin' a few houses down from Piper's, I jogged the remainder of the way. I didn't hear any noise as I climbed onto the porch. My heart halted in my chest as I eased the front door open to reveal a pool of blood soakin' into Piper's carpet.

Pushin' it fully open, my breath hissed out when I saw James lyin' in the blood, his eyes on me.

"Room. Gun. Cops coming quietly," he rasped. He lifted the phone in his hand slightly but the effort to talk or move clearly pained him.

I jerked my chin up. Unholsterin' my gun, I switched the safety off.

"Take care of her," he forced out. His eyes closed as his head dropped back to the floor.

My heart was poundin' in my throat as I moved slowly towards the bedroom. I pushed tight against the wall and heard the low rumble of Z's voice from Piper's room.

Gettin' closer, I carefully inched the door open so I could peek in.

I'm gonna kill that fucker.

Raisin' my gun, I steadied my aim. Z was so preoccupied that I could've walked right up to the bed.

One of his hands was around Piper's throat while his other worked at his pants. His gun was set to the side, almost out of reach.

I squeezed off a round, the sound echoin' in the small room. Blood spurted out as the bullet entered Z's thigh, forcin' him to roll to the side and fall off the bed.

Steppin' to where he sat on the floor, I pressed my gun flush to his temple.

When Piper's chest rose and fell steadily, I felt relief so strong it took everythin' I had not to sink to my knees.

I looked down at Z, his blood oozin' from his thigh all over Piper's rug. I waited, expectin' him to give some excuse or explanation. To at least say somethin'.

He didn't even look at me.

His eyes stayed glued to Piper as he stared at her with guilt, longin', and anger. He watched her as if he weren't currently bleedin' all over my woman's floor. As if I didn't have a gun pressed to his fuckin' head.

I was vaguely aware of more noises fillin' the house as I tried to remind myself that there was some downside to pullin' the trigger and blowin' his fuckin' brains out.

I trusted him. I trusted him with my woman, with my business. I treated him like a brother. And this is what he does? He scared my woman. He watched her. He touched her. Every word from his fuckin' mouth, voiced like a concern, like he had my fuckin' back, was to take Piper away from me. To take my sweetness. He hurt her.

I didn't protect her, and he hurt *her.*

"Piper needs you."

Those words flipped a switch and broke me from my thoughts. I looked to the side and saw Detective Oscar standin' close with her gun aimed at me. There was another cop next to her with his pointed at Z.

"Don't do something you'll regret, Jake. You can't see Piper every day if you're in jail," she pointed out. "We've got this, okay?"

I looked down at Z again. Despite multiple guns pointin' at him, he hadn't moved. His eyes were still locked on Piper.

My Piper, pale and unconscious because he'd hurt her.

"Piper needs you" Detective Oscar repeated.

Droppin' my arm, I handed my gun off to a startled cop.

Climbin' into the bed, I pulled Piper carefully into my lap. I pressed my lips to her head, the smell of cake filling my nose.

Moving On

Piper

"Wake up. Please, fuck, baby, wake up."

"What do you want, Mr. Bossy Pants? I'm sleeping." Yawning, I pulled the blanket tighter around myself.

"What? Now that you're gonna be Mrs. Bossy Pants tomorrow, you don't wanna fuck?"

"Suddenly, I'm not feeling so tired," I muttered, rubbing the sleep from my eyes before climbing onto my fiancé.

"You kept grindin' your ass against me, makin' all sorts of sexy little noises in your sleep. Havin' good dreams?" Jake leaned up on his elbows to kiss my chest as I straddled him.

"The best. I was marrying this super sexy badass with a huge dick and he was going to fuck me. And will you look at that, I must still be dreaming."

Jake's growl rumbled against me. Lifting me by my hips, he positioned himself to enter me but held back. I tried to push down but his grip tightened. "You know what I wanna hear."

"Please," I begged shamelessly. "Please fuck me."

Jake pulled me down as his hips thrust up.

Leaning forward, I clutched his shoulders.

One of his hands moved up my side and ribs, the tenderness a sharp contrast to the urgency of our movements. Rubbing gently under my breast, it came to rest in the center of my chest.

Anger flashed across his face, quickly followed by pain and relief.

Like I'd done for the past month whenever Jake did this, I brought my hand up to cover his, pressing it closer to me. I began moving faster until my heart beat pounded so quickly it would have been impossible for him not to feel it.

Even still, it wasn't until I inhaled deeply that I saw the last bit of tension leave his face.

On the night of the attack, one month before, I woke up hazily in my room to people rushing around. Globes of light floated around me, and everything seemed to switch between fast forward and slow mo.

I knew I felt safe, though.

When I came to more, I realized I was cradled in Jake's lap.

His voice was harsh, but his touch on me was light, as though he worried the slightest movement might shatter me.

"Baby," I rasped. My throat felt like I'd swallowed glass, then sea salt, and finished it off with a shot of flaming kerosene. As I leaned forward to sit up, the dull ache in my head turned into a jack hammering pain.

Though I tried to fight against it, the black edges pushed in again.

Things were far less hazy the next time I woke up. I tensed when I felt strong arms around me until I saw the ink and realized they belonged to Jake.

I opened my mouth, but he spoke first.

"Don't talk. I'll get the nurse, yeah?"

Looking around, I saw that we were in a hospital room. I nodded as he hit a button on the bed.

"What happened?"

Before Jake could answer, an older nurse came in.

"Glad to see you're awake. Let's check you out, and then we'll get you up and walking." She gave me a reassuring smile as she stopped to wash her hands. "Mr. Hyde, if you'd wait outside, please."

"No," he said firmly.

"I'm sure Miss Skye would feel more comfortable tending to her needs without an audience."

Jake looked down at me before sighing. He carefully shifted off the bed and stood. "I'll be right back."

"I'm Sally, your nurse for the day. Let's get you up." She helped me stand on unsteady legs.

After using the bathroom, I moved to the sink to wash my hands. I glanced up and caught sight of myself in the mirror.

Based on the look of pain and anger on Jake's face, and the sympathy on Sally's, I'd already guessed that I didn't look too hot.

Still, I was surprised by how awful my appearance was.

My hair was a tangled, dry mess and with the exception of a nasty purple bruise on my swollen cheek, my face was pale. There was also a dark, angry looking ring around my neck.

Bringing my shaking fingers up, I touched the mark. As the dull pain turned sharp, I saw Z with his hand on my throat as he worked at his pants so he could...

I flung open the door, startling Sally. Her face went soft as she took in my wide eyes and heaving chest.

Closing my eyes, I inhaled deeply and tried to remind myself I was okay.

Z's gone. Jake's here and he won't let anyone hurt me. I'm safe.

Sally helped me back into bed and began taking my vitals.

"How're you feeling?"

"Thirsty." My voice was rough, like the word had clawed its way up.

"I'll get you some water when we finish here."

"Thanks."

She was removing the blood pressure cuff when Jake came back in.

Gently lifting me, he sat on the bed and positioned me in his lap. His mouth moved against my forehead as he asked, "You okay?"

"Yeah. When can I go home?"

At my own words, panic seized me again. More flashbacks, like the world's worst slide show, played out in my head.

Jake's grasp on me loosened, but he murmured to me in soothing tones until I knew I was safe.

I also knew I was never going to that house again.

"When can I leave here?" I rephrased.

Sally's eyes were sympathetic and warm. "You have a concussion. There's a specialist on her way to look at your throat to make sure there's no lasting damage. You've already had an MRI, but you'll be heading for another one shortly. They want to be sure that, between the concussion and the lack of oxygen, there's no bleeding or swelling. If everything is okay, you could be discharged tomorrow."

"I already had an MRI? How long was I out?"

"They gave you a mild sedative, hon. It's only been a few hours. I'll go get your water and see what time the MRI will be."

After Sally left, Jake ran his hand through my hair, carefully avoiding the back of my head.

"James?" I asked.

"Slight concussion and a gunshot wound to the shoulder. But he'll be fine and headin' home in a couple days. We'll go visit him later."

Even though I hated to ask, I needed to know. "Chloe?"

"No," he said with a slight shake of his head. He didn't look too broken up about it.

"Z?"

Jake's jaw clenched. "I'm assumin' that crazy fucker is in a prison somewhere and headed for a padded room. It's better I don't know."

Though I wanted to know more about what happened, I was too drained to ask.

Sally brought me water, which I was only allowed to sip.

She obviously has no clue what it feels like to have a desert in her mouth.

After I drank, Jake put the cup on the table and pulled me closer.

"She's nice," I whispered when Sally left again. "I bet Jet would wanna rock her arch supporting, nonslip shoes off."

Jake let out a deep laugh that eased some of the tension on his face. "Yeah, you're probably right. Get some sleep, sweets."

"Yes, Mr. Bossy Pants."

"I'm gonna fuckin' kill him."

"Mr. Hyde, go wait in the hallway."

"*Fuck* the hallway."

"Go or I'll have security remove you."

"Try it," he warned.

While he often issued the same challenge to me, there was nothing playful about it this time. I knew if anyone attempted to make him to leave, it would not end well.

That being said, the nurse he was threatening had been an asshole from the time his shift had started, so he was kind of asking for it.

Reliving everything as I talked to the specialist wasn't easy. I didn't want to go through it without Jake if he got himself kicked out of the hospital.

"Baby, it's good news," I tried. "The doctor says I should be better within the week with no lasting damage."

"'Cause you didn't fuckin' fight back. That's the only reason there's no lastin' fuckin' damage! Sweets, he could've..." His strained voice broke, tortured. "He could've—"

"He didn't."

"But—"

"It sucked for you to hear." I grabbed his hand so he'd look down at me. "Imagine how I'm feeling talking about it. Now either shut up or leave. Please."

"Fuck. You're right. Shit, I'm sorry." He lifted my hand to kiss my palm.

"This was an extremely difficult situation," the doctor started, her eyes narrowing on the asshole nurse. "For you *both*. You deserve some patience and compassion."

Ohhhhhh. Someone's in trouble.

After meeting with the specialist, I was able to convince Jake to bring me to visit James.

By bring, I mean, he literally carried me.

James was still pretty out of it, but was happy to see me. We only stayed a few minutes, but it was long enough for me to see he was alright and for him to see the same was true for me.

As we were leaving the room, Jake looked back to James. "I owe you."

James shook his head. "Just keep her happy."

When we returned to my hospital room, Kase was waiting. His back was to us as he looked out the window. Turning stiffly, his expression was grim as he looked me over. "You okay, Pipe?"

I nodded, my throat having started to burn.

Kase stepped away from the window and headed towards the hall, setting something on the table by the bed as he went. When he reached the door, he paused to look back at Jake and me. "I'm so sorry."

Before anyone else could speak, he left like the room was on fire.

I looked at Jake, my face asking the question my throat was too sore to.

Jake set me gently on the bed before stretching out next to me. "I wanted to go to you. I knew somethin' was off. Kase held me back 'cause he thought you just needed time. He feels like it's his fault things got so far, and he's not listenin' to reason. He even put in his two weeks' notice."

I shook my head, cringing at the pain.

Jake pulled me to him and tucked my head into his neck. Reaching over to grab what Kase had set down, he slid my engagement ring back on my finger. He kissed my palm before placing my hand on his chest and covering it with his own.

"How?" I whispered.

"Kase. Don't know how long he spent out there searchin', but I know it was a long time."

"Good friend."

"The best."

Detective Oscar contacted us the following week to come in to the station.

"Did you know Z had a juvie record for stealing and stripping cars?" she asked Jake as soon as we sat down.

Jake nodded. "Yeah, why?"

"Given your law background and the high value of your business, it's surprising that you'd have two employees with records."

My brows shot up. "Two?"

I didn't even know there was one!

I watched Detective Oscar and Jake look at each other, a silent conversation happening between them. "Who else?" I pushed.

"No one, babe. Don't worry about it," Jake murmured to me.

"No. Who?"

"Kase. And, before you ask, I'm not tellin' you anythin' else. It's not my story to tell, and, more so, I know for a fact Kase *seriously* does not want you to know."

As curious as I was, I knew getting the information from Jake wasn't going to happen since he kept secrets like they were launch codes.

Plus, if Kase didn't want me to know, I'd have to respect that. I knew the kind of man he was, and that was all that mattered.

"Sorry, I thought she knew," Detective Oscar apologized, regaining our attention. "The reason I had you come in today was because with Z filling in the holes, we've been able to piece together what happened. I'm giving you the heads up right now, he'll probably go for the insanity defense. I'm not your dad, Jake, but I'd say it's also likely he'll get it."

"We already knew he was a fuckin' sicko," Jake muttered, his hand tightening on my thigh.

I looked at Detective Oscar. "It's worse than that, isn't it?"

She nodded her head slowly. "It's messed up and ugly," she warned before telling us Z's heartbreaking story.

Zachary Zane, then Double Z, before just Z, was Special Forces. In charge of a small group of men, he was known for being ruthless, conniving, and manipulative. He was also incredibly skilled with wires.

After his alcoholic father kicked him out when he was only eleven, he'd had to learn all of it to survive.

After spending seven years bouncing between juvie and neglectful foster homes, he put his skills to use by joining the military. Placing taps and traces, connecting and defusing bombs; if it had wires, he could do something with it. He had a high success rate. When he set a plan, he followed it to a T.

Until the one time he didn't.

On a mission overseas, he met a local woman at the market. She'd looked up at him and smiled shyly when they both reached for the same container of milk.

Because of her perfect, sweet smile, he'd called her "Doll Face".

Due to the nature of his job, they'd kept their relationship a secret. In a life full of hardness, she was the only soft he'd ever experienced. He fell quickly and deeply in love, to the point of distraction.

Leaving her one morning, he went to question a suspected terrorist. The interrogation was heavy on physical force. As the man hung by his bound wrists from a hook in his own warehouse, Z beat him. Savagely. Getting him close to death, one of Z's men would patch him up before Z started again.

After more than forty-eight hours, they were getting nowhere and Z lost his patience. He wanted to get back to his love.

She always worried when he was gone too long.

He started punching, absolutely brutal hits, one after another after another. The man was close to death when a shriek filled the air.

Z turned, wiping blood and sweat from his face, to see the sister he hadn't known the suspect had.

His Doll Face.

She was never supposed to be there.

She was never supposed to see what he did to protect people.

Her face was filled with fear as she dropped a basket of sweet breads. Turning, she ran from him.

He chased her without thinking, leaving his men behind.

Men he'd never see again.

His woman, in her frantic attempt at escape, ran off the path and onto the grass. Nearing the gate, she stepped on a landmine.

The blast blew Z back and knocked him unconscious. The detonation triggered another set of explosives wired to bring down the warehouse.

Z's instincts were correct; the man had a lot to hide.

Z never told anyone what had really happened. He was hailed a hero when backup found him unconscious.

His actions, lies, and mistakes all weighed heavily on him.

When he began seeing me at events, his obsession started. My tanned skin, long, dark hair and sweet nature reminded him of her.

But it was my scent that broke him.

His Doll Face loved to bake for her large family. Z would climb into her bed after a bad day, and the scent of vanilla would fill his nose, calming him.

I knew no one else felt any pity for Z. He'd hurt people and committed murder. On top of the emotional pain he'd caused, he'd almost killed me as he tried to hurt me in one of the worst ways you could.

In spite of all that, I mourned the loss of his Doll Face, his men, and the Z I thought I'd known.

The Z he could've been.

When the nightmares started, Jake put his foot down about me seeing a professional counselor. Since I knew I needed it, I didn't fight him.

It was hard to keep reliving what had happened, but my mind was doing it whether I wanted it to or not. At least when I went over it during therapy, I received the tools I needed to cope and move on.

Jake, just like Kase, felt incredible guilt for not protecting me. He knew I'd never have gone home alone had he not said such awful things.

While that may have been true, I explained that Z had intentionally goaded him into pushing me too far. He promised he'd try to tamp down his possessiveness, and I promised to keep being patient.

Keeping his word, I did the cake for Static in the Sun's album drop party without a peep from Jake. It probably helped that Blake Green was freaked way the fuck out and wanted nothing to do with me.

Having a crazy dude use you in his plot to kidnap a chick would calm anyone's shit down.

Jake understood why I'd been so harsh when I'd been forced to break up with him. However, I also knew the stuff that Z had made me say was real. They were insecurities Jake had and they ran deep. My vulnerable badass worried that I'd leave him and I knew that fear wouldn't disappear overnight.

Lucky for him, I was ready to spend every day of my life proving to him how much I loved him. I wasn't going anywhere.

Jake had wanted to get married right after we left the hospital. I wanted to wait until all the swelling and bruising was gone. It wasn't a vanity thing.

Okay, it wasn't *just* that.

I didn't want to look back at pictures and see the reminder of what had happened. I wanted my wedding day to be brightness with no dark cloud looming over it.

When I told Jake how I felt, he understood.

It was almost a month before he mentioned marriage again.

I woke, as the sun was just touching the sky, to Jake's fingers sliding slowly inside of me as his eyes studied my face intently. When I smiled sleepily up at him, he moved between my legs.

Tenderly, he eased into me as his fingertips drifted lovingly over my face and neck.

"Marry me tomorrow?" he asked, his lips brushing against mine.

"Yes," I answered simply.

Then Jake did another thing he'd sworn he couldn't do. His movements stayed slow as he savored me, worshipped me, made love to me.

It was beautiful in a way that was so profound I knew I'd remember it until the day I died.

Shortly after, I fell back to sleep with Jake's body curved along mine.

It was a few hours later that he woke me to straddle him so he could fuck me bossy.

I'd be hard pressed to say which I preferred, but I was looking forward to a lifetime together to decide.

When Jake said we'd get married the next day, he was *not* messing around. We were on a plane to Vegas that afternoon.

After getting in late, we checked into a gorgeous hotel that I barely saw through tired eyes. Collapsing into bed, we slept well into the next morning until a knock on the door woke us.

I lifted my head slightly and watched my fiancé pad across the room, the muscles in his back, ass, and legs flexing. He bent and scooped up his pants, pulling them on as he walked.

If I attempted something like that, I'd fall on my face.

Easing the door to our room closed behind him, his footsteps trailed off as he went through the rest of the suite to the main door.

I snagged his pillow and burrowed under the blankets. I started to doze back off when I heard voices filling the sitting room.

When Jake returned, I greedily enjoyed the view of his shirtless front.

His unbuttoned, loose jeans hung low on his hips. I knew where the deep vee of his pelvis and the sparse trail of blond hair led, but I still wanted nothing more than to explore.

My eyes slowly moved up the taut muscles of his abs, intricate swirls of ink, and the definition of his chest that had my name on it. I took in his broad, tattooed shoulders, masculine neck, and strong jaw with ever-present scruff that my fingers still itched to touch.

His full and slightly quirked lips, high cheekbones, and the harsh angles of his face made him so masculinely beautiful, I felt it was a disservice to womankind that he had yet to be sculpted in marble.

His green eyes were hooded, lit with a mix of amusement and arousal, and I knew my perusal had not been subtle.

Since I'd failed to notice that he'd stopped walking at some point, it had been in depth.

Oops.

When my eyes dropped down and I looked straight ahead, I saw something else that was far from subtle.

"You keep lookin' at me like that, sweets, and our family and friends out there are gonna hear a lot more than they want to."

I sat up quickly and the blankets fell around me.

Jake's eyes went even more hooded as he did a little perusing of his own.

Going back to the door, he opened it and said, "We got in late and Piper's still tired. We'll meet you in the lobby at one."

I heard muffled conversation fade as they left.

I got up on my knees. "Well, that was rude. Shouldn't we get dressed and go see everyone?"

Jake's eyes dropped to my naked body. "Fuck no." Prowling towards me, he pushed his jeans down and removed them as he walked with the same gracefulness as when he'd put them on.

God, that's hot. Why's that such a turn-on?

Maybe because I know all the other ways he's in control of his body.

And mine.

"No, I really think we should. I'll just get dressed." Turning from him, I leaned down and pretended to reach for my clothes.

My head shot back as he entered me hard, filling me.

His hands ran up my sides before reaching around to palm my breasts. He pulled me up so my back was pressed to his front. One of his arms wrapped under my chest to support me as he moved in me. His other curled up, his hand curving gently around the side of my neck as his thumb stroked my jaw.

The first couple of times his hand had gone to my neck, I'd flinched and jerked away. He'd understood, but I hadn't. I hated feeling the panic grip me, and seeing the pain and rage resurface in him. I missed feeling his rough thumb rub my jaw.

I'd made him promise not to stop doing it and he hadn't. As time passed, my reaction slowly but steadily improved until I was once again leaning into his touch.

I would have made him keep trying forever to get it back.

"If you wanna get dressed, I guess we could," he whispered harshly against my ear, his tongue edging the side. His thrusts intensified so much so that if his arms weren't around me, I wouldn't have been able to stay upright.

He stopped suddenly and began inching out of me.

"No!" Reaching around, I dug my nails into his ass to pull him back in.

Jake's deep chuckle turned into a groan. "Fuck, I love you."

"And thank fuck for that."

He might usually be Mr. Bossy Pants, but Jake was better at compromise than I'd once thought.

When we'd initially discussed wedding plans, the parents had ganged up on us to push for a traditional wedding. They still wanted that, except for my dad.

Dad was in favor of the wedding being wherever I wanted, as long as the end result was his only child being married to someone who would literally shoot a man to protect her.

Dad did tell Jake that given the chance, he'd be there in an instant so he could walk me down the aisle.

Jake ran with that idea.

We got our Vegas wedding, but with our family and closest friends. My mom, Thomas, Gregory, Sarah, Edge, Ray, Harlow, Rhys, and Kase had been ready to fly out on Thomas' company plane at a moment's notice. Nat and Dad drove up from California.

Everyone knew that as soon as the bruising was gone, there'd be no convincing us to wait any longer.

After loud and chaotic hellos in the hotel lobby, I asked, "So, what's the plan?"

"We're going to do all things girly to get ready," Ray said, looping my arm through hers and smiling huge at me.

"You all know the schedule," Jake's voice rumbled as he pulled me slightly from Ray to kiss me.

"I don't," I pointed out.

"And that's the fun of it. I'll see you tonight, sweets."

When the women left the hotel, we headed to a boutique.

I'd have happily married Jake in the jeans and t-shirt I wore. That didn't mean that once I saw the gorgeous dresses, I wasn't thrilled we were there.

Nat's eyes lit gleefully as she handed me a glass of champagne. "Have a seat."

Taking the glass, I narrowed my eyes as I studied her face. "Why do I get the feeling you're up to something?"

She shrugged, feigning nonchalance, but her valley girl lilt was strong from her excitement. "Because I am. We've been planning this for weeks."

Her use of 'we've' wasn't lost on me, and I grinned at her. It couldn't have been easy on her or my mom, but it meant a lot to me.

When I caught her eyes, I knew she felt the same way.

Sitting down, I watched as Ray and Harlow disappeared into what I'd correctly assumed were changing rooms.

Within minutes, they came out in matching shimmery, dove gray, one shouldered dresses that ended above the knee. The one strap was black ruched. Even with the black, back seam tights and gray three-inch pumps, I was surprised at how low-key the outfit was.

They totally rocked the look, but I got the feeling the moms played a heavy role in picking the attire.

This should be interesting.

"Oh my God, you both look gorgeous! Harlow, I had no clue your legs were so long."

Though she was only an inch or so taller than me, her legs seemed miles longer.

"Yeah, I get that a lot," she said, looking off to the side.

The moms and seamstress went to work on Ray, adding pins and walking around her as they discussed alterations.

I caught her gaze in the reflection of the mirror. After giving me her best model face, she rolled her eyes and blew me a kiss.

Standing, I moved closer to an unusually quiet Harlow. "You okay?"

"Yeah, I just… I'm so happy for you, Piper. I love you, and you're, like, the most kickass friend. I'm just so touched you wanted me here," she whispered, tears pooling in her eyes.

"Honey—"

"Don't say another word. If I cry, my eyes are gonna get puffy and my skin will get splotchy."

"I get Alice Cooper face."

"Then we both better get a handle on this."

Looking away as I tried to do just that, I saw the moms go into the dressing rooms.

I sat back to watch a relieved Ray get out of the hot spot as Harlow took her place, looking even more uncomfortable.

Her legs are seriously never-ending!

Within minutes, Nat, Sarah, and my mom came out of the rooms in similar gray, A-line, fifties style dresses.

"Those dresses are perfect!" I squealed.

"I'm thinking I'll make this my new look," Sarah joked, her lips twitching like her son's did.

When it was my turn, I went into a changing room. My knees gave out and I sank down onto a bench. Trying to stop the tears from sliding down my cheeks, I lifted my head to see my mom crouched next to me.

The others wiped at their eyes as they watched through the open curtain.

"I knew you'd love it," Mom said, reaching up to wipe a tear from my face.

"It's been one day since I said yes. How did all of this get done?"

"He's been planning everything with the owner of Ella's. He said she was almost more excited about the wedding than he was. Especially when he told her his idea for the dress. It's not my style, of course. But it's so you that I love it. And I love that he gave it to you. I couldn't have imagined anyone better for my beautiful daughter."

Obviously, Dad wasn't the only one shaken by what happened.

When my mom found out why I'd gone back to my house to change, she was wracked with guilt. We'd talked for hours about everything. She'd explained, which I already knew, that she just wanted better for me than she'd had growing up.

This wasn't to say she was magically the perfect mom, but she was much closer. She was happier, more relaxed, and I caught more than a glimpse of who she was when she let the walls down.

After getting control of my tears, I stood and helped my mom up. She hugged me tight before leaving me to dress.

My hands shook as I quickly pulled my clothes off. Sliding the dress on, I was cautious not to snag it on anything. I sat on the edge of the seat and slipped my shoes on before opening the curtain.

"Ta-Da!" I choked out as I tried not to cry on my dress.

The moms and my girls, upon seeing me, all burst into fresh tears that they hurriedly wiped.

The seamstress had me stand in front of the wall of mirrors as she pinned for alterations.

Once Jake had broken down my walls and closed the distance I'd tried to keep, I'd fallen hard and fast. There was no holding back.

As I looked at the dress, though I thought it was impossible, I loved Jacoby Hyde even more.

We went back to the hotel where an entire salon staff was waiting for us in my mom's suite. It may not have actually been the whole staff, but it felt like it.

After being split into different areas, everyone rushed to get ready.

Separated from everyone else, I was closed off in the master suite. My finger and toe nails were painted at the same time by two different people while someone fussed with my hair.

When the choice of hairstyles was given to me, I chose to leave it down. I also made sure they didn't put anything in it that would make it difficult for Jake to run his fingers through.

Or pull...

Shh, quiet, girly bits!

After my hair was set in rollers, my makeup was applied so quickly I feared the results. I slowly pried my eyes open to look in the mirror, bracing for the worst.

Instead, I saw that each line, color, and coated eyelash was nothing short of perfection.

I grinned at the makeup artist. "I seriously need to raise my makeup game."

Before I could figure out how she'd done it so fast, she left as two people came in to unwrap and style my hair.

It was chaotic, but it was the kind of chaos I liked. My favorite weddings were the rare ones when the vibe was electric with excitement, and that's what I felt.

I had no doubts or second thoughts. I wasn't screaming about some invisible flaw I wanted to focus on in order to avoid an actual problem. I wasn't crying and getting drunk in the ladies room.

Don't forget about the wedding where you walked in on the bride and the best man in the kitchen.

Though, from the bored look on her face, he was obviously far from the best.

I was nervous, of course. I was also out of my freakin' mind ecstatic.

As the stylist put the finishing touches on my hair, I heard the dresses being delivered. Someone from the boutique knocked on the door before coming in to hang my stuff up.

When I was finally alone, I took longer than I had available to get dressed. Smoothing the skirt down, I loved it even more than I had earlier.

For fear of busting my ass, I walked slowly on trembling legs out of the master suite. My mom was facing away from me and I was unsurprised to see her hair pulled back in her typical chignon. When she turned around, my brows shot up and I started laughing.

The front of her hair was pinned in victory rolls.

"You like?" my mom asked, preening. "It was my idea."

"I *love* it."

Someone from the hotel guided us from the room. Our charged energy bounced around us as we filed out and down the hall.

Taking the elevators up, we walked down another hall and stopped near a closed room. The moms stood close to the entrance while Ray and Harlow moved me out of sight.

When the doors opened, I heard a lot of voices.

"There's more than just the few people I was expecting, isn't there?" I asked, my voice shaking.

"Yup," Harlow confirmed with a smile.

"Don't cry. You've got so much mascara on, there's no way you wouldn't look like Alice Cooper," Ray laughed.

"Helpful! Thanks, that's *super* calming," I said sarcastically. "Quick, someone say something or I'm gonna start blubbering." I fanned my face.

"Rhys is escorting me down the aisle. Do you think he'd let me do a shot out of those dimples later?" Harlow raised her brows suggestively.

"I'd originally thought to eat cereal out of them, but I like your idea better," I admitted. "Not for me, of course. I'm a soon-to-be married woman."

Familiar sounding music started playing. Listening carefully, I realized it was a slowed down, instrumental version of one of my favorite X-ers songs. It had been playing when Jake and I danced at Jet's.

The moms disappeared into the room first. Harlow followed shortly after, turning to blow me a kiss as she went.

Ray grabbed my hands and clutched them tight as tears shimmered in her eyes. "Sometimes the road to happily ever after isn't smooth and easy. You have to fight through trials and obstacles to get there. There are dragons and big, bad wolves in disguise to defeat. Riding in a carriage with a prince wouldn't get you over those bumps and twists. Sometimes the road to your happily ever after is on the back of a bike with a badass knight that would kick the prince's ass if he came near you. I couldn't be happier you found your knight, Piper. I love you."

"I love you, too," I whispered past the lump in my throat. "Thanks for showing me that taking risks on a badass could pay off."

I pulled her to me and held tight as we tried to control our tears.

A minute later, Kase stuck his head out the door. "Hate to break this up, you know how much I love girl-on-girl shit. But there's a man waiting at the other side of this room who's starting to look tense and a bit pissed. Not sayin' Jake is the most patient man to begin with, but he looks about a minute, tops, from storming out here and making you walk down the aisle."

When Ray and I released our hold on each other, she air kissed my cheek before disappearing through the door with Kase.

I'd never been one to make decisions on the fly. When faced with any choice, I overanalyzed every detail until I reached my answer. More often than not, I was still plagued with doubt.

With Jake, though, I knew the risks would pay off. I'd strapped in, held on tight, and enjoyed the hell out of the ride.

And as I stood in the hallway, about to leap off the figurative cliff into the unknown, I knew wherever I landed would be beauty.

Inhaling deeply, I closed my eyes and let my head fall back. Warmth seeped into my soul as a calm peace settled deep in my bones.

"Most dads hate this day."

Opening my eyes, I saw my dad standing in front of me in a gray suit and black dress shirt. His expression was a mix of thrilled and heartbroken.

My eyes started to burn again.

"They dread it, the day their little girl becomes someone else's woman. I can't say that part is easy. But knowing you'll be with someone who would do all this, do everything he's done, to protect you and make you smile? Couldn't have picked a better man if I tried. You've made me proud with everything you've done, Lil' Rock. This is no exception."

Don't cry. Hold it back. Splotchy and streaked isn't a good look on anyone. Don't cry.

Oh, hell, I'm gonna cry.

Dad must have been able to tell. "Alright, alright, keep it together. You start crying, you'll have to go fix your face and all that junk. And

Kase was *not* exaggerating. That man up there is the epitome of restless."

I slid my arm through the crook in Dad's and we positioned ourselves near the doorway.

When the music changed, a strangled sob mixed with a laugh escaped from me.

The lovely, lilting instrumental was the first song Jake had held me during when we saw the band, Harington, at Rye. Though I'd wanted to kick him in the shin that night, I knew I'd never forget.

What I hadn't known was neither would he.

Though the melody sounded beautifully romantic, the unsung lyrics were actually about being so turned on by someone that the only thoughts you had were about fucking them in all sorts of kinky ways.

It was *perfect*.

Entering the room, I saw nothing but Jake.

And, just like the first time I saw him at Hyde's, my legs went to jello. As I was again wearing four-inch heels, I had to walk carefully so I didn't face-plant at my own wedding.

Forget congratulating yourself for walking without falling this time. Congratulate yourself for who you're marrying.

Standing at the end of the aisle, Jake looked scorchingly beautiful. His hair was down, making his cheek and jaw bones more prominent. The sleeves of his black dress shirt were rolled up to show his inked and tanned forearms. Slim fit, gray jeans tucked into his motorcycle boots, a matching gray tuxedo vest, and a hot pink tie made him look badass formal.

As soon as I was within arm's reach, Jake's hand curved around the back of my neck. Hauling me to him, my hands hit his chest as his mouth crashed down on mine.

Catcalls and whistles filled the room, though neither of us cared.

When Jake tore his mouth from mine, he pulled back slightly to look down at me, his eyes full of emotion. "Fuck, Piper. So fuckin' gorgeous. Thirty-four years of color-blind, lookin' at a lifetime of bright," he murmured, his voice ragged.

I knew I was right about why everyone else was wearing subtle colors when we were anything but. Standing up there, my girls and boys were dressed in gray and black.

Instead of the typical white gown, I wore hot pink with a dove gray lace overlay. The halter was attached to a thick, black band and came up as two separate pieces with a deep vee in the middle. The pink ended just above my breasts, leaving just gray lace to cover my upper chest and go around my neck.

The skirt under the banded bodice fell to the ground. Though my pink and gray pumps had a four-inch heel, the dress still dragged when I walked, creating a slight train and moving the slit on my left leg to near indecent levels.

Mom admitted that she and Sarah had convinced Jake to have a traditional white gown ready to go. Though he did, he'd been adamant that it wouldn't be needed.

He'd been right.

"No more tastin' bitter. You gave me sweet and bright, Piper. I'm gonna spend the rest of my life givin' you the moon."

When Jake jerked his chin, I dragged my eyes from him. Looking up, I saw the entire ceiling of the room was made of glass.

Thousands of stars twinkled brightly in the nighttime sky. The radiant full moon looked like it had been physically placed in the perfect position.

He might be a sex god, but even I know that's outside of his capabilities.

Maybe.

"Love you, Jacoby."

"'Til the day I die, sweets."

"If we can begin," Kase started, shifting to stand in front of Jake and me.

Glancing to the side, I saw that his and Rhys' outfits were similar to Jake's, though their ties were gray.

"Totally on board with this, but will it be legit?" I whispered.

"I got ordained, Pipe," Kase whispered back. "My gift to you. Well, that and a crazy, scary looking coffee maker. Look surprised when you open it."

I smiled. "Awesome."

Kase looked up at everyone and began the ceremony. "Love is anarchy. It's mayhem. You fight for it. *Live* for it. You hold tight and push through the ugly times, 'cause without them, you wouldn't fully appreciate the beauty. And that's what Jake and Piper have. A love that they'll work to grow over the lifetime I'm doubtless they'll spend together." Kase stopped to smile at Jake. "Jake's been like a brother to me for years, so I'm gonna do him a solid and make this fast. He's waited long enough for this day." Kase handed him something.

"With this ring, I give you me." Jake's voice was barely above a whisper as he slid a beautiful platinum and diamond band on my finger.

I turned and took the ring Ray held out to me before looking back at Jake. "That's all I've ever wanted." I ran my fingertips quickly along his jaw. "With this ring, I give you me." I slid the thick, platinum band on his finger.

Jake's newly ringed hand went to my neck. "It's only you."

"Jake, do you?" Kase asked.

"I do."

"Piper, do you?"

My heart pounded in my throat as my mouth rushed to get out the words. "I do."

"I ho'okahi kahi ke aloha," Kase said in Hawaiian, smiling wide. "Be one in love, Mr. and Mrs. Jacoby and Piper Hyde. Not that you've ever needed prompting, but you may now kiss your bride."

"Mine," Jake growled as his head came down.

"Forever," I whispered against his lips.

Perfection.

I'd thought it so many times. But nothin', fuck, *nothin'* was more perfect than hearin' Piper become my wife.

Mine.

I'd known from the very first time I saw her in the shop, lookin' like a porn star librarian, that there was somethin' more. Somethin' about her that screamed to me. It grabbed me and pulled me to her, wrappin' me in her, makin' me feel like my world started and ended with her.

It was only her.

And, as she stood next to me, so fuckin' sexy I was fightin' gettin' hard in front of our friends and family, she gave me *everythin'*.

Lookin' up at me like I was the only one there, like I was her dragon slayin' prince, she was only herself.

It was all she'd ever been.

It was all she would be.

And that was perfection beyond anythin' I could imagine.

Piper

After four days in Vegas, most of which was spent in our room, Jake and I continued our honeymoon in Hawaii. We spent a week and a half in our secluded cabana, naked, or on our private beach, close to naked.

And, occasionally, totally naked.

Like on our first night in Hawaii, when Jake stripped me down on a blanket in the sand and made love to me under a velvet sky.

Or in the ocean a few days later, when he grabbed my ass and lifted me so my legs could wrap around his hips. With the sun beating down, the clear water lapped around us as he fucked me hard.

We should get a pool.

After two weeks away, Jake and I came back to work together.

Jake had fixed up the break room and replaced some of the equipment he'd broken. He didn't do as much this time since we wouldn't be in the building much longer. The garage and the house, which I still hadn't returned to, had both been put on the market.

Everyone needed a fresh start.

Jake decided to have a new Hyde built from the ground up. His wedding present to me was the connected bakery.

I was excited about the idea. I'd still do custom cakes, but the storefront would allow me to also sell fresh items daily.

Jake was excited about the door in his office that opened to my kitchen.

"So, wife, what're your plans today?" he asked, looking down at me while his thumb stroked my jaw.

"I have some cakes to bake. Plus a few designs I have to sketch and send off to customers. And what're your plans, husband?"

"I have some cars to customize. Plus a few designs I have to sketch and send off to customers. And, in between that, I have to find time to eat the hot baker that works near my office. Hopefully, I'll get to fuck her up against some wall or bent over something."

I clutched the sides of Jake's t-shirt when a wave of desire hit me so hard that my knees nearly gave out.

Like most everything else, Jake didn't miss it. His eyes heated as his voice lowered. "Fuck, I love my wife."

"And I love you right back."

I felt his hardness against me as he pulled me close. Opening his mouth to talk, he was interrupted by a crash.

A cute as a button, but super pissed off, redhead stormed past.

Followed, surprisingly, by an equally pissed off Kase. "Harlow, hold up."

Two very nicely manicured middle fingers shot up over her head. "Fuck you, Kase!" she exclaimed as she slammed out of Hyde.

Kase followed after her, cursing to himself.

Jake raised an eyebrow. "Do I even wanna ask?"

"Probably. You guys are gossipy as hell. But I have no clue."

"Fair enough." Leaning down to my ear, Jake whispered, "I'm still hungry, wife." Cupping my ass, he lifted me.

I wrapped my legs around his waist. "I know someone who makes a mean cupcake. Maybe if you're lucky, you'll get one, husband."

"Hearin' you call me that, sweets, I already know I'm lucky. I just plan on gettin' luckier."

"What're you waiting for?" I kissed the underside of his jaw, his honeymoon grown beard rough against my lips.

"Not a damn thing, Piper. Not anymore." His mouth moved, taking mine.

My lips parted to give him what he wanted. What he'd always wanted.

Me.

About the author:

Layla Frost has always been a rebel. A true badass.
Growing up, Layla used to hide under her blanket with a flashlight to read the Sweet Valley High books she pilfered from her older sister. It wasn't long before she was reading hidden Harlequins during class at school. This snowballed into pulling all-nighters after the promise of "just one more chapter".
Her love of reading, especially the romance genre, took root early and has grown immeasurably.
In between reading and writing, Layla spends her free time rocking out (at concerts, on the couch, in the car... Anywhere is a stage if you get into it enough), watching TV (the nerdier the better!), and being a foodie. Though she lives in NY (the state, not the city), she's an avid Red Sox fan.

Rock out with me!

Follow me on Facebook:
https://www.facebook.com/LaylaFrostWrites

Tweet me on the Twitter:
@LaylaFWrites

Hit me up with some awesome emails:
LaylaFrostWrites@gmail.com

Visit my site:
https://www.LaylaFrostWrites.com

Made in the USA
Middletown, DE
26 September 2023